A Bradford Sisters Romance

True to You

Becky Wade

BETHANYHOUSE
a division of Baker Publishing Group
Minneapolis, Minnesota

Published by Bethany House Publishers
11400 Hampshire Avenue South
Bloomington, Minnesota 55438
www.bethanyhouse.com

Bethany House Publishers is a division of
Baker Publishing Group, Grand Rapids, Michigan

Printed in the United States of America

Library of Congress Cataloging-in-Publication Data
Names: Wade, Becky, author.
Title: True to you / Becky Wade.
Description: Minneapolis, Minnesota : Bethany House, a division of Baker Publishing Group, [2017] | Series: Bradford Sisters romance
Identifiers: LCCN 2016050049 | ISBN 9780764230332 (cloth) | ISBN 9780764219368 (trade paper)
Subjects: | GSAFD: Christian fiction. | Love stories.
Classification: LCC PS3623.A33 T78 2017 | DDC 813/.6—dc23
LC record available at https://lccn.loc.gov/2016050049

Cover design by Jennifer Parker
Cover photography by Mike Habermann Photography, LLC

Author is represented by Linda Kruger.

17 18 19 20 21 22 23 7 6 5 4 3 2 1

True to You

Books by Becky Wade

My Stubborn Heart

The Porter Family Novels

Undeniably Yours

Meant to Be Mine

A Love Like Ours

Her One and Only

A Bradford Sisters Romance

True to You

For Chris.

You're my husband, my best friend,
and the one who makes me laugh every day.

I love you.

CHAPTER One

Finding oneself at the mercy of a crazed gunman isn't all fun and games.

Nope, thought Nora Bradford. *Not at all*. Not even when said gunman was an actor toting a fake gun and you'd volunteered your time to play the role of hostage for noble reasons.

According to her sister Britt, Lawson Training Incorporated staged emergency situations just like the one they were in the midst of as the culminating exercise of every course they offered. Today's trainees were civil workers from the town of Centralia. Directly beyond the wall of the room where Nora and Britt had been stashed, the civil workers were attempting to respond strategically to a faux enemy trying to take over this faux office building.

Given the current state of the world, Nora certainly believed in the value of emergency preparedness and response training. In fact, Nora had agreed to come along with Britt today because Britt had framed this outing as something proactive the two of them could do to further the cause of world peace. Nora wanted world peace! It was just that, with every passing minute, she was growing more and more certain of her unsuitability for the role of hostage. Her decades-long love of reading had instilled in her a *very* vivid imagination.

To her ears, the agitated shouting of the gunman sounded all too terrifyingly real.

Tension had been mounting steadily within her, tightening her shoulder muscles and causing her stomach to constrict with unease, ever since the "attack" had begun. She should have opted to further the cause of world peace by volunteering in her church's soup kitchen. The soup kitchen was more her speed.

Angry yelling carried through the wall, followed by a few shrieks of fear.

Nora swallowed. *Shrieks of fear?* She could only hope that the volunteers who'd been cast as office workers were taking artistic license.

Britt, of course, seemed oblivious to the ominous commotion. She was four years younger than Nora, the baby of their family, and the bravest of them all.

Britt curled her fingertips around the bottom edge of the room's lone window and tugged. "I think we should try to escape." She smiled at Nora the same way she'd smiled at Nora whenever she'd suggested mischievous childhood adventures. Her eyebrows ticked upward delightedly.

"No," Nora answered firmly. "The gentleman who assigned us to this room told us all we'd have to do is wait." She infused her words with a calm she didn't feel. "Once we're discovered, we're supposed to react to the situation we encounter however we'd react in real life."

"I *am* reacting to this situation the way I'd react in real life. Which is to view it as a challenge. You know, like those Escape the Room games that are gaining in popularity."

"This is not an Escape the Room game. We're here to help provide an object lesson for the trainees. This isn't about us."

Britt gave the sash a few more hard tugs before stepping back and setting her hands on her hips. Slowly she turned, scrutinizing their environment. It held nothing but a desk and the chair Nora occupied.

Britt's attention stopped on an air vent mounted into the wall near the ceiling.

Nora narrowed one eye to a slit. "There's no way we'll be able to escape through an air vent. People crawl through them in movies, but they're not roomy enough for that in real life. Are they? More to the point, *we were instructed to wait*. We're not trying to get an A+ as fake hostages."

"Speak for yourself." Britt made shooing motions as she approached. "Scoot."

"Britt—"

"Scoot!"

Nora exited the chair.

Britt dragged it beneath the vent, stood on it, and peered into the duct.

Just as Nora lowered onto the carpet to sit, a heavy crash reverberated from the other side of the wall, sounding like a huge piece of furniture falling.

Was there any chance that this training exercise had been hijacked by a real attacker?

No. Even so, Nora felt the way she did when sitting inside an airplane as it hurtled down the runway for takeoff. Intellectually, she knew she was safe. Emotionally, she knew planes sometimes crashed.

She longed for the soup kitchen.

"Is the vent conveniently large enough to crawl through?" Nora asked.

"No."

"Well, we could always break apart the desk and use splintered pieces of wood to chisel a tunnel through the wall."

Britt hopped from the chair and gave a businesslike nod. "Okay. I'm game."

"I was kidding!"

"It might work."

"It'll never work. Also, we can't damage Lawson Training's property." Nora frowned and straightened the brown bandana she'd tied around her head to decorate her Rosie the Riveter updo. "Stop eying the desk in that hungry way, Britt."

Her sister returned to the window, her features holding a faint resemblance to those of a young Sophia Loren. This morning, Britt had woven her long walnut-brown hair into a messy side braid that totally worked for her. She wore skinny jeans under a loose silver top. If laid flat, Britt's top would look like a rectangle with sleeves. On the twenty-five-year-old Britt, however, it looked easy and sexy and trendy. Britt didn't care that much about clothes, but the feeling wasn't mutual. Clothes never failed to complement her.

On this first day of May, the Pacific Northwest forecast called for a peak temperature of sixty-two. Nora had dressed in her trusty cable-knit sweater. It was three years old and it, too, looked like a rectangle when you laid it flat. Unfortunately, it continued to resemble a rectangle while on Nora's body.

God, who must have diagnosed her to be very longsuffering indeed, had seen fit to give her two beautiful sisters. One older. One younger. Nora's genes had labeled her as the dotty spinster of the trio long before her ill-fated love life ever had.

She checked her watch. Five till noon. "We've been in here for almost forty-five minutes. How much longer do you think it's going to be? I'm craving my iPhone."

"You need a technology detox." More window wrestling.

If Nora had her phone, she could distract herself by checking her messages and social media platforms for communication from Duncan. Shutting her into this room without her phone was akin to shoving Linus into the world without his blanket.

Another booming thud rumbled the air. Two men shouted muffled threats.

Nora closed her eyes and scrolled down a mental list of all the things she'd planned to do on this Saturday. She'd planned to read book six in the Silverstone Chronicles. Design pinnable images for Merryweather's Summer Antique Fair. Make a batch of apple cinnamon soap from a recipe her great-great-grandmother had handwritten in 1888. If there'd been additional time, she'd hoped to do what she always did with leftover time on the weekends: rewatch episodes of *Northamptonshire*.

It had taken Britt and her thirty minutes to drive here, to the town of Shore Pine. Once they stopped at Mr. Hartnett's on the way home so that Nora could deliver the latest in a long string of bribery gifts, then continued on to their hometown of Merryweather, there'd definitely not be time left in the day to indulge in *Northamptonshire*.

A scent like that of burning chemicals mixed with sugar wafted to Nora. She glanced to the side in time to see smoke slide into the room from beneath the door. Smoke! "Um." She gestured to it.

"Huh," Britt said. "Cool effect."

Nora carefully drew in breath, making sure the smoke didn't smell like an actual fire. It didn't.

Commanding voices and the clatter of a scuffle drew closer to their location. Like a sewing machine needle increasing in speed, Nora's heart picked up its pace.

"Oooh," Britt said. "I'm liking this."

A grinding sound came from above. The sprinklers that had been embedded in the ceiling descended. "No!" Nora called out.

In the next instant, cold water hit her in the face. Squealing, she drew herself into a ball, tucking her head between her upraised knees and wrapping her arms around her shins. Across the room, Britt hissed with disgust.

"Thank you so much for inviting me to partake in this fun experience," Nora said to her sister, though the words went little further than her ancient clogs. "Next time I feel overly content and dry and warm, perhaps I can come again."

The door to their room banged open. Nora angled her face toward the entranceway just as a man filled the opening. A big man. Square-jawed. His grave gaze swept the square footage in a millisecond. He seemed not to notice the falling raindrops, though they peppered his wet, spiky brown hair and drizzled down his stubbled face. He radiated complete and total competency.

The force of his presence careened into Nora like a hundred-mile-an-hour wind. In response, she could do nothing but hold her ground and blink.

Deep within the building, an alarm began to blare.

A much smaller and more human-looking guy wearing a drenched business suit slipped into the room. The smaller one waved Britt forward. "Follow me, please. I'll lead you out." He moved off and Britt loped out of sight behind him.

Faint displeasure crimped the edge of the big one's lips as the full weight of his attention settled on Nora. The smaller one had been in training, she figured. This one must be the instructor, and he was irritated because his trainee hadn't noticed her in her huddled spot. The trainee had escorted out only the hostage who'd been standing directly in front of him, impossible to miss.

He slanted his body so that she had plenty of room to exit. "This way."

Nora spent a great deal of her time journeying to eras long past and places entirely fictional. Thanks to that and the nervousness she really *had* been feeling, it wasn't a stretch to imagine that this fantastical person was her real rescuer.

His hair was thick and well cut. It stuck up slightly in the front. She couldn't make out the shade of his eyes. Hazel? Subtle horizontal lines marked his forehead. How old was he? Thirty? Thirty-five? No trace of softness clung to his face. It looked like a face hardened by both experience and fitness. The same went for his tall, strong body.

He'd dressed in a black sweater, brown cargo pants, and worn-in leather Red Wing work boots. "Ma'am?" He regarded her with professional courtesy stretched thin with impatience.

Still staring at him, Nora used her fingertips to smooth water from her eyes in hopes of seeing him better. To be honest, he seemed a little too good to be true.

Then again, she was twenty-nine and single, and she'd purposely filled her life with things other than romance for three years straight. For the most part, she came into contact either with residents of Merryweather she'd known all her life or elderly people. In her regular life, she *never* met or even caught glimpses of men like this—

He strode to her.

She may have tarried too long. He probably thought her mute or so obstinate that she was playing the part of recalcitrant hostage on purpose.

Nora began to lever herself up, but he swept her into his arms before she could get any momentum. Her lips popped open. Her hand automatically rose to latch around one wide shoulder.

He walked from the room, through the fog-filled space beyond. Water continued to tumble from overhead.

She was being carried by him! Despite her additional weight, he walked with easy fluidity. Rescuing damsels from distress just might be an everyday occurrence for him. "B—" she began, then realized she had no idea what she'd been about to say. She, who was never at a loss for words.

A delicious masculine scent rose from his skin. He'd braced an arm behind her back and one beneath her bent knees. Her side was pressed against a male torso that had about as much give as a fir tree.

This was . . . incredibly intimate. Her hip was up against the abs of a man she hadn't even spoken one word to. Her palm was gripping his wet shoulder. And all she'd managed so far was "b." She needed to say something. . . .

Nora cleared her throat. "S-sorry about my slow response time back there. I was sort of stunned by," *you*, "the unexpected dousing."

He kept his attention focused ahead. His expression remained inscrutable.

"This is my first fake hostage experience. I'm a hostage rookie." Her limbs had begun to shake a bit from the cold and the wet.

No response.

"I probably would have been able to walk out under my own steam. Eventually."

They arrived at the top of a stairwell. Eep! Stairs. "If you'll let me—"

He carried her down.

A short foyer slid past, then they exited the building through sliding glass doors. The rest of the people who'd been a part of the exercise waited behind a temporary partition.

A small cheer went up at the sight of them. Nora spotted Britt right away. Her sister's eyes rounded with surprise. Or maybe hilarity.

Her rescuer set her on her feet, then met her gaze directly. "I apologize about the sprinklers. They don't usually go off when we deploy the smoke."

"Not a problem. I'm sure that deploying smoke is a tricky business." What was she saying? That wasn't witty. That just sounded inane.

"Are you all right?"

"Yes."

"Thank you for volunteering today." He nodded and moved to walk away—

"I'm Nora. Bradford."

He paused and faced her again. "John Lawson."

Intrepidly, she extended her hand. He gave it a firm shake.

"I live in Merryweather," she hurried to say, unwilling to let him go so soon. "I run the historical village downtown."

His chin dipped half an inch.

"I'm the director of the Library on the Green Museum." Mortification caused her cheeks to heat. Why was she rattling off her résumé as if trying to impress a prospective employer?

No reply. He wasn't exactly giving her a lot of conversational response to work with.

"I'm a genealogist and a historian. Anyway." She straightened and smiled brightly. "If I can be of assistance with . . ." She gestured vaguely toward the building. The distant alarm finally went silent. " . . . what you're doing here, let me know." Because genealogists were so famously helpful at staging crises.

His eyebrows drew together infinitesimally. "Did you say you're a genealogist?"

"Yes." Her pulse and her hope thrummed.

"I may give you a call about something."

"Great!"

Then he was gone, making his purposeful way toward a knot of people she assumed to be his coworkers. She didn't have her business cards on her. They and her phone were stashed in the purse she'd been asked to check in when they'd arrived. However, if John did decide to call her about the mysterious "something," it wouldn't be hard to locate the library's phone number. An Internet search for "Library on the Green" would pull it up in seconds.

A middle-aged man with ramrod military bearing stepped onto a crate and raised his voice to thank the volunteers for their time. He directed them toward a row of tables and invited them to help themselves to the pre-packaged sandwiches, chips, fruit, and bottled waters that waited there.

Everyone broke toward the free food, talking amongst themselves. Nora made her way back to Britt.

"What in the world just happened?" Britt asked.

"Well, when John arrived—"

"John? You're on a first name basis?"

"He carried me *in his arms*. That's the most intimate I've been with a man in years, so I thought it prudent that we exchange names."

"Why did he carry you?"

"I think I gaped at him a little too long when he arrived to rescue us."

"What do you mean, 'you gaped'?"

"I mean that I literally gaped at him. For a while there I was frozen. I think he got impatient. So he picked me up and carried me out."

Britt gave a disbelieving chuckle.

Nora raised her palms. "Is he or is he not one of the most striking men you've ever seen?"

"He's striking."

"He's mine, since I'm the one he carried and since you have a boyfriend."

"I broke up with Carson."

"What! When did this happen?"

"A couple of days ago," Britt said dismissively. "He was getting on my nerves."

"You were so happy."

"I fell out of happiness with him. He was more trouble than he was worth."

Britt's frequent romances always took off like rockets propelled by promise and power and star-crossed destiny. Then, a few months in, they all fizzled like a Tesla fifty miles from the nearest charging station.

The sisters retrieved their purses. No Facebook messages, tweets, emails, or text messages had come in except an automated text from Merryweather's smoothie shop letting Nora know about a weekend sale.

They took their places at the end of the food table line. As they inched forward, Nora kept trying to catch glimpses of John through the crowd. No luck. "So. About John . . ." She set a plastic-wrapped triangle of ham sandwich on the recyclable tray she'd been given.

"Still thinking about John?"

"You're kidding, right? I'll be thinking of nothing but John for months."

"If you're that into him, you should ask him out before we leave."

Nora selected a bag of kettle chips. "You don't actually think that I have the moxie to ask out a man I just met. Do you?"

"Asking John out might actually result in a date. Daydreaming about him won't."

Nora made a scoffing sound. "Does the name John Lawson ring a bell?"

"Well, this is Lawson Training Incorporated's event."

"Yes, but beyond that?"

Britt cocked her head to consider the question. She added two cookies and a bottle of water to her tray. "You know . . . it does ring a bell. A little."

"For me, too."

They decided to eat their lunch inside Nora's parked car, because there they could get heat flowing over their damp, clingy clothing. Once they'd closed themselves inside, Britt went to work on her food. Nora typed *John Lawson* into Wikipedia on her phone. A picture of John dressed in a naval uniform emerged. He looked younger in the photo than he did now, but exactly as compelling and serious and unflinching.

John Truman Lawson
Born: Seattle, Washington
Allegiance: United States of America
Service/Branch: United States Navy
Years of Service: Six
Unit: United States Navy SEALs
Awards: Medal of Honor

Nora sat back against the driver's seat. She'd just been rescued from a pretend emergency by a real Medal of Honor recipient. That explained why his name had seemed familiar—she'd caught some of the media coverage about his Medal of Honor a few years back. Everyone in the state of Washington had been filled with pride when the president had awarded the prestigious distinction to their own native son.

"Find out anything?" Britt asked.

"He's a former Navy SEAL and a Medal of Honor recipient. Good grief. Isn't the Medal of Honor the highest honor?"

"I think so."

Nora read through the rest of the information listed. "He was involved in a mission that resulted in the rescue of American and Canadian hostages. He saved a team member at risk to his own life, then held off the opposition until reinforcements arrived. The book *Uncommon Courage* and the movie of the same name are about him."

"Wow."

"It says that he lives here in Shore Pine and that he's the owner and CEO of Lawson Training Incorporated." The Wikipedia profile didn't provide nearly enough details to satisfy her. With a few quick taps, she ordered both the print and movie versions of *Uncommon Courage.*

Nora stared out the front windshield at a stand of aspen trees. The bright lime-green of their spring leaves contrasted boldly with their slender white trunks. Her sister crunched potato chips. Her car's heater whirred. Her own lunch waited untouched.

It had been years since she'd been attracted to anyone who wasn't fictional . . . or who wasn't an actor who played a fictional character. She was capable and scholarly and disinclined to gamble ever again on romance. Yet, something in John called out to something in her. It was unexplainable. Foolhardy, even.

And yet. Just thinking about him, just remembering the interaction she'd shared with him, caused warmth to curl deep within her.

• • •

Typed by John Lawson into the Reminders app on his phone:

○ Have building's sprinklers turned off. Can that be done and still be up to fire code?

○ Contact Nora Bradford at Library on the Green.

• • •

Facebook message from Duncan Bartholomew to Nora Bradford:

DUNCAN: How was your day, Librarian Extraordinaire?

NORA: Far better than average. I was a hostage in an emergency situation staged for training purposes. (I didn't particularly enjoy that part.) I ended up being rescued by a Navy SEAL. (I did particularly enjoy that part.)

DUNCAN: Just so long as you don't develop a crush on the Navy SEAL. Adolphus is prone to jealousy where Miss Lucy Lawrence is concerned.

NORA: Adolphus hasn't yet noticed the existence of Miss Lucy Lawrence. Much to my everlasting chagrin.

DUNCAN: But when he does notice Lucy's existence I do believe he'll be prone to jealousy.

NORA: When (and if) Adolphus finally notices Lucy's existence, she will be his. Heart and soul. Always and forever.

CHAPTER
Two

Nora answered the library's ringing phone the way she always did, with a cheerful, "Library on the Green Museum."

"May I speak with Nora Bradford?"

She instantly recognized the calm and confident timbre of the male voice on the other end of the line. For five unbearable days, she'd been waiting for John to call, praying the whole time that his noncommittal *"I may give you a call about something"* would turn into a reality.

She'd been sitting in her office at her desk, legs crossed. Now she plunked both feet on the floor and scooted to the edge of her seat, back snapping into a straight line. "This is Nora."

"Nora, this is John Lawson." He went on to explain when and where they'd met.

She didn't interrupt him. She didn't tell him that she was a professional researcher and that she'd scoured every detail about him available for public consumption.

She knew, for example, that he was thirty-three years old and that, like her, he was a Christian. Repeatedly in his book, he'd given God the glory for everything that had gone right on his most famous mission. *Be still my heart*, she'd thought each time she'd encountered one of his humble, plainspoken statements about his faith.

She'd learned that John was the eldest child of Ray, captain of a boat that took tourists on fishing expeditions on Puget Sound, and Linda, an elementary school administrator. She knew that he and his younger sister, Heather, had grown up in the Upper Rainier Beach neighborhood of Seattle. He'd graduated from Northern Arizona University before joining the Navy and getting himself on a track that led to the notoriously brutal BUD/S training, the first step to becoming a SEAL. She'd read his book and watched his movie and combed through every word of every page on his company's website.

"That's right," she said lightly when he finished, as if he'd just jogged her memory. "I'm glad to hear from you. Have you saved anyone from a fire sprinkler shower so far today?"

A beat of quiet. "Five so far. It's been a slow morning."

Nora laughed. "Your other hostages probably have legs that work faster than mine."

"Yes," he agreed.

"What can I do for you, John?" Oh, the deliciousness of saying his name. It was a plain name. The plainest name there was. Yet it was also timeless. Manly. Strong. A trendy name wouldn't have suited him. The uncompromising *John* was just right.

"Do you help people research their ancestry?" he asked. "As part of your job?"

"Yes, I do. I'm fairly well versed at accessing records online, plus I have a large collection of books and documents here at the museum that are often useful to people who are investigating their ancestry. The museum's primary focus is Mason County, but I have a fair number of resources from other parts of the state, as well."

Silence. She had the sense that John was weighing whether or not to enlist her help. How could she convince him to give her a try?

Nora bit her lip against the yearning washing over her and turned her gaze to the outdoors. Her second-story office windows provided views of spreading pecan branches and, beyond

the branches, glimpses of her kingdom—Merryweather Historical Village. Working in this office was like working in a tree house.
"Are you in the process of gathering information about your heritage?" she asked.

"You could say that."

"Well, I'd be glad to lend a hand. Assisting people as they assemble their family tree is one of the aspects of my job that I like best." Especially when those people were named John Lawson.

"Can we meet?" he asked.

"Certainly!" Had that sounded too eager?

"What time is good for you?"

Her mind raced. It was five o'clock, almost closing time. "Tomorrow afternoon?"

"I can be there around four."

"Have you finished your homework?" Nora asked Randall the next day. Eleven-year-old Randall Cooper had become as much a fixture at the Library on the Green as the display cases.

"Not yet." He paused the violent shooting game he'd been playing on his phone and lifted his face. As usual, he'd made himself at home in the rocking chair situated next to the museum's corner window. Nora had initially set the chairs near the Children's Area for parents to sit in. However, Randall occupied "his" chair far more often than anyone else.

"Ten more minutes of that not-very-redeeming-looking game and then homework?" Nora prodded.

"Okay."

"Would you like some tea? To go with all that gore?"

"No, thank you."

Nora had been doing her best to introduce Randall to the joys of tea. So far her efforts were faring about as well as Ahab's search for the white whale. "Hot chocolate?" she asked.

"Yes, please." He grinned. His big, straight, gleaming teeth flashed startlingly white next to his ebony-colored skin.

Nora had always been a goner when confronted with that grin. She disappeared into the museum's small kitchen to prepare his hot chocolate.

Randall had wandered into the Library on the Green two years ago after moving to Merryweather to live full time with his grandmother. Because the museum stood at the halfway point on Randall's walk home from school, it had become his convenient stopping place.

At first Nora had treated him in the polite, customer-service-oriented way that she treated all her patrons. But then she'd learned two things. That Randall's visits were going to become an almost daily occurrence. And that Randall's dad had died in a car accident. Nora herself had survived a heartbreaking loss early in life. Their growing familiarity with each other and their bond of childhood trauma had connected Nora to Randall. Nowadays, she treated him like a nephew.

To be fair, Randall didn't *technically* require an unofficial aunt. He was a responsible, smart, independent kid. But since Nora had no one at home to fuss over, Randall humored her. With equanimity, he allowed her to furnish him with snacks, odd jobs around the museum, occasional rides to basketball practices and games, homework accountability, and cautionary tales about middle school.

In return, Randall furnished Nora with a listening ear, thoughtful suggestions about the museum, and that heart-tasering smile.

Nora was never sure just who was ministering to whom in her friendship with Randall. It might be a tie.

Nora dutifully garnished the hot chocolate with mini marshmallows, then delivered the mug and two Walkers Shortbread cookies to Randall. She kept the cookies stocked for him—

Well. She also kept them stocked for herself. Anything that came in a container decked out in Scottish plaid couldn't be all bad for you.

"Thank you, Ms. Bradford."

"You're welcome, Randall. Just five minutes left before homework, okay?"

"Yes, ma'am." He moved his head in the way kids have of both saying yes and, at the same time, returning their attention to more pressing things. In this case, his phone's screen.

She checked her watch. John was due to arrive in fifteen minutes. Nervous excitement had been burrowing more and more deeply within her as the time of his arrival had drawn near.

"Nora?" One of the two ancient ladies standing near a map of Indigenous Peoples of the Pacific Northwest motioned her over.

"Yes, Mrs. Williams?"

She gestured to her companion. "This is my dear friend, Iris . . . oh, but of course you know Iris."

"I do."

"I was just telling Iris about my ancestor, Arthur Thacker, and of course, she's just as fascinated as can be and wants to see his journal for herself."

Mrs. Williams was a museum regular with a case of hypochondria and an endless thirst for information about her Mason County ancestor, Arthur Thacker. Nora had tirelessly unearthed every possible shred of information about Thacker, but Mrs. Williams hadn't given up hope of uncovering fresh details.

Poor Iris had been in with Mrs. Williams and seen the journal a minimum of three times previously. Iris was either the most forbearing friend alive or she had dementia and had forgotten the other times. "Certainly. I'll just go and get a few pairs of gloves." Opinions were mixed as to whether gloves were needed when handling antique papers, but Nora preferred to err on the side of safety.

Ten minutes before John's arrival.

The building's upper story contained Nora's office, as well as a roomy central space large enough for both a sitting area and Nikki's desk. Three days a week, Nikki worked inside the museum handling property management, billing, the website, event planning, and marketing. On Saturdays and Sundays she worked in the village as one of Nora's historical interpreters.

Nikki frowned at her computer. "I need a man."

"Good men are hard to find," Nora answered, pulling two sets of white gloves from their drawer.

"I didn't say I need a *good* man." Nikki looked up and released one of her throaty guffaws. She was fifty-eight, with fashion sense like a Best of the '80s highlight reel, heavy makeup, and a body that really did resemble an hourglass. Her bust, especially, was monumental. Almost as epic was the bouffant puff she teased up behind her bangs and in front of the barrette she used to pull back the sides of her long, dyed brown hair.

Nikki had loved and buried two husbands. Before, in between, and after those two, she'd fallen in love with several others.

"Would you mind coming down in five minutes?" Nora asked. "Mrs. Williams is here and it would be great if you could take over with her. I have someone coming in for a scheduled appointment."

"Is your scheduled appointment with a male someone?"

"I plead the Fifth." Nora made her way back downstairs.

The old ladies set about donning the cotton gloves.

Carefully, Nora removed Thacker's journal from its case.

"Nora, I think I may have consumption," Mrs. Williams said sadly. "I have a terrible cough, night sweats, and a high fever. I expect to start coughing up blood any moment, of course."

"I think they call it tuberculosis these days, and I was just thinking how well you looked. . . ."

John. John would be here in the flesh in just seven minutes.

The historical marker outside of Nora Bradford's Library on the Green Museum informed John that the structure had been built in 1892 as the town's first apothecary. In 1938, the city purchased it and turned it into a library. It functioned as a library until the seventies, when the city moved the books into a new location across town.

John let himself inside. Darkly stained pine floorboards supported numerous cases and bookshelves. Art filled the walls. In the corner, paper and containers full of markers and crayons covered a kid-sized table.

He spotted Nora across the room, speaking with two white-haired ladies. She raised a hand in greeting.

He gestured for her to take her time. He always ran five minutes early.

He paused to examine a collection of weapons that had belonged to early pioneer settlers. The longer he stood there, the more the room's heavy quiet pressed in on him. A middle-aged couple, with their hands clasped behind their backs, stood a short distance away, reading information mounted next to a painting. A boy sat in one of the rocking chairs, head bent to his phone.

He could hear every word of Nora's conversation—one of the ladies was describing her night sweats in detail—even though they were several yards away.

It was going to be hard enough to talk to Nora, a stranger, about the things he'd come to talk to her about. There was no way he was going to talk to her here, with this audience listening in.

When a brunette joined Nora and the white-haired ladies, Nora approached him, smiling.

Her hair drew his attention first. It was red. Not a brownish red, but a bright, coppery red. An unusual color. Just like on the day they'd met, she'd put it up in a style that made him think of pinup girls from the forties. Why would she wear her hair like that? Fashion statement? If so, he didn't get it. The whole retro thing had always struck him as strange.

"You made it," she said.

"I did."

"Would you like to sit down?" She motioned to the rocking chairs. "I'll send that cute boy over there upstairs. Between you and me, he's supposed to be working on his homework anyway."

The brunette was staring at him with intense curiosity.

"Actually, I noticed there's a coffee shop nearby." The outdoor seating at the coffee shop would give them more privacy. Fifty-yard-line seats at a Seahawks game would give them more privacy. "Can I buy you a coffee?"

Her eyes rounded slightly. "Sure." She turned. "Nikki?"

"Yes?" answered the brunette. Had he imagined it or had she just winked at him?

"I'm going out. I'll be back in a bit."

"You bet. I'll hold down the fort."

A long rectangular lawn stretched outward from the steps that led down from the library's door. Old-fashioned buildings of all shapes and sizes were positioned around the grass like houses on a neighborhood street, each one facing inward.

John cut a glance at Nora as they walked along the gravel path that framed the lawn. The top of her head came up to about his chin. If he hadn't carried her the other day, he'd have guessed her to be heavier than she was because of the way she dressed. The sweater she'd worn Saturday and the blue one she wore today were both huge. Her hair, her sweater, her long skirt, and her flat boots made her look very much like the librarian she was.

"Have you visited the historical village before?" she asked.

"No. This is my first time." He'd lived in Shore Pine for five years and came to Merryweather occasionally. Both cities had approximately six thousand residents, both were popular weekend and summer destinations, both had historic downtown areas that had been revitalized in the last decade, both were situated near water. Merryweather was located on the southern "Great Bend" section of the Hood Canal. Shore Pine, to its west, sat on the edge of Lake Shore Pine.

John knew that Merryweather was named after Meriwether Lewis of Lewis and Clark fame. And he knew that the logging industry had built this town. He hadn't visited Merryweather Historical Village until now because he spent his free time watching sports, on his boat, or working out. Girly little villages weren't his thing. Some of these structures were so small they looked like what Snow White would have lived in.

"When Walmart opened in Shelton," Nora said, "this part of Merryweather turned into a ghost town. My father bought up the warehouses that occupied this site and tore them down. He and I both love history, so our intention was always to transport historical buildings here. Which, as you can see, is exactly what we did." She didn't fumble or pause or say *umm*. She spoke quickly and intelligently.

"How long ago did your father buy this land?"

"Eight years ago."

"I visited a historical village with my family once when I was growing up. We bought tickets and walked through houses that were set up inside to look like they had when they were new."

"Right. Most historical villages are like that."

Not this one. The buildings were all in use. He saw a women's clothing store, an art gallery, a pottery shop, a flower shop. People were everywhere. Visiting the stores. Stopping to take photos. A few moms sat on blankets on the grass, watching their kids play.

"We wanted to attract large numbers of people downtown," Nora explained. "Also, it's my personal preference to keep historical things alive by utilizing them, so my dad and I decided we'd rent out the buildings to local businesses."

"It sounds like you and your dad make a good team."

"We did—I mean, we do. My dad serves as an advisor these days. He gave the village to me as a college graduation gift."

He looked across his shoulder at her. Raised an eyebrow.

Her lips curved. "I know. Generous gift, right?"

"I got a tie and a silver pen for graduation."

She laughed. "My father gave each of us, my two sisters and me, a graduation gift meant to help us gain a foothold in our chosen professions. Each of us has been solely responsible for the gift ever since."

They reached the coffee shop, which was housed inside a clapboard house with a wooden porch. The interior smelled like butterscotch. Now that he was inside he could see that it was more of a pie shop than a straight-up coffee shop. The workers behind the counter greeted Nora like a friend.

"What would you like?" he asked her.

She ordered hot tea.

"What else?" he prompted, drawing out his wallet. "Pie?"

"No, thank you. Tea is perfect."

He ordered coffee, and they took their drinks outside. His coffee had come in a to-go cup. Her tea had come in a fancy china cup with a saucer. He led her to the wooden table set farthest out on the lawn.

"How many of the buildings were here when your dad gave you this place?" he asked when they sat down.

"Three. The library is still in its original location. The only buildings we'd moved here at that time were Montgomery House and Hudson House." She pointed them out. "As soon as I took over, I started looking for locals willing to rent those two houses. Once I found them, I began renovating the library so it could function as a museum."

"How many buildings do you have here now?"

"Twelve." She took a sip of tea.

One company owner to another, he was impressed. "How did you grow it from three to twelve?"

"Rental income from the existing houses. Each time I'd saved enough money, I'd buy a new house and have it transported here. Somewhere along the way, Merryweather caught on. Tourists started to show up, just like I'd hoped they would, and they ended up giving new life to this whole section of town. B&Bs and restaurants opened their doors. Businesses moved into the office space near the village. Investors gutted old buildings and created apartments. Now we're bustling."

"Is the historical village under the jurisdiction of the city of Merryweather?"

She shook her head. "My dad and I have had to get permits and approval from the city every step of the way, but the village is privately owned."

"So you're your own boss."

"Yes." She met his eyes over the rim of her teacup. He caught a gleam of satisfaction and pride in her expression before she looked away and took another sip of tea.

The day of the training exercise, his first impression of Nora Bradford had been that she was pitiful, with her dripping hair and her inability to get up and walk out of the building. His second impression had been that she was plain. His third had been that she dressed old but was probably younger than he was.

He'd only been right about the young part.

She wasn't pitiful. And she wasn't exactly plain. Next to her bright hair, her skin was the color of milk. She didn't have the sort of features that would cause a man to do a double take. But her face did strike him as pretty in a gentle way. Nora Bradford was like the girl who was a sleeper in high school, then surprised everyone by going to Harvard.

"Just to make sure I understand," he said. "You're a landlady, a historian, and a genealogist?"

"Strictly speaking, yes. Nikki, who works with me, handles the landlady part. She's the one who deals with the tenants and rental income. I oversee the big-picture issues concerning the village, but on a daily basis, I'm more focused on the library. I spend a good bit of my time helping people research their ancestry."

He drank his coffee, tasting its rich, nutty, bitter flavor.

"The village required more of my attention back when I was acquiring buildings, but all that's slowed down now. I just need one more building, and then the village will be complete. See that open space, at the far end near the bank of the creek?" She indicated the area with her teacup.

He nodded. The library anchored one end of the development. The open space the other.

"I'm going to put a chapel there. I already have the MacKenzie Timber Barn situated next to where the chapel will go. It's been refurbished, so it's ready for receptions."

"Have you not been able to find a chapel?" he asked.

"No, I've found one. But I haven't been able to convince Mr. Hartnett, its owner, to sell it to me."

"Then why not bring in another chapel?"

"Because the Hartnett Chapel is perfection. It has a hand-painted stencil border along the top of the sanctuary and a *bell tower*." She shook herself slightly. "Anyhow. Enough about me."

She didn't say more, so he figured *enough about me* was her friendly way of inviting him to tell her his reason for today's meeting.

John shifted, peering at the empty space where Nora wanted her chapel to go. Her cup made a clinking sound as she set it on its saucer. A breeze rustled the branches overhead.

Sharing personal information with other people had never come easily to John. His time with the teams had only driven deeper his habit of playing his cards close to his vest.

He wouldn't have called Nora if his need to know his medical history hadn't become urgent. And his need to know his medical history wouldn't have become urgent if he hadn't been handed the diagnosis he'd been handed two months ago.

His phone chimed. "Excuse me."

"Of course."

He read the text and sent a brief text back, then returned the phone to his pocket and centered his attention on Nora. Should he trust her?

She was easy to talk to. She wasn't interrupting him or speaking over him. She wasn't too uptight or too mellow. She seemed smart and qualified and friendly. She made him comfortable. She was exactly the sort of person he should trust with this. "I wanted to meet with you because I'm trying to find my birth mother," he said.

She held his gaze calmly. "Okay. Tell me more."

"My birth mother put me up for adoption right after I was born. My parents adopted me shortly after that."

She sat still, hands in her lap. He could sense her mind turning. "Have your parents given you all the adoption agency paperwork they have concerning your adoption?"

"Yes, they gave me the paperwork a long time ago. I haven't talked to them yet about . . . my decision to search." He didn't want to cause his parents pain. Plus, he was well aware that he might never find his birth mother. If he didn't, then what was the point in telling his parents about his search?

"What do you know about your birth mother?"

"She was young and unmarried. My parents never met her, and she's never tried to contact them or me."

"I see."

"Washington unsealed adoption records a few years ago," he said. "So I applied for my original birth certificate, and they sent it to me."

"In that respect, it's fortunate for you that you were born in Washington. Only a handful of states have unsealed the records. In the states that haven't, searchers typically only have access to adoption paperwork and the birth certificate that lists their adoptive parents."

She knew her stuff. "Right. My father's name was left blank on the original birth certificate. My mother's name was listed as Sherry Thompson. I was born in Shelton at Presbyterian Hospital."

"Shelton." She chewed the edge of her lip thoughtfully.

Shelton was located twelve miles south of Merryweather. Presbyterian had been the largest hospital in the area at the time of his birth, and still was. People from Merryweather and Shore Pine and the rest of the towns in a thirty-mile radius of Shelton all used it.

"Where was your adoption agency located?" she asked.

"Seattle."

"I'm inferring that you contacted me because you haven't had success finding a woman named Sherry Thompson living in this region of Washington."

He wasn't used to talking with people who used the word *inferring*. "Exactly. Thompson is a common last name. I went on several websites to look for Sherry Thompson and contacted that registry. . . ." He couldn't remember its official name.

"The one that pairs you with your birth parents if they're also searching for you?"

"Yes. I didn't have any luck."

She tapped the pad of her thumb against the handle of her cup. Her forehead knotted like she was trying to solve a riddle. "I'm not surprised to hear that you weren't able to find Sherry easily. Chances are good that she's married and changed her last name at least once since your birth."

"True. Since I've already done the only things I know to do, I'm at a point where I could use some expert advice."

"I'd love to give you advice," she said immediately. Then hesitated, her cheeks turning pale pink. "However, I need to tell you that this isn't my *particular* area of expertise. I've only worked with a few other adoptees and only read three, perhaps, four books on the subject of adoptee search and reunion."

"That's more books than I've read on the subject."

"I'm certainly willing to educate myself as needed along the way. If we reach a dead end that I can't navigate past, then I'll put you in touch with organizations or private investigators who might be able to take you the rest of the way toward a reunion. Fair enough?"

"Fair enough. I'll pay you for your time, of course."

"No, no." She raised both palms. "I make my living from revenue generated by the village. I never charge the people I assist. Never. You're no exception."

"I *am* an exception."

She leaned forward, stacking her hands on the edge of the table. "Just between you and me, I adore history. I'm the one who should be paying my clients for the pleasure of getting to conduct their research."

"Good try, but no. I'm not going to work with you on this unless you'll let me pay you."

She frowned.

He frowned back. He wasn't a charity case. Nor was he a man whose mind was easily changed. Redheaded librarians who used big words didn't scare him.

"*Really*," she tried, "I'd much prefer not to charge you. It wouldn't be right to charge you for the same assistance I give to others for free."

"Email me a bill to cover the time you're likely to spend on my case over the next two weeks. If we're still at this two weeks from now, bill me again." He pulled a business card from his wallet and handed it over.

"I'd rather—"

"No."

She sighed, looking down at his card.

"John!" A woman called to him from across the grass.

He twisted in his seat and saw Allie walking toward them. When she'd heard he was coming to the village today, she'd immediately pitched the idea of joining him for shopping, followed by dinner. He'd explained where she could find him in the text he'd sent a few minutes ago.

"Are we agreed?" he asked Nora, standing up.

She stood, too. "We're agreed. Can you gather all the documents you have? I'd like to go over them together at our next meeting."

"Sure. As soon as you send me your bill, we'll set up a time for our next meeting." He'd taken whole courses on negotiation.

"Hey." Allie gave him a warm smile as she drew near.

"Hey. Allie, this is Nora. Nora, Allie."

Nora grinned as wide as someone who'd just been told she'd won the lottery. "So nice to meet you!"

"Likewise." Allie interlaced her fingers with his, and the two women exchanged small talk.

John half-listened while wondering how long he'd have to pretend to enjoy shopping and whether any of the restaurants around here served steak. "We better get on our way," he said to Allie during a gap in the conversation.

"Sounds good."

"See you later, Nora," he said.

"Yes!" Nora responded. "Indeed. Indeed!"

The librarian was a little odd.

Nora stood like a statue, watching John walk toward the building known as Doc Hubert's office. He was still holding the hand of his girlfriend. Could—could Allie be his *wife*?

No, no, no. Nora's thorough study of John would have turned up information about a marriage. Allie must be his girlfriend. His very attractive girlfriend with long, dark blond hair, a fit body, and lots of natural, relaxed confidence.

Nora's smile ached with effort. It felt like the Cheshire's cat's smile, except more foolish. *Of course he has a girlfriend, Nora! Of course he does. How could you have imagined that he didn't? He's the definition of handsome masculinity and full of legendary bravery to boot.* She wasn't the only woman in America who'd noticed his appeal. Every woman he came into contact with every day, all day long, had to notice.

She'd been in her element during their entire exchange, talking first about her village and then about his search for his birth mother. Nora loved nothing better than when people turned to her for help. She relished being useful, and she'd been lapping up his need of her and feeling somewhat cute in the new cardigan and skirt she'd bought last night especially for this meeting. She'd even dared to think that John might be picking up on the chemistry between them, too.

Disappointment solidified in her midsection like concrete.

It was only because she'd been on such a high that the return to reality felt so steep. Once she'd had more time to think about this, she'd feel better.

The Dreaded Harrison and Rory, his pregnant wife, chose that moment to exit the children's boutique housed in Golding's Mill. Harrison gave Nora a friendly wave. She returned the gesture, Cheshire cat style. No doubt the two of them had been busily accumulating tiny newborn clothing and lovely little accessories for the nursery.

Cold envy shafted like an arrow through Nora's heart. She rapidly bustled her teacup back to The Pie Emporium.

The Dreaded Harrison and his wife were shopping for baby things.

And the Most Delectable John had a girlfriend.

• • •

Text message from Nora to Willow Bradford:

Nora
I'm self-medicating my emotional distress with ice cream. How much can I safely prescribe? I wouldn't want to overdose on Ben & Jerry's.

Willow
Just one pint.

Nora
Uh-oh.

Willow
I'm arriving in Merryweather tomorrow, so from then on we can eat ice cream together. Ice cream eaten in the company of a sister isn't nearly so pathetic.

CHAPTER Three

The next day Nora stood sentinel on the covered front porch of Bradfordwood, the home she'd grown up in. The gray sky slid by like a moving watercolor painting. Raindrops plinked off the roof, the stone steps, the red bricks that formed the driveway. The murky, opaque quality of the light was the result of both the rain and the fact that somewhere beyond the clouds, the sun had begun to set.

Nora slipped her hands into the pockets of her sweat shirt. She'd dressed in work-out gear this morning because she'd had an industrious plan to hit the gym at some point this Saturday. But then she'd spent ages agonizing over how much to charge John before finally crafting and emailing him a bill. She'd picked up the Silverstone Chronicles, sunk two hours into reading, visited her favorite fiction blogs, updated her progress on Goodreads.com, and switched out her winter wardrobe for her summer wardrobe. She never did make it to the gym, yet here she stood in her yoga pants, Hogwarts Alumni T-shirt, and sweat shirt.

Her older sister, Willow, was due to arrive any minute, and tradition dictated that the family be standing outside, waiting and waving, when she pulled up. Nora was *certainly* one for tradition even if Willow's string of arrivals and departures occasionally made her feel dull. Trusty Nora. The sister who'd never lived outside of Merryweather except during her college years. Still here. Rooted in the town of her birth.

The truth? She loved Merryweather. She'd actively chosen to live here, so there was no reason for her choice to make her feel drab—

Nora almost snorted. When had any comparison between herself and Willow or Britt *not* made her feel drab?

She could still remember the moment that had crystallized her role in her family in her mind. She'd been thirteen and sandwiched between her sisters, sharing the same bathroom mirror as they prepared to leave for a stage production of *The Lion King*.

She'd peeked to one side and watched fifteen-year-old Willow lean forward to apply mascara. In the light from the wall-mounted bathroom fixture, Willow's face looked breathtakingly lovely. She had big, almond-shaped eyes and amazing cheekbones. Perfect bone structure, really.

Willow was the beautiful one.

Nora peeked to the other side and watched Britt brush her thick, long hair. At the age of nine, Britt had already been recognized by their parents as a creative genius. For months, she'd been churning out dessert masterpieces that seemed better suited to magazine covers than to their family's table.

Britt was the talented one.

Nora then turned her attention on her own reflection. Mouse-brown hair, because she hadn't started dyeing it red until midway through college. Ordinary face and body. Braces.

Okay, she thought pragmatically. The reality of her sisters hadn't snuck up on her, after all. She'd been living with the truth of their extraordinary qualities all her life. But in that one moment, the truth demanded a decision from her.

Your sisters will always be prettier and more naturally talented than you are. How are you going to respond, Nora?

She'd firmed her lips and lifted her chin. *I'm the smart one. That's how.*

That choice had informed everything that came after. Nowadays, Nora looked back on her plucky thirteen-year-old self proudly because that awkward girl had chosen the right track.

The year Willow left home to attend UCLA, she was discovered by a modeling agent. She'd been circling the globe ever since, captivating the world with her beauty.

A freight train couldn't have stopped Britt from following her passion. She aced culinary school, then studied abroad for two years under legendary French pastry chefs. She became a Master Chocolatier and opened a shop in Merryweather Historical Village named Sweet Art.

Willow and Britt had done very well for themselves, yes. But Nora knew them through and through. They had flaws and vulnerabilities, too. Also acres of goodness. She loved them. She was closer to them than to anyone else in the world.

These days she spent very little emotional angst on the topic of her appearance or her God-given talents (or lack thereof) relative to theirs. She did sometimes make wisecracks to herself about it. And it did prick her when she was introduced to people and they responded with a baffled, "*You're* Willow's sister?"

But emotional angst? Not much.

She'd been looking forward to Willow's homecoming.

How long had it been since Willow was home last? Five months? Even though they made an effort to visit each other—Nora had flown to LA for a long weekend in February—they were never able to spend as much time together as Nora would have liked.

This particular visit promised to be extra special because Willow would be staying in Merryweather for more than six months. She hadn't spent that much consecutive time in Washington since she'd left for college.

Footsteps approached, bringing Britt to a halt next to Nora. "No sign of her yet?"

Nora shook her head and lifted her phone. "Any minute now, I'm guessing. I'm waiting for her usual, 'I'm at the gate turning in' text."

They watched the rain sprinkle the drive. "I escaped out here away from prying ears so I could get the scoop about your meeting yesterday with the Navy SEAL."

"He has a girlfriend."

Britt wrinkled her nose. "Well, that stinks."

"Doesn't it?"

"Maybe they're about to break up," Britt suggested hopefully.

"Their relationship looked pretty well established to me. They were holding hands, and she was beaming at him. They seemed at ease with each other."

"Perhaps what appears to be ease is really serious dissatisfaction on both their parts."

"Yes, and perhaps Adolphus Brook will come cantering up this driveway on a stallion, pull me onto the saddle with him, and ride away with me."

"I'd pick John Lawson over Adolphus Brook any day of the week," Britt said.

"Blasphemy!" Nora had spent three years watching and rewatching episodes of *Northamptonshire* and mooning over Adolphus, one of the characters on the show.

Britt zipped her puffy vest up to her neck. "Brr." The wind teased free a few sections of her hair and sent them wisping around her forehead and cheeks. She'd caught the rest into a topknot that looked effortlessly chic. "How did things go between you and John before his girlfriend showed up?"

"Things went very well. He's . . ." Nora groaned. "I can't adequately put it into words. . . ."

"That's a first for you."

Nora chuckled. John had that effect on her. He foiled words! Even artful words. "He gives off this aura of complete . . . ability. It's in his face and his bearing and his body language. It's not pretentious or anything. It's just . . . well. I'm guessing he has a crazy amount of confidence."

"Go on."

"If a *dragon* had swooped down during our meeting, I think

John would have stood up, wiped the crumbs from his hands, and taken care of it."

"I love men who can fell dragons."

"I can fell dragons." The masculine voice came from behind them.

Nora angled to watch Zander exit Bradfordwood's grand front doors carrying a plate covered with six small and crispy potato pancakes, each topped with a swirl of sour cream, a thin slice of smoked salmon, and a sprig of dill.

"At the moment," Nora told him, "the ability to steal Valentina's appetizers is a skill I value above felling dragons. I'm starving."

"How'd you manage to sneak these without Grandma noticing?" Britt asked him.

"I have my ways." A twist of humor on his lips, Zander extended the plate toward the sisters.

Alexander "Zander" Ford and Britt had met when they'd both been in the ninth grade. They became the best of friends. Zander had spent so much time with the Bradfords over the years that he'd earned a place as a de facto family member.

Sometimes, when Nora looked at Zander, she could still see the shadow of the ashen, undersized, sullen kid he'd once been, though he was a grown man now. His almost-black hair and the dark shadow of scruff on his cheeks contrasted with his fair skin and ocean-blue eyes. Sleeves of tattoos covered his arms down to his wrists. He always dressed starkly and simply. Today's outfit consisted of worn jeans and a black T-shirt.

Zander and his older brother had lived with his aunt and uncle during their high school years because Child Protective Services had removed them from their mother and father's care. Nora hadn't forgotten his aunt and uncle's junky house on Merryweather's ragged edge. Nor had she forgotten the tough, street-kid clothes Zander had worn like protective armor in those days.

He no longer needed armor. His lean, six-foot-tall body communicated toughness very well all by itself. He was serious and introverted, with a dry sense of humor you'd never be treated to unless you'd gained his hard-won friendship—or happened to be standing next to him when he murmured something funny under his breath.

No stranger would guess that the guy with the tats and the intense eyes had a photographic memory. But they might guess, if they were very observant or especially skilled at deciphering the charge in the air, that Zander was in love with his very good friend Britt. And had been for a long, long time.

"When you were inside," Britt told Zander, "Nora told me that the Navy SEAL has a girlfriend."

"The ones who can fell dragons are usually taken." He tipped up his chin and popped one of the potato pancakes into his mouth whole.

"Dating words to live by." Nora nibbled on the delicious appetizer. Zander had only stolen two for each of them. It would require willpower to make her portion last.

"You're going to be seeing him more," Britt said to Nora. "Right?"

"Right. I'm helping him research his genealogy." Which was the extent of what she'd divulge to her sisters or anyone else on the subject. John had told her he hadn't yet informed his parents about his search for his birth mother. She certainly wouldn't be the one to shatter his privacy.

"You never know what might happen between the two of you in time," Britt said. "The future is wide open."

"Yeah," Zander agreed. "The Navy SEAL might get eaten by the dragon."

"John Lawson would never get eaten by a dragon," Nora replied, with no small amount of indignation. "You serfs clearly haven't read *Uncommon Courage*."

Zander and Britt laughed. "Your sister called us serfs," Zander said, flicking a potato crumb in Britt's direction.

"Calling John's prowess into question will always get you categorized as serfs," Nora assured them.

"You big serf you," Britt said to Zander.

"You're such a serf, Britt."

"You are."

"No, you."

"Where's Willow?" Nora frowned toward the point where the driveway disappeared in the direction of the road. The actual road couldn't be seen from the porch. Bradfordwood reigned over a two-hundred-acre plot of land. "She said she'd be here in ten minutes what seems like fifteen minutes ago."

Just as she awoke the screen on her phone to check the time, a text from Willow arrived.

Turning in, it read.

"Good! She's here. Hide the evidence."

Zander slid the plate and napkins out of sight beneath one of the porch chairs.

Nora leaned inside the front door. "Grandma," she called. "Valentina. Willow's driving up."

Willow stored her white Range Rover near Sea-Tac airport. Each time she flew in, personnel from the storage facility brought the SUV to the gate to meet her. The car's headlights glided into view.

Nora, Britt, and Zander started waving. Grandma's diminutive frame and Valentina's plump one took up places nearby, also waving. Even though there were five of them, their welcome party seemed woefully small without Mom and Dad, who were usually such an integral part of every porch greeting and farewell.

When the Range Rover stopped, they all hurried forward. Willow hugged them, smelling of Chanel and bringing light to the overcast day with her bright green eyes and gentle smile. "Hi, Nora. Britt! So good to see you, Zander. Hi, Grandma. You look wonderful. Valentina, did you make the potato pancake appetizers you promised?"

Willow wore black skinny jeans and a pale gray sweater that sheathed her body like a stylish cocoon. At five feet nine, Willow was on the short side for a model. Nonetheless, as they climbed the steps and entered the house together, Willow stood four full inches taller than Nora.

Willow answered their questions about how her travel day had gone while they made their way past the front dining room and sitting room, the library, and a powder room. For all Bradfordwood's ten thousand square feet, the family mostly congregated in just two rooms: the kitchen and den. Those spaces flowed together and lined the rear of the first floor. Enormous windows captured the view off the home's back terrace, a long sweep of manicured lawn that stretched downhill to the Pacific water of the Hood Canal. On the far side of the canal, land rose into a hump that resembled the back of a great, green slumbering dinosaur.

"Eat!" Valentina encouraged in her thick Russian accent, her stout arms motioning to the appetizers she'd set on the bar. "I make potato pancake for you, miss! Yummy. So yummy!"

Their father had hired Valentina as their housekeeper/nanny when Willow was a baby. Valentina's round, pink-cheeked face complemented a personality that shined with a perennial case of happiness.

Grandma, in contrast, must have excused herself to use the restroom right at the moment when the Holy Spirit handed out the fruit called joy. "I'll just take a broccoli spear," she said in her usual anguished tone. Nora suspected it gave her pleasure to slight Valentina by never eating anything but mouse-sized portions of her cooking. "There's dairy on the potato pancakes and dairy doesn't agree with me."

Each morning, Grandma donned her trademark pearl earrings and rolled her long white hair into an elegant bun at the nape of her neck. She'd been gifted with the smoothest and prettiest complexion of any seventy-nine-year-old woman alive. Never had she spent a day in the hospital. She had enough income to live comfortably and to dress gorgeously, yet she could look on any glass brimming to the top with Dom Pérignon and find a way to regard it as half empty.

The rest of them helped themselves to the potato pancakes, mixed nuts, and crudités. This spread was a mere precursor to the roast Nora could smell baking.

The room's lamps and recessed lights cast them all in golden light as they made themselves comfortable in the den with their plates, glasses, and paper napkins.

"I don't know why she didn't use the good linen napkins," Grandma groused to Nora.

"Has anyone heard from Mom and Dad since the group email they sent out a few days ago?" Willow asked.

"No, that's the last one I got, too," Nora answered. "They're still in Zambia receiving discipleship training."

"I love that they're finally fulfilling a dream that Mom's had for so long." Britt sat cross-legged on the sofa, plate balanced on one knee. "Some of my earliest memories are of her reading books to me about Africa and missionaries."

"She read those to me, too," Willow said. "Was it their anniversary, do you think, that finally tipped the scales and motivated them to serve overseas?"

"I think so," Britt answered. "It made them take stock."

"I agree," Nora said. "My theory is that Dad wanted to give Mom the only anniversary gift he hadn't given her yet."

"You *would* take the romantic approach." Zander had remained standing, one shoulder casually braced against the fireplace. "I think their anniversary reminded Garner that they're getting older, and if they were ever going to be missionaries, it needed to be now."

Nora arched an eyebrow. "You *would* take the death-is-imminent approach."

"Overseas missionary work is for the young," Grandma put in. "Kathleen and Garner are too old for it, as I've told them more than once."

"I don't think there's an expiration date on service," Britt said calmly. They were all used to disagreeing with Grandma.

"They're not too old for service," Grandma explained. "It's *overseas missionary service* that they're too old for. I certainly believe that the Lord expects all of us to suffer in His service until death."

"Um." Britt pulled a skeptical frown. "I don't think that suffering necessarily has to be a part of the service."

Grandma sniffed and held her broccoli spear airborne between two thin fingers. "In the Bible it says, 'Take up your cross and follow me.' Our service to the Lord should cost, otherwise it's not service."

"What about the verse that says, 'God loves a cheerful giver'?" Nora asked.

"It's entirely true. We're called to suffer cheerfully for God." Spoken by the lady who wouldn't recognize cheerfulness if it served her a hamburger.

"Well!" Nora made her voice bright to counteract Grandma's gloom. "Even though I'll miss them, I think it's great that Mom and Dad took the opportunity to go to Africa."

"And all because you"—Britt extended an arm with a grand flourish toward Willow—"made it possible."

In some ways, Willow had kept to the oldest-child stereotypes. She was hands down the sister who'd achieved the most. And like most firstborns, she was a rule follower. She wasn't pushy or bossy, however. If and when she guided the family, it was always through listening first, thinking second, and then speaking in her thoughtful way. "I'm glad I could take over the Inn at Bradfordwood so that Mom and Dad could go. I don't get many chances to help them these days." She rubbed a fingertip into the sofa's chenille fabric. "I needed a break from work anyway."

Grandma launched into a monologue about how the current generation worked too hard and never turned off their electronics—*Guilty*, Nora thought—and how they were too ambitious in general.

Nora would have loved to see Grandma try to scold Frederick Bradford about ambition, seeing as how all three sisters had his ambition to thank for this home, their family's company, Bradford Shipping, and their charmed upbringing.

Frederick, their many times great-grandfather, had been a reasonably successful East Coast railroad man. He would have remained a minor footnote to tycoons like Vanderbilt and Hill except that he'd had the foresight to turn his gaze to the Northwest before anyone else. He moved to Seattle in the late 1870s and by 1881 completed the first rail line linking Seattle to Chicago. Suddenly a journey that had taken five months could be accomplished in five days.

Several years later, the Klondike gold rush brought thousands of prospectors rushing to Washington via Frederick's railroad en route to Canada. That did it. Frederick's respectable net worth swelled into a bona fide fortune.

He'd ended up falling in love with a young Englishwoman, marrying her, and taking her to her home country on a lavish honeymoon trip. According to family stories and his existing letters, he'd been so enamored with his bride that, while in England, he'd purchased a house on the hills of Northumberland for her as a wedding gift. He'd then had the house taken apart brick by brick, shipped around the cape, and reassembled in Washington. They'd named it Bradfordwood.

Eventually Frederick's mother-in-law had come to live with them. Either out of a gracious wish to give the woman independence or because she annoyed the tar out of him—accounts were mixed—Frederick built a dower house on the edge of his property for her.

Several years ago, Mom had latched onto the idea of turning the dower house into an inn. She'd painstakingly renovated it and had been running it ever since with equal parts dedication and love.

The moment Nora's parents had decided to move forward with their bucket list missionary plans, Mom began looking for someone to take over the running of the inn for her while they were away. She'd found a wonderful candidate with plenty of experience in hotel management, but he had a family and lived in Vermont. He needed time to sell his house and move his wife and kids cross-country. He wouldn't be arriving for duty until November.

Willow had volunteered to take up the reins of the inn until the hotel manager arrived. Mom had only needed to close the inn for two weeks, just long enough to bridge the gap between their departure for Africa and Willow's arrival.

"Do you think it will be strange to live in this house again for such a long stretch?" Britt asked Willow.

A pause. "Maybe," Willow allowed. "This house is so familiar to me, and yet it feels like a time capsule . . . like a piece of my past more than my present."

"I reinstate my offer for you to come and live with me," Nora said. "I can supply Ben & Jerry's, excellent books, and all the tea you can drink."

Willow chewed a cashew, a pretty curve on her lips. "Tempting. But I think I'll get along fine here with Valentina to keep me in line. Right, Valentina?"

Valentina had been crooning and beaming during the preceding conversation. "Yes, miss!"

"Will you make Belgian waffles sometime soon?"

"Belg?" Valentina tilted her head questioningly. Valentina was sort of like Gilligan in the sense that she'd come to America with her husband on a three-hour tour and stayed more than thirty years. Even after thirty years, Valentina's grasp on the English language was loose. Nora suspected this was partially because Valentina realized that if she didn't understand what was being said to her, she could go ahead and do things the way she wanted and smilingly blame the end result on a lack of comprehension.

"Do you still have the Belgian waffle iron?" Willow asked her, slowly and clearly.

"Waffles! I make them for you, miss. So yummy!"

"You can stay at my place," Britt told Willow. "I have chocolate."

"Or at my place," Zander said. "I'm handsome."

They all laughed. Except Grandma, who gave a disapproving *tsk*.

Willow set aside her plate. "Are you dating anyone these days, Zander?"

Every face turned toward him. Even Grandma's. Especially Grandma's. She wasn't usually privy to conversations regarding their dating lives.

He shrugged. "No one special."

"I've been trying to convince him to ask out this girl named

Audrey that he works with," Britt said. "I've met her and she's very cool." Britt rose and sailed toward the bar. "Anyone need an iced tea refill?"

"It's never a good idea to drink too much tea at this time of the evening. All that caffeine," Grandma said accusingly.

Nora cut a look in Zander's direction and noted that his hooded gaze surreptitiously tracked Britt's movements.

When exactly was Britt going to wake up and notice that the very best man, the one who'd die for her, the one who'd been there for her in every moment big or small for the last ten years, was The One?

So far none of the Bradford sisters had been lucky in love. In Willow's case that was because she'd yet to find the right man. Nora was 95 percent certain that her own destiny included nothing but imaginary men. In Britt's case, she already had the man. She just hadn't recognized him yet for who he was.

"How's the book coming along, Zander?" Willow asked.

"It's coming along well." For the past several months, Zander had been working on a manuscript. He'd finished it a few weeks back and was currently polishing it up before shopping it around. He hadn't given any of them, not even Britt, so much as a peek at it.

"Can we read it?" Nora asked him.

"No."

"*Still* no?"

"It's nice to have a few secrets," he said.

Grandma moved her weight forward as if gathering herself to stand. Nora grasped her forearm and helped her up.

"I hate to leave, but the knitting circle at church can't function without me," Grandma said. "I keep telling and telling the ladies that I don't knit and they keep adding me back onto their roster and insisting that they can't have their meetings without me. Since they knit baby blankets for underprivileged mothers I can't very well not go, can I?"

"No. It's probably best that you go and suffer cheerfully," Britt answered.

That night Nora lay in bed concertedly trying to keep her thoughts focused on Adolphus Brook. Replaying her favorite swoon-worthy scenes from books, movies, and television in her mind usually staved off loneliness and ushered in sweet dreams.

Tonight? Not so much.

She couldn't sleep because she couldn't get John out of her head. John, who was the most *man* man she'd ever met. John, who was not on the market. John, who was adopted and wanted, for a reason he had not disclosed, to find his birth mother.

Why did he want to find his birth mother now, at this particular stage of his life?

She knew enough about adoptee search to know that there was often a catalyst that flipped a switch in the life of the adoptee, driving them to take action. Usually the people she assisted gladly told her why they'd decided to research their history. That John hadn't relayed this information made her doubly curious. She wanted to know that piece of his puzzle. She wanted to know the *why* of his search.

Irritated with herself, she tossed back the covers, revealing her purple pajama top and drawstring plaid bottoms. She padded in the direction of the living room.

Her glorified shoe box of a house sat in a secluded spot on a wooded hillside overlooking the canal. Canal was a misnomer. The body of water known as the Hood Canal was actually a fjord, and she wished it had been named appropriately way back when. She valued proper nomenclature.

She'd decorated her house in a country-meets-the-1950s vibe. The shades of distressed white, cherry red, and Dutch blue she'd chosen spoke to her of welcome. The bookshelves covering her walls spoke to her of old friends and adventures.

She slid a disc from season two of *Northamptonshire* into her DVD player. Five minutes later she'd settled into her chair, holding a mug of her homemade concoction of decaf chai tea. Gently, she tucked a throw blanket around herself.

This little obsession with John wasn't the healthiest thing in the world. She couldn't have John. She could, however, have the company of Adolphus.

Nora had always been an avid fan of period dramas. Three years ago, when her heart had felt like ground beef, they'd become somewhat of a lifeline for her. She'd watched them whenever her heartbreak had threatened to drown her.

She'd sighed over Richard Armitage in *North and South*. Tumbled into love with Colin Firth in *Pride and Prejudice*. Spent a great deal of time considering the merits of William Hurt's Rochester next to Michael Fassbender's Rochester next to Timothy Dalton's Rochester. She'd shaken her fist at Julian Fellowes when he'd killed off Matthew in that famous season-ending car crash on *Downton Abbey*.

And then, *then*, she'd discovered the BBC's *Northamptonshire*.

She'd become an instant addict. The gorgeously produced and acted series was set in England's Regency era and followed the loves, dreams, trials, and intrigues of both the lowly and the gentrified residents of the British county of Northamptonshire.

Most of the show's female viewers clucked and cooed over the dark and powerful Earl of Cumberly or the brawny and earnest horse trainer, Craddock. It took a very discerning and erudite woman to notice the appeal of Adolphus, the Viscount of Osgood and Lady Amelia's scholarly and bespectacled younger brother.

Upon discovering *Northamptonshire*, Nora had joined every online gathering of fans she could find and gone on to found the Devotees of Adolphus Brook group on Facebook. Through the Devotees, she'd caught the attention of Duncan Bartholomew, the actor who played Adolphus.

To her utter astonishment, her initial fawning correspondence with Duncan had developed into a genuine online friendship. They didn't talk on the phone. They'd never met. However, they communicated often via Facebook.

She actually knew THE Duncan Bartholomew! *She* was his pal! *She* was! Every single time she received a message from him, joy sang through her. He'd even taken to calling her Miss Lawrence after he'd found out that she, like the Lucy Lawrence character on the show, was a librarian with a heavy case of amour for Adolphus.

Much to Nora's frustration, *Northamptonshire* had only attained moderate success in England and in America via PBS. Also, despite the valiant support of Nora and the Devotees, Adolphus could not be considered one of the stars of the large cast. His supporting role was far too small.

Nora had spearheaded numerous social media and email campaigns aimed at increasing the show's visibility and securing more and bigger plot lines for Adolphus. So far, without measurable success.

She nursed her tea as she watched *Northamptonshire* through weary eyes. When Adolphus strode into the picture, she smiled. *Hello, darling.*

• • •

The quote emblazoned across Nora's purple pajama top:

"I am happily married to academia."
—Adolphus Brook

• • •

Text message from Willow to Nora and Britt:

Willow
I just remembered that Grandma's 80th birthday is coming up at the beginning of July. Since Mom and Dad are gone, I do believe that means the birthday fanfare is up to us.

Nora
I nominate Willow as Handler of Birthday Fanfare.

Britt
I second.

Willow

Slackers.

Britt

We could take Grandma out to lunch at Flemings again this year. Eating at the most impeccable restaurant in town makes it difficult for her to find things to complain about. You know how she enjoys a worthy challenge.

Nora

I don't think we can get away with lunch at Flemings for an 80th birthday.

Willow

I agree. An 80th birthday = a party at Bradfordwood.

CHAPTER *Four*

Until now, Nora hadn't realized that she found punctuality sexy in the extreme.

John strode through the doors of Shelton's library five full minutes ahead of their scheduled meeting. Nora was glad that she'd made an effort to arrive even earlier. The extra time had allowed her to select a table, arrange her office supplies, compose herself, and smooth a stray piece of hair into her Victory Curl updo.

He'd dressed more casually today than in the past, wearing jeans and a brown T-shirt with *Hurley* written across it. Even so, he walked toward her like a high-ranking naval officer ready to brief his team on their mission. All broad shoulders and relaxed leadership.

"Hi, Nora."

"Hi, John."

"The requested documents." He handed her a manila file folder.

"Thank you very much." She motioned to the table. "Shall we make ourselves comfortable?" *Wait here, John, while I slip into something more comfortable—*

Stop it, Nora! This is a business meeting.

They settled into side-by-side chairs and, wow, he smelled good.

Like some edible, very appealing combination of cedarwood, bergamot, and maybe a hint of . . . rosemary?

She rolled the fragrance around in her mind, entranced by it and priding herself on the fact that she knew what bergamot smelled like. She'd been congratulated on her excellent nose more than once during the courses she'd taken on tea.

"Right. Well." She may have just spent a few *too* many moments smelling him. "Let's see what we have here." With an air of clinical professionalism, she opened the file folder.

Nora was a naturally curious person. The genealogies of the people she assisted never failed to interest her. John's genealogy, however, interested her *keenly*.

His birth certificate sat on top. It contained the information he'd related to her at their last meeting as well as a few details he hadn't mentioned. Sherry Thompson, his birth mother, had been twenty-two at the time of his birth. Oregon was listed as the state of Sherry's birth, and John's delivering physician had been a Dr. Paul Douglas.

Nora pointed to the name of the physician. "If Sherry was a patient of this Dr. Douglas and if he's still practicing, then his office will likely have a file on Sherry, her pregnancy, and your delivery. That file should contain her address at the time."

"Can you explain how her address at the time of my birth could help us find her now? She's probably not still living at that address, right?"

"Right," Nora agreed. "However, at this stage of our search, our goal is simply to collect as much information as we possibly can. So, for example, if we could meet and speak with Sherry's old landlord, then maybe he could tell us something about her that might prove to be useful. Or, say her old address leads us to an outreach for unwed mothers. The outreach might have further documents about Sherry."

"Got it."

"It's impossible to know which innocuous piece of information might later become the clue that makes all the difference. So . . . no detail is too small."

John studied her in a way that caused her pulse to throb in her neck. "Okay."

Nora flipped to the next page, an information sheet that the adoption agency had no doubt given to John's parents. The name Sherry Thompson wasn't listed here, but other pertinent facts were.

Physical description: 5' 7", 135 pounds. Brown eyes. Brown hair.

Birthdate: March 18

Nationality: American

Religion: Christian

Occupation: Teacher

"Could the fact that she was a teacher help us at all?" John asked.

"Absolutely, it might." She turned her ring around her finger a couple of times, pondering. "I've seen a few background sheets like this in the past. In those cases, information about the birth father was also provided." She glanced at him.

His eyes were a mellow shade of hazel that brought to mind glinting rocks at the bottom of a mountain stream. The attention he leveled on Nora through those eyes was anything but mellow, however. It was concentrated, smart, forceful.

"My birth father wasn't mentioned on the birth certificate, either," he said.

"No."

"Do you think that's because Sherry didn't know who he was? She may have had more than one boyfriend at the time I was conceived."

"It's possible. Or maybe she knew exactly who he was but had a motive for wanting to keep his identity to herself."

More of that crackling silence. She was bookish! She had no experience at holding eye contact with Navy SEALs. All the practice she'd put in with Mr. Darcy and Rochester and Adolphus didn't seem to be holding her in good stead. "I suppose," she said, "you can ask Sherry about your birth father when you meet her. If you want to."

He nodded.

She tugged her focus to the tabletop, where his hand rested. His black watch with its black band, round black face, and white numerals whispered to her of the precision timing necessary for special ops so far away and dangerous that they boggled her mind.

Nora turned to the next sheet in his folder. "Interesting."

"What's interesting?"

"This waiver of confidentiality that your parents signed means that they rescind their rights to any implied or explicit confidentiality they had with their attorney or adoption agency. In other words, they're opening the door for you to learn all the facts you can."

He looked unsurprised. "This waiver's been with these other documents for years."

"According to the date, you probably would have been in . . . high school at the time your parents printed this out and had it notarized."

"The date listed there was my eighteenth birthday."

"Had you mentioned to your parents that you were interested in finding your birth mother?"

"No."

"Well, this paper may make our search easier. Individuals and companies are hesitant to share information they think other people might want kept secret. Because of this paper, they're likely to be more willing to work with us."

John's parents may have had reservations about John connecting with his birth mother while he was still a child. But at eighteen, he'd technically become an adult and this paper indicated that on that day John's parents had decided to give him access to his history when and if he wanted it.

She knew from his book and movie how decent his parents were. Yet this one sheet of paper, quietly added to John's adoption folder, revealed much more to her about the generosity of their character.

Together they went through the rest of the file. The amended birth certificate named his adoptive parents as his mother and father. His Final Decree of Adoption. A business letter from the attorney John's parents had used, a Mr. Harvey Morrow. A business card from the adoption agency who'd placed John.

No Petition to Adopt. No foster parent paperwork either, which might mean he'd never been fostered. Some hospitals allowed adoptive parents to visit their newborns while they were in the hospital's maternity ward and to take them home once the baby passed health checks and all the official procedures were complete.

"I've already scanned all these papers and saved them on my computer," John said.

"Great. I brought along a binder. So, if you're in agreement, we can use it to store the physical copies of the documents we collect."

"That's fine."

Whenever working "in the field," she always packed her monogrammed canvas bag with her laptop, a binder, a coin purse full of change to use on copy machines, a notepad, pens, highlighters, sticky notes, and two emergency packages of M&Ms. She'd already taken the liberty of stocking John's binder with dividers and enough clear sleeves to make a landfill groan.

Overly obsessive compulsive? Possibly.

She slid his documents into sleeves, then freed the notepad and a pen and started jotting a to-do list. "I think we should contact the attorney who handled your adoption. Among other things, he may be able to give us a copy of the Petition to Adopt, which may in turn list Sherry's address. We can query Presbyterian Hospital for their records of your birth. We can look for Dr. Douglas via the American Medical Association Directory."

Nora spared a peek at John to see whether he was tracking with her or whether she'd inadvertently left him by the road miles behind. A bemused expression graced his face. Almost as if he found her to-do list, or her—or both—humorous.

"Everything I just said may have been *too* large of an information dump," Nora confessed.

"No, I was just thinking that this is exactly why I hired you. You know your way around research."

"From what I've heard, you know your way around Navy SEAL-type . . . stuff."

His face went blank. "Huh?"

"I know about your past with the SEALs."

"I don't have a past with the SEALs."

Terror flashed through her. Had she—had she gotten it all wrong?

No. No, she'd seen his picture—*his* face—on the Wikipedia profile and again in the shiny, picture-filled pages in the middle of his book, and in all the online articles. "You *do* have a past with the SEALs," she stated.

"I run an emergency preparedness and response training company."

"Yes, but you're also a Medal-of-Honor-winning SEAL."

A gap of quiet. Then a small, crooked smile broke across his rugged face. "I am?"

"Yes!" She laughed, because as positive of his background as she'd been, he'd had her going there for a second. "After I flunked out of your hostage exercise, I looked you up. Your name was familiar to me."

"It was?"

"Yes. You're pretty famous in these parts."

"I am?" His eyes twinkled beneath straight, no-nonsense brows. His jaw formed a pronounced, indomitable line.

"You're pretty famous everywhere, truth be told. You may or may not have heard, but there's a book and a movie . . . ?"

"You read the book?"

"And watched the movie. They were both excellent. But as is usually the case, the book was superior. It was an exquisitely written book."

"I didn't write it, so I can't take credit for it."

"Someone else wrote the book, but it was about you, so I do believe you can take *some* credit."

He shrugged.

"I gather you prefer not to tout your past glories?"

He chuckled as he sat back in his chair, casually resting a forearm across his abdomen.

Her heart did a goofy little somersault.

"Did you just say *tout*?" he asked.

"Do you or do you not prefer to tout your past glories?"

"I don't mind people knowing. But I'm definitely against touting. Definitely."

"Understood. Even so, I'll now know whom to call when I need Navy SEAL-type . . ."

"Stuff?"

"Exactly."

"I'm expensive," he answered immediately, deadpan.

She released a peal of laughter. Was he picking up on this uncanny, rare, wonderful *click* between them? Of course, the *click* she perceived could just be her heretofore dormant hormones talking.

"You're expensive, and yet here I am," she said, "trying to give you my help for free."

"You practically still are. That thing you called a bill was sort of a joke, Nora."

"It was the best I could bring myself to do."

He regarded her for a long moment, looking unconvinced. Then he moved his gaze to the to-do list. "I'll contact the attorney who handled my adoption," he said. "And I'll call Presbyterian Hospital."

"Before we leave the library, we should take a look at the medical directories to see if we can locate your delivering physician."

Within the pages of the American Medical Association directory they found Dr. Paul Douglas. Fortunately for them, he was still a practicing obstetrician, though he now worked in Pullman, Washington. John entered the number for Dr. Douglas's practice into his phone.

Nora watched him while furiously brainstorming ways to prolong their meeting. She wanted more time with him. She shouldn't want more time with him. He had a girlfriend.

He looked up as he pocketed his phone.

"Would you like to take the binder?" She extended it a few inches, hoping she didn't look like the mother in the Bible story who was asked by Solomon to hand over her baby so it could be cut in two. This was John's search, yet Nora already felt deeply invested. She wanted to keep the binder.

"No, that's fine." He barely spared it a glance. "I have the computer files."

"Ah, yes." As if she'd forgotten.

"I'll follow up on my end and be in touch."

Two days later John stood before his home's floor-to-ceiling windows, holding his cell phone to his ear, waiting while it rang. The sun sat directly overhead, covering the navy blue water of Lake Shore Pine and the green hills that climbed from its edges with bright light.

Since his meeting with Nora, he'd done nothing to further his search for Sherry. Several times he'd thought about making the calls he'd told Nora he'd make, but each time a sense of reluctance that felt like a low-pitched hum had held him back. The hum reminded him of the intuition of danger he'd experienced at times during his years in the service.

Even before he'd contacted Nora, he hadn't been 100 percent sure about his decision to search for Sherry. He didn't think any adopted person could ever feel 100 percent sure about something as full of divided loyalties and unknown consequences as this was. Searching for a birth mother meant stirring up the past, potentially hurting his parents, and barging into the life of a person who might not welcome him.

The fact was that he wanted to find Sherry. And he didn't.

In the end, he decided to look for her because he needed answers about the medical condition that had thrown his life onto its side. He'd finally made himself dial the office of his delivering physician just now for the same reason.

"Obstetrical Associates of Pullman," a woman's voice answered.

John explained his reason for calling.

"What year did you say you were born?" she asked kindly.

He told her.

"I wish I could help you, but I've been Dr. Douglas's office manager for twenty years, and I can tell you without a doubt that he was a resident at Presbyterian Hospital that year. He wasn't in private practice at the time, so he didn't have patients, per se. I'm afraid we won't have any records concerning your mother or your birth."

"I understand."

"However, if you'll give me your phone number, I'll certainly ask him to call you. He's delivered a lot of babies over the years, but it's possible that he might remember something about your mother or you."

John gave over his information, and they disconnected. He Googled the main number for Presbyterian Hospital and dialed. After making his way through a few different "please listen carefully as our options have changed" messages, he reached a live person in the records department.

This time John simply asked for his birth records without explaining that he'd been adopted. He told the man his birthdate and his birth mother's name, then waited. He could hear computer keys clicking.

John watched a bird fly along the lake's surface. He'd had the house built into a steep hillside, so when you looked out from indoors, it almost seemed like you were hovering above the water.

The sound of the man's typing faded. "I see here that you were adopted."

John frowned. "Yes."

"Because of that, I can't provide your birth records to you."

Anger tightened slowly within John like fingers curling into a fist. This stranger on the other end of the phone could look at his records, but he could not? "My adoptive parents signed a waiver of confidentiality that I can fax or email to you."

"That won't make any difference."

"Washington State has opened sealed birth records."

"Yes, but this hospital is independently owned. Our policy is to respect the privacy of birth mothers. They were patients of ours, and when they left our care they believed that their records would remain closed."

"The records belong to two people. My birth mother. And me." He spoke evenly but without apology.

A frustrated sigh. "I realize that. However, our policy stands. We do not make closed records available. To anyone."

Tense quiet followed. John's brain turned, searching for solutions. "Could you block out the identifying information and send me the medical details only?"

"No."

His jaw tight, John ended the call, stuck his phone in his pocket, and pushed open two of the glass doors that had been built to fold in against one another along a track. He paced up and down his deck, scowling, struggling to cool his irritation.

The hospital records department viewed him as if he were still the baby in their documents. He was no longer an adopted child. He hadn't been a child for a long, long time. He was a thirty-three-year-old adult with every right afforded to adults by the United States of America.

He could understand the hospital's desire to protect his birth mother's rights.

But what about his rights?

He wasn't having any success at cooling his irritation. Knowing he could trust the lake to calm him, he headed down the path leading to his dock. As he walked, he studied the small ripples on the lake's surface to gauge today's wind.

He'd always loved the water. His grandfather had felt the same way about it. His dad, too.

John had grown up making the drive to his grandfather's cabin in Shore Pine on weekends and school vacations. He might have been raised near Seattle, but Shore Pine had always been where he belonged. From as far back as he could remember, he'd liked the valleys and mountains here. The quiet. He liked his grandmother's pancake breakfasts, the card games his family played after dinner, and the bowling alley in town his dad took them to. He liked being surrounded by nature, breathing air that smelled like fir.

The water, though. The water had been the biggest draw of all.

When he'd been with the SEALs, he'd held on to God during his worst moments. In those moments, he prayed for God to fill his head with something other than physical agony and fear. Each time, God answered that prayer by giving him memories of Shore Pine.

God had kept him alive. And God had used Shore Pine to keep him sane.

When he left the Navy, there'd been no question where he'd live. He parked himself in his grandfather's cabin for an entire year. It was a simple, hand-built house. Familiar. He'd valued simple and familiar during that first year, when he'd been trying to get his head around what had happened in Yemen and adjust to life as a civilian.

He could have lived in that cabin for a long time, except that the whole Lawson family shared it.

His grandfather had passed away when John was in college and left the cabin to John's dad, Ray. John's dad continued his father's open-door policy with the cabin. John's parents, his sister, Heather, and her husband all made an effort to spend as much time at the cabin as their schedules allowed. Aunts, uncles, and cousins used it, too.

John hadn't felt right about monopolizing their vacation spot, so he purchased this piece of land five miles down the road and built a house of his own.

He reached his boat and released its cover. Once the moorings were free, he started the motor and pointed the bow toward Shore Pine. His own home stood in one of the lake's many undeveloped coves. As the boat glided past a series of cliffs and around a few wide turns, the land grew more developed near Shore Pine.

The town's streets marched back from the water like rows of soldiers. Good restaurants now dotted those streets, thanks to the customers Rhododendron Lodge and the new high-tech orthopedic rehab center had brought with them.

John steered standing up, keeping his speed slow, letting the wind rake through his hair. He catalogued the other craft on the water, most of which he recognized.

He'd spent the morning catching up on work from his home office, something he did when he needed to focus or preferred to be alone. When you owned the company, you could work from home when you wanted. And you could take your boat out at one p.m. on a Thursday when you wanted to think about your search for your birth mother.

When he'd talked to his parents about being adopted as a kid, his mom had told him that she believed his birth mother was brave and sacrificial. She said his birth mother loved him so much that she'd given him up so he could have an opportunity at a better life. His mom always followed that up with, "*We prayed for you and you're God's answer to our prayer, John. You're our son, born into our hearts. God meant you for us and us for you. We love you.*"

He'd been curious about his birth, but for the most part he'd just nodded and accepted what his parents said.

Then he'd reached middle school. Like a lot of kids that age, he was miserable. He started to question what his mom had told him about his birth mother. His mom had never met his birth mother, so how could she know why she'd given him up? It seemed more likely that his birth mother rejected him because she hadn't loved him or wanted him.

Then in high school, baseball became the most important thing in his world. That, girls, and working on his dad's boat. Not knowing about his origins hadn't seemed all that important. More baseball, thanks to a partial scholarship, and a lot more fun had followed him into his college years.

When he'd graduated, he moved into a boring apartment and took an entry-level corporate job. He hated it. His restlessness with his life brought back all the old doubts about his roots. Desperate, he started searching for a job—any job—that didn't involve sitting at a computer for eight hours a day.

A friend suggested the SEALs. The instant John heard the suggestion, it connected with him.

The more he researched the SEALs, the more right it felt. Eight months later he finished Indoc and started the First Phase of Basic Underwater Demolition/SEAL training—also known as six weeks of torture—in Coronado, California.

Just like in the movies, guys quit the First Phase of BUD/S right and left because they couldn't hack it. And just like in the movies, they had to ring the brass bell in the courtyard when they left.

His first day there, John looked at the bell with one single, focused, ferocious thought in his mind: *Never. I will never ring you. If I die, I die. But I will never ring you.*

He hadn't rung the bell, and he hadn't died—though there'd been times when death seemed like a better option than SEAL training.

He'd been too consumed by exhaustion and determination over the next seven months and three phases to have the luxury of thinking about the details of his birth. Every time he went through medical testing, though, he was reminded by the questions they asked about his family history.

Six years after BUD/S, news reports about what had happened in Yemen caught the interest of a publisher. While he'd been getting Lawson Training off the ground in Shore Pine, he'd also worked with the writer assigned to him. The writer wanted to know everything about him, but John put limits on what he would and wouldn't share. His adoption had been off the table.

The book became a runaway bestseller, a fact that still seemed incredible to him because he didn't think his story was all that interesting. He certainly didn't think his actions had been unusually brave. He'd done exactly what any SEAL would have done in the same situation.

The movie followed the book. Money poured in—was still pouring in like sand. Add that to the income he generated from the eight or ten speaking jobs he agreed to every year. Plus, the current American climate of mass shootings and terrorist threats had put the emergency training his company offered into high demand.

His career success had given him the luxury, or maybe the curse, of time to think again about his birth mother. He shifted the boat into neutral and pulled out his phone. There was one more call he'd told Nora he'd make.

The memory of the redheaded librarian caused him to smile. She was quirky. Very quirky and sort of fussy with her tight hair and her to-do lists and her huge bag of office supplies.

Even so, during their last meeting, it had felt to him like they'd known each other for a long time. Or maybe like they'd been meant to know each other when the time was right. He liked her honesty, her sense of humor, her quick intelligence.

Beneath his feet he could feel his boat rocking as he called the law firm of the attorney who'd represented his parents in his adoption.

"Smith and Morrow," a young woman answered.

"Hello. Does Harvey Morrow still work for the firm?"

A beat. "I'm sorry, Mr. Morrow retired twenty years ago and passed away three years ago."

"Ah."

"Don't feel bad! People call all the time asking for him." She laughed lightly. "He was a Seattle institution."

"He represented my parents in my adoption. Is there someone else I could make an appointment with? To discuss my case?"

"Absolutely. His daughter, Melissa Morrow, is one of our partners."

Twenty-four hours later, John sat across the desk from Melissa Morrow in her high-rise Seattle office.

"My dad practiced family law for forty-five years," Melissa said. She was a heavy-set woman, middle-aged, and friendly. "He handled *a lot* of adoptions during that time."

"I can imagine."

"One of the joys of following in his footsteps has been getting to meet people like you, people who were in some way involved in my father's cases."

John nodded.

"We used to have whole rooms dedicated to files. No longer. We went digital a while back. As a result, my secretary was able to pull up your adoption records in no time." She rested her palms on her desk blotter. "Thanks for supplying us with the waiver of confidentiality, by the way, and for letting us know which documents you had in your possession already."

"You're welcome."

"The only relevant piece of information we have that you were missing is the Petition to Adopt." She reached toward a paper tray, pulled free a printed sheet, and extended it to him. "Here you are."

He scanned it. *There.* Right there, beneath the name Sherry Thompson . . .

Was her address.

Bingo.

• • •

Written in a card from John's mom, Linda, to John:

I just wanted you to know that your dad and I watched Uncommon Courage again last night. We went with you to the premiere, and then saw it at least three times when it was in theaters, but we love watching it on our own TV. It gets better every time!

You've proved to the whole country that you have the heart your dad and I always knew you had. We're so proud of you, John. And we're praying for you.

You're on my mind all the time. Ever since you told us what the doctors said, I've been asking the Lord to "strengthen you with power through his Spirit in your inner being." Ephesians 3:16.

Dad and I are coming to Shore Pine next weekend, so we'll check in on you then.
I'll bring lasagna.
Love, Mom

• • •

Facebook message from Duncan to Nora:

DUNCAN: I can't sleep again tonight. Insomnia bites.

NORA: Cup of warm milk?

DUNCAN: I wish. I gave up dairy and gluten last month.

NORA: In that case, healthy eater, is there anything of actual value I can do? I'd like to help.

DUNCAN: I'm just discouraged. I've been working quite hard, but no one seems to notice or care. I'm not getting the type of traction I hoped I would.

NORA: You're extremely talented, Duncan. Extremely!

DUNCAN: If only you were a casting director.

NORA: If only. I'm a very discerning layperson and believe me, your talent is a rare, rare gift. In time, you WILL gain traction.

DUNCAN: Not every talented person does.

NORA: You will. You must! I think it's time for me to organize another email and letter-writing campaign to the show's producers on your behalf. What say you to that?

DUNCAN: I say thank you. What would I do without you, Miss Lawrence?

NORA: Perish?

CHAPTER
Five

Nora's phone dinged to signal an incoming text message while she was skimming the village payroll Nikki had assembled. She'd heard once that constant distractions from text messages, social media notifications, and incoming emails had a deadly effect on deep concentration and productive work.

Yeah, but . . . but . . . Look! A new text.

The moment she saw John's name, adrenaline bolted through her. "It's only a text," she whispered to herself. Nothing could come of her crush on John. Zero. He was already in a relationship. Nonetheless, her body continued its breathless clamor.

It had been three days since he'd offered to follow up on the course of action they'd discussed earlier in the week. Rationally, she understood that three days was a perfectly appropriate amount of time. John was a busy man! Yet to her, the distance from Tuesday to Friday had seemed endless.

Nora could plow through research more quickly and powerfully than oxen through fresh, soft dirt. Since her meeting with John, she'd been aching to pick up the phone and greedily make all the phone calls he'd said he'd make.

She restrained herself because, regardless of how much she wanted to overstep, this was John's search. He had the right to pursue it at his own pace, to handle as much of it as he wanted, and to keep as much of it private from her as he wished. She was restricted to her usual role: Genealogist Who Gives Advice.

Her phone's screen revealed his full text. *The daughter of the attorney who handled my adoption gave me an address for Sherry Thompson. 3476 Regent Drive, Shelton.*

Her eyebrows climbed upward. An address already! Quite a development.

If she opened his text immediately, scrolling ellipses would appear on his end. Not wanting to seem overzealous, she made herself wait several minutes before finally tapping on his message and typing her reply. She thought about it, deleted it, reworded it, then finally sent, *Outstanding news! Good work. I'll check the Central Appraisal District site to see who owns the house currently.*

Almost immediately, he answered. *I already did. The house is owned by Travis and Whitney Hillcrest.*

She wasn't sure whether to be impressed that he'd thought to check the appraisal district's site or disappointed that she wouldn't be able to do it for him. The latter would have allowed her to amaze him with her productivity. *I'm pleasantly surprised! You may have skills above and beyond Navy SEAL-type stuff.*

What's our next step? he typed.

We can find out who owned the house in Shelton at the time of your birth by visiting the Mason County auditor's office and researching the house's deeds.

I can meet you there on Monday morning if that's good for you.

10? she asked.

See you there.

The next afternoon, Nora and Willow went to Britt's shop in search of bliss by chocolate. "I'd like the dark chocolate cashew, please," Nora said, mouth watering.

"Creature of habit," Britt accused. She plucked the asked-for truffle from the display case and handed it over.

Nora admired the chocolate sitting on her palm, tucked into its pristine white paper crib. Then she took a bite. Britt had fairy-dusted salt on top of the dark chocolate cashew. That faint salty tang enhanced the perfectly balanced flavors of dark chocolate, cream, and cashews. Nora's muscles relaxed by degrees.

"Milk chocolate caramel for me," Willow said.

"Two creatures of habit." Britt handed Willow the caramel with a shake of her head. "Go find a spot, and I'll bring you something new to try. You guys need to branch out."

When Britt had returned from her years overseas and announced her plan to open a chocolate shop, Nora had insisted that she locate her shop inside the historical village. Britt, Nora, and their dad then launched a hunt for just the right old structure to transport to the village for Britt's purposes. They eventually found a bank that looked like an escapee from a London set for *Peter Pan*.

Despite its cuteness, Nora was at first skeptical of the bank. The building seemed too staid for Britt's vivid personality. Britt, however, was able to envision its potential right from the start. Her certainty had paid off.

The bank's faded brick façade had needed little restoration. Indoors, Britt removed the old partitions and counters. She dedicated the front half of the square footage to the store and the back half to her kitchen. After some debate, she left the scarred floors just as they were and whitewashed everything else.

Windows marked two of the walls. Britt had covered the remaining walls with black-and-white photographs depicting America's chocolate-making history. A display case highlighted row upon row of chocolates. On the wall behind the display case, a blackboard listed the prices per pound.

Almost every day of the week, Britt stopped by the library or Nora stopped by Sweet Art. As much as she loved her library, Nora loved Sweet Art almost as much. It smelled of cocoa powder and the espresso beans Britt used in some of the chocolates. The bank's windows invited sunlight in and multiplied it, so Sweet Art glowed with a welcoming and warm ambience. The shop portion of the building didn't offer room enough for tables, so Britt had installed a bar and bar stools around the interior's perimeter.

Nora and Willow settled onto two of the stools and polished off their chocolates just before Britt arrived. She placed a cup of ice water and a chocolate before each of them.

Ordinarily, Britt didn't wait on customers unless there was a rush. She'd hired her friend to work the floor so that she'd be free to spend her time the way she preferred: in the kitchen, hair in a high ponytail, chef's coat in place, sugar crystals floating. She always came out, however, to wait on Nora and Willow when they stopped by. It was their sisterly privilege: free chocolate plus personal service from the chocolate maestro.

"I've been experimenting with gold flakes, slivers of almond, and candied citrus peel," Britt explained. "This is my most recent attempt."

Nora and Willow both made a fuss over the beauty of Britt's creation. The rectangular base of the chocolate swept upward into a firm curve. Gold flecks shone from just beneath the chocolate's surface, like amber leaves poised beneath a frozen pond.

"Is this real gold?" Willow asked.

"Yes," Britt answered. "Twenty-four-karat gold, pounded into extremely thin sheets, then flaked."

"I didn't realize gold was edible," Nora said.

"It is in this form. Actually, the Japanese have been using it in food and drinks for centuries. It has a long European history, too."

As much as Nora liked to think of herself as the smart one, Britt's knowledge of the culinary arts could probably give Nora's knowledge of genealogy a run for its money.

Willow reached for the chocolate—

Britt made a *tsk*ing sound. "Cleanse your palate first, please."

"You haven't been around in a while," Nora said to Willow. "You've gotten rusty."

Both older sisters took dutiful sips of water. When tasting chocolate, Britt had taught them to cleanse their palate, smell the chocolate, ensure the chocolate was served at room temperature, and hold each bite on their tongues for ten or fifteen seconds to notice how the different elements melted.

"Give it a rub and a smell," Britt said. "What do you notice?"

"A hint of orange?" Nora offered. "Vanilla?"

"Mostly just dark chocolate smell," Willow admitted.

Britt made a gesture to proceed. "Okay, give it a try."

Nora did her best to eat the chocolate like an expert, instead of like the novice she still was. Only Zander, who'd educated himself on chocolate, was adept at picking up on nuances.

Britt leaned forward, her features sharpened in concentration. "Does it have enough essence of wild strawberry?" she asked when the fifteen seconds had passed.

"Huh?"

A sheepish smile. "Essence of wild strawberry. Does it have enough?"

"Mm, yes," Willow said emphatically. "The essence of wild strawberry is coming through."

Britt narrowed her eyes. "You're just saying that."

"Fine. Yes. I'm just saying that."

"We're only qualified to enjoy your chocolates, Britt," said Nora. "You know we're hopeless as critics."

"Hopeless," Britt agreed. "How are things going at the Inn at Bradfordwood?" she asked Willow.

"Since Clint cleans each day, I've mostly spent my time learning the reservation and billing systems."

"Have you made Mom's baked French toast recipe yet?" Nora asked. Like a B&B, the inn served breakfast to its guests each day.

"What about her egg and sausage casserole?" Britt asked. "Or cranberry scones?"

"I've tried all of the above. The scones, especially, need more work." Willow dusted chocolate from her hands. "Overall, I think I'm off to an okay start."

"Call me if the scone recipe continues to give you trouble," Britt said.

"Have you decided what Britt and I can do to help with the planning of Grandma's party?" Nora asked.

"Not yet. But I'll assign responsibilities soon. You know . . ." she murmured thoughtfully. "I've changed my mind. I think I might make a good critic, after all, Britt. Give me another"—she put out her palm and crooked her fingertips—"so I'll know for sure if there's enough essence of wild strawberry."

"Get out of my shop, freeloaders." Britt winked at them and disappeared in the direction of her kitchen.

"I think that was the first time I've ever eaten gold," Willow said to Nora. "I wonder if that means I'm now worth my weight in it."

"You're worth way more than your weight in gold, and you know it."

"You're worth way more than your weight in gold, too," Willow said.

"Funny, Adolphus Brook told me the very same thing just last night."

Nora hoped her older sister would laugh. Instead, Willow's extraordinary catlike eyes considered Nora without blinking. Willow was soft-spoken and well-mannered, but she was also incredibly observant.

"Nora Bradford?" Willow asked.

"Yes?"

"How long has it been since you and Harrison split up?"

The question impacted Nora the way a tiny sharp knife thrust deeply into her chest cavity might have. Which *infuriated* her. She'd been praying against bitterness and envy and hurt for so long now. She'd gone down on her knees and pleaded with God to cleanse her heart over and over and over. She didn't want those awful, insidious emotions. *Take them*, she'd begged Him. *Take them!* Yet here she still was, experiencing pain at the mention of his name, which made her feel like a failure. She'd give away her house not to feel pain at the mention of Harrison's name. "Three years," Nora said.

"Is he the last nonfictional person you dated?"

"Um . . ." Nora pretended to think it over while scratching the side of her chin.

"I'd like to punch him," Willow said companionably, "right in his dumb nose. I never liked him very much."

"Yes, you did."

"I liked him. But not *very* much. I definitely never liked his dumb nose."

The conversations of shop patrons filled the air with a cozy purr. The pleasantness of her surroundings contrasted harshly with the gloom of this particular topic. "He and Rory are expecting a baby. Did you know that?"

"No."

"She's due in a few months." As the words left her mouth, Nora could hear that she'd spoken them too lightly. They sounded suspiciously jovial.

Willow blew out a breath. "After he broke off your engagement to start dating Rory, I wish the two of them had moved to another town. How often do you see him?"

"Pretty often. Maybe weekly?" She didn't add that her quickest route from home to work took her straight past his orthodontic office, which amounted to a twice *daily* reminder of him. She sometimes detoured around his office. But every time she did, the need to take the detour ended up reminding her of him anyway.

"That must stink."

"I'd probably see him less if he didn't insist on being so friendly. As it is, he catches my eye and waves or makes an effort to talk to me every time we come within a hundred yards of each other. He invites me to parties at their house. He even stops by the library."

Willow wrinkled her nose. "That's not normal."

"I think it is normal for a lot of couples these days. An amicable split, you know?"

"Amicable splits are for divorced couples with kids, not dating couples."

"I think they *are* for dating couples whose parents are friends, who grew up together."

"You were engaged, and he called things off two months before the wedding. You don't owe Harrison amicable. You don't owe him anything. He owes *you* about a thousand apologies and a replacement groom."

Nora chuckled, but it was a chuckle undergirded by heartache.

She and Harrison were the same age and had gone through Merryweather schools together since kindergarten. He was outgoing, a bit of a showman, and classically handsome in an Ivy League kind of way. She'd been self-concious, bookish, and just a little bit smarter than Harrison in every subject. They'd operated on opposite sides of the same group of friends and kept in touch through college. Stanford for her, Duke for him.

When he kissed her under a maple tree at sunset the summer after they graduated college and before he headed to dental school, she mostly remembered feeling overwhelmingly flattered.

Merryweather didn't offer many eligible single men. An extroverted dentist: her clear best choice. She and Harrison had gotten along beautifully throughout the four years that they'd dated. No fights. No uncontrollable passion. Just two mature people in a secure relationship. She'd wondered why other people found relationships so difficult. *Relationships are a pleasure*, she'd thought, with an enjoyable sense of superiority. She and Harrison were exceptional at this!

When he'd proposed, she'd once again been overwhelmingly flattered. She was going to marry before either of her sisters, which seemed like a hugely surprising and fortunate outcome. Her future was settled, and whew, wasn't that a load off her mind? She felt safe. Smug.

Until. Until Harrison had met the love of his life.

And it hadn't been ordinary, hometown her.

It had been fresh and creative Rory. Even her name was fresh and creative. Rory. She'd come out of the sort of East Coast family that summered on Nantucket. She possessed a calm demeanor and a face and body that were, if you looked closely, rather normal. However, she came across as dazzling thanks to her amazing sense of style. Impeccable makeup, an ability to layer clothing artfully, and a knack with accessories went a long way. As did her perfect bangs (too few appreciated how hard it was to get bangs to lay perfectly), coupled with the sleek mahogany bob she wore tucked behind both ears.

On her blog, *Say Yes to Beauty*, Rory discussed style, makeup, hair, interior design, art, and cooking. She'd started the blog in high school and amassed such a staggering number of followers that she now made her living blogging.

Harrison and Rory met at a coffee shop near the University of Washington, where he'd been finishing dental school. It had only taken him fifteen days of friendship with Rory to realize she was the one for him.

Fifteen days.

He'd come to Nora and broken their engagement as honorably as possible. He'd not yet asked Rory out at that time, and he'd been properly remorseful. Tearful, even. With anguished candor, he told Nora that it couldn't be explained, but he believed he'd suddenly found, in Rory, his *soul mate*. Which had been honest of him and all. Kudos to him for his forthrightness. But his confession left Nora feeling wretched.

In order to assuage his guilt, Harrison had doted on Nora in the days and weeks following their breakup. His cloying care had made the whole situation worse. If he'd been a jerk, she could have cut him out of her life and told herself she was glad to have discovered his true character before the altar.

Rory had ended up saying yes to Harrison the same way she said yes to beauty on her blog. The two of them married ten months after Nora's canceled wedding date.

For a good long while, Nora had tortured herself by reading Rory's blog. Via her posts, Rory detailed her beautiful and tasteful romance, her beautiful and tasteful home, her beautiful and tasteful clothes, cooking, makeup, and knowledge of art. Rory had flair and an understated sense of humor. She was a gifted writer. The posts caused Nora to like Rory about as much as she'd automatically loathed her on principle.

When this past New Year's Day had rolled around, Nora had given up *Say Yes to Beauty* as a New Year's resolution. Thank goodness for that. A beautiful and tasteful pregnancy would have been more than she could have handled.

Before Harrison had ended things with her, Nora had believed that her boyfriend loved her, that he was trustworthy, that she'd found her partner for life, that they'd honeymoon on Fiji, and that she'd have baby #1 by the age of thirty.

She'd been completely wrong. She'd been completely wrong about *all of it*.

The predicament with Harrison, even three years later, was still a miserable and confusing emotional stew. "Did you ever have to see Corbin again after the two of you broke up?" Nora asked. Willow had had a handful of boyfriends over the years, but Nora sensed that her sister had only deeply loved one: NFL quarterback Corbin Stewart.

"No. I had a close call once. I learned at the last minute that we were both scheduled to attend the same charity event. Luckily, I found out in time and skipped it."

"But you could have gone and been all stunning and haughty and sent him into an agony of regret."

"True. But then I'd have had to see him with his date, which might have sent *me* into an agony of regret." Willow sipped her water and carefully folded and re-folded the tiny paper wrapper that had held the gold-flecked chocolate. "Remember how you insisted I start dating again after Corbin and I broke up?" Willow asked.

Uh-oh. She could see where Willow was headed.

"You prodded me to go out again after four months," Willow continued. "You haven't dated anyone in *three years*, so I think I'm past due in demanding that you put yourself back out there."

Nora pulled a face.

"You haven't sworn off dating forever, have you?" Willow asked, completely serious.

"No!" Not forever, anyway. Just for the next forty years or so.

Nora liked to think she might enjoy dating when she was an elderly person. "Merryweather doesn't exactly have a bustling singles scene."

Nora had a wide pragmatic streak. After Harrison, she'd decided to abstain from dating and focus instead on old buildings and older genealogy records. Whenever anyone asked about her love life, she boldly announced her contentment with her singlehood.

She was scholarly and dependable, but not particularly pretty. She'd self-diagnosed herself with a low libido and often thought that God had no doubt wired her that way so she'd be well suited for a life as an unmarried auntie to Willow's and Britt's kids.

Willow extended her palm. "Let me have your phone."

"My phone?"

Willow waited. Nora passed it over, and Willow went to work. "You have lots of apps on here, but I don't see any dating apps."

"Goodness, no."

"I'm going to download one that will show us the single guys in this area."

"I will murder you if you put a profile of me on a dating app."

"I'm already doing it. Go ahead and try to murder me. I'm taller and stronger." Willow looked up with a bemused smile. "Remember when we used to wrestle with Dad when we were kids?"

"What if *someone I know* sees me on the app?"

"Then that'll mean they're on it, too, and they'll have no room to judge."

"Willow," she growled.

"We'll just jump on for ten minutes and check out some of the men. If you don't like it, we'll delete it. No biggie."

Nora bared her teeth.

Willow busily punched things into Nora's phone. "You're right about the singles scene in Merryweather," Willow said. "So why not get a little help from online dating services or apps?"

"Do *you* use online dating services or apps?"

"Certainly not." One final tap. "There. You're on. And look.

Here's someone to consider." Willow set the phone on the bar's surface and the sisters bent their heads over it.

A picture of a plain man with a massive Adam's apple filled the phone's screen. Even though the picture revealed only his head and shoulders, he appeared to be extremely tall and skinny.

"Swipe right if you're interested and left if you're not," Willow said.

"But I feel horrible about rejecting this poor guy based on nothing but his looks! He might be really sweet or funny or smart."

"Do you want to go on a date with this man? Yes or no?"

Nora didn't harbor the smallest speck of attraction for the guy with the Adam's apple. While apologizing to him mentally, she swiped left.

Instantly, another man appeared.

"No!" Nora wailed. "That's Evan from the post office. This is all your fault, Willow. I can't unsee this. Every time I visit the post office I'll remember that Evan's looking for love."

"Looking for love is nothing to be ashamed of. He's decent looking."

"And he's perfectly nice, but he lives with his mom and has several pet ferrets. Plus, he smells like mustard."

"Left or right?"

"Left!"

An image of a man who resembled a sumo wrestler materialized. His LA Dodgers baseball hat sat on his head like an acorn cap on top of an orange.

"Left," Nora sighed.

A message came up announcing that there were no more matches in their area.

"That's it?" Willow demanded.

"Is it too late to go back and give the guy with the Adam's apple a second chance?"

They giggled.

"Now delete it," Nora said, "before Evan sees me on there. I'll be mortified if he asks me over to meet his ferrets."

More giggles as Willow deleted the app and handed back the phone. "This situation is more serious than I thought."

"I'm happy with my non-dating life. I have *Northamptonshire*." *And I have my working relationship with the mouthwatering John Lawson.*

"I think we need to take drastic measures." Willow tilted her head, then slowly swept her attention down to Nora's toes and back up to her eyes.

"You're frightening me."

"I'm constantly worked on by makeup artists, hair stylists, manicurists, fashion people, and on and on and on. I'd love a chance to work on someone else for a change."

"You think I need a makeover." Nora tried not to take offense. When she and her sisters were young, they'd freely criticized and made fun of each other. They'd stopped that years ago, however. Nowadays, they operated on a plane of mutual respect. Pointing out one another's flaws violated their unspoken code.

"Not a makeover," Willow answered. "I think you look great. But it's been three years since Harrison, and maybe now's the time to leave the past behind. If you're ready for a change, I'd like to help. That's all."

It would be churlish not to accept makeover help from a successful model. Yet it was humiliating to accept makeover help from a sister. "That was very diplomatic. Everything you just said."

"It would be a treat for me. A creative outlet."

"The baked French toast recipe isn't creative enough for you?"

"It's not creative at all. That's just me trying to follow Mom's steps exactly."

Change. The siren song of change *was* enticing, Nora had to admit. It had been ages since she'd changed anything about her clothes or hair.

"C'mon." Willow rose without waiting for an official okay. "We'll start with your closet."

"You own a lot of cardigans, Nora." Willow zipped hanger after hanger along the bar mounted on the inside of Nora's small walk-in closet. "A whole lot of cardigans."

Nora sat on the edge of her mattress. "I live in a cool, rainy climate."

"Hmm."

"I really like cardigans. You've convinced me of the benefits of change, but I don't . . . well, I don't want to wear clothes that aren't me. You know?"

"I want to make you more you, not less. This is about enhancing your sense of style." Willow selected a heather-gray cardigan and a white collared shirt. "Do you have a pencil skirt?"

"Plenty of skirts but no pencil skirts."

Willow pulled out a navy, knee-length A-line skirt. "Can you try this outfit on for me?"

"Sure." This was exactly the kind of outfit Nora already wore to work every day. She came out of the bathroom moments later.

Willow approached, opened the neck of the white shirt, and turned up the collar. She unfastened the cardigan and then snapped Nora's wide belt around her waist on top of it. "Do you have any clothespins?" Willow asked.

"No. This is the era of the clothes dryer."

"Chip clips, smart aleck? You know, to hold your chip bags closed?"

Nora retrieved three chip clips. "If my Ruffles go stale, it's on you."

Willow gathered the back of the skirt against Nora's legs, rolling the excess fabric in and clipping it to hold it in place. "This will simulate the lines of a pencil skirt." She selected a pair of high heels.

Nora dutifully stepped into the heels. "I'm not a fan of high heels—"

"Keep an open mind."

Willow retreated a few paces to assess. "Can I take a look at your jewelry?"

"Yes."

"Any brooches?"

"A couple of vintage ones."

Willow sorted through Nora's jewelry. "You could do a big chunky necklace with this outfit. Since you're wearing neutrals, accent jewelry in a color like jade green or pink or turquoise might be fun. Or strands of silver beads. That kind of thing. Today, though, let's try this." She pinned a fifties-era sunburst brooch above Nora's heart and clicked three bracelets around her wrist, bracelets Nora never would have thought to pair together.

Once again, Willow moved back to study her progress. A slow smile moved across her lips. "I'm good at this."

She positioned Nora squarely in front of the full-length mirror mounted on the inside of her closet door.

"Wow," Nora breathed, somewhat stunned. "You *are* good at this."

• • •

Written by Willow:

To Do . . .

1) Take Nora shopping

2) Get her eyebrows threaded

3) Purchase all new makeup for her

4) Think about how to convince her to get a new haircut without in any way offending or criticizing her

CHAPTER Six

John entered the Mason County auditor's office five minutes before ten o'clock only to find that Nora had already arrived. He was used to running earlier than, well, everyone he knew. Except her.

She was in the middle of a conversation with three of the office's employees. They were talking like close friends, which probably meant that Nora spent quite a bit of time at the county auditor's office.

As John approached, something within him eased at the sight of Nora's reddish gold hair and wry expression. He was . . . glad to see her, he realized.

She motioned him forward with a smile.

He was *very* glad to see her. Almost as if he'd . . . missed her?

"I'd like you to meet John Lawson," Nora said to the others. "He runs Lawson Training Incorporated in Shore Pine."

"Yes." One of the ladies nodded. "I've heard of it."

All three of the strangers watched him with interested faces.

"We're working together," Nora stated. "We met when I served as a volunteer for one of his company's training exercises. It turned out that I was ghastly at the role of hostage."

"That's true," John told the ladies. "She was bad."

"I'm not used to being bad at things," Nora said. "If I could have another turn, I really do think I could be an exceptional hostage."

"No more turns for you."

The employees looked hesitant for a moment, then laughed.

"John!" Nora protested. "The fact that I froze was all the fault of the sprinklers."

"Everyone else had to deal with the sprinklers that day, too. None of them froze."

"It's very uncharitable of you to point that out. I want another turn."

"No."

Another round of laughter.

When they parted from the ladies, Nora led him toward a deserted corner of the building. She hadn't asked any of the employees to help her find the deeds belonging to 3476 Regent Drive, the house Sherry Thompson had lived in at the time of his birth. She didn't seem to need help.

Nora located an aisle of shelves, then skimmed her fingertips over the spines, searching volume after volume.

Her hairstyle reminded him of Lucille Ball. She wore jeans and a pale blue blouse with white dots on it, with sleeves that she'd pushed up her slim forearms. She carried the same big bag over her shoulder that she'd brought with her the last time he'd seen her.

"This is the one." She started to tug at one of the books.

"Let me." John freed it and followed her to a table at the end of the row.

Nora glanced at the book's index, then flipped to the page for 3476 Regent Drive. "Here we are." She scooted the volume toward him and leaned back slightly so that he'd have plenty of room to study it.

He read the property's location details and age. It had been built in 1925. Carefully, he turned pages in search of the title deed that covered the year he'd been born.

Here. This was it. The grantor, the seller, of the house had conveyed the property to the grantee, the buyer. The grantee's name was Deborah Thompson. "I think we've found a relative of Sherry's," he said.

"Yes." Nora's brown eyes sparkled. "I was worried that we'd come upon a landlord's name. This is much more helpful."

"Are you thinking that Deborah Thompson might be Sherry's mother?"

"Maybe. She could also be Sherry's older sister. Or a cousin. Or some other relative."

He reread the record. Deborah had purchased the house two years before his birth. The next deed revealed that she'd sold the house two years after his birth. "No husband's listed," he commented. "Deborah was the sole owner of the property."

"Yes. Just to be sure they didn't keep the house in the family, let's make our way through the names of the owners that followed Deborah to see if *Thompson* appears again either as a middle or a last name."

They checked, but the name Thompson didn't reappear.

Once Nora had photocopied Deborah's deed and added that page to the binder, she set her laptop on the table between them. "I'm interested to see whether anyone named Deborah Thompson still lives in Shelton or its surrounding towns."

He watched her fingers speed across the keys. She ran searches on three sites back-to-back for Deborah's phone records, property records, and ancestry records.

No hits.

"She doesn't live near here anymore," John said.

"Maybe."

He grinned. "That's twice now that I've tried to draw a conclusion and you've said maybe."

"That's because I'm an investigator. Until the data gives us a definitive answer, I have to keep an open mind and consider all the things that *could* be true."

"I was thinking maybe you just liked to shoot me down."

She met his gaze, amusement tipping up the edges of her lips. "Well. There *is* that."

A long moment passed. John caught himself staring and jerked his gaze away.

Nora turned back to her computer. "It might be that Deborah really doesn't live near here anymore. Or she might have passed away. Or she might have gotten married and changed her last name." She studied the screen as if it held hidden answers. "I'm going to try one more website real quick."

"Okay."

A necklace with several silver strands hung around Nora's neck. When she moved, the beads made a soft clinking noise. The sound the beads made, like the woman who wore them, relaxed him. He didn't have to work hard to have a conversation with Nora or to fill up the silences between them. Being in her company came easy.

He felt at home in the Mason County auditor's office, a building he'd never visited before. It sure wasn't because of the décor. He felt at home here because Nora was with him.

He furrowed his brow. The fact that he hadn't known Nora very long made the effect she had on him surprising, but no less true.

He could be himself around her. He could be himself around her because she was exactly herself around him. She was genuine. Confident and slightly vulnerable at the same time. It was that piece, that vulnerable piece, that made her authentic, that led him to think she might make a good friend, that made him believe he could trust her.

"No luck at this site, either." She angled toward him. "How do you feel about driving over to 3476 Regent Drive? We can check out the house Sherry lived in. It's not the best time of day to catch neighbors at home, but we can try to knock on some doors anyway."

"To see if any of the residents on the street remember Sherry or Deborah?"

"Exactly! Certainly." She looked to be on the verge of laughter. "One hundred percent right. Correctamundo! Notice how good I can be at *not* shooting you down?"

Looking at the house Sherry Thompson had once lived in was like looking into the mysteries of the past. His past.

John stood on the sidewalk in front of number 3476 with Nora beside him, trying to get his head around the fact that his birth mother had lived in this house when he'd been born. *This* was where she'd lived. It was more than he'd ever known about his birth mother in a lifetime of wondering.

The bungalow-style house was positioned in the middle of a block of similar bungalows. All the houses looked well kept. This neighborhood appeared to be popular, probably due to its nearness to Shelton's downtown and Oakland Bay.

3476 had a deep front porch supported by two thick columns at the front corners. Gray paint. White trim. In recent years, a modern addition had been added to the back. The original part, the part that Sherry would have lived in, was small. Even so, Deborah Thompson must have been at least a middle-class professional woman back in the day to have afforded the payments.

He imagined a shadow image of Sherry climbing out of a car parked on this driveway. Walking up these front steps. Opening this door.

He glanced at Nora. Her profile looked very white and clear against the colors of the street in the background.

"Ready?" she asked, face still forward toward the house.

How had she known he was looking at her? "Ready." He took a step, lost his balance, and quickly righted himself.

"You okay?" she immediately asked.

He cursed inwardly. She'd seen. "Yeah."

They walked up the path. "I respect that you'd like to keep this search as private as possible," she said. "If someone's home, we don't need to go into detail about our reasons for asking for information on Deborah."

"All right."

"If a woman answers, I volunteer myself to do the talking." She knocked on the door. "I'm less intimidating."

"I'm intimidating?"

"You're as intimidating as a Humvee. Wait, that's not a very good analogy because you're a Navy guy. You're as intimidating as a submarine. What do you think about that analogy?"

"It's just so-so."

"I can do better. How about a torpedo? You're as intimidating as a torpedo."

The door opened to reveal a young woman with a baby on her hip.

"Hi, I'm Nora Bradford of the Library on the Green Museum in Merryweather. We're researching two women who lived in this house thirty-three years ago."

"Oh, really? Wow. That's great."

"I know." Nora smiled widely. She had a way with people, he'd noticed. "Do you happen to know anything about either a Sherry or a Deborah Thompson?"

The woman slid her attention to him shyly before moving it back to Nora. "I've never heard those names. Sorry! I wish I could help. Did . . . did something happen with . . . these people?"

"No, this has to do with a genealogical search."

"We've lived here for a couple of years. I'm afraid I only know a little bit about the family who lived here before us." She continued talking to Nora, telling her that she thought the previous family had had three teenagers and then filling her in on the renovation work she and her husband had done before they moved in.

Behind her, the walls that had likely once divided the front areas of the house were mostly gone. He could see through the living and dining areas all the way back to a new kitchen. The only old things remaining from Sherry's era were the baseboards, crown moldings, window casings, and floor.

Nora thanked the woman and handed over her card in case her husband had anything to add.

John and Nora then went door to door along Regent Street. At the majority of houses, no one answered. The only people they did catch at home were retirees and stay-at-home parents. They had the same conversation with each of them that they'd had with the young mom, but no one had lived on the street long enough to have known Sherry or Deborah.

"If we come back, we should come back at a time when more working people will be at home." Nora lifted her gaze from her phone, where she'd been recording the address numbers of everyone on the block who hadn't answered their knock. "Say, around seven on a weeknight. People are usually back from work or errands at seven, but the sun's still up. We don't want to knock on anyone's door after sunset. That's just creepy."

"I wouldn't want to be intimidating *and* creepy," he said.

She laughed. He grinned in response. He liked to make her laugh.

She put away her phone and set her hands on her hips. "To be honest, it's a bit of a long shot to think that we'll come across anyone who remembers the Thompson ladies even if we do come back on a weeknight. I think our time might be better spent pursuing other avenues. Did you speak with the obstetrician listed on your birth certificate?"

"He called me and told me he wished he could help, but he doesn't remember anything about Sherry or my delivery."

"What about the hospital where you were born?"

"Presbyterian won't release my birth records to me."

"Okay. Well, we know from the adoption agency's information sheet on Sherry that she was a teacher and a Christian."

"What are you thinking?"

"That we might be able to find old yearbooks or directories from local schools. We can check with churches in the area to see if they have or had members named Sherry or Deborah Thompson."

He nodded. "I'm booked tomorrow. Wednesday?"

They set up a time, said their good-byes, and got into their separate cars. She drove a PT Cruiser painted as bright a blue as her hair was red.

From behind the wheel of his black Suburban, John watched Nora's car turn, then disappear from sight. He could feel his enthusiasm for the day draining from him. Compared to the time he'd just spent treasure-hunting with Nora, the rest of the things he had planned for the afternoon and evening stretched before him like gray fog.

Irritated with himself, he turned the key in the ignition, wrapped a hand around the gear shift—then stopped. He dropped his hand and stared blankly at his dashboard.

Between his health and his search for Sherry, he already had more on his plate than he could deal with without feeling depressed because his meeting with Nora had ended. What was going on with him?

Yes, he felt comfortable with Nora. Yes, her personality and her sense of humor fit together with his more serious personality and his own sense of humor. The two of them were destined to be . . . friends. It wasn't like he was into Nora in a romantic way.

A lot of his buddies had female friends. His best friends had all been guys up until now, but that didn't mean it was too late for him to add a female friend or two. He could have female friends in addition to his girlfriend.

Over the years, he'd had several girlfriends, and his experience had taught him that Allie was the best kind of girlfriend for him. The independent kind.

Allie was an event planner. They'd met last fall in Tacoma when he'd given a speech at a Christian conference she'd been running. He'd asked her out and they'd been dating ever since, for six months now.

Allie didn't need to see him constantly. She had a successful career and a life of her own. Allie was beautiful, nice to everyone, full of common sense. She hadn't pressured him to make things exclusive, although it had gone that way after a couple of months. She didn't expect him to say *I love you* and hadn't pushed an *I love you* onto him, either.

When he'd told Allie about his condition, she'd hugged him for two minutes straight and kissed the side of his neck and told him that she'd be at his side every step of the way and that it would be all right and that he could count on her.

She could count on him, too. Not once in his life had he cheated on a girlfriend. Not even when his high school girlfriend had been a senior and he'd been a college freshman and he'd been at a party in Flagstaff with that gorgeous dark-haired sorority girl who'd wanted him. Not even then.

He knew how to act appropriately with women who weren't his girlfriend. He understood where the line was, and he'd committed to never stepping over it. Allie could trust him around anyone. That went double for the librarian.

Yet his dark mood remained. The day continued to stretch like gray fog. His car engine continued to idle.

His phone rang.

"Hey," he said.

"Hey, yourself," Allie replied. "Want to come over tonight? I'm in the mood to make you dinner."

Let's drive to Seattle tomorrow, Willow texted Nora later that day. *Those three cute outfits I put together for you from your closet aren't going to last long.*

Nora paused the episode of *Northamptonshire* she'd been watching. She hadn't really been paying attention, anyway. She'd mostly been remembering all the things John had said earlier today and how he'd looked while saying them.

No other man had ever cast such a powerful spell over her. Harrison had certainly never thrown her into this sort of a crush/daze. The crush part was pure happiness. The daze part came from the acute pain of knowing John wasn't, and couldn't be, hers. He couldn't be hers! *So quit pining over him, Nora!*

There's no hurry, she replied to Willow. *I can wear my normal stuff until we have a chance to go shopping this weekend or next week.* Though, to be strictly honest, she couldn't muster much passion for her "normal stuff."

John had given her goose bumps more than once today, but he'd never given the slightest indication that he'd noticed any change in her clothing. That fact hadn't diminished her pride in her new look, which was telling. *She'd* really liked how she'd felt today. She hadn't needed a man's compliment to validate it.

No! You're not allowed to wear your old clothes! Willow responded. *Shopping for new things is a matter of some urgency.*

Nora laughed. *Pencil skirts are a matter of some urgency?* Accepting Willow's help had so far proven to be more fun and less humiliating than she'd feared.

Some of the tops you have need to be altered. Some of the rest will serve you well if styled differently. But to make any of them work, you really need pencil skirts, trousers, and skinny jeans. Plus, a sundress or two.

Skinny jeans? What's the world coming to?

In this world, the world that Adolphus Brook DOESN'T live in, women your age wear skinny jeans. We can knock out Phase 2 and Phase 3 of the Enhancing of Nora Bradford in Seattle tomorrow.

Lord help me, Nora thought. She wasn't brave enough to ask what Phase 2 and Phase 3 involved.

• • •

Post from Nora to the Devotees of Adolphus Brook Facebook Group:

> Hi, all! Just in case some of you didn't see the announcement in the Fans of *Northamptonshire* group, I wanted to let you know that American viewers of the show will be engaging in a Twitter campaign for the next two weeks, aimed at thanking the companies who sponsor the show on PBS. This is in addition to the current email and letter campaign to the producers on Adolphus's behalf, but I think you'll all agree that we can't pass up this chance to come alongside the rest of *Northamptonshire*'s enthusiasts to support and encourage those who make TV's best show possible!
>
> Be sure to tag the show using their Twitter handle, @Northamptonshire in your tweets. We'll all be using the hashtags #IHeartNorthamptonshire and #grateful.

Before I go . . . did anyone else notice the look that Adolphus gave Lucy on last night's episode? When she handed him the book he'd requested, he peered at her under his lashes. It was brief, but (I hope?) meaningful. I almost missed it the first time. But after rewinding it four times, I can definitively say that there was significant eye contact between them in that moment! And I can optimistically say that the eye contact between them may have contained some tenderness.

CHAPTER Seven

Phase 1 of Willow's Enhancing of Nora Bradford? Wardrobe.

Phase 2 turned out to be eyebrow sculpting. Whenever Nora had seen people at the mall reclining in chairs and getting their eyebrows "threaded," the treatment had appeared peaceful. When you were the one in the chair, however, it *hurt*. Nothing peaceful about it. She'd been limp with relief when it was finally finished and she was handed a mirror.

At first, Nora had been concerned about the reddish areas above and below her eyebrows. The redness had quickly faded, however, and as it had faded, her appreciation for her newly sculpted brows had grown. Her eyebrows hadn't been shoddy before. But the wizened gentleman had taken her from looking like a person with a pleasant face to a person with a fashionable face.

Phase 3? Makeup. Willow had ushered Nora to the MAC counter at Nordstrom in downtown Seattle. The staff there had instantly recognized Willow and, of course, been agog over her. The consultant who'd done Nora's makeup had collaborated over every part of the process with Willow as if the two of them were trusted co-workers and Nora was their joint project.

Nora was once again handed a mirror when the job was complete. Her fears that she'd end up resembling a geisha had come to naught. The consultant had highlighted her best features while camouflaging her flaws. The natural, sheer colors they'd picked for her eye shadow, blush, and lipstick complemented her light complexion and fiery hair.

Nora mulled over her makeover from the passenger seat of Willow's Range Rover as her sister drove them back toward Merryweather. She was now a woman with updated clothing, eyebrows, and makeup. It surprised her how much these superficial improvements meant. As their shopping day had progressed, she'd caught herself standing straighter, walking more purposefully, finding plenty to like when she caught sight of herself in mirrors and shop windows.

Was it unchristian of her to be enjoying her spruce-up as much as she was? The Lord looked at the heart, after all. He didn't care a bit about what she looked like. Duly noted. Inarguable. Yet, she didn't think the Lord would begrudge her some new outfits and improved eyebrows.

Glossy water slid by far below them as Willow steered across the Tacoma Narrows Bridge.

Her reaction to her updated appearance made Nora suspect that her self-image may have been decimated by The Dreaded Harrison's betrayal more than she'd realized until now. She'd never thought much about how their breakup might have colored her feelings toward herself. She'd thought a great deal about how it had wrecked her relationship with Harrison. She'd thought quite a bit, too, about how it had dented her relationship with God.

Up until Harrison had broken her heart, her faith in God had been clear-cut. So much so that not even her early-childhood trauma had shaken it. She'd been unable to imagine why anyone *wouldn't* trust God. Childlike faith had seemed to come with nothing but upsides. While Harrison had loved her and wanted to marry her, it had been easy to affirm that yes, God's will was best. Absolutely!

Then one day Harrison hadn't loved her or wanted to marry her anymore. He'd chosen someone else over her. The pain of that had been so excruciating that Nora had lost hold of her certainty in God's will.

She still loved God. Undoubtedly she did. However, life and Harrison had weathered her. In the months that followed her broken engagement, her childlike faith had been replaced by something more adult, more jaded, and a whole lot less naïve. After Harrison, it no longer seemed safe or wise to depend on God to provide the sort of happy ending He'd never guaranteed her in Scripture anyway. It had seemed proactive to take more responsibility for her own life.

She could trust herself. That, she knew. So she'd decided to make her own happy ending. Forging ahead, she'd worked hard and pursued success doggedly, fueled in part by a deep desire to save face and prove her worth. She'd dug her nails into her dignity and refused to let anyone see how much Harrison's dismissal had shredded her on the inside.

At least that was what *she'd thought* she'd been doing. Despite her determined efforts not to, she may have been inadvertently wearing Harrison's rejection and her defiant "I'm the smart one and that's enough for me" message around town like a scarlet letter thanks to her appearance. Which was too embarrassing to contemplate.

Nora swallowed and rubbed her fingertip along the car door's armrest. Back and forth. Back and forth.

Over the last three years, she'd told everyone—most of all herself—how content she was in her singleness. But was that really true? Down deep? At gut level? Or had that mantra mostly been motivated by that same insecure need to save face and prove her worth?

Shame burned her stomach like acid because she didn't like the truth.

Man, this was hard to admit even to herself because she wanted wholeheartedly to be content in her singleness. Instead, ever since Harrison had consigned her to the single life, she'd felt as though she'd been handed a ticket to a second-class ship cabin when she'd paid for first class.

What a horrible thing to confess! God was all she needed. Singleness was not second-best. She had to get her head straight on those facts before she could consider dating again.

Dating. The word alone roused fear in her, confusion as to how to begin, and—worst—a disgusting, chilling whisper that assured her she wasn't attractive enough or woman enough or *whatever* enough to keep a man long term.

Yikes. Um . . . no wonder she'd been hiding behind dowdy clothes and her beloved spinster persona.

It was time, past time, to stop hiding. To move beyond the scars Harrison had left. To repair her self-image. And to step into the future wearing a pair of fashionable high heels.

John's sense that he and Nora were destined to be friends was no fluke. No, it was a fact that became more and more clear to him over the next two weeks.

They met every few days to work on their search for Sherry. Together, they dug up all the thirty-three-year-old school directories and yearbooks they could find. No luck locating Sherry there.

They called or visited each of the churches that had been around thirty-three years before. No luck.

They hunted through old Shelton newspapers in hopes of coming across a mention of Sherry or Deborah. No luck.

They searched for marriage announcements and marriage certificates for either woman. No luck.

Their efforts had hit a frustrating wall. That didn't mean, though, that the time they spent together was frustrating. For John, the time they spent together was golden. Nora cracked jokes. She charmed every person they came in contact with. She used ridiculously big words. When he was with Nora, he forgot for whole spaces of time about his diagnosis. When he was with her, he could breathe.

He began to think about Nora even when they weren't together. At work, driving home, or running on the treadmill, he'd find himself wondering what Nora was doing and whether she was busy or happy or tired.

He and Nora both behaved professionally and respectfully. They said nothing that fell outside the boundary of friendship. They did nothing Allie would disapprove of. Each time he saw Nora, he talked to Allie about their meeting and updated her on the progress of the search.

So while he didn't exactly feel guilty about Nora, he did sometimes wonder how much time he should be spending with her. How much was okay? How much was too much? When you put hours of concentration into something or someone, you got to know that thing or that person well. He'd spent a lot of hours with Nora, and every meeting, every text message they exchanged, every phone call they made to plan strategy had helped him know her. In fact, he knew Nora better after a month of friendship than he knew Allie after more than six months of dating.

That wasn't a slam on Allie. There were just some people you felt close to after an hour because you had chemistry with them . . . and others you felt the same amount of closeness to after a year. Maybe it also had to do with the difference between friendship and dating. Friendship was more relaxed. You weren't hung up on trying to impress the other person.

John prayed over it. He didn't hear God leading him to call off the search or to limit his friendship with Nora, which was good because he didn't *want* to hear God leading him to call off the search or limit their friendship.

When they'd tried everything Nora could think of to turn up information on Sherry, and failed at all of it, it started to look like the decision to call off the search might be taken out of John's hands. Nora had told him that first day at the Historical Village that if she could no longer help him, she'd pass him off to a private investigator or an organization that handled cases like his. She hadn't suggested either of those things to him yet. But John could feel those options coming for him, like two buses he didn't want to ride.

Nora wasn't good at accepting failure. However bad she was at it, he was worse. He was the guy who hadn't rung the bell during BUD/S.

How about we return to Regent Street? he asked Nora at the end of May via text. *We can go back and knock on the doors of the neighbors who weren't there the first time.*

It's worth a try, she wrote back. *Let's go in the early evening this time. In my professional opinion, we're long overdue for a break in this case.*

"Yes, I knew Deborah. My husband and I have lived here for forty-five years."

Nora stilled. After this house, she and John only had two houses left to try on Regent Street. They'd received so many blank looks and so many friendly and unfriendly "Sorry, but I didn't know Deborah or Sherry" responses so far this evening that Nora had grown accustomed to disappointment. She hadn't expected the cute little lady at 3423 to be the needle in their haystack.

Goose bumps shimmied down her arms. "You . . ." Nora chased after her thoughts, which had raced off excitedly in all directions. "You knew Deborah?"

"I did," the woman answered. "Deborah and I were friends." She extended a hand. "I'm Sue Hodges."

Nora and John took turns exchanging handshakes with her.

Sue looked to be in her mid-seventies. She had curly light brown hair and a slim build. Her outfit of jeans, white shirt, and a royal blue sweater came across as both informal and classy. "Come in." She encouraged them to make themselves comfortable on her floral sofa, then disappeared into the kitchen to prepare glasses of ice water.

Great Scott.

The man who'd led worship at their church since Nora and her sisters were young often peppered his speech with a hearty, "Great Scott!" Nora, Willow, and Britt had adopted the phrase and also taken to calling the man himself Great Scott, though his name was Arnold.

Whenever Nora spoke with him after the service or ran into him around town and he tossed a "Great Scott!" into the conversation, she had to pinch the inside of her elbow to keep from laughing. If Nora spotted Great Scott while with one or more of her sisters, she'd rush them into the nearest restroom until danger passed. They all knew that the tiniest knowing glance from a sister in response to a "Great Scott!" would be enough to bring on a storm of inappropriate giggles.

Of all the words Nora knew, *Great* and *Scott* were the two that seemed most equal to today's state of affairs. Their patience had finally paid off!

Nora met John's eyes. "A lead," she whispered.

"Maybe." He gave her an uneven smile. "Possibly. It depends on the data." A five-o'clock shadow cast a faint darkening across his cheeks. He was looking at her with his rock-in-a-clear-mountain-stream hazel eyes and projecting his usual aura of competency.

"I stand corrected by my own protégé," Nora said. "Everything will depend on the data. That's very true."

"In order to be your protégé, wouldn't you have to be older than me? And wouldn't I have to be interested in becoming a genealogist?"

"Ah, protégé of mine. There's much you don't know."

"There's much *you* don't know."

"About Navy SEAL-type stuff?" The phrase had become an inside joke between them.

His smile widened. "About the definition of protégé."

"Shh! Here she comes."

Sue placed two tall glasses on the coffee table for them, then took a seat in one of the chairs opposite. "What was it you said when I answered the door, about why you're looking for information on Deborah and Sherry?"

"We're researching the genealogy of one of their relatives," Nora answered.

"We've hit a dead end," John added.

"Which relative are you researching?" Sue asked.

"Sherry Thompson's son," John answered.

"Mmm." Sue nodded. Her gaze appeared to focus on a point beyond her living room window. Though if Nora had to guess, she'd say Sue was actually focusing on a point several decades before. "Deborah and I were around the same age, so we naturally gravitated toward each other."

If Deborah was around the same age as Sue, then Deborah was also the right age to be Sherry's mother and John's grandmother. "Do you have a best guess as to how old Deborah would be now?" Nora asked.

"Seventy-seven, maybe? I like to think we would have become close if our schedules had been more alike. Deborah was single and worked long hours. I was married and a full-time mom. My husband, Adam, and I have three kids. They were in high school during the years when Deborah lived on the street."

"I see," Nora said. Her heart thumped eagerly. She and John had been working hard to uncover information on Deborah and Sherry without a shred of success. Concern that her best efforts at guiding him might not be enough had been keeping her up at night lately because she wanted, badly, to provide him with the information he sought.

"Deborah and I would visit whenever we saw each other out in the yard," Sue continued. "She came over a few times for dinner parties Adam and I hosted. She was a nice person. A generous person. I remember that she used to run a garage sale at her church every year to raise funds for church programs."

"Which church was that?"

"Bethel. It closed down long ago."

Which explained why their investigation into local churches hadn't paid off.

"Deborah was successful," Sue said. "She had a wonderful career going."

"What kind of work did she do?" John asked.

"She worked in banking. She always wore suits." Sue chuckled fondly. "In those days, professional women like Deborah wore power suits and had, you know, big hair and"—she gestured expressively—"big shoulder pads."

"Do you know which bank she worked for?" Nora asked. She took a drink of water to be polite, even though she was technically too riveted by Sue's revelations to be thirsty.

"She worked for Myer Bank. It's gone now, too. So many things have changed."

"Do you know why she sold the house down the street?" John asked.

Nora peeked at him proudly. He was actually beating her to some of the questions. The way a protégé might.

"Deborah moved because she was offered a promotion in Elma. We sent each other Christmas cards for a few years after she left, but then I'm afraid we lost touch."

"Would you happen to have her Elma address?" Nora asked.

Sue paused, thinking. "I might. In my old address book. I'll go and check."

Sue made her way to the office across the hall. Nora had a direct line of sight into the small room. She watched Sue bend and open a desk drawer.

Her intuition tingled the way it did whenever she was on to something with one of her searches. Finding a birth mother brought with it a different set of challenges than did tracing a person's ancestry. But the two pursuits also had plenty in common. In both cases, you followed one piece of information to the next to the next. And along the way, you typically needed fortune to smile on you a time or two.

Sue was carefully copying something onto a piece of paper.

Nora reached over and squeezed John's forearm with exultation.

He froze, and instantly regret flooded Nora. What had she just done? The corded power of his wrist and forearm brought back sensory details from the day he'd carried her through the faux office building. The feel of him . . . of touching him . . .

It wasn't like she'd taken hold of his hand. Even so, this was way too intimate. Too dizzying. A mistake.

Awkwardly, she patted his arm twice in a motherly way, then returned her hand to her lap. She didn't dare look at his face. "I think Sue has the address," she whispered.

"Maybe," he said. Was she imagining the strain in his voice? "Possibly. It will depend on the data."

Sue handed Nora the sheet of paper before returning to her chair. "I'm surprised that I did still have Deborah's address in Elma. No wonder Adam calls me a pack rat."

"Thank you." Nora trained her attention relentlessly on Sue while willing away the blush that threatened. She'd just *squeezed John's arm*, something she had absolutely no right to do. "Do you know where Deborah was from originally?"

"Oregon. Let me think for a minute." The older woman tilted her face toward the ceiling. "The name of the town will come to me."

Nora sure hoped so. Oregon was a big place.

She was excruciatingly aware of John's big body sitting beside her motionless, his weight dipping down the sofa cushions.

Sue snapped her fingers. "Blakeville. She was from a town called Blakeville . . . I think."

"This is so helpful. I can't tell you how much we appreciate your time." Nora pulled a pen from her purse and wrote *Blakeville, Oregon* on the back of the paper containing Deborah's Elma address. "Do you think you might have a picture of Deborah somewhere?"

"No, I'm afraid I don't. I didn't take as many pictures back then, before cell phone cameras."

"What did she look like?" Nora asked, curious.

"She was nice-looking. Very much so. Dark blond hair, down to about here." She indicated her shoulders. "Average height and build."

"What about Sherry?" John asked. "Do you remember her at all?"

Sue peered at John for a few moments, clearly trying to dredge through her memory. "Vaguely."

Based on the fact that Sherry had been just twenty-two at the time of John's birth, it was possible that she'd been away at college the first few years that Deborah had lived at the house.

"She kept to herself." Sue shook her head. "I can't remember now if we ever spoke or not. She was pretty, I do remember that. She had long, dark hair."

"Was Sherry Deborah's daughter?" John asked.

Sue's eyes widened at the suggestion. "No, no. Certainly not. Deborah had no children."

"Yet again, the computer searches I'm running are yielding nothing," Nora said.

John could only see the upper half of her face over her laptop's screen.

She growled. "*Arrgh*. So frustrating."

Had the librarian just growled? He would have laughed, except he didn't think Nora would appreciate him laughing in the face of her irritation.

They'd driven straight from Sue's house on Regent Street to the nearest coffee shop, and John had carried her big bag inside for her. While she'd gone to work on her computer, he'd ordered a tea for her, a water without ice for himself, and two plates of what the girl behind the counter had told him was their specialty: cinnamon apple cake with cream cheese frosting.

He moved the last of the items from the tray to their table. "I'm starting to think you don't know how to run computer searches."

"That's exactly what I'm afraid you'll think! You'll have to trust me when I say that, despite the evidence to the contrary over the last few weeks, I'm excellent at running computer searches. A search is only as good as the records in the system. If there are no matching records, then the search yields nothing."

"Thanks for explaining that, Nora. When you have a moment maybe you can explain why two plus two equals four."

"Oh, John," she murmured apologetically.

He leaned back in his chair and smiled across the table at her. "Do the people around you need for you to explain every little thing to them? Or do you just enjoy explaining things?"

"To be honest, it's probably more that I enjoy explaining things. Sorry for talking to you like you're a first grader."

"A sixth grader, maybe."

"It's only that I want you to think I'm adding something to this process so you won't fire me."

He stilled in the middle of sectioning off a bite of cake. "You are adding something. There's no way I'm going to fire you."

Her shoulders relaxed.

"We wouldn't have found out anything that we have so far if not for you," he said.

"My inability to generate new information these past few weeks has been hard for me to accept. I'm a high achiever."

Yeah, he'd noticed. He'd also noticed that her brown eyes were the exact color of gingerbread. That she always fidgeted with her teacup until the handle was positioned exactly to the side at a right angle. That she clicked her key fob twice to lock her car as if the first time hadn't already successfully locked it. That she loved ice cream. "I feel like I'm a low achiever as your employer," he said.

She blinked at him. "How so?"

"I'm not paying you enough."

"How about you let me work for free? Please? After all, I've hardly helped your search along so far." She slanted her head hopefully. "What do you think?"

"No way. Send me another bill. I can't imagine why you'd want to continue working on this without getting paid."

"Because I'm fascin—really interested in your . . . case, of course."

"Send me another bill, Nora." He took a bite of cake.

Turning her focus to her computer, she scrunched her nose and thumped her fist on her keyboard lightly, as if scolding it. "I ran searches for Deborah and Sherry in both Elma and Blakeville. It looks like Blakeville only has a population of two thousand, so there's no telling how much information they've made available online. Admittedly, hoping for a hit there might have been a bit of a stretch."

Admittedly. It amused him, the way she talked.

"Elma is slightly bigger, so I was hopeful. Alas." Who said *alas* these days? "No trace of Deborah or Sherry there, either."

He nudged her plate toward her. "Eat cake."

"You bought me cake?"

"You're just now noticing?"

"Yes."

"I bought you cake and tea."

"Thank you."

"Sure."

He watched her admire the dessert, then take a few bites. She ate in a ladylike manner, spine straight, one hand and her napkin politely in her lap. A strand of her hair had fallen out of her bun. It rested against the side of her neck, curling a little. Red hair against that pale skin—

He looked away. Drank water.

When she'd grabbed his arm back at Sue's house, the contact had felt like lightning. Ridiculously powerful. He'd drawn in a breath without meaning to and braced against it.

On the spur of the moment, Nora had squeezed his wrist. That's all. It had been harmless.

Her action, anyway, had been harmless.

It was his reaction that had him concerned. Even now, he had no idea why he'd overreacted to such a small, innocent thing.

Nora was the sort of woman who'd feel right at home as a *Jeopardy!* contestant. He was the sort of man who'd feel right at home rappelling from a helicopter onto the deck of a ship in the dead of night. They were nothing alike. He'd have a hard time explaining the reason for their friendship to anyone who asked. He'd have an even harder time explaining why her hand on his arm had messed with his head the way it had.

"Why do you think Sherry would have been living with Deborah if they're not mother and daughter?" Nora asked.

"I don't know. It seems strange that a twenty-two-year-old woman would have been living with a relative in her mid-forties."

Nora sipped her tea. "If Sherry was a teacher at the age of twenty-two, then she must have been a first-year teacher. Or maybe even a student teacher. I guess it's plausible to think that she lived with a relative right out of college, while she was still getting her feet under her as an adult."

No one could have paid him to live with a relative after he'd graduated college, but that was him.

"There's another possibility that occurs to me," she said.

"I'm listening."

"Back in the day, unmarried women were occasionally sent away when it was discovered that they were pregnant. Some families were so ashamed that they wanted to cover the whole thing up."

His gut tightened. He didn't want to think his conception had been so unwanted that Sherry's family would have taken that step. "If a woman had a family like that, wouldn't they have pressured her to abort the baby?"

"A lot of these families were religious. So it was a catch-22. The families were strongly against abortion. But their daughter's pregnancy out of wedlock wasn't acceptable, either. So the pregnant woman would leave her hometown and stay, sometimes several states away, at an outreach for expectant mothers or with a relative. Have her baby. Give the child up for adoption. Then return home."

"And pretend that nothing had changed?"

"Oftentimes, yes."

"That's crazy."

"The case studies have shown that many of the birth mothers had a hard time. They were expected to forget about the baby they'd put up for adoption, but of course, they couldn't forget. Even if everyone around them never mentioned it again, something major *had* happened to them. Stuffing it down and ignoring it didn't make it go away."

She wasn't talking about him, but her words hit him in the chest anyway. *Stuffing it down and ignoring it didn't make it go away*. Stuffing it down and ignoring it pretty well summed up how he'd been getting through the days since his diagnosis. If he really thought about his condition long enough, it grew so big and black that he'd begin to feel like he couldn't get enough air into his lungs.

"Sherry might have grown up far from here," Nora said, "and stayed in Shelton for the months leading up to your birth. Then returned home."

"And who was Deborah to her? An aunt?"

Nora shrugged.

He was getting tired of waiting for the data. He was ready to start speculating. "Since they have the same last name, Deborah might have been Sherry's father's . . . sister?"

"It's possible," Nora allowed. "With the age spread between them it seems like too much of a leap to think they could have been sisters."

"A big leap," he agreed. "What's our next play?"

"Blakeville. It's our most likely source of new information. If Sue was right and Deborah really is from there, that is." She took another thoughtful sip of tea. "I'll call whatever kind of city office I can find in Blakeville tomorrow. I'd like to know whether they have a collection of city directories and, if they do, if they've been digitized."

"What kind of information would we be able to get from a city directory?"

"The names, addresses, and occupations of every resident of the town. If we can find Deborah's family in a city directory, then we might be able to begin to assemble a family tree. And a family tree would be enormously helpful."

"How likely is it that Blakeville has city directories?"

"Seventy thirty? Many towns had them. Up until about fifty years ago, anyway." She set her cup back on the table, carefully adjusting the handle so that it lined up directly to her right.

"The woman I spoke with in Blakeville told me that they do have city directories, but they aren't digitized. Their town library closed, so now they store the books inside their courthouse," Nora informed John the next day over the phone.

She was making a work-related phone call to relay information! However, even before she'd started dialing John's number, her breath had gone a little shallow with anticipation. Hearing his deep, resonant voice on the other end of the line was causing her blood to rush with the swoony, heady joy of her crush on him . . . which hadn't abated in the least. No, it had only grown more stubbornly insistent.

"None of Blakeville's records are available online?" he asked.

"Not only are they not available online, they're located in what I'm very much afraid might be the bowels of Blakeville's courthouse."

He laughed. "The bowels?"

"Indeed."

"So let's call back and ask someone to go into the bowels of the courthouse and find the city directories for us."

"I already did ask that, and the lady who answered my call said that the same budget cut that cost them their library also cost them their librarians. Blakeville's small. The courthouse staff is miniscule. The employees were spending so much of their time digging around in the basement trying to answer people's requests for information that her boss finally put a stop to it. All the documents in storage are available to the public, and anyone who wants to search for information is welcome. But if we want to go that route, we'll have to help ourselves."

A long pause. "There's no one there I can strong-arm into doing some research for us?"

"You can try," she said doubtfully.

"Will you text me the number of the lady you spoke with?"

"Sure."

"Thanks. I'll call you right back."

They hung up and Nora watched the clock on her office computer screen tick off the passing of two minutes.

Her phone rang. "We need to drive to Blakeville," John said.

"No success at strong-arming?"

"That woman was about as flexible as a rock. She kept insisting in that sweet way of hers that rules are rules."

"We could try another line of inquiry instead." Nora was working hard to remain impartial toward the possibility of a trip to Oregon in order to compensate for the impartial part of her that wanted, very much, to hang out with John all the way to Blakeville and back. That much time in his presence would be the decadent equivalent of a visit to the world's best spa. "What do you think?" she asked. "Do you have any ideas?"

"Elma?"

"I called Elma to make sure their records are all online. They are. I can't find any evidence of Deborah or Sherry in Elma."

"Then we go to Blakeville."

Quiet settled between them. She bit the side of her lip.

"It'll take us about five hours to drive there," he said.

"Yes."

"Can you leave tomorrow?"

She hadn't expected him to be in a hurry. Maybe the search for his birth mother had sunk its hooks more deeply into him than she'd understood. "Are *you* free? Can . . . *you* leave tomorrow?"

"I'll have to move some things around at work, but yes. My staff can cover for me. Can you go tomorrow?"

It occurred to her that admitting that she could go, that she could easily reschedule her work, tomorrow night's planned date with *Northamptonshire*, and quality time in front of the mirror trying to master the art of eyeliner, might make her seem pitiful. "Yes. My staff can cover for me, too."

"If we leave at nine in the morning and make one stop for lunch, we'll get to Blakeville in the afternoon. That'll give us a few hours before the courthouse closes."

"Right."

"In case that's not enough time, I'll find us a hotel and book two rooms. So pack for two days. Okay?"

Two whole days with him. Two. Whole. Days. "Mm-hmm," she murmured weakly.

John was Allie's boyfriend. Allie was John's girlfriend.

Nora had once suffered a huge amount of agony when The Dreaded Harrison had broken up with her because of Rory. There was absolutely no way that she'd allow herself to become a Rory. *Please! As if John would ever give you a chance to be a Rory.*

Nora would go to her grave respecting John's relationship with Allie. Respecting herself. Upholding her half of a very platonic interaction with John.

There was no reason to feel badly because she'd gotten exactly what she'd secretly hoped for.

"I'll pick you up in the morning. . . . Oh, wait," he said under his breath.

"What?"

A few seconds of humming silence. "My Suburban's a company car, and the guys will need it over the next few days. I also have a 1968 Plymouth Road Runner Hemi—"

"Hmm?"

"—but we don't want to take that on such a long trip."

"I can drive," she automatically offered.

"You don't mind?"

Had she really just volunteered to chauffeur John Lawson, the man of *Uncommon Courage* fame, into the heart of Oregon? Her? Even amongst her family members, she was almost never nominated to drive. "No," she said. "I don't mind."

John's conscience pricked him painfully as he set his phone onto his desk at work. Meeting Nora for an hour here or there was one thing. But driving with her all the way to Oregon?

So? So what if they drove to Oregon?

Male/female coworkers traveled for business together all the time. This was no different. He talked to Nora about Allie. He knew for a fact that she supported his relationship with Allie.

Nora was his friend!

His friend who'd frozen him yesterday with a single touch.

It's okay. He'd had a day to think about yesterday. He'd concluded that moments of attraction to people you weren't dating or married to happened. It was how you responded that mattered. If you were an ethical person, you guarded yourself. You made the right choices. You refused to act on the attraction.

He didn't expect to have to deal with attraction to Nora on the trip to Blakeville. But if he did, he had faith in his ability to handle it.

These second guesses of his were wasting his time and energy. Blakeville was the best lead they had, so they'd travel there together. It was as simple as that.

She was just his coworker. She was just his friend.

• • •

Text message from Willow to Nora and Britt:

Willow

Grandma's on board with a birthday dinner party the evening of July 3rd. Here's your mission, should you choose to accept it. (And you better.) Britt and Valentina will oversee the caterer. Nora will handle invitations and RSVPs. I will handle the renting of party tables, chairs, dishes, linens. Together, we'll visit the florist to pick out flower arrangements and together we'll decide on a gift.

Britt

Aye aye, captain!

Willow

Nora?

Britt

Nikki came by the chocolate shop this afternoon and told me that Nora's preparing for a road trip to Oregon tomorrow with the Navy SEAL. I'm guessing Nora's away from her phone, planning.

Willow

What Navy SEAL?!

Britt

One named John Lawson who once was awarded a little thing called the Medal of Honor.

Willow

WHAT!!!

Britt

She's helping him investigate his ancestry.

Willow

If two sisters exclude the third sister from juicy information, that's a serious infraction of the sisterly code. I might have to petition the court to grant me two new sisters.

Britt

The information wasn't juicy enough to be mentioned to you for one simple reason. John has a girlfriend.

• • •

Facebook message from Duncan to Nora:

I see no green circle by your name, Miss Lawrence. You're not online and I have to confess, it's very depressing to come to Facebook in search of you and find you absent. Insomnia is bad enough. But insomnia without you?

Unacceptable.

I'm bereft, Librarian Extraordinaire.

CHAPTER
Eight

Nora had her car professionally cleaned inside and out. She took it in for an oil change and tire pressure check. She filled its tank. Then she surreptitiously sprayed Summer Flowers room freshener onto the floor mats. No need for John to think her a car maintenance slacker.

They'd decided to meet at the Library on the Green Museum for their road trip. Knowing John's penchant for arriving early, Nora pulled into the museum's small parking lot at 8:40 a.m. When she spotted Nikki sitting behind the wheel of her decade-old Camry, waiting, her heart sank.

Nora had been forced to trust her employee with her travel plans because she needed Nikki to cover for her while she was gone. Telling Nikki anything, however, carried with it a considerable level of risk. Nikki was nosy under ordinary circumstances. If she suspected that a handsome man might be in the offing, she became unbearable.

Nora rolled down her window.

Nikki rolled down her window. "I want to see the Navy SEAL," she declared. "I didn't get a good look at him the day he stopped by the museum."

"As I recall, you stared at him the whole time."

"But he was only inside for a minute or so. I really, *really* need a shot of estrogen, and the Navy SEAL is better than hormone replacement therapy."

Warmth climbed from Nora's neck toward her cheeks. She knew good and well that she wouldn't be able to convince Nikki to leave before John arrived. Her best hope of mitigating this impending disaster was to lay ground rules. "Nikki, my voluptuous and very smart office guru slash historical interpreter?"

"Mmm?" Nikki's peach lips curled with wicked delight.

"I command you to act politely toward John. We're going on a *business trip*. Do not mention any part of his anatomy."

"Who, me?"

"Do not ask about his relationship status."

"Nora! I'm surprised at you."

"Do not make any bawdy suggestions—" For the love! John's shiny Suburban turned into their parking lot.

She and Nikki climbed from their cars into the sunny morning. Nikki had doused herself in enough Yves Saint Laurent Opium to choke a skunk.

John hauled a duffel bag from the Suburban. A man Nora remembered from the Lawson Training hostage exercise sat behind the wheel of the Suburban. He raised a hand in greeting to her and Nikki, then drove off.

"Good morning." John approached, wearing battered jeans and a simple navy T-shirt.

Oh, heaven. His handsomeness always flustered her most when she first saw him. In a minute or two, she'd begin to adjust to it. Somewhat. Never fully. "Morning!" Nora chirped, popping her trunk.

He'd barely set his bag inside when Nikki extended her hand. "We haven't met officially. I'm Nikki, Nora's office manager."

John shook her hand. "Nice to meet you."

"Ready to hit the road?" Nora asked John, a trifle desperately.

"My, you've got a strong grip," Nikki purred. She reached out and squeezed his upper arm with her free hand, her brightly painted fingernails like drops of blood against his skin. "It must be these big biceps."

Nikki had ignored the first ground rule and mentioned his anatomy.

John studied Nikki with bemused confusion.

"You're a gorgeous, gorgeous man," Nikki told him, point blank. "Do you have any friends who are slightly older and single, but who look just like you and have a military past?"

He threw back his head and laughed.

Nora cleared her throat and edged toward the driver's-side door.

"Well?" Nikki asked. "Do you have any friends like that?"

"I'll have to think about it."

"Because I'm looking for someone like you," Nikki said. "*Actively* looking."

"Okay."

"You're dating someone, right?" Nikki asked.

Nikki had ignored the second rule and asked about his relationship status. Nora was going to kill Nikki!

"Yes," John answered. "I'm dating someone."

Nora's stomach twisted at his words, which was maddening because she was extremely aware, every second of every day, that he was dating someone. His spoken confirmation of it shouldn't make a fig of difference.

"That's too bad," Nikki rumbled, looking like a woman who'd just spotted a mouthwatering slice of chocolate cake, then been told the customer in front of her had purchased it out from under her.

"Well, I think it's too bad that you're looking for someone slightly older," John said to Nikki. "Otherwise, if and when Allie and I break up, you and I might have—"

"For you," Nikki interrupted, "I'll make an exception on age. Anytime. Anywhere."

"John!" Nora interjected before Nikki could break rule number three and make bawdy suggestions. "We should probably get going." She slipped into the driver's seat and started the engine.

"Anytime!" Nikki declared, tracking John as he took his seat. "Anywhere!"

He chuckled. "Nice to meet you, Nikki."

"Nice to admire you, John." She stuck out an ample hip and set a hand on it. "Come back soon."

Nora reversed before another word could be said. *Not one more word, Nikki!* From now on she'd be keeping all meetings with John top secret from Nikki Clarkson.

Her thoughts tumbled as if in a clothes dryer. She couldn't believe Nikki has just squeezed John's bicep. She herself would very much like to squeeze his bicep but couldn't, of course, because she was a well-behaved person and because—as he'd just very clearly stated—he had a girlfriend. Also, with every indrawn breath she could smell bergamot, not Summer Flowers. And of the two, she preferred bergamot hands down. Also, John was *sitting beside her*, quietly occupying her passenger seat, his body relaxed.

John. Who she was driving to Oregon. She was. Driving him.

"Nice office manager you have there," he said.

"I'm very sorry about that."

"About what?"

"Nikki's flagrant flirting."

"I can handle flagrant flirting."

"It was in ill taste."

"I liked her."

"*You did?*"

"Yeah. Do you mind if I slide this back?" He indicated his seat.

"Not at all."

He slid it way back, then tilted it to recline more.

When they came to a light, she glanced across the small space in time to see him slide on a pair of sunglasses. Nora sighed inwardly. She might literally combust from the force of her attraction to him and be reduced to nothing but vapor. If that happened, it would be totally worth it. A good way to go.

Peering back toward the road, she wrapped her hands tightly around the wheel and tried not to combust.

“Are you going to drive all the way to Oregon with your nose one inch from the windshield?” he asked.

“What? Oh. No.” She laughed nervously and leaned back. The light turned green.

She was on a road trip with John Lawson. They were going to Blakeville, potential hometown of Deborah Thompson, to see what they could learn about John’s birth family.

Great Scott!

A new outfit, new shoes, and a bulging travel kit full of new cosmetics filled her suitcase. Since their shopping day in Seattle, Willow had been murmuring about Phase 4 of the Enhancing of Nora Bradford: a new hairstyle. Nora hadn’t decided yet whether she should pull the trigger on Phase 4. Her bright hair and pin-up-inspired hairstyles were her signature. Without her signature, she might really become a textbook example of the invisible middle child.

“Do you like music?” she asked. “We could listen to music. Or we could just chill. I don’t want you to think I’m one of those annoying people who’ll make you fill every minute of a five-hour trip with conversation. I’m sure you have work to do. During the drive. So go ahead. I’m cool.”

“Nora?”

“Mmm?

“Your nose is an inch from the windshield again.”

John spent a good deal of the drive studying Nora. His chair was pushed back farther than hers, and she was concentrating on the road, which meant he could watch her all he wanted without her knowing.

She had delicate wrists. Short fingernails painted dark gray. Her profile was marked with a gently swooping nose and a mouth that, if you took the time to notice, was perfectly shaped. Not too thin or too puffy. Always slightly tilted up at the corners.

The small bumps of her vertebrae ran in a straight line down the back of her neck. Her tiny silver hoop earrings were set with what appeared to be real diamonds.

In the details of her appearance, he found ties to what he already understood to be true about her personality. Nora was high-tech in some ways and old-fashioned in others. Her watch was high-tech, her hair old-fashioned. She was capable and vulnerable. The way she drove, following every rule of the road and braking smoothly, was capable. But the girly shirt she had on, with its little puffy sleeves, was vulnerable. She was intelligent and wry. Real and guarded. And he could find clues to all of that if he looked close enough.

When had Nora become so pretty? He clearly remembered that she hadn't been pretty at all the first time he'd seen her. But now? Now she was very pretty.

He narrowed his eyes with confusion. Had she become more pretty to him as he'd gotten to know her because of who she was? Or would anyone—even people who didn't know her at all—say she'd gotten prettier?

He didn't know. Maybe both?

If anything about her had changed, he couldn't put his finger on what. Except—wait. She'd stopped wearing bulky clothes. At the training exercise and at their first few meetings she'd worn huge sweaters. He hadn't seen her in a huge sweater or skirt in a while. Had he?

It was warmer now than it had been then. She'd probably put her cold-weather clothing away and would bring it out again this fall. If she did, it would be a crime because those sweaters and skirts had been hiding a good body.

He rested the back of his head against the seat and rolled his face toward the passenger window. May's clouds and rain had stepped aside to make room for an early June full of sun and quiet wind and mild temperatures. Summer had arrived.

Their drive would take them through Portland and national forests. He knew the area well, and he knew he could expect beautiful scenery most of the way. In these surroundings, with Nora nearby to make him laugh, his future didn't seem so dark.

He was happy, he realized with a start. It had been a while since he'd felt this particular thing. In fact, he hadn't felt this way since the day he'd sat in his doctor's private office. There'd been framed diplomas on the wall that day, bookshelves, and a miniature globe on the desk's corner. There'd also been an apologetic steadiness in his doctor's expression that John had hated.

None of that had the power to overwhelm him today, though.

Today, he was happy.

Blakeville sat in the shadow of Mount Bachelor, a nine-thousand-foot-high volcano located on the eastern side of the Cascade mountain range. It had been christened Mount Bachelor because it stood off to the side of the famous trio of peaks named the Three Sisters.

John used his phone's GPS to guide Nora through the historic town of Blakeville toward the courthouse. Nora followed his directions. It was clear, however, that trusting someone else's map-reading skills didn't come naturally to her.

"Take a left here," he said.

"Left?" she asked skeptically. "Okay."

"Straight through the light."

"That's not it there?" She pointed to a two-story beige building in the distance. Stone accented its corners, a central stairway led to its front doors, and a flag flew out front.

"That's it, but some of these streets are one-way, so we have to go straight here."

"Ah," she said, as if she thought he'd just fed her an outright lie. As if finding the Blakeville courthouse was tricky for him. As if he hadn't spent the bulk of the Third Phase of BUD/S proving his land nav skills.

"Are you usually the navigator?" he asked.

"No."

"Yes, you are."

"Yes," she admitted. "How could you tell?"

Ten minutes later they'd parked and been given maps that listed the contents of each of the courthouse's three basement levels. Nora's prediction had come true. Blakeville's city directories were located in the bowels of the building.

John held open the elevator door for her when they reached B2, a space filled with white-washed cement walls and stained industrial carpeting. Metal shelves held everything from cardboard boxes to rusting pieces of junk that Nora would probably call antiques. It smelled like dust.

They followed the map to the basement's rear wall. Worn drawers rose from the floor to a waist-high counter. Above the counter, open-faced cubbies contained records, rolls of paper, and stacks of who knew what.

John and Nora separated and began searching the cubbies from opposite ends.

"Here," Nora said after a time.

He neared.

She indicated a group of books with matching black writing on their spines.

During the drive, they'd gone over their plan. They'd start their search of the directories by looking for Thompsons living in Blakeville at the time of Deborah's birth, seventy-seven years ago.

John did the math in his head, found the volume from that year, and set it on the counter. When Nora came to stand next to him, his awareness of her heightened. The rhythm of her breath. Her height. Her body heat. The basement felt suddenly, heavily silent. The fluorescent lighting buzzed loudly.

The book's index showed that the contents were divided into sections. An alphabetical listing of inhabitants. A list by street address. A list of businesses and community buildings. Maps.

"Aren't you going to tell me what to do?" he asked Nora.

"What? And treat you like a sixth grader?" She smiled. "I wouldn't dream of it."

He flipped to the alphabetical listing of inhabitants and made his way to the *T*s. Four men with the last name of Thompson had lived in Blakeville that year. John squinted, trying to understand how the information was arranged. If a man was married, his wife's name was listed in parentheses next to his. Then came his home address.

Deborah's parents had likely been married at the time of her birth, so he focused on the names of the three married men and their wives. Albert and Virginia Thompson. George and Ruth Thompson. Homer and Mary Thompson.

Nora bent closer to the book and the outside of her arm brushed against the outside of his arm. Nothing. There and gone.

Yet warmth spread from the spot through the rest of John's body. He drew in an uneven breath. Let it out slowly.

Nora pulled a notepad and pen from her bag. "Care to do the honors?" She extended the notepad and pen toward him.

"How about I read it and you write it?" he suggested.

"Good."

He moved his finger along one line at a time, spelling out the names, saying the addresses and occupations so Nora could take them down.

"No children are listed," John said when he was done. "Does that mean that these people didn't have children? Or that these directories only listed adults?"

"These directories only listed adults." Nora leaned against the counter. "The federal government takes a census every ten years that includes children." She chewed thoughtfully on the tip of her pen. "The government makes the census data public seventy-two years after it's taken. The most recent one came out about five years ago."

"So you're saying that the census they made available five years ago would have been taken around the time Deborah was born?"

She met his eyes. "Yes. If we're fortunate, we might be able to find Deborah there, now that we know who to look for." She motioned to the names she'd written on the notepad.

"Then let's check the census."

"Can you get cell phone reception down here?" They both pulled out their phones.

"No bars," he said.

"Me either. C'mon." She reached to lift her giant bag.

"Seriously, Nora. Stop trying to carry it. I've got it." And he did, even though he felt like a wuss every time he put her bag with its green trim and bright pink monogram over his shoulder.

They made their way to the courthouse's ground floor. Their phones immediately reconnected to the network. "I have bars." Nora walked toward a bench set against the hallway's wall. The beige marble floor had been buffed so much that John could see his reflection in it.

They sat. Nora tugged her computer free, settled it across her knees, and went to work searching for census data.

"All right," she said when she had all the fields filled in for the first of the three couples named Thompson. "Whew. This is making me nervous all of a sudden."

"Why?"

"Maybe nervous isn't the right word. Excited is better. This is a big moment. Ready?"

"Ready."

She submitted the search. John's concentration homed in on the census page that appeared. The scanned image showed rows and columns that had been filled in by hand. Nora scrolled down until they located Albert and Virginia Thompson. They had no children.

She ran a new search for the second couple, George and Ruth Thompson. They had five children. John read the first child's name under his breath. Nora joined in, and they read the next four names in soft unison.

None of them were named Deborah. Just one couple left to try. It could be that Sue had been wrong, that Deborah wasn't even from Blakeville. Or it could be that Deborah's family had moved to the town after this census. Or it could be that Sue had given them an incorrect age for Deborah.

Nora ran a new search for the third couple, Homer and Mary Thompson. They had three children. "Lucas," John and Nora read. "Kenneth. Deborah."

John stared hard at Nora's computer screen, at the neat black cursive on the white background, clearly spelling out the name *Deborah*.

"Ha!" Nora gave an excited clap.

John continued to stare.

"For a few weeks nothing was going our way," Nora said. "But this, right here? This just went our way. Discoveries like this are my favorite part of the job."

"I can't believe we found her."

"Believe it." She grinned widely at him.

He dug his hands into his hair, paused, then ran them the rest of the way through. "Do you remember the name Sherry gave me on my original birth certificate?"

"Mark Lucas Thompson, wasn't it?"

"Deborah's brother's name is Lucas."

Nora reread the record. "It sure is."

They let that sink in.

"Birth mothers often give their babies names that have personal significance to them," Nora said.

"So maybe Lucas is Sherry's father. Which would mean that Deborah *is* Sherry's aunt."

"Maybe. Could be. Possibly. It depends on the data." A small dimple flashed in Nora's cheek. "When this census was collected, Homer Thompson was twenty-six. Mary was twenty-five. Lucas was five. Kenneth was three. And Deborah was ten months old. Homer was a clockmaker and watch repairman." She added the new details to her notepad.

They still didn't know for sure that Sherry was related to these people. But the evidence was stacking up, making it look more and more like John had blood ties to them. "The address that's given for Homer and Mary here is the same one that was given in the city directory," John said. "There's an *R* under the own or rent column. So they were renters?"

"Yes."

"Would looking up the deed to the property give us any information we could use?"

"Since they were renting, probably not. I think we're better off heading back to B2 and trying to track Homer and Mary from one city directory to the next. That will tell us whether they stayed in Blakeville. When their kids become adults, we'll hopefully be able to locate them in the directories, too."

John carried Nora's bag back to B2.

The Blakeville city directories spanned the period from 1936 to 1960. John and Nora started at the beginning and began working their way through, locating Homer and Mary in each book. Homer and Mary had moved a few times, but they'd never left Blakeville. John and Nora had finished with fifteen of the volumes and were approaching the time period when Lucas Thompson would have become old enough to be mentioned in the directories, when a voice over the PA system let them know that the courthouse would be closing in ten minutes.

Already? John checked his watch and was surprised to see that it was ten till five. It would take them the remaining ten minutes to put the directories back in their cubbies.

"When we come back tomorrow, we can go through the rest of these," Nora said.

"I'm glad I booked us rooms."

"Good foresight, John."

"Thank you very much, Nora." She handed him the books and he pushed them into their slots. "Hungry?"

"Starving."

"Once we check in at the hotel, I'll order us some appetizers."

I didn't make the suggestion because I want to spend more time with her, he told himself almost angrily. He refused for it to be about that. They were both hungry, and she'd come all this way to help him. Offering her food was the least he could do. It was only polite.

Her face swung toward his. The power of their eye contact sent a knife of pleasure driving into him.

"Sounds good," she said.

• • •

Facebook message from Duncan to Nora:

DUNCAN: Hard at work today as usual? You know what they say about all work and no play . . .

NORA: I'll have you know that I'm on an adventure! I'm sitting in my car at a gas station on the outskirts of Blakeville, Oregon. The Navy SEAL is insisting on filling up my tank before we drive to the hotel, even though my tank's not yet empty. He's nice like that.

DUNCAN: Is this a road trip for work or for pleasure? I seem to remember cautioning you not to develop a crush on the Navy SEAL.

NORA: It's a road trip for work. We're hot on the pursuit of research.

DUNCAN: If you could see me, you'd see that I'm frowning.

NORA: Not only am I on a road trip, but I'm also in the throes of designing an invitation for my grandmother's 80th birthday party. The invitation is going to be impeccable. So there, famous person. My dance card is filling up. Take that!

DUNCAN: Impressive. Message me a picture of the invitation once you have it finished. I want to live vicariously through your impeccable-ness.

NORA: Your wish is my command. Now I'd better dash. The Navy SEAL is back.

DUNCAN: One last thing. Did you see on the events page of my site that I have an appearance coming up on Tuesday?

NORA: Thanks for the heads-up! You can count on me, Duncan. I'm on it. I'll drum up as many attendees for it as I can. Cheerio!

• • •

Quote from Uncommon Courage*:*

> "I learned that I needed to be very honest with myself. There wasn't room in SEAL training for ego or assumptions or desires or self-deceit. If I was going to make it through, I was going to have to do it on what was left of my true character once all the surface parts of who I thought I was had been stripped away."

CHAPTER
Nine

Did John know for sure where they were going? Because a large number of people, who were perfectly effective in other areas of their lives, were hopeless when confronted with phone maps and concepts like north and south.

They'd left the gas station twenty minutes ago. John had directed her onto a road that climbed through a forest populated with towering pine and glinting streams. They'd swept past alpine lakes and meadows dotted with snowberry. It was all tremendously lovely, and Nora would have appreciated it more if they hadn't very clearly been journeying away from civilization instead of toward it. Following this course, they were more likely to find themselves in Idaho than at an establishment that served appetizers.

She bit her lip and wondered whether she should question his directions.

John saved her from having to make that decision.

"The hotel's coming up in half a mile," he said.

Sure enough, an understated marker announcing Conifer Crest Lodge appeared. She turned in, feeling chagrined for having doubted John and relieved that she'd kept her mouth shut.

A bend in the drive brought the lodge into view. Nora gaped through the windshield at it, wonder settling over her. In the style of so many buildings of the Northwest, it had been built to complement its natural setting. Cedar shake siding, towering beams, and sparkling rectangular windows composed its exterior. It oozed the kind of rustic elegance that Condé Nast was so fond of. Rory, who'd been endowed with an overabundance of good taste, would definitely have said yes to this lodge on her *Say Yes to Beauty* blog.

Why had she just had that wayward thought about Rory? Rory wasn't welcome here, thank you very much, in this unexpectedly charming place.

"When you said you were booking rooms, I assumed you meant you were booking rooms at a hotel along the lines of a Holiday Inn Express," she murmured.

"This . . ." he said, "isn't that."

The valet met them and soon Nora was standing at the check-in desk, engaging in an imaginary scenario in which she and John were married and were about to go from here to a room and a bed they shared. He'd have to take his shirt off to get in the shower, of course, and . . . well, yummy. She'd love to know what he looked like shirtless. To feel his arms around her. To have all that strength and intensity focused entirely on her.

Was it warm in here?

The check-in attendant behind the desk kept shooting glances at John, each one longer than the last, until the sound of his fingers clicking computer keys faded to silence. "Are you the author of *Uncommon Courage*?"

"William Reed wrote it," John answered.

"But it's about you," the man stated. "Right?"

"Yes."

"That was a terrific book!" He laughed with surprised delight. "I'm so glad to meet you. Thank you for your service to our country, sir."

The men shook hands.

"I listened to the audio version of it on my phone," the attendant continued. "I listen to a lot of books when I'm commuting.

Anyway, by the end of it, I felt like I knew you. That's crazy, huh? I don't know you. But it was just that well-written."

Nora studied John, amused. He'd set his jaw in a way that was both formal and distant. He said little. The man who could slay dragons wasn't exactly lapping up the praise.

The staffer continued to extol John and John's book before sliding two key cards toward them. "Have a wonderful stay here at Conifer Crest, Mr. Lawson and Ms. Bradford."

"Thank you."

Their luggage had already been taken to their rooms, so John led her straight to the restaurant off the foyer. He bypassed the indoor seating and held open one of the thick doors leading to the patio.

Nora caught her breath as she stepped outside and took in the panoramic view. It reminded her of a scenic stop along a highway.

People filled the patio's tables. In both directions, walkways beckoned, hugging the sides of the lodge and wrapping all the way around the building.

Nora moved to the edge and peeked over. It wasn't a particularly steep drop. The tips of the trees below reached almost to her toes. The land sloped down and away gradually, melding into a wide valley, until it finally reached the lazy, curving line of the Deschutes River in the distance. Beyond the river, peak after soaring, craggy peak jutted heavenward like raggedly torn pieces of construction paper in an impressionist collage.

Nora turned her back to the sun, still hours from setting, and walked along the balcony in the other direction, her fingertips trailing the flat-topped log that formed the railing. She stopped at the walkway's far corner. The muted noise of the guests on the patio filtered over her while she drank in the rippling mountainsides flanked with lush trees and the hazy river at the base of it all.

"Beautiful," she whispered. It was the sort of beautiful that made your heart hurt and tugged at the bravest and most fanciful parts of you.

John stopped a few feet away from her position. He placed his forearms on the railing and leaned forward onto them, one leg cocked.

For long moments neither spoke.

True peace wisped through Nora, as gentle and sweet as the breeze on her cheeks. Peace. And companionship, too. She and John had spent most of the day side by side, but she didn't want a break from him. In fact, the opposite was true. She didn't want to let him go—

Don't, she warned herself. *Don't cherish his companionship*. His companionship wasn't something she'd be able to hang on to. She'd have to let him and his friendship go, and maybe soon, depending on how long it took them to locate Sherry.

A waitress approached, offering them a shy smile.

"Do we want to grab a table or are we good here?" John asked Nora.

They'd spent too much of the day sitting and this spot was perfection. "I'm good here," Nora answered.

"Me too."

They ordered two iced teas and, after some debate, a cheese and meat board.

"I'm pleased with the progress we made this afternoon," Nora told him when the waitress had gone.

He nodded. "You said once that you'd helped a few other people who were trying to find their birth mothers."

"Yes."

"Were you able to find them? The birth mothers?"

"We were. I'm always determined to help my clients. Any type of client with any type of genealogical goal. But because I'm half-adopted myself, I think I'm wired to feel extra determined on behalf of my clients who are adoptees."

He focused that intent and powerful gaze of his on her. It was *so* powerful that the backs of her knees tingled in response.

"What do you mean, you're half-adopted?" he asked.

"I'm only biologically related to my dad."

He waited.

When she didn't offer more, he said, "Explain."

She arched an eyebrow. "How about we make a deal?" He was a private, self-contained man. She needed a stick she could use to prod information out of him. "If I tell you about me, then you'll tell me something about yourself in return."

"What kind of something?"

"The kind of something you're willing to share. If I ask a question that's too personal, just let me know, and I'll move on to another."

His masculine lips quirked. "You have a whole list of questions waiting for me?"

"Yes."

"Just how intrigued do you think I am by your half-adoptedness?"

"Sufficiently intrigued to agree to my terms."

He smiled, and she didn't know whether to laugh because of the joy that smile brought her or cry because he loved someone else.

"I agree to your terms," he said. "Go ahead and explain."

"It's all a bit confusing, so hang on to your hat. As you know, I have two sisters."

"I'm hanging on to my hat pretty well so far," he said dryly.

"I'm the middle sister. Willow is two years older. Britt is four years younger. We have the same father, but all three of us have different mothers."

Upon hearing this information, people always reacted in the same whistling, eye-rounding type of way that basically communicated, *Your dad must have been a world-class womanizer*.

John didn't react that way. He merely watched her, hazel eyes serious.

"When my dad was in his early twenties, he met this beautiful French woman named Sylvie," she said. "Sylvie was backpacking through America at the time. They were the same age, but she was much more worldly and adventurous and freewheeling than he was. She was a painter. Extremely creative and talented . . . the kind of person who might talk about philosophy for two hours, then smoke a cigarette, then make crepes, then skinny-dip in the lake. She's still that type of person."

"Skinny-dipping? Suddenly Sylvie is sounding like someone I'd like to meet."

"Did I mention how beautiful she was? She was *very* beautiful. Not the normal kind of beauty. The I-can't-believe-my-eyes kind. Sylvie's daughter, my sister, became a model, but Sylvie's rumored to have been even more exquisite in her day."

"And your dad fell for her."

"Like a stone."

"They had a fling."

"Yes, even though my dad was raised by sensible Christian parents and even though he was a believer and should have known better. He fell totally and completely in love with Sylvie."

"And she got pregnant."

"Exactly. My dad wanted to marry her more than anything. But she refused."

Their waitress arrived and carefully set their food on the balcony's ledge. Three kinds of cheese. Nuts and olives and dates in tiny matching bowls. Crostini. Wafer-thin crackers. Small mounds of capicola and peppered salami. Lovely fanned-out slices of pear and green apple. All arranged on a wooden platter.

Before Nora had finished marveling over it, the waitress had returned with their iced teas. "Can I get you anything else?" she asked.

"I think we're good," John said, and she left them to it.

John, always gentlemanly, motioned for Nora to go first. "You were telling me about the skinny-dipping French beauty."

Nora took a bite of crostini, sharp cheese, and salami. She almost moaned aloud but caught herself at the last second.

John went for the olives first.

"The skinny-dipping French beauty stayed in Washington with my dad during her pregnancy," Nora said. "A month after Willow was born, she put Willow in his arms and continued on her tour."

"She was never a mother to Willow?"

"Not in the traditional sense. She didn't want custody. She lives in France, where she's made a celebrated career for herself with her art. She calls Willow or sends cards or blows through for a visit now and then. When she does, she treats Willow like an amusing friend. Willow calls her Sylvie and she calls Willow Cherie."

"So what's your mom's story?"

"My mom's story is sadder, I'm afraid."

John stopped eating, and his regard turned solemn.

Nora toyed with the corner of a downy paper napkin that lay half-pinned beneath the platter. "My dad works for Bradford Shipping, the import/export company that's been in my family for generations. The company had been worth a fortune in prior eras, but right around the time that Sylvie left, it was on the brink of collapse. The company needed him, and of course Willow needed full-time care. On top of those pressures, I think the loss of Sylvie completely devastated him. He hired a Russian housekeeper slash nanny named Valentina who's still with us to this day. And he set about finding a wife."

"On the rebound?"

"He's never said that to me. In fact, no one has ever even hinted at that within earshot of me. But, yes. If I had to guess, I'd say he was on the rebound big time. The timeline alone points to it. Only five months passed between Sylvie's departure and my mom's entrance into his life. What that tells me is that he was lonely and overwhelmed and maybe also bent on the path of repentance after what had happened with Sylvie."

"What was your mom like?"

"My mom, Robin, was Sylvie's opposite. She grew up in church, and everyone I've ever talked to about her says that she was family-oriented, kind, and dependable. I think my dad knew that, above everything else, he could trust her. Finding someone he could trust must have seemed like a shelter in the storm. It couldn't have hurt her cause that she was the type of woman who'd obviously make an excellent mother to his motherless baby. They got married when Willow was one and had me a year later."

"And did she make an excellent mother?"

"The best, according to everyone." Nora's throat began to tighten. The topic of her mother was not new to her. It was an old familiar road she'd been driving over all her life, conversationally and emotionally.

She could remember whispering about it to her fascinated elementary school friends when their teachers or parents weren't listening. During her high school years, when her peer group had loved to wallow in all things tragic, her friends had wanted to plumb the depths of what had happened to her mother for hours at a time.

Nora had grown up with a bedroom full of pictures of her mother in expensive frames. And every year until she'd left for college, her family had celebrated her mother's birthday with cake and shared memories. In the Bradford family, her mom held a sainted place of respect and fondness. Sort of like a beloved heirloom Bible.

There had been times when, considering her mother's fate, Nora had felt guilty about the normal, stable, mostly happy life she'd gone on to lead. But there had never been a time when Nora had felt she couldn't talk about her mother. All that talking didn't prevent fresh eddies of grief from washing over her, however. She missed a woman she couldn't even remember. Loss was woven into the fabric of her life just like her memories, her family, her faith, and everything else that made her who she was.

"My mom and a friend of hers used to meet four times a week to go walking," Nora said, "often at Blue Heron Park. It has lots of jogging trails through the woods and along the lake. Do you know the place?"

"I do."

"Sometimes my mom and her friend would bring their kids along in strollers for their walks. But if their husbands were home, they'd go without the kids. And if my mom or her friend couldn't make it, they'd occasionally go alone. Which is what happened the night my mom . . . was killed. Her friend couldn't make it, so she went alone."

He frowned. The lines of his face were a study in grave, war-hardened beauty.

"She died on a night that had seemed totally ordinary. My dad came home from work and took over with Willow and me. My mom told him about the dinner she'd made, they exchanged a kiss, and she darted out the door. It was late summer, so she had a few hours left before darkness fell."

"She never came home?"

"No. A man named Brian Raymond dragged her off the walking path at Blue Heron Park. He duct-taped her mouth and her wrists." She refused to be ashamed of the facts surrounding her mother's death. She spoke about them to anyone who asked, and she never sugarcoated them. She wanted people to know her mother's story. She did. That said, these facts were ugly and brutal and disgusting. Always heavy to acknowledge. Always difficult for someone who knew nothing of them to hear. "He raped her," she said quietly. The words brought a flash of inward pain. "Then he strangled her."

Silence sifted between them.

"Nora," he finally said.

Tears pricked her eyes at the sound of her name, spoken by him with compassion.

She drew herself up. "I was seven months old when she died. It wasn't until many years later that my dad told me about the violence she'd endured at the end. To my dad's credit, he held himself ruthlessly together after her death. He stepped up and poured all his energy and focus into his daughters. He's a wonderful dad."

The mountain air smelled of pine, earth warmed by sunlight, and the honeyed fragrance of the lupines growing in shocks of vertical color from a nearby pot.

"What happened to Brian Raymond?" he asked.

"Just to give you some background, Brian was raised by a mother who battled alcoholism and a father who committed suicide when he was ten. It's unsettling because in pictures he looks somber but also handsome and athletic. We know for a fact that he was intelligent. He had a good job. He had friends. But beneath the normal trappings, he was broken and vicious." She considered

John. "You've come face-to-face with some vicious men during your time with the SEALs."

"Yes."

They were both adopted. And both her life and his had been marked by encounters with cruel people. She and John might look like a strange pair. The genealogist and the Special Ops vet. But the more she knew him, the more she realized how well their backgrounds qualified them to understand each other. "Brian Raymond was thirty when he killed my mom. By then he'd already raped five other women."

"Did the other women survive?"

"Yes. He was increasingly brutal with each one, but my mom was the first and only one he killed. Evidence from her murder led the police to him."

"Is he serving time?"

"No. After his sentencing, he hung himself in his jail cell."

Nora wondered what John's astute eyes saw as he assessed her.

"After what happened with my mom, my dad decided that love and marriage were *not* for him." She gave a rueful laugh that came out sounding sadder than she'd intended.

"Yet you have a younger sister."

"My dad had decided love and marriage weren't for him, but God hadn't." Time to steer this conversation to something more hopeful. Seriously! She didn't want, and surely her mom wouldn't have wanted, their spirits to sink with depression while surrounded by the stunning evidence of God's majesty. "Two years after my mom's death, my dad met Kathleen. They both worked at Bradford Shipping. My dad says that he tried his hardest to resist her, but over time, he couldn't help falling in love with her. They've been happily married now for a long time."

"And Kathleen is Britt's mom."

"Yes, she's Britt's biological mom. Shortly after she married my dad, she legally adopted Willow and me so she's been a mom to me since I was three and to Willow since she was five. She's the one who gave us baths, made us do our homework, nagged us to clean our rooms, took us to the DMV for our driver's test, and bought us prom dresses. I have a special place in my heart for my mother. But Kathleen's the only mom I can remember." She shrugged. "She's our mom."

"That's how I feel about my mom."

"I understand completely."

Their waitress came to check on them.

"Is there anything you need, Nora?" John asked.

You. To love me in sickness and in health till death do us part. "Not a thing."

"Just the check, then," John told the waitress.

"This, and anything else you'd like, are complimentary," she replied. "Stefan, at the front desk? He told the chef about, you know, who you are. So . . . this is the chef's treat."

John's posture stiffened. "That's very kind, but I'd like to pay."

The waitress replaced Nora's bent napkin with a fresh one. "No, no," she said cheerfully, walking off. "It's already been comped. Enjoy!"

Nora nibbled a sliver of pear. "You seem a trifle uncomfortable, John."

"Hmm?"

"You were uncomfortable at the check-in desk, too."

His eyebrows dipped together in the center. "Thanks for pointing that out, Nora."

She laughed.

He piled a cracker with cheese as if that ended their discussion.

"So?" she asked. "How come recognition makes you uncomfortable?"

"According to our deal, you get to ask me one question. Is that your question?"

"No, no," she hurried to say. Goodness, she didn't want to spend her one question like a kid who accidentally asked a genie for a wish before thinking things through.

He finished his cracker, then funneled nuts into his mouth, his vision trained far away. His black watch glimmered. Over the month of their friendship, Nora had noticed everything there was to notice about things like John's watch, eyelashes, the scuffs on his boots, and the network of veins on the undersides of his wrists. It also hadn't escaped her attention that he occasionally hummed what sounded like "Sweet Child O' Mine" when concentrating. Or preferred his water without ice. Or never seemed cold and often wore T-shirts in weather that made her shiver.

Weighing her options, she selected a slice of apple and balanced a scoop of cheese on top. In the end, she decided to ask him the question she wondered about the most often. "Why are you searching for your birth mother?"

A hurricane of black feelings stirred within John at Nora's simple question.

Should he tell her why he was searching for Sherry? He was searching because of his diagnosis, but his diagnosis still felt raw, like he'd received it yesterday. In the time since he'd learned about it, he'd only brought himself to tell his family and Allie. No one else.

It seemed like a betrayal of Allie, to tell Nora something so personal. Yet, Nora was his partner in this search, so in some ways, it seemed like she had a right to know.

He wanted to tell her because he wanted her to know him.

And he didn't want to tell her because he needed to keep the distance between them in place.

Why are you searching for your birth mother? she'd asked.

Because I'm going blind, Nora.

The words waited inside of him. *It's an inherited condition. So you see, if I can't keep my sight or my independence, which I value more than just about anything, then I want answers.*

If he said that to her, she might pity him. It made his heart stop just to *think* about her pitying him. He'd rather her go on thinking he was better than he was.

Nora waited patiently for his answer, golden light behind her. He felt a pull toward her—a loyal and intense pull.

Careful, John.

"Your question's too personal," he finally said.

"John!" she scolded, laughter in her tone. "I just spilled my heart out, telling you about my mother."

"I'm glad you did."

"And?"

"And you said from the beginning that if your question was too personal, I could tell you, and you'd move on to another."

"Fine," she said lightly, obviously deciding not to test the boundary he'd put down between them. "In that case, I'd like to know what happened that night in Yemen."

"You already know. You read the book and saw the movie."

"I want to hear about it from you. In your own words." Nora rubbed her arms.

"You're cold." His voice held a rugged edge of concern.

"I don't want to leave, though." Kneeling, she grabbed a light green sweater from her purse. She slid her arms into it. "I'm good. So . . . spill. You were a member of SEAL Team Six . . ." she offered encouragingly.

"People still call us SEAL Team Six because it sounds cooler than our official title, which is Naval Special Warfare Development Group."

"Your focus was counterterrorism."

He smiled. "Who's telling this?"

"You are."

"The objective of our mission in Yemen was to extract hostages from a group of militants. They were holding two American journalists, one American aid worker, and two Canadian aid workers. We'd been following the situation for a while, but it became urgent when the terrorists announced that they planned to execute the journalists within forty-eight hours. The president gave the order, and we were on our way to Yemen."

"You didn't have much time to plan."

"We had enough time," he stated. "Intel on the compound where we suspected the hostages were being held had come in a few days before the execution threat. Our people had been working on a strategy since they'd received the intel."

"Okay."

"Two Ospreys transported us to a position about seven kilometers from the compound."

"In the dead of night, right? You SEALs seem to like nighttime missions."

"We SEALs are all about concealment. Hostage extraction is extremely difficult. Our mission was to protect hostages from captors who were very close, in proximity, to them. We did everything we could to ensure that we'd be able to neutralize the captors *before* they suspected we were there."

"I'm trying to look like I'm accustomed to talking about the neutralizing of captors. How am I doing?"

"You're doing fine."

"Continue." She made a *go on* motion.

"Two of our snipers simultaneously took out the night guards. One guard was sitting outside. One was walking by a window inside. When those shots went off, several of us were already waiting close to the rear of the house. We entered, engaged with the guard in the hallway and the two who'd been sleeping. It couldn't have taken us more than twenty seconds to deal with all five of them."

"That part went according to plan."

He nodded. "None of us heard the guy in the hallway alerting reinforcements on his walkie-talkie right before we entered the house. It wasn't until much later that we found out that's what had happened. The Ospreys landed at the compound. We'd started loading hostages and team members onto them when we saw three open-topped trucks speeding toward us. As soon as they were within range, they started spraying us with machine gun fire. The first Osprey lifted off safely. I was in the second Osprey. It got up, but they fired an SA-7 surface-to-air missile and hit the tail of our aircraft."

Nora looked worried that he wouldn't make it out of the story alive.

"You know all this already," he reminded her.

"Hearing you tell it is bringing home the fact that you really did *live this*. It's not fiction, like what I'm used to. You were actually trapped in a doomed helicopter."

He'd relived it through nightmares for a long time afterward.

"How many of you were inside the Osprey?" she asked.

"Seventeen. Three of the hostages. Two medics. The rest of us were military. The pilots pulled off an incredible piece of flying to get us down as well as they did. Even so, it was rough. Two SEALs died in the crash. Two more were pinned inside the wreckage and died in the fire." His felt a muscle in his neck tick. "All but three of us were injured."

"You say that, but the three of you who were still on your feet did have injuries."

"Right, but not the kind that would slow us down. The three of us pulled everyone from the Osprey that we could, then loaded up with guns. The other two guys took up positions between the militants and the crash site. Their goal was to hold them at bay. I stayed behind with the survivors. I got them down into a gully so they'd be out of range, then climbed to the top of the ridge and waited in a stand of trees."

"Did you think that reinforcements would make it to you in time?"

"I knew they'd make it to us, but I didn't know if they'd make it in time. The terrorists were on us fast and I was spending all the ammunition I had. Lobbing grenades. Shooting. Reloading. We were outnumbered. They were well-armed and well-organized."

"You were shot twice."

"Both were flesh wounds."

"But they bled." She looked deeply offended on his behalf. "A lot!"

"They weren't the kind of injuries—"

"That would slow you down?"

He grinned wolfishly.

"Continue your tale." She reached for her iced tea.

"The militants killed one of the SEALs in the forward position. They wounded the other."

"Who you then rescued at risk to your own life."

He lifted a shoulder. "I continued to do what I could to hold the attackers off. Let's put it that way."

"While relaying information to the reinforcements," she added.

"If you say so."

"And did our guys really make it to you in the nick of time?"

"*Just* in the nick of time."

"So tell me something that's not in the book or the movie."

He'd been trying to talk sense to her about what had happened in Yemen, yet her expression was full of softness and respect, and he knew she was building it all up in her mind. He'd admitted to himself a few minutes ago that he wanted her to think he was better than he was. But never about this. "I'm going to tell you the honest truth about it. You ready?"

"Ready."

"I'm not a hero, Nora. To me, a hero's someone who weighs the situation and searches his soul and then sacrifices himself. That night in Yemen, there was no time to weigh the situation or search my soul. I didn't decide to sacrifice myself." He needed to make this point clear. "I just *did my job*. My instincts and my training took over, and I picked up my gun and started firing. I reacted the same way any other SEAL on that mission would have reacted. It's just that I was able to do what others weren't because I was uninjured and because I was standing farther back, in the trees."

"Okay."

"Okay?" he asked, relieved.

"You were doing your job. That day in Yemen was another day at the office."

"Another day at the office," he agreed. "A very bad day. But just a day."

"The praise of others makes you uncomfortable because you feel as though you were fulfilling your duties, same as everyone else."

"Several SEALs gave more than I did that night. I knew them and their families. They were brothers of mine, and they deserve thanks."

"Yes, but the people who cross your path only have you. In their path. To thank. They won't have the opportunity to thank the others."

He scowled.

"You did something for America and for those people that a lot of us would have loved to have done in theory, but could never do in reality. So thank you, John. Very much. For what you did."

The link of their eye contact grew heavy and meaningful.

Protectiveness of her, fierce tenderness for her, swept through John. So strong that his lungs physically tightened. So strong that sexual desire rocked him.

He wanted her.

He wanted her badly.

"I'd better go in," he said.

"John . . ."

"I'll see you in the morning." He didn't look at her. He was already stalking past. He was afraid of what he'd do or say if he looked at her.

Not one more glance.

"Bill your dinner and breakfast to your room," he growled. "I'm paying."

• • •

Phone conversation between Allie and her best friend, Lizzie:

Allie: John is on a trip with the genealogist he hired to help him find his birth mother. Should I be worried?

Lizzie: Is she pretty?

Allie: Not in a conventional way. But she is sort of . . . cute. And John's always telling me how smart she is.

Lizzie: Then maybe some degree of worry is in order.

Allie: That's what I was afraid you'd say. I've been playing it cool with John because I'm no dummy. I would have scared him off if I'd told him from the start how much I care about him. Do you think I've been playing it too cool?

Lizzie: Based on the time I've spent with you and John, I think you've played it exactly right. Do you trust him?

Allie: I trust him. But that doesn't mean I'm not a little concerned. We've been dating for six months, Lizzie. I keep thinking and hoping that he's going to decide that he loves me. But so far, he hasn't.

Lizzie: That doesn't mean he won't.

Allie: But I have no guarantee that he will, either. John's never fully let me in. He's never given me his heart.

• • •

Text message from Allie to John:

Hi, sweetheart. How're things going in Oregon?

CHAPTER
Ten

John paced his hotel room until he couldn't stand pacing it any longer.

He changed into work-out clothes and went to the gym, which was full of loud silence at this hour. While all the rest of the guests ate dinner, he lifted weights. Did stomach crunches. Ran on the treadmill.

None of it offered an escape from what he'd just felt for Nora.

When she'd told him about her mother, sorrow had poured into him. Then he'd told her about Yemen and seen that same sorrow looking back at him. Her story had brought down his defenses. His story had crushed what was left of them.

He'd wanted to know about her life and to tell her about his. He'd wanted that, so that was what he'd allowed to happen. But, in retrospect, they shouldn't have shared so much.

A man got to know himself well, living through situations like those he'd been through. He was almost never surprised by his own responses. Ever since he'd moved to Shore Pine, he'd become predictable to himself.

But the surge of desire he'd just felt for Nora—was still feeling for her—surprised him. It had thrown him off-balance the way an earthquake might, and now aftershocks of self-hatred continued to rattle through him. Sins of the mind and heart were every bit as wrong as sins of speech and action.

He'd been explaining away the chemistry between them. He'd been telling himself he could manage it.

He'd been lying to himself.

He'd been a fool. Worse than a fool. He was flirting with infidelity. And that? That was unforgiveable.

He returned to his hotel room and jerked his sweat-stained T-shirt over his head. Standing at the window, he could see nothing of the day's view now that night had stolen it. Only his blackened reflection stared back at him.

He'd underestimated the power of his feelings for Nora. And he'd overestimated, big time, his own sainthood.

He was a fraud. Many times he'd spoken to groups about how he'd rooted his identity in Christ. Then he'd learned he was losing his eyesight. Ever since, God had been showing him just how much his identity had been and still was rooted in his own abilities.

He'd spoken to groups about the value of honor. Now God was showing him how little his own honor was worth.

It was humbling. It was disturbing.

Nora had thanked him for what he'd done for America, for pity's sake. And Allie was at home, trusting him.

He had no one to blame but himself. His own rationalizations had brought him to this point. Now he needed to find a way to get through tomorrow, return Nora to Merryweather, and cut ties with her.

He *hated* what he'd have to do.

She'd done nothing wrong, and she wouldn't understand why. Just the thought of ending their friendship made him sick. Yet he couldn't do their friendship anymore without wanting her, so he couldn't do their friendship. Which made him furious at himself for having failed at controlling his body and his mind. He'd ruined what he and Nora had when what they had was good. Or . . . it *had* been good. Right up until that moment on the balcony. That was the moment when he'd stepped across the line between good and wrong.

Moments of attraction to people you aren't dating or married to happen. His lecture to himself came back to haunt him. *It's how you respond that matters. If you're an ethical person, you guard yourself. You make the right choices. You refuse to act on the attraction.*

He picked up his phone and saw a text waiting from Allie. Guilt fell over him like a blanket. With a groan, he tossed his phone on the bed and scrubbed his fingers across his forehead.

He was a fraud. He was a fraud who needed to beg God's forgiveness, then do what was needed to make things right.

Frustrated, Nora turned her face toward the alarm clock on her hotel room's bedside table. It read 6:12 a.m. John had sent her a curt text message last night suggesting they meet in the lobby at nine this morning, to which she'd said sure, which meant she should still be sleeping. Especially because she'd stayed up thinking about him until after midnight, then slept in fragments full of dreams of him.

Now here she was in this luxurious bed, surrounded by cool air, darkness, and the pleasant drone of the lodge's heating and cooling system.

She should be sleeping. Problem was, her thoughts wouldn't quit returning to John and that fiery moment between them last night. It had seemed to her that it had been important, that moment. That it had meant something. She'd thought, when they'd been standing there, gazes locked, her pulse tripping, that she'd read hunger in his eyes.

To be strictly honest, she might have been mistaken. It wasn't like she had a lot of current experience with longing looks, except those given by Colin Firth's Darcy. It felt hugely presumptuous of her to conclude, based on one silent stare, that John was interested in her romantically.

However, if she'd been mistaken about what she'd seen, then why had he left like that? So suddenly?

She didn't know. John Lawson was about as open as a bank vault.

Nora socked her pillow and rolled onto her other side. When she closed her eyes she saw John's face—resolute jaw, blunt cheekbones, straight brows, wind-mussed brown hair—against a background of mountains.

It had been much easier to be certain of her own morals before John had looked at her like he had last night. When he'd been looking at her in that way, primitive and open and full of need, it had felt indescribably *good*. It had been so good that every time she went back over it in her memory, longing curled deliciously in her midsection.

When she'd diagnosed herself as having a low libido, she'd misdiagnosed herself completely. Her libido was plenty active. It had just needed a certain Navy SEAL to nudge it awake.

It shamed her to admit it, but she'd wanted that—whatever *that* had been between herself and John last night—to go on and on and on. Even more shameful, if he'd tried to do something—for example, if he'd moved in and wrapped a hand around the back of her neck and kissed her—then she worried that she wouldn't have had the strength or the will to stop him. Her ideals might not have been sturdy enough to stand up to her overwhelming affection for him.

That was an awful thing to admit to herself. Surely she would have found the strength and the will if she'd needed to find them. God would have helped her resist John. Wouldn't He?

She hoped so, but she wasn't sure because the mere possibility that John might feel something, even a little something, for her was causing hope as sweet as caramel and as sharp as broken glass to press upward within her.

John was off-limits, like a mansion behind an eight-foot-tall metal fence! She was a horrible person for hoping that he liked her.

Lord, it's not right. Before, when it had been clear that John thought of her as his friendly genealogist, it had felt harmless to nurse her crush on him. But now? It didn't feel so harmless. It probably wasn't harmless, ever, to nurse a crush on someone else's boyfriend. Because these sorts of things, cheating sorts of things, weren't to be toyed with. Even if you thought nothing could or would ever happen. Naturally, you *would* think that . . . right up until the moment something did happen.

She'd wanted to come on this trip with John for her own selfish reasons, and she'd gotten her wish. She'd told herself with such superiority that she could never be a Rory, back when she'd assumed she'd never be given the chance to be a Rory.

She wasn't a very nice person, it turned out. She'd been positive about her niceness all her life. She'd been even more positive about it since her broken engagement. While fanning the flames of her hurt, she'd clung to her own niceness like one of her throw blankets. Harrison and Rory were the mean ones. She was nice.

She'd thought.

Really, Nora. All that had occurred was a single heated look that she may have misinterpreted. Her good manners—and John's—were still intact. They hadn't done anything, so it was too early to classify herself as not-nice. No doubt things would return to normal between herself and John today.

If John were ever to ask her out, it would only be when he was free to do so.

And in what sort of fantasy world would *that* come to be? It would have to be a very lavish fantasy world indeed, with unicorns, cathedrals made of roses, and bunnies who spoke Swedish.

She tossed aside the covers and reached for the room service menu. If she couldn't sleep, she may as well be productive.

She called down an order for a waffle, fruit, bacon, and tea. After donning the hotel-issued robe over her pjs, she propped herself up in bed and checked her phone. Idly, she scrolled through emails concerning the annual Summer Antique Fair she spearheaded in order to provide a shot in the arm to the economy of Merryweather.

If she ever did re-enter the dating world, she'd do best to download that dating app again and swipe right on Evan, owner of ferrets. He was at approximately her same level of attractiveness.

Rich, famous, Medal-of-Honor-winning John would only ever be available to her in the unicorn world.

A knock sounded. Nora helped the lodge employee transfer her scrumptious-smelling breakfast to the room's corner table. She watched the clouds drift across the morning sky as she ate her meal.

Everything was fine. She and John were coworkers and friends. That tiny stretch of electric silence between them last night hadn't been that big of a deal.

Nora was a nice person. John was honorable. They were both Christians. John and Allie's romance was perfectly safe.

Today, she and John would concentrate on finding Sherry.

When Nora came downstairs before nine, she immediately spotted John waiting for her outside. He'd already asked the valet to pull the car around and was leaning against it, arms crossed. He wore dark gray cargo pants and a black long-sleeved shirt with a tiny Nike swoosh on one side of his chest.

Even as Nora towed her rolling carry-on across the lobby, she could tell that things had shifted between them. John's face had a hard, closed-off quality to it.

Great Scott, she thought dejectedly, sadness yawning up from the floorboards and threatening to engulf her.

Nope. She refused to be sad about this.

One of the bell staff swung the door open for her with a flourish.

"Good morning," she said to John, her carry-on bumping over stone.

"Morning." He didn't look at her as he lifted her luggage into the trunk.

"Have you already checked out?" she asked.

"Yeah. The keys are in the ignition."

Dutifully, she climbed behind the wheel, and they set off. Uncomfortable quiet reigned. She darted a look at him. He'd turned his face to the passenger-side window. She swallowed. "Did you do anything interesting last night?"

"I worked out. That was about it."

"Glad to hear you worked out. It's important to stay in shape for Navy SEAL-type stuff."

He grunted. No smile. No joking response.

She was not going to be sad about this!

It was difficult not to be, though.

This new sense of distance between them proved that last night's interaction *had* impacted him, that he believed they had done something wrong. He was making a countermove in order to protect his relationship with Allie, which left Nora feeling miserable and also faintly indignant because, after all, she hadn't been the one with the hungry eyes or the significant other.

No, she'd been the one making hungry eyes at John since the day they met. She'd been the one who might not have had the willpower to say no to the man with the significant other.

She was culpable, too.

The truth of that filled her with guilt and regret, because now she'd lost her easy camaraderie with John, and she *treasured* her camaraderie with John. She'd never, never wanted to risk that.

She wished she could go back and undo the entire talk on the balcony and reset their relationship to pick up where it had left off when they'd exited the courthouse yesterday. If only a person *could* go back and undo things in life. If only there were do-overs.

"Are you thinking we should begin today by going through the rest of Blakeville's city directories?" he asked.

"Yep. Exactly."

God bless Homer and Mary Thompson's generation, Nora thought as she and John successfully tracked the couple through every single Blakeville directory. Theirs was a hardworking generation who fought in wars and who, except for those displaced by the Great Depression, largely had the grace to stay put.

Unfortunately for their purposes, the same could not be said of Homer and Mary's children. It seemed that none of their three kids had settled in Blakeville because none of them ever made a debut in the directories.

"What should we do next?" John asked, sliding the final directory back into its place.

"We can try to look up Homer and Mary's death certificates."

"What will those tell us?"

"When and where they died. We might also be able to learn when and where they were born, their parents' names, and cause of death. It's the first piece of information that's of most interest to us because if we can find out when and where they died, then we can search newspapers for their obituaries. And if we can find an obituary, well . . . that could provide all kinds of details about their family."

"How do we look for death certificates?"

"The Oregon death index is online. If Homer and Mary died here in Oregon, they might come up." Back to the hallway bench on the main floor of the courthouse they went.

A few efficient clicks later, Nora had instigated a search of the death index. She valiantly tried not to notice that John smelled like the soap the lodge had provided . . . a piney lemon mixture. He sat a good distance away from her. Even so, she could sense the banked strength in the weight and lines of his body.

"There." He pointed. "Homer James Thompson."

"Right." *Focus!* "I feel obliged to say that this record could belong to another man with the same name." She clicked on the record. The document stated that Homer James Thompson had died on May fifth, nineteen years ago. In Blakeville. The page also listed his birthdate and the name of his spouse, Mary. The last two pieces of information confirmed that this was *their* Homer.

"It's him," John said.

"Yes." The opportunity to glimpse people who'd been born long before her, sometimes centuries before, was one of the rewards of Nora's job. At times it was almost as if she could reach out and touch her fingertips to theirs through history.

Based on the information they'd gathered yesterday and today,

Homer, the clockmaker from this scenic small town in Oregon, had been coming alive in Nora's imagination. Thus, this evidence of his death saddened her in the same way that walking through a cemetery and reading his tombstone would have. Homer had been a man with a rich life. He'd had a family and dreams and hardships and successes.

"I could have met him," John said evenly. "If things had been different. I was fourteen when he passed away."

Nora nodded. If John was Homer's illegitimate great-grandson, would Homer have wanted to meet him? Had Homer's heart been big enough for that? Had Homer even known of John's existence?

They couldn't find Mary in the Oregon death index. The index didn't provide information on deaths that had occurred in the last several years so Nora pulled up one of the genealogy sites she subscribed to and eventually located Mary's death certificate there. Mary had died just ten years ago. She, too, had remained in Blakeville to the end.

"I say we try to find an obituary for Homer," Nora said. "I'm guessing that we can count on Mary to have made sure that his obituary was thorough and accurate. Now that we know exactly when he died, we can concentrate our search on newspapers printed the week after his death."

John had seen people on TV shows and movies using microfilm, but he'd never had need of it himself until now. Like a lot of things that had seemed very high-tech when they were invented, microfilm now seemed very low-tech.

The *Blakeville Herald* had been published weekly from 1904 through the present. Old issues were kept on the third floor of the courthouse in an area called the Microforms Collection. Nora had used the library catalog to find the film containing the issues of the *Herald*, which were indexed by date of publication. She'd slid film from the year of Homer's death into the large microfilm reader and was currently searching through the images.

The print zipping past the screen made John dizzy, so he looked down. Nora had crossed her legs. She had on a narrow black skirt that ended at the knees and a pair of red high-heeled sandals. She was slowly bouncing her toe.

Immediately, he looked in another direction. He'd been trying not to look at her because every time he did, his gut clenched with longing for something he couldn't have. If there was ever a pointless waste of a feeling, that was it.

He'd slept very little the night before. Around three in the morning it had occurred to him that, in view of the fact that he was about to end his friendship as well as his business relationship with Nora, he needed to make sure she'd cashed the checks he'd given her.

He didn't usually spend much time following his accounts. He had an accountant on his staff. But he'd gotten out of bed, opened the banking app on his phone, and looked carefully through the list of withdrawals for the payments he'd made to Nora. He couldn't find a single one.

She hadn't cashed his checks.

He thought he'd outsmarted her by making him send her bills. Instead, she'd outsmarted him by taking the checks he'd sent her and doing what? Ripping them up? Sticking them in a desk drawer?

He never would have let her help him if he'd known she wouldn't accept payment. While they were working their way through the directories earlier, he'd excused himself and withdrawn cash from the branch of his bank, located two storefronts down from the courthouse. He couldn't see her again after today, but he definitely could make sure she was paid in full.

"You're a praying man, right?" Nora asked.

"You read the book and saw the movie," he said, repeating verbatim one of the things he'd said to her the night before.

She laughed, and the sound affected him like a shot of tequila. John set his molars together hard.

"Well, this might be a good time to send up a prayer," she said. "Lord, if you could help us find an obituary for Homer, that would be awesome."

"Amen."

"Here's the paper from the week Homer died. It looks like the obituaries are on page eight." Carefully, she slid to the correct page. Once there, she leaned toward the screen for a few seconds, then sat all the way back in her chair, quiet.

He'd noticed that whenever she'd hit on something, she retreated to give him space to see for himself what they'd found.

He squinted at the screen until he located Homer's name.

> Blakeville—Homer James Thompson, 84, died May 5th after a brief illness.

In this old-fashioned courthouse in the middle of Oregon, Nora had found the obituary of the man who had likely been his biological great-grandfather.

> He leaves his wife of sixty-five years, Mary (Wellington) Thompson; his son Lucas Thompson and his wife, Judith, of Bend; son Kenneth Thompson and his wife, Donna, of Portland; and daughter Deborah Tanner and her husband, Timothy, of Portland. He also leaves behind grandchildren Jeffrey Thompson of Seattle, Sherry O'Sullivan of Grants Pass, Tony Thompson of Bend, Jack Thompson of San Francisco, and Wendy Masterson of Phoenix, four great-grandchildren, and many close friends.
>
> Mr. Thompson was a lifelong resident of Blakeville. In his early years, he worked at Hanson Sawmill, where his father was employed. He met his wife at Blakeville High. A year after her graduation, in 1935, the two married at Holy Cross Christian Church. In 1942, Homer joined the U.S. Air Force, where he served as a gunner in World War II. Upon his return from the front, he was employed by the sawmill for three years. Then he opened his clock and watch repair business, Thompson Timepieces, which he ran until his retirement. He greatly valued his customers and was twice named Blakeville Business Owner of the Year.
>
> Homer loved the Lord and the congregation at Holy Cross, where he served on the board of deacons and taught fifth grade

Sunday School for more than forty years. He was an avid fisherman and an excellent banjo player.

A funeral service will be held May 10th at Holy Cross, followed by a private burial.

John thought for several seconds, then read back over the announcement. "My birth mom's married name is Sherry O'Sullivan."

"This tells us that her married name was O'Sullivan at the time this was written, nineteen years ago."

"And she lives in Grants Pass." Grants Pass was a small city in the southern part of Oregon.

"Well . . ."

"We know she lived there nineteen years ago," he finished for her.

"Correct."

"It's a big deal, though. That we learned this information. Isn't it?" He angled a questioning glance at her.

Pride glittered in her eyes. "A very big deal."

He peered at the screen. "It looks like Deborah married, too. Her last name is listed as Tanner here."

"Right. At some point after she sold the house in Shelton and before Homer died, Deborah married."

For a long time, neither of them spoke. "Should we run a search for Sherry O'Sullivan in Grants Pass?" As John said the words, he realized how close they were to finding Sherry. The sense of foreboding he'd had on his deck the day he'd called Sherry's delivery room doctor came over him again.

Was he ready—completely ready—to dig up the past and push his way into Sherry's life? The question sent a chill down his neck.

"Listen," Nora said gently. "How about we go to the coffee bar downstairs and take a break? I'll buy you a cup of coffee. You look like you could use some caffeine."

"I do?"

"Yes."

"Could you use some?"

"Always."

"Then I'm buying."

Nora snapped a picture of Homer's obituary with her cell phone before returning the film to storage.

At the small coffee bar off the courthouse foyer, they ordered a coffee and a tea. At this late morning hour, only one other customer, a middle-aged lady, occupied the single table's far end. John made sure to put plenty of space between himself and Nora when they took their seats. He didn't want their knees or feet to accidentally touch.

Nora made small talk. She asked questions and seemed fine with it when he said little in response.

Surely it was normal to feel conflicted about digging up the past and pushing his way into Sherry's life. He didn't know what information he'd find or how she'd react. He hadn't even found Sherry yet, and he already regretted any pain or inconvenience he'd cause her. His goal wasn't to interrupt her life. His goal was to find answers, and in order to find answers, he'd have to contact her. There was no getting around that.

A big part of him was ready. A small part of him wasn't. But no matter what, he'd move forward. He'd come this far because he wanted his medical records. He needed to know who'd passed his condition down to him.

Their drinks sat before them, empty now. Nora's words drifted away.

"Okay," he said. "You can go ahead and run the search for Sherry in Grants Pass."

She lifted one brow, asking him without words if he was sure. Nora had a sharp, observant mind. Obviously, she'd either sensed or seen his reluctance. She could read him better than anyone had been able to in a long time. "We can run the search later," she said reasonably. "Even days from now. Whenever you'd like."

We won't be in contact days from now. "You're dying to run it now," he said.

"Yes. But the pace of this search is yours to set. Not mine."

"You're good at this, you know. At research."

She sat back a fraction, pleasure in her expression. "You think so?"

"Yes." He wanted her to know that.

"Thank you."

"Go ahead." He gestured to her bag, where her computer waited.

Nora began by combing through online telephone and address listings for Sherry O'Sullivan in Grants Pass.

She received nothing but messages saying that no records matched her criteria.

"Foiled again." She wrinkled her forehead. "Don't worry, John. I'm not dissuaded."

"Never thought you were."

"Let's check marriage records." She opened a new tab on her Internet browser. "We've inferred that Sherry might be Lucas's daughter, because she named you Mark Lucas. In Homer's obituary, do you remember where it said Lucas lived?"

He didn't need to check the picture of the obit on Nora's phone. He remembered. "Bend."

"And what county is Bend in? Is it here in Deschutes County?"

He Googled it on his phone. "Yes."

"A lot of brides get married in their hometowns. So if Lucas is Sherry's dad and she was raised in Bend, then we should check for marriage records filed in Deschutes County after your birth and before Homer's death." She began filling in the website's various fields. "We're looking for a wedding between Sherry Thompson and someone—we don't know your first name, sir—O'Sullivan." She hit enter.

Several hits turned up. The very first one listed Sherry Thompson and Edward O'Sullivan. Nora sank her upper teeth into her full bottom lip.

John groaned inwardly and forced his attention to the computer screen.

The marriage record named the bride as Sherry Anne Thompson, the groom as Edward Dean O'Sullivan. They married three years after his birth.

Thanks to his birth certificate, he'd always known Sherry's age. The birth year given for her here was exactly right. The groom was two years older than she. It listed Sherry's birthplace as Bend, Oregon. Edward's birthplace as Aberdeen, Washington. Her parents: Lucas and Judith Thompson. The record also provided Edward's parents' names, the minister's name, and the names of witnesses.

"We were right," John said. "She's Lucas's daughter."

"She's Lucas's daughter," Nora confirmed. "Now we also know her husband's first name."

This search was coming along the way a crossword puzzle did. The first few answers had been slow and difficult to come by. But now that they'd figured out a good portion of the clues, the empty squares were filling in fast.

"Let's look for Sherry and Edward in Bend." Nora returned to her first tab and ran a search.

No hits.

"We have to keep in mind that many things could have happened since Homer's death," she said. "Sherry could have divorced and married someone different and have a new last name. She and Edward could have moved overseas. She or Edward could have died—oops. Sorry. That's not a very optimistic thought. I didn't mean to speak that one out loud. Let's run a search for Sherry and Edward in his hometown of . . ."

"Aberdeen, Washington."

The moment she input the data, the site brought up an address and phone number for Sherry and Edward O'Sullivan in Aberdeen.

Beside him, Nora froze.

Tightness banded around John's chest. His birth mother was living in Aberdeen, Washington, with her husband. Here was her address. Here was her phone number. She hadn't divorced and remarried. She hadn't moved overseas or died. She was living in a city just over an hour's drive from where he lived in Shore Pine.

They'd found her.

Nora's job was done.

• • •

Text message from Willow to Nora and Britt:

Willow

Valentina is making an enormous pot of borscht for dinner. It smells delicious but she's filling a pot large enough for a dozen people. There's just me! I need reinforcements. Join me for dinner. Have borscht. Will host.

Britt

I'm in, but I haven't heard from Nora today. I'm hoping she and the Navy SEAL decided to elope.

Nora

The Navy SEAL has a girlfriend! He and I are on our way back from Oregon and just pulled into a 7–Eleven for a pit stop. We completed our research today and now it occurs to me that I did my job so well that I managed to promote myself out of my one connection to him.

Britt

Invite him and his girlfriend to Grandma's birthday party. That will give you a new connection to him.

Nora

That will give me a new connection to him, yes. But that will come at the agonizing cost of having to watch him and his girlfriend together during the party.

Britt

Then kick him to the curb. No man is worth agony.

Britt

p.s. If you do decide to invite him and his girlfriend to the party, be sure to ask him to bring along one of his guy friends for Willow.

Willow

Excuse me? After seeing the selection of available bachelors in this area on Nora's dating app, I'm 100% sure that I will not be finding the love of my life in Merryweather.

Britt

Nora has a dating app?!

Nora

I had one, at Willow's urging, for about two minutes. I'll see you at Bradfordwood for dinner. I'll be the one crying over John into my borscht.

CHAPTER
Eleven

The instant Nora spotted the sporty little silver Audi parked on John's driveway, she comprehended her grave mistake.

An hour ago she'd informed John that she'd drop him off at his house at the end of their journey home from Blakeville. He'd assured her that one of his friends or employees could pick him up at the Library on the Green, but she'd held firm.

She'd wanted to take him all the way to his house for two reasons. One, she'd been dying for a glimpse of his house. Two, on their drive to Blakeville, the spaces of quiet between them had rippled with comforting familiarity. The spaces of quiet on today's drive had crackled with strain, despite the fact that he'd been perfectly polite. She'd been hoping to end their trip on a high note of kindness.

Nearly a mile ago they'd exited the road onto his private drive. When she'd caught sight of a roof line through the dense cover of trees, her anticipation had heightened. Then she'd driven a little farther and spotted the Audi, and her anticipation had nose-dived like a mortally wounded fighter plane.

That car was entirely too cute to belong to a man.

"Allie's here," John stated.

She pulled to a stop behind the Audi. "Oh, good!" Her enthusiastic response sounded as patently false to her ears as it felt to her heart. She'd overcompensated.

"I told her around what time we'd be back, but she hadn't mentioned she was coming over."

"Mmm! A nice surprise, then."

He let himself out. While he was retrieving his duffel bag from her trunk, the front door of his house—his new and modern and huge house—sailed open. Allie emerged wearing cut-off jean shorts and a white eyelet off-the-shoulder top. She had an acre of hair and two acres of slim, tan legs. Her feet were bare. She could have walked straight out of the J. Crew summer catalog.

Allie waved and smiled, making her way toward Nora's car. She was chewing something and cupping something in her hand. Clearly, she'd been relaxing barefoot here at John's house, snacking casually. She looked supremely comfortable, as if she belonged in these surroundings. Which, of course, she did.

Nora called herself an idiot ten different ways for insisting on bringing John here and, in so doing, forcing this wretched pain on herself. She rolled down her window and gave an answering wave.

Allie intercepted John near the back of Nora's car. In her rearview mirror, Nora saw Allie come into view, arms open for a hug, face lifted for a kiss. With a jagged inhale, Nora averted her gaze to her lap. She just . . . *oh my goodness*, she just could not bear to watch them hugging and kissing.

Despite that you feel like you're dying, you're not actually going to, Nora. Heartbreak isn't fatal.

"Hi, Nora," Allie said warmly. "Nice to see you again."

Nora lifted her face as Allie approached. "Nice to see you, too."

"It sounds like you had a successful trip."

"Yes! Yes, we did."

"John told me that the two of you were able to find a name and address for his birth mother."

Red grapes. That was what Allie had in her hand. That was what she was snacking on. Nora shouldn't be surprised that John had kept his girlfriend, who ate grapes at his house when he wasn't here, up to date on the specifics of their search for Sherry. Until this moment, however, the search for John's birth mother had felt like something that belonged mostly to her and John. "That's right."

"What great news," Allie said.

"It really is. Well, I better be on my way."

John came to a stop a few yards behind Allie on the path leading to his house. His duffel bag rested over one wide shoulder. His expression was guarded. His posture rigid.

"Let me get you a drink or something before you go," Allie said. "You've been driving for hours."

Nora stared at the genuinely likeable person in front of her, feeling and thinking so many things simultaneously that her mind had gone blank. "No, no" was all she managed.

Allie popped the final grape into her mouth and wiped her palms against her shorts. "Come inside," she insisted. "Stretch your legs, and I'll get you a drink. It'll only take a minute."

There was probably a graceful and laughing way to decline, but Nora couldn't dredge it up. She wanted Allie and John to think her fine with this scenario because a true friend of John's *would be* fine with proximity to his girlfriend. "Okay," Nora murmured, turning off her ignition. "Just for a minute."

"Isn't this house wonderful?" Allie asked as they entered the foyer.

"Incredibly so," Nora answered honestly.

"I'll give you a quick tour."

Allie led the way, keeping up a stream of relaxed conversation. Nora could feel John's glowering presence behind them. Hear his gait.

Her pulse had begun to boom like a church bell signaling a funeral. *Bong. Bong. Bong.* A feverish clamminess crept over her skin. *Heartbreak isn't fatal!*

A hallway ran along the back section of John's house. On one side, windows faced a wooded mountainside. The other side contained bedrooms, bathrooms, a media room. Everything looked gleamingly new. He'd furnished the house in a simple, faintly mid-century modern way. Extremely unfussy. Smooth gray concrete floors stretched beneath Nora's feet. Pale cream paint covered the walls. Everywhere she looked, windows invited the outdoors in.

John set his bag on a king-sized bed in one of the rooms.

His bedroom.

Despite her avid interest in his house, Nora remained discreetly in the hallway throughout the tour. Not only did she loathe her role as the third wheel in John and Allie's happy reunion, but this Allie-instigated peek into John's life made her feel as if she was invading his privacy.

Once she'd followed Allie down a few steps into the portion of the house that faced the lake, she had to slow for a moment to catch her breath at the grandeur surrounding her. At this early-evening hour, auburn light flooded in through walls of glass that towered toward a ceiling two stories above.

The kitchen and dining table were tucked back on her left. To her right, a TV was recessed into bookshelves that reminded her very much of the bookshelves at her own house. Sofas and leather chairs dotted the rug between the TV and a stone fireplace.

She was no expert in the field of architecture, but this house seemed to her to be a masterpiece. Not a cold masterpiece. A masterpiece that managed to give off the impression of welcome and nature and calm.

Allie rattled off five different drink choices, then asked Nora which one she'd like.

"A bottled water, please."

Allie headed toward the kitchen.

John went ahead, freeing a latch on the rear glass doors. At his bidding, the tall panels slid open along a track, folding in until no separation remained between the interior and exterior living spaces.

If this was *Northamptonshire*, John would be the earl, and this house would be the grand castle on the hill. In the TV world, she preferred Adolphus. But in the real world, she'd fallen quite unoriginally for the earl.

John and Nora walked onto the expansive deck. The lake spread below them like a royal blue sequined scarf.

He came to a stop, his hands thrust deep in his pockets. His hair was in disarray, Nora noted, probably from Allie's fingers riffling through it. His profile appeared to have been sketched with firm, unapologetic lines. "This is my favorite part of the house," he said.

"This outdoor space?"

"Yeah."

"I can see why. Your house is amazing, John."

"Thank you." He met her eyes. He'd hardly looked at her all day. He was a powerfully handsome man, but the ache of yearning that tugged at Nora wasn't borne of his outward beauty. It was borne of every single inward part of him she'd come to know.

"I appreciate everything you've done," he told her. "I never would have found Sherry without your help."

A lump formed in her throat. "You're welcome." She forged ahead with a voice that she hoped rang with optimism. "Look for an email from me soon. I'll include attachments of those resources I mentioned earlier. They'll provide ideas and suggestions about how best to craft a letter to a birth mother. Not that you have to rely on the suggestions, of course. I'll just send them to you in case they're helpful."

"Okay." He looked as if he wanted to say more.

Nora waited expectantly—

Allie arrived. She handed Nora the bottled water, then wrapped a hand around John's elbow.

Bubbling hot jealousy turned Nora's entire midsection to lava.

She had to get away from Allie and John, the couple. But that meant leaving John, and she'd never wanted to leave a person less.

Would she ever see John again? She hated for their friendship to end like this . . . on this big downbeat and with Allie as a witness. She didn't have a choice, however. This was exactly how it *was* going to end. "I'd better get going," she said. "I'm meeting my sisters for dinner. Valentina made borscht, a Russian stew of beef, carrots, and potatoes. And cabbage, of course."

"Sounds delicious," Allie said.

"Thanks for the water."

"You're welcome." Allie regarded her fondly.

John stood stock-still, eyes glowing hazel fire, features withdrawn and grave.

"I'll let myself out." Nora turned on her heel, desperate to retain her dignity at all costs. "See you guys later."

"Enjoy the stew!" Allie called.

"You bet. Gotta love cabbage!" She strode at a fast clip, hot tears sheening her eyes. Mortified, she willed them away. She climbed quickly into her car and steered along John's driveway, her thoughts a whirlpool. Gotta love cabbage? Was that what she'd just said?

It *hurt* to care about a man who cared for someone else above you. Who'd chosen someone else over you. It hurt, hurt, hurt.

Once again, like with Harrison and Rory long ago, she found herself on the outside, looking in. The first time she hadn't had a choice. But this time, she'd willingly opened her heart to John. So futile!

Could it be that she was subconsciously bent on injuring herself? Or maybe subconsciously bent on protecting herself, which was why she'd let herself fall for a man who already had a girlfriend? After all, one didn't have to risk the vulnerability that came with a real relationship when the subject of your crush was already in a real relationship with someone else.

Nora weighed the two possibilities in her mind, testing them the way a person might press a bruise to measure its level of pain.

In this case, no. *No*. She didn't think either an underlying desire to injure or protect herself had motivated her friendship with John. Or, at least, neither desire had motivated it much.

The cause of her current distress wasn't as nefarious as that. The cause was far simpler.

She'd looked up from her crouched position on the floor of a fake office more than a month ago, and she'd laid eyes on John Lawson. That was it. She'd looked up and laid eyes on him. And in that split second, less than the slice of time between heartbeats, she'd become enamored with him. Her dazzled, loopy, devoted feelings had been the culprit all along. *They* had caused her to make the mistake of caring for him. And then caring more. And then more.

She'd cooked up such an acute case of heart-slaying tenderness for John that it had now become harmful to her. She should be glad that they'd found Sherry and that their association had come to an end!

But she wasn't.

When Nora entered Bradfordwood, both Britt and Willow looked up from where they stood at the island in the kitchen.

"Hey." Willow, who wore calf-length exercise leggings and a turquoise work-out top, smiled in greeting.

"Well?" Britt paused the motion of the knife she'd been using to slice a baguette.

"My last words to John Lawson were 'gotta love cabbage.'" Nora leaned over and rested her forehead on the lip of the marble-covered island.

"What?!"

"Gotta. Love. Cabbage," Nora reiterated miserably.

Her sisters laughed. Ill-bred sisters.

"Why in the world did you say that?" Britt asked.

Nora straightened. "John's girlfriend was there to greet him when I dropped him off at his house. She looked so pretty, and they seemed so chummy, and I was rattled and desperate to leave. So I babbled about borscht, blurted out, 'gotta love cabbage,' and practically ran."

"I'm sure it wasn't as bad as all that," Willow said consolingly.

Britt snorted. "Did you invite him and his girlfriend to Grandma's party?"

"I considered it, but no. I didn't." As much as she wanted another chance to see him, she couldn't trust that her motives for asking him to the party would be honorable. Nor could she stomach the torture of watching him and Allie together. Nor did she think, if she'd asked him to the party today, that he would have said yes.

Willow poured sparkling water into a goblet filled with ice cubes and slid it toward Nora. "So that's it, then? The end of the line with the Navy SEAL?"

"The end of the line."

"I know what will cheer you up," Willow said.

"I'm terrified of whatever you're about to say," Nora replied.

"Phase 4."

"My hair?"

"Yes." Willow's jade-green eyes sparkled. "I'll make an appointment for you with Javier." Willow had discovered Javier, a hair salon owner in Bremerton, during her latter high school years. Every time she came home, she visited Javier for a trim. Her great faith in him was no small thing; Willow's hair had been styled by some of the most talented hair aficionados on the planet.

Nora gritted her teeth.

"You're going to have to trust me," Willow said. "You'll come out of the salon with everything you love about your hair intact. We're just going to gild the lily."

"I don't know."

"Well, I do know. It's going to be fabulous. Once we've tackled the hair, we'll address Phase 5, the search for the perfect dress for Grandma's party."

"You're both loco," Britt announced. Britt, who had on a headband, old jeans, and a sweat shirt. Britt, who didn't care how she looked. Britt, who'd already secured the undying love of an excellent man without even trying. Britt, who was oblivious to Zander because her head and heart were sunk deep into chocolate.

"We want men to fall in love with our underlying qualities." Willow picked up a wooden spoon and held it like a professor would a pointer. "Our character, our heart, our personality. The things that make us uniquely us—"

"I'd be fine if a man fell in love with me because of my Death by Chocolate truffle," Britt said.

"And I'd be fine if a man fell in love with me for my *Northamptonshire* DVD collection," Nora said.

"We want them to fall in love with us for our underlying qualities," Willow reiterated, unperturbed. "But . . ."

"But?" Britt asked.

"Never underestimate the power of looking your best or the power of making the man in question *think* that you're hard to get," Willow said. "Those two things seem to help motivate men to fall in love with underlying qualities." She winked at Nora, then moved to the stove to whip off the pot's lid. "Let's eat."

"Gotta love cabbage!" Britt crowed.

Valentina had been cooking borscht for them since they were girls, which made the rich, spicy, meaty stew extraordinarily comforting. They sat at the kitchen table and blessed the food. Even though they were eating an informal sisterly dinner, Willow had set the table gorgeously with place mats, linen napkins, and the good silverware. Golden peonies burst from a squat crystal vase.

"Who can we fix Nora up with for Grandma's party?" Willow asked Britt.

"Willow!" Nora squawked. "Earlier today you shot Britt down when she floated the idea of fixing you up for the party."

"Yes, but I'm not the one mourning a Navy SEAL. I like the idea of a date for you. Wouldn't it be nice to have someone to flirt with at Grandma's party?"

"No. So, Willow, how are things going at the Inn at Bradfordwood?" Nora asked, making a sad attempt to change the subject.

"They're going well. Everything I do with reservations and billing is still taking me twice as long as it should because I can't get the hang of the computer programs. But I haven't burned any of the breakfasts. The guests have all been very friendly. Clint and Valentina are great. They know what they're doing way more than I do."

"How many hours a day are you putting in?" Nora asked.

"Maybe four? The guests do self check-out, but I need to be there when they tell me they'll be arriving. I make them cookies and Mom's raspberry lemonade and give them the welcome tour and their keys—"

Britt snapped her fingers. "Sorry to interrupt," she told Willow.

"But I just thought of who Nora can flirt with at Grandma's party. Evan. He'll be there."

Evan? Of the ferrets? *Set your cap for Evan, Nora*, her logical self nudged. *He's at your level*. "He will?"

"Yep," Britt said. "He's great about helping us ship out Sweet Art's orders. Plus, Grandma likes him."

"Is Evan the one who smells like mustard?" Willow paused her bite of soup in mid-air.

"One and the same," Nora replied grimly.

"Evan can be the mustard." Britt grinned. "And Nora can be his soft, salty pretzel. A perfect pair."

Late that night, Nora's vision caught on an envelope. The slim, opened-ended kind. She'd been digging through her purse for her cell phone when she'd spotted it.

Scrunching her nose, she lifted it free. The illumination from her kitchen's recessed can lights revealed the name of a bank printed across the envelope. She turned it over. Someone had written in blue pen on the back.

I noticed that you hadn't deposited my checks.

John? John.

It was certainly true that she hadn't deposited his checks. She'd been hoping he wouldn't notice.

He must have . . . slipped this into her purse at some point today? But how? She'd had her purse with her—

How, Nora? He's a former member of SEAL Team Six.

She counted the stack of cash out onto the counter. Every dollar she'd billed was accounted for.

She stared at the money for long moments while a confusing welter of sorrow and chagrin gathered in her chest.

John was fair-minded. He'd told her more than once that he wanted her to receive payment for the time she'd devoted to his search. She should view this money in that light, as evidence of his respect and courtesy and generosity.

People were always elated to receive envelopes full of money, *right*?

Not her. Not this time, because it felt like this was John's way of putting her in her place. He was reminding her that she was, first and foremost, a contract employee. And now he'd paid his employee in full.

This was good-bye.

Dully, she walked to her kitchen window. She stared out at the darkness blanketing the land beyond.

Her sisters weren't here now to make her feel better. The make-believe people in her bookshelves and DVD collections didn't have the ability to wrap her in their arms, to listen, to understand.

She was alone, truly alone.

For many years, she'd been charging past even the thought of loneliness. Her default responses to loneliness had been to fill her time with things she cared about and to stuff her head with sermons about singleness not equaling incompleteness and women not needing men and the great benefits of independence.

However, the day of her Seattle shopping trip, she'd dug past those default responses and gotten real with herself about her own discontent. Her dissatisfaction with her singleness was a subtle, creeping, evil, hard-to-pin-down thing. She'd been trying to work on it, but it wasn't cooperating. Nor could it be cured with a pat of Neosporin and a Band-Aid. Fixing her discontent was going to be less of a quick fight and more of a long, drawn-out battle, she could tell.

Today had been a seriously lousy day on the battlefield.

She was twenty-nine years old, and she'd fallen for a man who'd ended their friendship with an envelope full of money. So, yeah. The fact that loneliness had come for her tonight was probably to be expected. Her instinctive response was to sweep it under the rug. But she refused to this time.

Loneliness was real. It existed within her.

The tears she hadn't let fall earlier, when she'd left John's house, filled her eyes. They eased over her lashes in slow tracks. She rubbed them away with the heels of her hands.

She cried out of sheer loneliness. Because her work with John was over. Because she was out of Ben & Jerry's. Because she'd miss John. Because she'd lost a friend.

• • •

Email from Duncan to his personal assistant:

DUNCAN: See the attached invitation to a birthday party in Washington, USA. I'll be in Los Angeles with the press junket for *Over Sunlight's Bridge* just before the birthday party, yes?

PERSONAL ASSISTANT: Yes. I have you booked in at the yoga and detox retreat in Napa Valley for five days. Followed by the press junket, which winds down two days before the birthday party. As it stands, you'll be en route between LAX and Heathrow during the party.

DUNCAN: How long does it take to fly from Los Angeles to Seattle?

PERSONAL ASSISTANT: About two hours and forty-five minutes. Would you like me to change your return itinerary?

DUNCAN: Maybe. I think I'd like to fly to Seattle in time for the party. Stay for a few days. Then return home.

PERSONAL ASSISTANT: I've been working for you for some time, but this is the first birthday party for an eighty-year-old woman I can remember you attending.

DUNCAN: A female friend of mine will be attending the party. (A female friend somewhat younger than the birthday girl.) We've never met in person and I have half a mind to surprise her.

• • •

Phone conversation between Allie and her best friend, Lizzie:

Lizzie: How's John? Is everything okay with you two?

Allie: John's not himself. He's quieter than usual, and he's troubled about something.

Lizzie: Well, he's had a rough few months, with his health and the birth mother thing.

Allie: I know. Maybe it's wrong of me, but I'm actually hoping he's struggling for those reasons and not because of his unconventionally cute genealogist.

Lizzie: Now that they found his birth mother, the two of them are done working together, right?

Allie: Right.

Lizzie: Excellent. Disaster averted. Every man I know wants to date you, Allie. John would have to be crazy not to appreciate you.

Allie: I'm going to be the perfect girlfriend as I help John through whatever it is he's going through. Non-clingy and confident with just the right amount of fun thrown in. Oh, and I purchased a new bikini because we're going out on his boat tomorrow. A new bikini never hurts.

CHAPTER Twelve

John missed Nora.

He and Allie sat in the stands at Safeco Field, watching the Mariners play. They'd eaten Seattle Dogs. The air was crisp and bright. The home team was winning. Allie was wearing a Mariners ball cap and a tight, V-necked Mariners T-shirt. She was such an obvious knockout that the college guys in the row in front of them kept twisting around to glance at her.

The fun he was supposed to be having only made John's depression that much more obvious to him.

Back in Blakeville, he'd decided to say good-bye to Nora and focus his attention on Allie. Ever since then, he'd been trying. Thing was, his attention wasn't listening. He hadn't seen Nora for five days, and still, he couldn't seem to focus on anything but her and how incredibly crappy he felt without her.

For the first couple of days, he'd told himself it was just that his guilty conscience was plaguing him. He'd prayed over and over for forgiveness. He'd done the right thing when he'd cut off his friendship with Nora. Admittedly, too late. But he'd done it. And he hadn't contacted her since. So while there was definitely some guilt there, it had finally occurred to him that he couldn't get Nora out of his head for a whole separate reason. . .

Because he missed her.

He'd missed people before, when he'd been a Navy SEAL. During those years, he'd spent months at a time far from home and family. Far from girlfriends. He'd missed his family and girlfriends in a mild kind of way. The loss had been there, but always low-level and at the back of his mind. He'd been able to deal with it.

Missing Nora, though, was like a cold, heavy ache square in the center of his torso that made him feel hopeless and pointless. He woke up to the ache. Couldn't get rid of it all day. Went to bed with it. Slept horribly. Then got up and did the whole thing over again. In between, he remembered the tiniest things about her.

The bracelet she wore. The odd way she held a pen. How she sometimes bit her lip in concentration.

He resettled the bill of his cap. His dad and grandfather had brought him to his first Mariners game when he was six. They'd sat in the cheap seats with hot dogs and tall cups of icy soda. John had loved every minute of it. He could still remember the sound of the battery-operated radio his grandfather had brought along. He could picture his dad's smile when John had decided to wear a ball glove to the game just in case a home run came their way.

The day after he'd returned from Blakeville with Sherry's address, he'd called his parents and told them about his search for Sherry. He'd explained how they'd found her contact information. And he'd let them know that he planned to send Sherry a letter.

His dad had said little, but what he'd said had been encouraging. His mom had been full of thoughtful, supportive questions.

John had been aware, during the whole conversation, how hard it must have been for them to hear their son tell them he'd been looking for his *other* mother and father.

Allie offered the open bag of peanuts to him.

He shook his head and squinted, trying to bring the baseball diamond into focus. It was no use. The center of his field of vision was fuzzy because of the deterioration that had already taken place. It would never improve. It would only get worse. In time, there'd be no point in coming to watch his favorite team play his favorite game because he wouldn't be able to see the field at all. Nor would he be able to view the games on TV or even read about them in the sports section.

A sense of panic expanded inside his body so fast he had to breathe steadily to fight it back.

When Nora had been around, he'd been better able to deal with his condition. But now his condition felt more unbearable than it had before he'd met her.

What was he going to do?

He had two choices. He could tough it out and walk through this valley he'd been in since Blakeville.

Or he could break up with Allie and contact Nora. It scared him, how much he wanted to break up with Allie, because it sounded like something a crazy man would do. Maybe he was cracking up.

Allie was awesome. She'd been one of the best parts of his life since his diagnosis. She'd joked with him when he hadn't felt like smiling. She'd listened when he'd needed it and baked her famous cheese enchiladas for him when he'd needed those. She'd promised him that whether or not he could see didn't matter to her and that he could depend on her.

And she'd done all that while looking beautiful and putting no romantic pressure on him. He had a huge flaw. He was *going blind* and yet Allie was sticking with him. She had no flaws . . . and he was thinking about breaking up with her?

Nora had never even hinted that she wanted to date him. After he told her about his diagnosis, she was even less likely to be interested. So if he broke up with Allie, then he'd be giving up a woman he'd been dating for six months to take a chance on a woman he'd worked with for one month.

It was idiotic even to think about breaking up with Allie for Nora.

He needed to tough it out and walk through this valley. He needed to have faith that he'd come out the other side. Soon, God help him.

One of the college guys sent a stupid, star-struck look in Allie's direction.

The cold, heavy ache remained stubbornly in the center of John's torso.

A bustling Saturday afternoon tourist crowd filled Merryweather Historical Village's green. They'd been drawn by the charming buildings and the great shops, yes. They'd also come for the historical interpreters, a fact that filled Nora with a pleasant dose of smugness. Adding historical interpreters to her village on Saturday and Sunday afternoons had been her brainchild.

Colonial Williamsburg had impeccably trained, thoroughly knowledgeable actors. She had Nikki, a brainy bombshell; Amy, a frazzled mom; and Blake, a male Goth teenager.

So, almost the same thing.

Nora typically stationed Blake at the village's outdoor fireplace, dressed in homespun clothes and a blacksmith's leather apron. Nikki and Amy roved across the property, chatting with visitors. Sometimes they gave tours. Sometimes they answered questions about Washington's history while churning butter, gardening, sewing, or cooking.

She spotted Nikki working in the vegetable garden next to Crownover House and moved in that direction, Randall walking alongside her.

Randall was already dressed in his red-and-white basketball uniform for the game she'd be driving him to in an hour. His basketball shoes had seen better days. Even so, he carried them around in a backpack that also contained a small towel, wristbands, and a sports bottle of water stuck in the outside pocket. He'd patiently explained to Nora that his basketball shoes were for basketball only. He'd ruin them if he wore them on other surfaces. So he wore his regular sneakers to the games, then, like Mr. Rogers, sat down and changed his shoes.

Nora had never been good at any sport, and she'd certainly never cared whether she won or lost the games she'd been forced to play in gym class. She'd classified herself as a noncompetitive, sportsmanlike person. Thus, it had come as a surprise to sit in the bleachers at Randall's games and find it necessary to battle the urge to chew her fingernails, scream in indignation at the refs, and boo the opposing players. She permitted herself the occasional burst of applause or polite "Woo-hoo." Keeping it at that required Herculean self-control.

Since they had time to kill before the game, she and Randall were on their way to help the historical interpreters set up the children's craft scheduled for this afternoon.

Nora had spent the morning doing laundry, buying groceries, making insightful comments on her favorite book blogs, updating her Goodreads status, and promoting the events on Duncan's upcoming American tour to publicize his independent film. Even after all that, she'd had an overabundance of time, so she'd made a Bundt cake recipe that had been passed down through her family since 1896.

Every single thing she'd spent the morning doing had been tinged with a tang of desperation because she was working very, *very* hard not to think about John.

Two kids were hanging over the white picket fence that framed the side garden at Crownover House, watching Nikki hoe weeds. An older man, probably the boys' grandpa, stood behind them, eyes glazed at the sight Nikki presented.

"So here I am hoeing. Here in my vegetable garden. Here at this house I own," Nikki was saying.

Nora had given Nikki, Amy, and Blake the title of interpreter for a reason. They weren't reenactors. They were simply charged with the task of introducing details of pioneer life to the people who came through. For her own entertainment, though, Nikki sometimes liked to take a little holiday to nineteenth-century Washington in her imagination.

"It sure is hard to be me." Nikki sliced at the weeds with her hoe. "My chores are pretty much endless. I'm the gardener, dishwasher, cook, maid, mother to my ten children, seamstress, keeper of the chicken coop, and butcher, which is . . . disgusting, if I do say so myself. I'm not the kind of woman who's okay with grabbing a chicken by the neck and spinning it around in the air." She raised her face, a look of tragic determination on it, Scarlett O'Hara style.

Randall giggled. He was a fan of Nikki's.

Nikki's beleaguered gingham dress strained to confine her hips and bosom. She'd accessorized the dress with a straw hat, pink Swatch watch, long fake French-manicured fingernails, cubic zirconia earrings, and the Fitbit she'd recently purchased to help motivate her to lose weight. Her silver eye shadow and burgundy lip gloss appeared to have been applied with a trowel.

"Sometimes I wish I could jump into the future." Nikki wiped her brow dramatically.

"You're here!" one of the boys called. "You're here, in the future!"

Nikki started. "I am?"

"You don't need to work in a garden to grow your food," the other boy said. "We have grocery stores."

"What!" Nikki exclaimed.

"And we have microwaves! And nobody has to grab chickens by their necks and spin them around."

"Well, in that case"—Nikki set her hoe against the side of the house—"I think I'm done gardening for the day."

"And we have computers!"

"And Wii!"

"Can I have your number?" their grandfather asked.

Nikki released a throaty laugh. "Sir, I've just arrived here in the future." There was no shyness in Nikki Clarkson. She spoke directly to the gentleman with humor and a fair amount of purring fondness for his gender. "Now that I've arrived, I'll need time to figure out grocery stores and computers before I'll be ready to give out my number. You *are* mighty handsome, though, I must say."

Nora caught Nikki's eye and shook her head. No hitting on the tourists.

The boys looked back and forth between Nikki and their grandpa.

"If you live near here," Nikki said to the man, "stop by the Library on the Green next week. We'll talk."

"I'll be back," answered the grandpa. Then he and the boys moved off.

Nikki let herself out of the fence. "Hey, cutie pie," she said to Randall. "Did you hit anyone up for hot chocolate and marshmallows today?"

He nodded. "Ms. Bradford."

"And? Did she deliver?"

He nodded.

"That's because Ms. Bradford is a pushover."

"I object!" Nora said, but Randall was already running ahead to Golding's Mill. Nora and Nikki followed at a slower pace. "Collecting hearts as usual, I see," Nora said.

When in motion, Nikki's hips undulated more than the Nile River. "If that man has any sense, he'll drive to the nearest department store and invest in the best cologne money can buy." A lusty sigh. "I do like a man wearing good cologne. The men I dated before my first marriage all wore Polo and to this day, every time I get a whiff of it, my uterus trembles."

"Ah."

"If that man comes back to see me and he's wearing Polo, I'll marry him."

"A bottle of Polo is all it'll take?" Nora asked.

"I'd marry your Navy SEAL even without Polo. If given half a chance, I'd sop him up with a biscuit."

"With a biscuit?"

"With a biscuit!"

"He's not *my* Navy SEAL, as I believe I've mentioned about one hundred times this past week."

"Then I suggest you move heaven and earth to make him yours, Nora. Take it from me, men like the Navy SEAL are as rare as wealthy gamblers."

"He's taken!" *And thanks so much, Nikki, for bringing up the one subject I've been struggling—a huffing and puffing while I tread water kind of struggle—to avoid.*

They'd reached Golding's Mill, where an outdoor patio offered shady square footage and a fireplace that climbed charmingly up the exterior wall. She'd shut off the fireplace's inner opening and created an outside opening instead. Weathered old beams held up the tin patio roof, and stone pavers created the patio's floor. Custom-ordered tables of native timber built with antique tools completed the space.

They used the patio often for village events: pioneer cooking demonstrations, evening wine tastings, talks from visiting authors or historians, al fresco dinners prepared by Merryweather's best chefs the first weekend of September during the Antique Fair.

Amy and Blake stood at one of the tables, unpacking a box of craft supplies. The kids would be making summer mobiles today out of sticks, yarn, pom-poms, and felt.

Randall, Nikki, and Nora went to work distributing the supplies among the tables while Amy filled them in on the rigorous demands of her three teenagers' sports schedules. Amy spent the bulk of her time driving them around. She fueled herself with caffeine and reassurance.

"Grace has been invited to play on the touring team for club volleyball," Amy said, with the tone of a parent whose child had been invited to walk the gallows.

Amy had a softening body, a blandly pretty face, and a blond bob she rarely found the wherewithal to style properly. Though Amy was sixteen years older than Nora, Nora had always felt protective toward the perennially uncertain Amy.

"Do you think I should let her play on the touring team?" Amy asked. "I just . . . I don't know."

"Sure," Randall and Blake said.

"Of course you shouldn't!" Nikki answered. "You're not Cinderella. And I'm not talking about when she's fabulous at the end. I'm talking about when she's being worked to death by undeserving family members at the beginning."

"It's just that, I mean, the touring team is a good opportunity, and Dan thinks—"

"Take that man to a hotel for the weekend and remind him why he's enslaved by your charms!" Nikki demanded. "Then tell him what *you* think about the touring team."

"There's a minor present!" Blake interjected. He placed his hands over Randall's ears.

Randall grinned the grin Nora loved, full of gleaming teeth.

"Randall and I aren't old enough for this conversation," Blake told Nikki.

"You're eighteen," Nikki said to Blake.

"I'm around the same age as Amy's kids, so it's grossing me out to hear about moms and dads enslaving each other with their charms."

"Grow up, Bram Stoker," Nikki said with a smile.

Amy twittered nervously and glanced at The Pie Emporium, no doubt desperate for another hit of coffee.

Nikki continued to flood Amy with marital and parenting advice, despite the fact that she wasn't married or a parent.

Blake ushered Randall nearer to Nora.

Each time Blake arrived for his shift, he set out blacksmith tools. Bellows, tongs, hammer. Then he hung wrought-iron items available for sale on pegs around the hearth.

He talked about blacksmithing to everyone who stopped by. He did a great job keeping the fire stoked. And he did a fair business selling iron items. Nora *never* let him anywhere near red-hot metal, however. Most of Blake's life experiences to date had been gained from horror movies, horror books, and scary video games.

She watched him carefully set stacks of colored paper at each spot along the table. His dyed, matte black hair swooshed across his pale oval face as he moved. Was he wearing eyeliner today?

Sometimes Nora imagined the muscular, testosterone-laden, real-life blacksmiths of the 1870s scowling at her with accusation from their graves.

"Ms. Bradford?" Blake said. "Hey, I've been meaning to ask you . . ."

"Yes?"

"Well, since you're a librarian, I was wondering if you know anything about the business of publishing."

"Only a little."

"I have an idea for a children's book."

Blake was interested in a pursuit both educational and productive? Thank God. "That's wonderful, Blake."

"I was thinking about doing a graphic novel, you know? But for kids. And it's going to be about this evil guy named The Beheader, and he's going to chase after people and behead them. Then this young kid is going to get powers given to him by zombies, and he's going to confront The Beheader in an epic fight scene."

"Mmm."

"And everyone will be rooting for the kid and expecting him to win. But then—here's the genius part—he doesn't. The Beheader takes the kid's severed head and uses it to obliterate the zombies."

"Sounds cool," Randall said.

"I see." Nora had been a fiction lover all her life. She wasn't about to discourage Blake's creativity, even if his book sounded to her like the kind of fare that might scar kids for life.

"And then The Beheader will have a zombie feast," Blake said.

Why, yes, of course, Nora thought.

And on the heels of that, *I love my employees*.

And on the heels of that, *I miss John*.

They'd returned from Blakeville a week ago yesterday. Instead of diminishing, her sorrow over him kept multiplying and multiplying.

She could recall exactly how he'd looked striding through the library in Shelton, smiling over two plates of apple cinnamon cake, slipping on his sunglasses in her car, standing on a balcony with heat in his eyes. She went back over everything she could ever remember him saying. She reread every text and email he'd sent and listened to the two voicemails on her phone.

Nora straightened, colorful pieces of felt in her hands, and peered across the green toward the table she and John had shared at their first meeting.

The day after she'd last seen him, she'd compiled the online articles and PDF documents she'd told John she'd email to him. She'd yet to send them, because she knew her email might very well be the final communication between them. She'd been hesitant to send the thing that would screw the lid onto their joint efforts. Plus, she'd been unable to decide whether or not to add an invite to Grandma's party to her email.

Every day she'd told herself to make a choice and send the email. What if he was waiting to read those papers before formulating a letter to his birth mother? It wasn't likely he was waiting. But if he was, he'd be wondering what was taking so long. Nora's name had never, ever been attached to the adjective *inefficient*. Just the idea that John might think her inefficient gave her hives.

She filled her lungs with air, then gradually exhaled. She'd go straight to her office inside the library. Right now. She'd send that email, and in it, she'd invite John and Allie to the party because she was suddenly positive that she could invite him with the right motives. Not steal-someone's-boyfriend motives. But I'd-like-us-to-share-a-social-circle motives.

She'd been dumb to think she couldn't bear to see him with Allie. Of course she could bear it. The awful eight days she'd just endured had brought her to a crystallizing realization.

She'd much, much prefer to see John from time to time in a friendly way than never see him again in her lifetime.

• • •

Email from Nora to John:

John,

I hope this note finds you well! I'm sending over the resources I'd told you about. I've attached them below.

On another topic entirely . . . Do you remember me mentioning my grandmother to you? She's turning 80 soon, and my sisters and

I are planning a birthday party for her. Willow, Britt, and I would love for you and Allie to attend if you're available. It will be held at Bradfordwood on the evening of Saturday, July 3rd. If you're free that night, I'll mail an invitation.

All the best, Nora

• • •

Nora,

Thanks for the attachments you sent.

Unfortunately, Allie and I have other plans on July 3rd and won't be able to come to the party. I hope your grandmother has a great birthday.

John

CHAPTER

Thirteen

Nora's heart jumped into her throat when she spotted John's name in her email inbox mid-morning on Monday.

Since Saturday, when she'd sent her email to John, she'd been praying that God would help John understand the spirit in which her email had been written. She'd also been praying that she'd respond well to John's response to her party invitation, whether it was a yes or a no.

It was a no. She stared at the few lines he'd typed.

It was a no.

She grabbed her purse, left the library, and drove straight to the Hartnett Chapel. As she drove, disappointment drilled down into the sense of numbness laboring to protect her.

Lord! I prayed against this. You know I did! You remember, right?

When she came to a stop in front of the chapel, she drank in the sight as if it were the antidote to disappointment. Which in a strange way, it was.

She mounted the chapel's familiar steps. Like always, the knob turned easily beneath her palm and the chapel's interior welcomed her with a hushed atmosphere and the scent of old wood. She simply stood, letting the comfort of the place sink into her.

From the time when Merryweather Historical Village had been nothing more than a wish list on a yellow legal pad, Nora had longed for a chapel.

A year after she'd graduated from college, she'd come across a mention of the Hartnett Chapel while reading a letter written by Lena Sussex, one of Merryweather's early residents, to her sister. Nora had scoured old records and found the plot of land belonging to the Hartnetts. Further digging had confirmed that the Hartnett family still owned the property.

She'd called Mr. Hartnett. When he'd informed her that the chapel was still standing, she'd been euphoric. He'd given her directions and assured her that she was more than welcome to have a look.

She immediately drove out to see the chapel. All these years later, she could still remember the rush of unalloyed joy she experienced when she saw the simple, boxy one-room building. Quite utilitarian, except for the loving embellishments that had been added. Instead of the usual white, the clapboard exterior was painted palest blue. The chapel boasted a peaked front door. The elegant, scrolling woodwork of the overhang above the door bore witness to the skill of the long-gone carpenter who'd fashioned it. The original bell still hung in the chapel's bell tower. A sturdy, roughhewn wooden cross reached heavenward from the tower's highest point.

Nora had been dating Harrison when she'd first come to the chapel. They hadn't been engaged at that time, but that hadn't stopped her from concocting a rosy vision of the Hartnett Chapel's role in her future wedding.

She'd determined that she'd purchase the chapel and bring it triumphantly to her village. She'd restore it lovingly and tastefully. Since her wedding guests would be too numerous to fit inside its walls—her family was one of the bedrocks of the community, after all—she'd seat the guests outdoors in rows of white chairs. She'd use the chapel's raised front stoop as the platform for her vows and bedeck the door with a crown of flowers. The bell tower would jut into the blue sky and all the guests would swoon over the beauty of their love and the perfection of the setting.

That's how it was *supposed* to have gone.

The first problem had occurred when she'd asked Mr. Hartnett if she could buy his chapel. Mr. Hartnett was a robust, white-haired retired logger. He'd granted her permission to spend time at his chapel whenever she wished, and he even tolerated her frequent visits to his home bearing bribery gifts. But he would not sell his chapel to her.

The Hartnett Chapel had stood empty for a few generations, but that didn't mean it wasn't important to Mr. Hartnett. He'd made memories at the chapel during his boyhood. It represented a piece of his family's history, and he was set on retaining it for his grandchildren.

Whenever he told Nora these things, she explained why she loved the chapel and how dotingly she'd take care of it. She promised to put a sign out front declaring it the Hartnett Chapel. She assured him that his descendants would always have an open invitation to use the chapel for events at no cost. She went on and on about how nice it would be to share this particular piece of his family's history with all the residents of Merryweather and the many tourists who visited her village.

Alas, Mr. Hartnett liked his chapel exactly where it was.

Which was all perfectly reasonable yet left Nora feeling like a sorority girl who'd been rushing a particular pledge with all her might and zero success.

She reached the front of the chapel and slowly swiveled. Carefully, she catalogued the details around her to make sure nothing had dared change since the last time she'd come. Some of the windowpanes tipped at jaggedly broken angles in their frames. The once-white paint on the walls had become a crust of peels. Cobwebs arched like buttresses beneath the beams supporting the roof. A rug of dirt and grime covered the hardwood floor.

The original wooden pews remained amazingly intact, however.

So did the hand-painted green stenciling that formed an enchanting border along the top rim of the walls.

She let herself out of the building and took a seat on the stoop.

From this vantage point, no other man-made structure could be seen. The Hartnett Chapel had been rooted in a meadow ringed with nothing but rolling land.

It had rained on the drive here. The sky hovered close above, a dull gray mass. However, sunlight had found a faraway crack in the cloud cover. It slanted across the land, touching tree branches and turning their leaves a bright, alive, almost eerie green.

There was no way for her to know if John and Allie really did have plans the night of July third. Or if John had said they had plans because he wanted to avoid her. The idea that he might want to avoid her stung. At the same time, if he wanted to avoid her in order to guard his romance with Allie, then it only proved what she'd always known to be true about his character. Perhaps in a few days, when it didn't sting so much, she'd be able to commend him for that.

She rested the side of her head against one of the spindles in the handrail that flanked the chapel's front steps.

This building centered her in part because she loved it, in part because it helped her hear what God was saying to her.

Today, God was reminding her that she shouldn't expect to receive everything she wanted in life.

The things you wanted and prayed for and didn't receive left holes in your heart and sometimes in your historical village, too. As much as Nora wanted to rail against that, she had to concede that the holes were what the Lord used to mature and humble His people. The things you didn't receive added value to your life, the same as did the things you received.

Life had holes. Life was still beautiful.

Nora could sense God's nearness, hear Him in the sounds of nature, see Him in the rays of sunlight. He hadn't given her this chapel or John, but He had given her Himself. He was enough.

He's enough, Nora.

She knew it in her head, that He was. But her heart continued to waver. Her heart had a long memory. It hadn't forgotten what had happened the last time she'd trusted God fully.

Her heart was preoccupied at the moment, anyway, by its efforts to patch the hole that John had left.

"Why are you smiling?" Allie asked.

"Oh." He'd just wheeled his suitcase from his closet into his bedroom so he could start packing. The suitcase had reminded him of Nora's huge monogrammed bag, and he'd been smiling over the memory of how she'd carried half of Office Depot around inside of it. "I was just thinking about the last trip this group of guys and I went on together."

"I'm glad you're excited about it. You're going to have a great time."

He nodded.

He was leaving in the morning and would be gone for ten days. Three days in New York, where he'd be giving seminars on emergency preparedness. The rest in Maine, fishing with a group of former SEALs.

Maybe they'd do Navy SEAL-type stuff. He opened his mouth to tell Allie how Nora had joked about Navy SEAL-type stuff—

He closed his mouth. That wasn't something he could tell Allie.

She sat on the edge of his bed, the toes of one foot sunk into the carpet, her other foot tucked behind her ankle. She'd bent her head to check something on her phone. Her thick blond braid trailed down her back.

She'd made dinner for them in his kitchen tonight. Cheese enchiladas, rice, salad, and something she'd called an ice cream pie. His brain had registered the fact that all of it was good, but he hadn't really tasted any of it.

Two weeks had passed since he'd seen Nora, and still, all he wanted to smile about was Nora. The only subject he really wanted to talk to Allie about was Nora.

After he'd received Nora's email, he'd thought about how to respond for two days. He'd finally done what he hadn't wanted to do and turned down her invitation. He was trying to be ethical. To be a decent human being. To be a trustworthy boyfriend.

"Would you like me to send a care package to you and the guys in Maine?" Allie asked without lifting her attention from her phone's screen.

"No, that's okay."

"It says here that the resort will accept deliveries for guests."

"Huh."

"You know, I haven't been to New York in years. I'd love to return. I wonder if there are any last-minute deals on flights. . . ." Her fingers tapped at her phone. "We could go to museums and see a musical or two."

Right then, in the middle of his bedroom with the handle of an empty suitcase in his hand, he realized he was done. He didn't want Allie making him any more enchiladas or sending him care packages or coming with him to New York. He didn't want to feel obligated to check in with her during his trip. He didn't want her waiting for him at the airport when he returned.

On paper, Allie was the perfect girlfriend for him. Everyone loved her: men, women, kids. She had it all together. She was full of good qualities.

But she didn't click her key fob twice to lock her car. She didn't have fiery red hair and pale skin. She didn't use ridiculous words.

There was something about Nora and him together, about *them*, that fit. It didn't make sense. Nora was much more widely read than he was. She loved tea, for goodness' sake. She wasn't athletic at all. She was a fan of some British show with a long name that he'd never heard of because he avoided PBS like the plague. And her hairstyles confused him.

In a way he couldn't explain, the things that made Nora who she was—her good heart and her flaws and all the rest—also made her exactly right for him. Which meant that everyone else, even Allie, was exactly wrong.

Regardless of whether Nora wanted to date him or didn't want to date him, he couldn't go on dating Allie any longer. He was grateful to Allie for helping him through the days following his diagnosis. Very grateful. But his desire to be free had outrun his affection and gratitude.

All girlfriends everywhere deserved more than what he'd been putting forth since he returned home from Blakeville. Allie, who'd done absolutely nothing wrong, definitely deserved more.

Pressure to say something to her, to end it, mounted within him so strongly he was surprised he'd been able to fight it up until now.

He left the suitcase behind. "Allie?"

Her face lifted to his, smiling.

He didn't want to hurt her, and he was already sorry, incredibly sorry, for the hurt he was about to cause.

John watched clouds steal Washington from view as his plane gained altitude on its flight to New York.

Allie hadn't screamed or sobbed or cursed him when he'd ended things with her yesterday. She had way too much pride for that. Even so, their breakup had been painful. It left John feeling two ways.

Like a world-class jerk.

And relieved.

He didn't doubt that he'd done the right thing. It was just that the doing of it had sucked.

This trip had come at a good time.

He needed a vacation and distance to get his head straight.

Over the next ten days, he'd pray and think and rest. When he returned home, he'd decide what in the world to do about Nora.

Deciding what in the world to do about Nora would have been easy if it weren't for his eyesight.

The day after arriving in Shore Pine from his trip, he stood on his deck. He could barely make out the lake through the morning mist. It wasn't a hard or a cold mist. It was a soft, summer mist that suited his mood.

Before he could ask Nora out, he'd have to tell her about his blindness. She deserved all the facts before making a decision about him, but man . . . He sighed. He didn't want to tell her.

He'd prefer for Nora to go on thinking he was the man she'd read about in *Uncommon Courage* and watched in the movie. Which was rich, considering he'd always known, even before his diagnosis, that the man in the book and movie was better and bigger and braver and a whole lot more immortal than he'd ever been.

He didn't have to contact Nora. Their relationship was already over. He could just leave it like it was. Nora would never have to tell him she didn't want to date him or watch him weaken.

Except he missed her too much not to contact her. Almost a month had passed since their trip to Blakeville. In all that time their only communication had been her email to him and his to her. Yet the cold, heavy ache of missing her had never gone away.

Somehow, during the search for Sherry, Nora had become the bright spot in his days. She was still his bright spot, and he couldn't make himself let her go.

His finger paused over his cell phone's screen and the text he'd begun typing to Nora. He slowly hit backspace backspace backspace.

Angrily, he combed a hand through his hair. He couldn't make himself let her go, and at the same time he hated the idea of dragging her into the struggle that was coming for him . . . the struggle that had already begun.

Blindness wasn't pretty. He'd lose his ability to drive himself places. He might even lose his ability to walk places without being led by someone. His mind spiraled whenever he thought about waking up to darkness, not being able to look at his lake, having to fumble his way through life.

He wanted better for her.

But, selfishly, he also plain old *wanted her*. So he'd tell her his secret and explain what it meant. He'd tell her, and then the ball would be in her court.

Growling, he typed a text message. Before he could stop himself, he pressed send.

Nora's phone binged to signal a text message.

She was sitting inside Sweet Art, savoring a dark chocolate cashew truffle when she heard the *bing* and reached over to pull her phone from her purse. The instant she saw *John Lawson* as the sender's name, her heart stuttered. The truffle sat in her mouth, melting, while joy and caution gusted within her.

John.

Oh, John.

If there'd been any thought that she'd moved on from him, which to be factual there hadn't been, seeing his name appear on her phone blasted that away. If one equated physical hunger to Nora's hunger to hear something from John, then Nora had been at the point of cannibalism.

"I'm guessing from the look on your face that you've heard from John." Britt neared, tucking the dustcloth she'd been using into her apron's pocket.

Nora peeled her gaze from the phone to Britt.

"Breathe." Britt made sweeping motions in front of her lungs. "Chew. Swallow. Speak."

Nora did as she was told.

"What did he say?" Britt asked.

"Let me see." She clicked to reveal the full message. "He says he knows Grandma's party is just a few days away and he's sorry because it's short notice and because he realizes it's rude to change his RSVP. But he'd like to come if the invitation is still open." This was way too good to be true. She'd all but given up hope.

Britt pursed her lips. "He didn't say *we'd* like to come if the invitation is still open?"

"No. Just *I'd* like to come."

"For the record, I'm going to have to hurt him for causing you this much happiness if he's still with his girlfriend."

"I'm going to have to hurt you for causing me a stroke by suggesting he might not still be with his girlfriend. Surely they're still together. I mean . . . Don't you think?" She searched Britt's face.

"I think you and I need to know the answer to exactly that. Like now. Text him back and say, 'Certainly! You and Allie are still welcome to come to the party.' That's the subtlest way to fish for information."

Nora thought it through. "Perfect." She typed Britt's suggested text with quivering fingers and the taste of chocolate in her mouth.

Neither of the sisters attempted so much as a hiccup as they waited for John's reply.

Bing. They almost bumped heads as they leaned in to read his words.

Allie and I broke up. It'll just be me.

"Great Scott," Nora wheezed. Her free hand flew up to cover her heart and keep it in its place.

"I'd kind of like to pump my fist and squeal," Britt said calmly, "but I'm not sure that's the correct response to news of someone else's breakup."

"I'm having the same dilemma. What if *she* broke up with *him* and he's heartbroken about it?"

"Nora." Britt gave her a longsuffering look. "I can just about promise you that no woman has broken up with that man. Ever. He was the one who broke up with her. It's you he likes."

"What! We don't know that he likes me."

"Think about it. There's only one reason why he'd ask to come to Grandma's party. It's not because he's hoping to have a raging good time at an eighty-year-old's birthday. It's not even for the supremely good cake I'll be baking. He wants to come to the party for you."

Glorious hope, terrified hope swelled within her. She would love to believe Britt. But Britt's conjecture felt too farfetched to trust. "How should I respond?"

"By saying, 'It's about time, slow-moving Navy SEAL.'"

"Take pity on me and give me a suggestion that's in the realm of how normal, non-Britt people actually speak to one another."

"Well, for starters, I don't think you need to mention his breakup at all at this point. There'll be time to discuss that with him later."

Good advice. She carefully typed, *Grandma's birthday dinner will begin at 7:00, but feel free to arrive at my parents' house anytime—*

"Because any time's a good time for lovin'."

"That's *so* not helpful, Britt." Nora continued formulating her message: . . . *between 6–7. 423 Briar Cliff Road, Merryweather. I feel it's only right to do you the favor of warning you that Grandma doesn't call a gathering a party unless the women are wearing fancy dresses and the men are wearing suits.* She read it over three times, checking for typos. It seemed to hit the right note.

"I approve," Britt said.

Nora sent the message.

He responded immediately. *Thanks for the warning. It sounds like I owe you a favor.*

"Ask him to bring a friend for Willow."

"I don't know . . ."

"Nora Bradford! Think about your poor sister. Don't even consider hoarding all the handsome guys for yourself."

"Yes, because I'm so well known for hoarding *all* the handsome guys."

"You're known for your caring generosity," Britt shot back. "So prove it."

Nora bit her lip and wrote, *Willow likes to balance out the tables, and we have one more spot for a guy at our table. If you bring a friend with you, then it'll be me who ends up owing you a favor.*

I'll do my best.

Great! See you then.

"Well done, sister." Britt scooted the unfinished truffle closer to Nora. "Now eat chocolate."

Nora took a bite. "How come you didn't ask me to have John bring two friends? One for Willow and one for you?"

"I'm still on hiatus from dating after my last train wreck of a romance. Anyway, Zander will be there. He's better company than a boyfriend, and he's handier, too, because he'll help me serve birthday cake."

"As far as you're concerned, this whole party is about the cake, isn't it?"

"Well . . . yeah."

"There's more to life than dessert, Britt."

"Touché, coming from the woman who up until a few weeks ago poured all her energy into *Northamptonshire* and books." Britt disappeared in the direction of the kitchen.

Nora finished the chocolate slowly. She allowed her emotions to execute a long row of ecstatic cartwheels, then tried to settle herself enough to think rationally.

Britt's opinions aside, it was certainly possible that Allie had been the one to break up with John. It was also possible that John didn't like Nora in the way Britt thought he did. He might have texted her because he was sad and in need of a distraction. It wouldn't do to build a fiction worthy of one of her epic fantasy novels to explain John's motives for attending the party.

She'd wait. She'd be prepared for whatever came.

For this one beautiful, cocoa-powder-covered moment, it was enough simply to have heard from John. And to know that she'd get to see him again.

John.

Oh, John.

Nora had been experiencing a wide range of misgivings since she climbed into Willow's Range Rover en route to the hair salon. They intensified as she sat in Javier's chair and he gently took down her hair.

Her updos were the one aspect of her appearance that people

seemed to remember, that people commented on. Was she really willing to give up her one memorable, comment-worthy feature?

She'd finally told Willow she'd consent to a new hairstyle because she *earnestly* wanted to look her best for Grandma's party now that she knew John would be there.

Willow had laughed and confessed that she'd made a hair appointment for Nora the day after they'd eaten borscht. Willow hadn't informed Nora about the appointment because she'd been employing the technique their mom used to use on them for dental appointments. When they were kids their mom would announce, "We're having our teeth cleaned today!" immediately before pulling into the dentist's parking lot. She'd never given her daughters time to wail or stoke their anxiety. It had been stealth attack dentistry.

Willow had been planning stealth attack hairstyling.

"Were you just going to kidnap me?" Nora had asked.

"Yes. But I won't have to now that you've come to your senses, which I applaud you for, by the way. I'll pick you up tomorrow at three thirty."

So here she was. And even though Nora hadn't been kidnapped . . . even though she'd raised her hand for this . . . *yikes*.

Javier listened carefully to Nora's ideas, concerns, and limits. Then, just like at the makeup counter several weeks back, he and Willow did a great deal of talking back and forth amongst themselves. The two experts, the two taste-brokers. Nora felt like an eight-year-old at the mercy of adults.

As he worked on her color, Nora became more and more certain that she was going to end up with brown hair the color of blah. Just how much would she infuriate and offend Willow if she went to the drugstore and bought her usual box of Firelight Red and dyed it all back tomorrow?

An assistant shampooed and conditioned Nora, then Javier flashed his shiny scissors around her head. It looked to her like he was cutting it too short. Her heart dropped like a rock down a canyon. Unlike the color, there'd be no way to change this back before the party.

Javier spun her to face the center of the salon, away from the mirror, while he blew her hair dry. "No peeking!" he kept saying in his accented English. Could it be called peeking when you were trying to look at your own hair?

Finally, he set aside the blow dryer. He swept a flat iron along the strands. Willow beamed. Nora felt queasy. The chicken salad sandwich she'd had for lunch hadn't been the best choice, perhaps.

Her hair was her thing. Why had she subjected herself to this?

Because Willow's a beauty genius and because you really do want to look your best for the party. Take heart! Be brave!

Javier considered her critically.

I don't think I like you, Javier. You, with your accent and shiny scissors.

He reached out and brushed a lock into place with the kind of familiarity that only hair stylists and massage therapists were permitted. "Finished," he declared. "You look beautiful."

This was at least the fourth time he'd told her she looked beautiful. Nora knew very well that he was doing it unconsciously. No doubt he told all his clients they were beautiful with perfunctory regularity. Which went a long way toward explaining his salon's roaring success.

Slowly, Javier turned Nora to face the mirror.

Nora watched her own eyes round in the mirror's reflection.

Oh. My. Goodness.

Willow came to stand at her shoulder, looking self-satisfied.

Javier had dyed Nora's hair a deeper shade than it had been before. Instead of resembling a brassy copper penny, it now resembled burnished cinnamon. A little darker near her crown, with a few lighter, more honey-colored strands around her face. It was just as striking and eye-catching as Nora had always wanted but no longer one flat shade. This red had depth. A Dutch master could have used the color palette of her hair in a painting.

Javier had parted it on the side and cut a light fringe of bangs that swept across the edge of her forehead, then melded seamlessly with the rest of her hair. He'd done a lot of layering, but it had all been subtle under-layering, because, for the most part, her hair appeared to be all one length. It ended in a perfect line at her shoulders.

Nora was too surprised to speak.

She looked . . . Did she look better? She'd been braced for displeasure, so it was taking some mind-bending to figure this out. But, yes. She thought she might look better. The side bangs complemented her features. The length of the cut flattered the shape of her face.

She looked classy.

"You're welcome," Javier drawled.

"See?" Willow said. "You're still exactly yourself. We've just surrounded your beauty with the best possible setting." She waved a hand down Nora's hair. "Like a Tiffany setting is to a diamond, this hairstyle is to your face."

"I . . ."

Javier chuckled deeply. "You're welcome," he said again.

• • •

Unsent letter from John to Sherry Thompson O'Sullivan:

Dear Sherry,

My name is John Lawson and I was born at Presbyterian Hospital thirty-three years ago this past November. I learned your whereabouts by speaking with Sue Hodges who lives on Regent Street in Shelton and by traveling to Blakeville and searching through Thompson family records.

I was adopted by Ray and Linda Lawson and raised in Seattle. I have one sibling, a sister.

I graduated from Northern Arizona University and was fortunate to play baseball during my years there. Shortly after graduation, I joined the Navy and served for six years. For the past five years, I've been living and working in Shore Pine. I own Lawson Training, a company that offers emergency preparedness and response courses.

If you're the woman that I'm looking for, I'd like an opportunity to meet you. I won't contact you further until I hear from you via the phone number, email, or address I've included below. I'd appreciate the chance to speak with you and ask you a few questions.

Sincerely, John

• • •

Email from Duncan to his personal assistant:

Go ahead and book me on that flight into Seattle. I fancy some Pacific lobster, a trip up the Space Needle, and time with my American friend.

CHAPTER Fourteen

Willow Bradford considered herself to be an accomplished hostess.

She was probably the least talkative Bradford sister, but luckily for her, you didn't have to be extraordinarily talkative to host a good party. You simply had to be skilled at planning, at introducing people, and at keeping the food, drinks, and conversation flowing. Those things, she excelled at.

Willow stood on Bradfordwood's back patio, assessing with satisfaction the scene that awaited Grandma's party guests.

She and her sisters would have appreciated a rustic/chic party. That type of party would have suited the outdoor summertime setting perfectly, but it wouldn't have suited Grandma. "Rustic" would have confounded the older woman. Margaret Elizabeth Burke appreciated formality.

So, after much thought, Willow had decided to derive her party inspiration from the pair of pearl earrings Grandma wore every day. She'd chosen an elegant white-on-ivory color scheme. Because the weather had been gracious enough to cooperate with her hopes—*thank you, Lord*—the party rental company had arranged round tables on the brick terrace behind Bradfordwood. She'd selected linens and plates in hues of white. Pearl napkin rings. White hydrangea centerpieces. Numerous votive candles in silvery holders. Every tablecloth, fork, glass, and hydrangea petal was in place.

She'd rented dozens of white lanterns of various heights and shapes and filled them with flickering LED lights. Some of the lanterns lined the edges of the patio. Some stood at the French doors that marked the boundary between the interior and exterior of the house. Many more lanterns hung from the branches of the trees bordering the terrace.

Thin strips of gauzy clouds striated the blue sky, and the air was just beginning to take on that gilded, late-afternoon quality. Beyond the terrace, the emerald swath of lawn swept like a carnival slide down the acres that separated the house from the Hood Canal.

She'd talked Grandma into a sit-down dinner that started at seven o'clock, despite the fact that Grandma typically ate no later than five fifty. The guests were invited to arrive anytime between six and seven—which meant that Grandma's early-bird friends could be expected to appear at any moment. Willow checked the time. Five forty.

Willow made her way inside and spotted Nora in the living room near the fireplace, pinning a corsage to Grandma's blue raw silk coat while Grandma grumbled.

Willow paused for a moment, struck by the picture Nora presented. The Enhancing of Nora was complete, and Willow had enjoyed it so much that she was almost sad that it was over. Watching Nora's transformation had been sweeter than watching the best renovation show HGTV had to offer because it had been happening to Nora. Her Nora. Who deserved it. Who'd basically retreated to a cave of her own making after Harrison broke up with her.

They'd shopped for Nora's dress together. A pale blue strapless bodice and wide skirt formed the dress's base. On top of that rested a sheer, intricately embroidered overlay that added a scalloped neckline and three-quarter sleeves to the top half of the dress and additional detail to the bottom half. The vintage flair of it suited Nora, as did the golden high heels, complete with decorative bows over the toes that Willow had insisted upon. All of it, the whole package, absolutely worked. So much so, it was hard not to congratulate herself a little.

The doorbell rang. Taking a bracing breath, Willow hurried forward to answer it.

Guests arrived in a steady stream. The conversational volume rose. Drinks were poured. A respectable portion of the prosciutto-and-melon skewers, shrimp cocktail, and crispy veggie egg roll appetizers were eaten.

Britt kept an eye on the food. Nora helped people find the bathroom and their name on the list of assigned tables. Willow remained in the front part of the house, greeting guests as they arrived.

Thirty minutes before dinner was scheduled to begin, Willow made her way through the downstairs rooms and terrace to take a quick head count. She expected sixty and was only missing a few.

She rounded the corner from the living room into the central hall on her way back to the foyer. Her face lifted—

Her steps immediately cut off.

Terrible, *terrible* surprise clenched her heart.

Two men had just entered. They were both tall, athletic, and handsome. Both wore expensive, well-cut suits and ties.

But only one of them had broken her heart.

The old bitterness, misery, and fury came rushing back, causing her pulse to pound. What in the world was he doing here? This was *her* house. Her territory. Private property! She'd never wanted to see him again in her lifetime, and until this moment she'd felt confident in her ability to achieve that goal.

Shock paled his chiseled face. Clearly, he was as appalled to see her as she was to see him.

Corbin Stewart. Here. She wanted to shove him hard in the chest and tell him to leave. She was a famously composed person. Of all men, however, he was the one who had the power to break that composure like a brittle stick between his hands.

Only if you give him that power, Willow.

Every good model knew how to perform for the camera. She'd

had years of practice at looking into lenses and communicating desire or boredom, amusement or questioning inquiry. With effort, she called on her experience, channeling both calm and indifference. She stood tall in the simply cut teal sheath dress she'd chosen for the evening and approached them, her high heels rapping against the hardwood floors.

The man standing beside Corbin must be John, Nora's Navy SEAL. She'd been expecting John, and she'd known he was bringing a guest. Of all the people on earth, *this* was the friend John had chosen to bring?

She gave John a smile she did not feel in any corner of herself. "Hi, I'm Willow. Nora's sister."

"I'm John Lawson. This is my friend, Corbin Stewart. Do . . ." He looked back and forth between them. "Do you two already know each other?"

Clearly John had noticed the painful clang of recognition that had passed between her and Corbin. "We do," Willow said.

"We dated once," Corbin told John.

Corbin's voice was agonizingly familiar to her. She lifted her chin a fraction and did her best to concentrate on John, though it was hard to ignore the huge, glowering presence of one of the NFL's most successful former quarterbacks. "It didn't end well," she said.

John winced. "Nora asked me to bring a friend."

"I didn't know this was your family's party," Corbin stated, voice flat.

"This is your first time to come to the house?" John asked him.

"Yes."

"When we dated," Willow said stiffly to John, "I lived in LA, and he lived in Dallas. We didn't date for very long, so there was never a reason for him to come to Washington to meet my family."

Animosity filled the silence.

"Ah," John said.

Corbin said nothing.

"How do you two know each other?" Willow asked John.

"We met a few years ago at a charity golf event. We were paired together on the course. Who else was in our foursome, Corbin? I can't remember now."

"A couple of rich businessmen."

"That's right," John said, his tone relaxed. He was obviously trying to bring his buddy and himself back to less awkward ground. "Corbin came to Seattle about a month ago to have his shoulder operated on."

Willow already knew this information. She hadn't watched Corbin's press conference back in March—she wasn't a masochist—but she'd been unable to avoid learning that he'd announced his retirement. Both the career-ending shoulder injury he'd suffered in his final game and his subsequent retirement had made national news. He'd undergone his second surgery in Seattle because Dr. Wallace, America's most renowned orthopedic surgeon, was based there.

"After the surgery, when he came to Shore Pine, he called me," John said. "I live in Shore Pine, so we've been hanging out."

With effort, Willow made herself meet Corbin's eyes. The power of it resonated all the way down her body, as if she were a tuning fork. "Why did you come to Shore Pine after the surgery?"

"Dr. Wallace has a rehab center there."

It disoriented her to look at Corbin again after four years. He was a complete stranger and simultaneously someone she knew intimately.

He still kept his hair shaved close to his scalp. It was the exact color, a brown caught between mahogany and auburn, that it had been when they were together. His dark eyes were the same, except that they'd once glowed with tenderness for her and were now frozen over with coldness. The muscles defining his six-foot-three frame were distributed so perfectly that when you saw him in pictures or on TV, you didn't have an inkling of how large and solid he was in person.

When she'd known him, the driven, hardworking quarterback side of him had been balanced by an easygoing, charming, humorous demeanor off the field. Tonight, there was no humor in him at all.

"Had you heard about the rehab center in Shore Pine?" John asked her.

She glanced at him. "No, I hadn't."

"Dr. Wallace built it about a year and a half ago. It's state of the art."

"I see." She wished Corbin had chosen a state-of-the-art rehab center in Dallas, where he lived.

A version of Bogart's line from *Casablanca* slid through her mind. *Of all the homes, in all the towns, in all the world, he walked into mine.*

"Can I get you something to drink before dinner?" Willow motioned to the back of the house and the mingling guests.

"That's not necessary," Corbin said. "I can leave."

"There's no need. What happened between us is ancient history." Willow did her best to say the last smoothly. What had happened between them might be ancient history, but it still bothered her. It was usually a low-level type of bother. However, being confronted with him made the pain big and fresh all over again. She gave him an expression that said, *I can handle this fine. Can you?*

"Okay," Corbin said grimly.

She escorted them to the bar, then sailed outside. Each round table sat eight. At her table, she, her sisters, their cousin, the post office worker Evan, Zander, and John had place cards announcing their names in calligraphy. No card waited at Corbin's place because they hadn't known who John was bringing. Nora and Britt had been adamant about seating her next to John's guest, so that was how she'd arranged things. Unknowingly, she'd positioned Corbin Stewart right next to her.

She *refused* to sit next to that man during dinner. Surreptitiously, she slid her cousin Rachel's place card in front of the plate next to Corbin's, then sat herself a safe distance away, next to Evan.

"Changing the seating plan?" Nora came to a stop beside Willow.

"Yes." Willow's heart continued to beat as fast as a rabbit's. "John's here."

"Oh?" Nora's face lit up.

"He brought Corbin Stewart as his guest."

Nora's eyes rounded. "What? No!"

Almost a month had passed since Nora had seen John. They'd gone to Blakeville in early June, and now the electronic calendar on her smartphone had glided into early July.

Not a day had gone by during that time that Nora hadn't thought about him and missed him and wished, painfully, to see him. She'd been fairly certain during the past month that she'd never get that chance again. It had been agonizing to think that her parting glimpse of him, standing on his deck alongside Allie, was the last glimpse she'd ever get.

Then his out-of-the-blue text had ended the separation between them. The text after that, the one informing her that he and Allie had broken up, had turned Nora's world from black and white into Technicolor.

Never could she remember anticipating something as keenly as she'd been looking forward to seeing John tonight. Not even when she'd counted down the days until Christmas as a child or when she and her sisters had packed for their long-planned trip to Bali or when she and Harrison had set a date for their wedding.

All day today she'd been swinging between hoping that John might be interested in dating her to firmly reminding herself that she shouldn't place any unrealistic expectations on him. He'd never told her he felt romantically toward her. . . . But that could be because he'd had a girlfriend. Nothing in his recent text messages had indicated he felt romantically toward her, either. . . . But that could be because he wanted to see her first, let things progress slowly, then tell her himself.

Arrgh!

After spending a few minutes with Willow, doing her best to put out the unexpected fire that Corbin's appearance had lit, Nora made her way toward the house. Self-consciously, she adjusted one of her sleeves.

She loved this dress with unreasonable fervor. Its lines were understated, yet the decoration at the neck and hem was so lavish that she'd never have chosen it for herself no matter how enchanting. *What? So fancy? I'll call too much attention to myself!*

Willow had talked her into buying it, and once again, Willow had been right. This dress was all whimsy and beauty. It made her think of galloping horses and secret gardens and great loves.

She paused inside the French doors. Nervousness and anticipation coursed through her bloodstream as she scanned the den full of people for—

There.

John stood at the bar, his attention on Corbin as the two men talked.

He wasn't made of fairy-tale stuff and her imagination; he was real and he was actually here. Flesh and blood *John* was standing inside her childhood home, bounded by people and surroundings she knew very, very well. Emotion—elation and wonder and worry and gratitude—clutched so hard within her, she almost wanted to cry.

Almost. She wouldn't let herself because goodness, what would he think if he looked over and saw her crying?

He wore a sleek charcoal suit, a simple white shirt, and a pale gray tie. His cheeks were clean shaven. His hair gleamed with a trace of dampness. He projected his trademark dragon-slaying confidence.

Nora started toward him. When she was about halfway there, he turned and their gazes met.

She smiled, fireworks of joy detonating inside.

He walked toward her and when they were a few feet apart, opened his arms to her. She stepped immediately into his embrace.

It was a friendly hug, the kind of hug people often share when greeting one another after time apart. Only she'd never hugged John before. In a friendly manner or in any other manner. Sensations flooded her mind. His strong hold. His warmth. The smell of his soap. A feeling of destiny.

Longing suffused her and . . . *oh no*. The moisture she'd contained moments before pooled in her eyes.

"It's really good to see you," he said, his voice slightly gravelly.

"It's really good to see you, too."

Go away, tears! Oh, dear.

They stepped apart. Nora instantly bent and made a show of adjusting the strap on her shoe in order to give herself a moment to regain full control. She would not be caught crying during their reunion as if she were a child who'd been handed a long-lost stuffed animal. *So here I am, John, correcting the fit of my shoe. No biggie. This is completely normal of me.*

Her skirt swished into place as she rose.

He regarded her with an uneven smile, as if entertained by her, as if glad to see that she was still as quirky as ever.

"You look beautiful," he said.

"I do?"

"Yes."

She knotted her hands at her waist. "Thank you. So do you."

"I don't wear a suit that often these days."

"That's an unpardonable shame."

His brows lifted. "Did you just say *unpardonable*?"

"I did." They held each other's eye contact. Pleasure at being together again flowed between them.

He gestured in Corbin's direction. "Did your sister tell you that I brought her ex-boyfriend?"

Nora nodded.

"Sorry," he said. "I didn't know."

"I know you didn't. Don't worry about it."

"We can leave—"

"No." Gracious, no. "It's all right. Willow is the most well-mannered person I know. She'll be able to handle having Corbin here."

John introduced Nora to Corbin, and the two of them exchanged small talk. Nora wasn't a football fan. Who had time to watch football when there were so many fantastic books in the world yet unread? Nonetheless, Corbin's face was familiar to her both because of his fame and because Willow had sent pictures of the two of them to the family, back when they'd been dating.

It had always been easy for Nora to dislike the men who'd broken up with Willow or Britt. Especially if they'd done so in a hurtful way. She'd been actively disliking Corbin for years on Willow's behalf. Now that he'd shown up at Bradfordwood as John's friend, though, she decided to suspend her disapproval until after the party.

"Good evening, gentlemen," Britt said, taking up a position behind the bar next to the overworked bartender Willow had hired. Britt's dark hair hung free in loose waves. She wore an Indian-print maxi dress in jewel tones.

"This is my younger sister, Britt," Nora said to John and Corbin.

"I was there with Nora the day of the emergency drill," Britt told John. "I got soaked right along with her, thanks to your office sprinklers."

John's features registered recognition. "That's right. You were the one who had the sense to leave when I opened the office door."

She grinned. "That was me."

"I'd like you to meet Corbin Stewart," John said, indicating his friend.

Britt's lips parted. She stared at Corbin. "No kidding."

"No," Corbin said wryly.

"This is who you brought to the party?" Britt asked John. "Corbin Stewart?"

"This is who I brought," he confirmed.

Britt laughed. "Awesome. Every party needs at least one good villain."

"Hey," Corbin protested.

"Have you seen Willow?" Britt asked Corbin.

"Yeah. She . . . met us at the door."

"And she let you stay?"

"Yes."

"I underestimated her abilities as a hostess. I knew she was good. But to let *you* stay?" Britt whistled. "She's better than I thought."

Corbin narrowed his eyes and cut a disgruntled look in John's direction. He was one of the greatest players in the history of the NFL. No doubt he was usually adored by everyone.

"What can I get you?" Britt asked. "Despite that Jesus himself turned water into wine, my grandmother believes that alcohol is unchristian. So we have virgin sangria, Arnold Palmers, and virgin peach daiquiri punch."

"An Arnold Palmer, please," Corbin said.

Britt went to work fixing Corbin's drink and simultaneously peppering him with questions.

"Meet you at the table?" John murmured to Corbin.

"If I survive her inquisition," Corbin murmured back.

John motioned for Nora to precede him outside.

This past month, John's memory of Nora had been powerfully clear. So it surprised him that the real Nora was much prettier, even, than his memory of her.

When he'd seen her across the room just now, the sight of her had struck him like a crashing wave. He still felt dazed.

She led him outside toward one of the short, cement-topped brick walls that ran outward along both edges of the terrace, forming makeshift benches. They sat, and she angled her crossed knees toward him.

This was the first time John had ever seen her with her hair down. Her hair was darker, maybe, than it had been before and much softer looking. The old styles had been tight and hair-sprayed. Now the strands brushed against the tips of her shoulders, distracting him, making him want to run a finger along the upper line of her shoulder.

Long, dark lashes framed her brown eyes, and she must be wearing pale pink lip gloss, because every time it caught the light it sparkled.

What was the matter with him? *Quit staring at her lips, John.*

He'd come to this party for just one reason.

Her.

Being here with her made every minute of the past month worthwhile. The pull between the two of them hadn't lessened. It was still there, mysterious and forceful, and it steadied him. For the first time in weeks, it was as if the earth had found its level beneath his feet. He wasn't home alone with his depressing future. He was here, with Nora.

Problem was, she was gazing at him as if she believed him to be a hero, which filled him with a guilty sense of his own selfishness. She didn't know the full truth. He needed to tell her about his vision.

"Catch me up on what's been going on with you," she said.

"I'd rather hear what's been going on with you."

"I asked you first."

He told her about New York and Maine and some of the things they'd been working on at Lawson Training. She told him about her sisters and her parents in Africa and her efforts to prepare for the upcoming Summer Antique Fair.

"What about Sherry?" she asked. "Have you written to her yet?"

"I've written to her, but the letter's still sitting on my kitchen counter. I don't know why I haven't mailed it yet. I guess I just haven't felt ready."

"I get that. Contacting her is a big step."

"Would you be willing to look over the letter sometime and tell me if it sounds okay?"

"I'd love to."

Beyond the patio, an awesome view of the Hood Canal spread out like a painting. He'd known that Nora had come from a wealthy family, because she'd told him that her father had given her the historical village as a graduation gift. Still, he hadn't expected her to have grown up in the sort of mansion that the Vanderbilts could have owned.

"What happened between you and Allie?" she asked.

He tried to decide what to tell her.

"If I'm being too nosy, just say so," she said.

"No, it's all right. Allie and I have always gotten along really well, but things were never very"—he knit his brow—"serious between us. Lately, it became clear to me that we weren't meant to stay together. I guess it's as simple and complicated as that."

"When did you break up?"

"Two weeks ago."

"Are you all right about it? The breakup?"

"Yes. It was the right decision."

She studied him. "What about Allie? Is she all right about it?"

"Allie will be fine. She and I are still friends."

"That's good," she said softly.

Just then the clinking sound made by a fork striking the side of a glass carried to them. John looked over and saw that Willow was the one who'd called for everyone's attention. "Dinner is about to be served," she announced. "We invite you to take your seats. Once everyone is in place, Pastor William has graciously agreed to offer a word of prayer. Enjoy your meal."

The guests moved to the tables.

"Listen," John said just as Nora had been about to rise. "I'd like to . . ."

She stilled, waiting.

"I'd like to talk with you later. . . ." *About my diagnosis.*

"We can talk now if you'd like."

People were taking seats nearby. "Later's fine."

Grandma's birthday dinner was, for Nora, like a dream. In part because of the twinkling lanterns. In part because of the exquisite table settings and delicious food. In part because of her fanciful dress. But most of all, and it really wasn't even close, because of John.

He sat next to her, talking and laughing with both her and Britt, who was seated on his other side. Whenever he looked at Nora, which he did constantly, there was both a heat and a tenderness in his eyes that hadn't been there before. It had her thinking crazy things. Did he *like her* like her?

She drank in the details of him. His hands. The cords of muscle running down his neck. The button on the outside of his suit sleeve's cuff.

A princess didn't technically need a prince to make her big night out at the ball complete. Even without a prince, that ball meant a break from a difficult past and the drudgery of everyday life. This party meant the same to Nora. That, alone, was something to celebrate.

Thing was, even if the presence of a man you cared about wasn't integral, it had the ability to improve things *incredibly*. John made her buzz with happiness and sigh with longing and tingle with awareness. So, definitely yes. If a woman had a chance to be a princess at a ball, she should opt for the package that included a prince.

The only fly in the wine of Nora's delightful night was the palpable hostility between Willow and Corbin.

Evan of the ferrets sat next to Willow. Corbin sat next to their cousin Rachel, who'd been peering at him like a toddler with separation anxiety. Corbin and Willow were seated directly across from one another, as far apart at they could possibly be at a round eight-top. Both of them were trying so hard to act as if they were having a great time and as if the other didn't exist that they were proving the opposite to be true.

When the meal concluded, the sisters, Valentina, and Zander gathered at the cake table. In keeping with the ivory-on-white theme, Britt had coated her chocolate cake's two circular tiers with white frosting as smooth as fresh snow. She'd dotted tiny edible candies that looked like pearls here and there and added one artful mound of hydrangea blossoms to the cake's top.

Grandma tottered in their direction, and Nora saw that she'd donned her mink coat. Silently, Nora groaned.

Grandma had owned the mink for thirty-five years. Whenever she wore it, Nora feared she'd be doused in red paint by protestors. Also, it smelled dank and boasted massive shoulder pads. Willow, Nora, and Britt had nicknamed it Old Musty. Grandma didn't care that they loathed it. She wore it relentlessly, even in mild weather.

"Thank you for coming this evening," Grandma said in her lemony voice once the crowd had hushed. "I'm sure you all have many more important things to do tonight."

Her guests responded in the negative with murmured "No, nos" and shaking heads.

Grandma sniffed. "When my granddaughters told me of their intention to plan a party on my behalf, I asked them not to bother. But they held firm, so I asked them to plan something modest. It says in the Bible, 'Sell your possessions and give to the poor.'"

An interesting sentiment coming from a woman in a mink coat.

Britt leaned near Grandma and whispered, "It also says that if you give all your possessions to the poor, but do not have love, you gain nothing."

Nora's lips warbled as she struggled not to laugh.

Grandma looked down her nose at everyone. "As I'm sure you've all noticed, this party is very grand."

Nora and Britt didn't have the money to pay for this kind of party. But Willow did, and she'd been in charge.

"So," Grandma continued, "I don't know whether to sit my granddaughters down for a Bible lesson or thank them."

"Thank us!" Nora and Willow answered in unison, both smiling.

"How about we sing 'Happy Birthday'?" Britt asked the guests.

The happy birthday song rose into the night air.

Nora glanced at John. He gave her a grin as slow as honey. It was a private smile just for her, complete with a flash of white teeth, relaxed humor, and crinkly eyes.

Great Scott.

The song wound down. Britt went to work slicing cake, and Zander helped plate.

"Anything we can do?" Nora asked, Willow at her side.

"Would you mind grabbing another cake server?" Britt lifted Zander's wrist to show them the utensil he held. It looked like a spatula, except angled to a point. "And more napkins, please. This pile looks too small to me."

"We're on it," Nora said.

She and Willow made their way to the formal dining room and located the cake server in one of the china cabinet's drawers. "Ah ha!" Nora lifted it free.

"I'd like to take that thing and stab it into Corbin's chest," Willow said. "Repeatedly."

"Willow, I . . ." Nora's attention caught on the driveway outside. A dark sedan idled there, headlights lit. A man exited the back seat, and another man—the driver?—came around to pop the trunk and hand the first man his suitcase.

The cake server fell from Nora's hands and hit the floor with a clatter.

Willow startled. "Oh! You okay? What . . ."

Shock raced over Nora's skin. She couldn't be seeing what she was seeing. Right? Stunned, she moved toward Bradfordwood's front door.

"Nora?" Willow's voice seemed very far away.

Nora let herself onto the porch, then stepped down the first step.

She could hardly believe it. Her mighty imagination had not conjured him. She *was* seeing what she was seeing.

Duncan Bartholomew walked toward her wearing a European-looking knit scarf and a crooked smile.

• • •

Post from one of the co-moderators of the Devotees of Adolphus Brook Facebook Group:

> I've been as busy as one of Santa's elves, creating new memes of Adolphus for us to share. And, of course, for us to enjoy personally. I've uploaded them to our shared files. I'm partial to the photo of him in his study, wearing the muslin shirt with the ruffles at the neck and his spectacles. Those ink-stained fingers! I die! A thousand salutes to jolly old England for creating such a fine specimen of a man.

If you haven't mailed your letters to *Northamptonshire*'s producers on Adolphus's behalf, now's the time. We want more screen time for our favorite character!

Here's hoping your day is full of *Northamptonshire* skies and a certain Mr. Brook's swoon-worthy smile!

CHAPTER Fifteen

Miss Lawrence, I presume?" Duncan said.

That voice! With the clipped, upper-crust British accent. Nora gaped at him.

He came to a stop at the bottom of the porch steps, his face tilted up to hers. He held a leather suitcase. Beneath a worn blazer and scarf, he had on a T-shirt and jeans. The strap of his cross-body messenger bag bisected his chest diagonally. "Have I shocked you into silence?" he asked.

Astonishment bubbled from her in a breathless laugh. "Yes! Sorry! You officially shocked me into silence there for a minute." She descended the steps, arms outstretched. "Duncan!"

"Nora."

They shared a quick hug. She stepped back, beaming. "What are you doing here?"

"I thought it was high time we meet."

"Oh. My. Goodness."

"You sent me a picture of the invitation to your grandmother's birthday party. Remember?"

"Vaguely."

"So I booked a ticket. I wanted to surprise you."

"I'm having trouble thinking of a word that adequately captures what I'm feeling. Maybe . . . flabbergasted?"

"In a good way?"

"Yes." She was his fan girl! The president of his fan girls. Really, she was too old to be a fan girl. A fan woman, that's what she was. How were fan women supposed to behave when the object of their infatuation arrived? Squeal? Faint? "What . . . what are you doing in Washington? I thought you were only going to be in LA. You should have told me you had an event here! I could have arranged . . . something."

"I'm just here to meet you."

"You're *just* here to meet me?" she repeated, finding his statement wildly hard to believe. "That's it?"

"That's it. You don't live terribly far from LA, after all."

"Wow." Where was a defibrillator? This sort of thing did not happen in her life. Nora was so honored and, at the same time, pointedly aware that John awaited her in the backyard. John, who she was three-quarters of the way in love with. John, who was newly single. John, who meant the world to her. She didn't want to do anything to hurt him or her chances with him.

In that regard, Duncan had chosen a somewhat horrifying time to surprise her. She now needed to think of a way to . . . insert Duncan into her evening with John. "How long will you be in Washington?"

"Four days."

"Where are you staying?"

"I thought I'd just grab a hotel in town."

Her memory raced back over the years and years of Facebook messages between them. She couldn't boot him out of Bradfordwood sans car to search for a last-minute hotel room. "My sisters and I would love for you to stay here." She indicated the edifice towering over them like a nosy guardian. "You should feel right at home. The house is British."

"Whatever's easiest," he said lightly. "It wasn't my intention to inconvenience anyone."

"It's not an inconvenience. There's plenty of room. My sister Willow is the only occupant at the moment." Come to think of it, Willow might not be all that thrilled about sharing the house with an unexpected houseguest she'd never met.

Nora had very little practice at spur-of-the-moment decisions. She preferred research and careful plans laid out months in advance.

"You don't live here?" Duncan asked.

"No. This is where I grew up, but only my parents live here now. Come." She started to turn, then remembered that he was weighted down with luggage. "Can I carry something for you?"

"No, I've got it."

She led him into the sitting room off the foyer. He deposited his things.

It was almost dizzyingly surreal to have him here. She'd always thought that he resembled Orlando Bloom's character in *Pirates of the Caribbean*. Longish brown hair full of just the right amount of curl. A pointed chin. Fine, even features.

Nora guided him down the central hallway, panic beginning to circle inside her. How *could* she insert Duncan into her evening? Her only choice was to introduce him in a straightforward way to John and the others. "Are you hungry?"

"I've already had dinner, but I wouldn't turn down cake or champagne."

"There's no alcohol to be had at this party."

He chuckled. "You Yanks. So conservative."

"How about a flute of sparkling grape juice?"

"That, I'll gratefully accept."

She slipped behind the bar to pour his drink. Duncan was her friend. As of right now, John was also her friend. So maybe neither man's presence would rock the other man's boat? The possibility of that seemed slim, even to her.

She passed over the champagne glass.

"Many thanks."

"Right this way for cake." They fell into step. "I haven't tasted the cake yet, but I'm sure it's delicious because my sister made it. Britt's a master chocolatier. Which"—she took in an uneven inhale—"you know already. I've told you about my sisters many times, haven't I?"

"You have. Willow's a model and Britt is a baker and you're a candlestick maker."

"Sorry! I'm a bit rattled."

"Aww," he said indulgently. "It's to be expected."

Her cheeks felt abnormally warm against the air gently gusting off the estuary. They approached the cake table. The elderly guests had all returned to their tables with their slices of cake. Only Britt, Willow, Zander, Valentina, and, a short distance away, John and Corbin, remained.

The instant John spotted her and Duncan together he abruptly stopped talking to Corbin. His features hardened with suspicion.

Nora's confidence quavered. "I'd like to introduce Duncan Bartholomew," she said. It was clear to her that her sisters already knew exactly who'd arrived. She'd mentioned Duncan to them plenty and even regaled them with pictures of Duncan over the years. No doubt Willow had recognized him and forewarned Britt. Both sisters gawked at Duncan with ill-concealed fascination.

"Do you remember me telling you about the TV show that I love?" Nora asked the group. "*Northamptonshire*?"

"North what?" Valentina's round face crumpled with confusion.

"*Northamptonshire*," Nora repeated. "It's a TV show."

"TV!" Valentina dimpled. "Yes, miss. Yes."

"Well, Duncan is one of the actors on the show. He's a bit of a celebrity, really." As soon as she said that, she regretted it. He was a huge celebrity in her world, the world of a *Northamptonshire* mega fan. But to most Americans, Corbin, Willow, and John would all rank higher on the celebrity chart than an actor who portrayed a minor character in a BBC drama that had attained mediocre success. She was flubbing this!

John scowled.

She made herself wade in deeper, even though water was lapping higher and higher up her face, almost submerging her. "Duncan plays the role of my favorite character on the show, Lord Adolphus Brook."

"Should we call you 'milord'?" Britt joked.

"Meatloaf?" Valentina whispered to Willow. "We going to call him Meatloaf?"

"No need to address me as milord," Duncan replied cheerfully. "Just Duncan will do."

"What brings you to Washington?" Zander asked.

"I came to visit my biggest fan."

A blip of silence.

"Who's that?" Valentina asked.

"Why, Nora here. She's so brilliant that I couldn't resist the chance to meet her while I'm in America."

"So this is the first time you've met?" Zander asked.

"Yes," Nora answered. "Until now, we've only chatted through Facebook messages."

"Amazing how well you can get to know a person through Facebook messages," Duncan said.

The group gazed at Nora and Duncan blankly, obviously struggling to process the astonishing fact that a British actor had just stepped from the screen into Bradfordwood's backyard.

"Are any of you the Navy SEAL?" Duncan asked.

No! Would it be rude to dig her fingers into Duncan's blazer and yank him backward?

"I'm a former Navy SEAL," John said.

"Are you! Nora's told me a lot about you."

"Really?" John asked, unsmiling. "What has she said?"

"Only good things." Duncan laughed and clapped John on the upper arm.

Duncan's slender frame reached a height of about five foot nine. John was several inches taller, several inches broader, and far more forbidding. Duncan had never looked brawny onscreen or in photos and interviews. Never that. But somehow the camera had made him seem a bit larger than he was.

"How did you two meet?" John asked.

"Nora sent me an email a few years back," Duncan answered. "I can't keep up with all the correspondence I receive, but my personal assistant sometimes passes along a letter or email or message if it's particularly good. She forwarded Nora's email to me. I enjoyed it so much that I messaged her to thank her, and we've been communicating ever since."

"Yep," Nora managed.

"Nora's one of the moderators of the Fans of *Northamptonshire* Facebook Group," Duncan continued, "and she founded the Devotees of Adolphus Brook group. She works tirelessly promoting the show and me. She's a godsend."

"Oh, I don't know about that," Nora said.

"She's a godsend," Duncan repeated.

Duncan had just publicly outed her obsession with Adolphus and the show. Until this moment, her obsession had been somewhat of a personal thing. The people closest to her knew about it in a general sense, but even they didn't know the scope of it. She'd rhapsodized about *Northamptonshire* to John more than once, but she'd never said a peep to him about Adolphus or Duncan in particular.

The Devotees would be green with jealousy when she told them that Duncan considered her a godsend and had shown up at Bradfordwood in person. However, she understood that non-Devotee people—John included—would view her passion for Adolphus as kooky and maybe a tad desperate.

She'd rather he hadn't found out at all and *really wished* he hadn't found out this way. Sheepishly, she glanced at John.

He scratched the side of his face, looking approximately as amused as a man might look while being briefed on a terrorist threat.

So much for Duncan not rocking John's boat. This was very bad.

"Excuse me, but are you one of the actors on *Northamptonshire*?" an elderly lady asked Duncan. Three of the lady's friends flanked her, all of whom were at least eighty.

Duncan turned to address his admirers with a beatific smile. "I am!"

Nora faced John and Corbin. "I designed the invitation for this party," she said, her voice pitched low. "I sent Duncan a copy of it so he could see my handiwork, but I—I never imagined he'd get it into his head to attend."

"It sounds like you two are pretty close," John said.

"No. I mean, yes. I guess we are close in a way. In a Facebook messaging way. Not in a real world way. Until now."

John didn't answer.

Corbin's attention flicked to Willow. A frown line notched the skin between his brows.

Nora buried her trembling hands in the folds of her voluminous skirt. "You haven't had cake yet, have you? Let's get some cake, and then we can all go back to the table and hang out. I'm sure most of the guests will be heading home soon to strap on their CPAP machines, but I'd love for you both to stay."

"I think it would be better if we go," John said.

Nora attempted to sound less distressed than she felt. "The cake's the best part."

"No," John said quietly, looking into her eyes. "For me the cake isn't the best part."

The sweetness of his words seized her heart. "We were going to talk. Remember?"

"We'll talk another time," he said.

"John, I . . ." She couldn't think of what to say, how to give the sentence closure.

"Good night." He passed by.

Corbin thanked her for dinner, then moved off. By the time she'd swiveled toward the French doors, John had disappeared.

She stood for long seconds in her fancy dress, staring at an empty doorway. How and when was she going to see John again? Should she rush after him? And say what? *Do you have feelings for me? Because I have feelings for you. So for the love of all things holy, please don't let Adolphus—I mean Duncan—throw you off track. I'm sorry about him. And please, please believe me when I say that I never ever expected Adolphus to enter my non-fictional world.*

"Cake, Miss Lawrence?" Duncan arrived at her shoulder.

She accepted the plate of cake with numb fingers.

Nora had been pining for a romance between Lucy Lawrence and Adolphus for three seasons. And now Duncan had, in coming to Bradfordwood, made the sort of grand gesture toward her that she'd been waiting for Adolphus to make toward Lucy. He was even giving her the kind of affectionate attention she'd been longing for Adolphus to give Lucy.

It seemed that the princess, who'd been working hard for ages without even a glimpse of a suitor, had just been left at the ball by one prince and passed a slice of cake by prince number two.

"What are we going to do with the cute British guy?" Willow asked in a hushed tone.

An American friend of Duncan's had just called him on his cell phone. The moment Duncan had stepped into the sitting room to talk, Willow had tugged Nora and Britt into the downstairs powder room and shut the door behind them.

The Bradford sisters, who'd kicked off their high heels long ago, had just finished setting the house back to rights after the party. Duncan had been in the mix with them the whole time, cleaning, keeping up a nonstop stream of conversation, consuming virgin sangrias.

"First of all," Nora said, "I'm really, really sorry about springing Duncan on you as a houseguest, Willow. In the heat of the moment, inviting him to stay here seemed like the polite thing to do. Is that going to be super weird for you?"

"A stranger sleeping in my house with me. Why would that be weird?" Willow asked dryly.

"Okay." Britt spoke with the resolve of a field general. "How about I march out there and tell the cute British guy that he'll be bunking at Zander's house?"

Willow placed a staying hand on Britt's arm. "No. It's all right for him to stay here. I guess. My bedroom door locks. He's an actor, and actors aren't usually axe murderers, right?"

"Right," Nora answered. "They're too easily recognized to get away with axe murder."

"Comforting. What I'm wondering is what we need to *do* with him, exactly. I mean, he can't just hover around here for four days. Should we take him to see the sights around Merryweather? Book him a ticket for a boat tour of the Sound? Who's going to feed him?"

"Me," Nora assured her. "I'll come back first thing tomorrow. I'll make him breakfast and then take him . . . somewhere for the day."

Britt pushed her lips to the side. "Tomorrow's Sunday, so I have the day off. You and Duncan and I could go hiking at Olympic National Park and have a picnic lunch up at Wagonwheel Lake."

"Sold."

"I cannot believe he showed up here," Britt stated.

"Me neither," Nora said.

Willow contemplated Nora. "I didn't realize that you and Duncan were such good friends."

"We're pretty good friends," Nora conceded.

"Do you guys chat online every day?" Britt asked.

"Some days we chat several times a day. Some days not at all."

"Do you think he has romantic intentions toward you?" Britt asked.

Both sisters waited, their curiosity trained on her. Nora was far more used to training her curiosity on one of them. Usually Willow and Britt led far more interesting lives than she did. "I don't know what to think. We flirt online, but in a harmless type of way that I never thought would lead to anything. The dynamic between us in person feels new and a lot more . . . careful."

"What about John?" Britt asked.

"I think John's upset with me."

"It looked like you two were on a date tonight," Britt said.

"It did?"

"Yes," Willow and Britt said in unison.

"It felt like we were on a date," Nora said honestly. "Then Duncan arrived."

"I like John," Britt said.

"I like him, too," Willow said. "Even if he does have bad taste in friends."

"However," Britt said, "the operative word concerning the cute British guy is—"

"British?" Nora asked with false innocence.

"Cute," Willow supplied.

• • •

Text message from Duncan's personal assistant to Duncan:

Personal Assistant
Well? How's the mysterious American woman in real life?

Duncan
She's even better than I imagined.

Personal Assistant
You like her, then.

Duncan
I like her very much.

• • •

Text message from Corbin to his friend, Gray:

Corbin
I ran into Willow Bradford tonight. Remember her?

Gray
I remember. How does she look?

Corbin
Like a supermodel.

Gray
My condolences.

Corbin

It's not right or fair how beautiful she is. It's not even normal.

Gray

My sincere condolences.

Corbin

It's bad enough that I have memories of her I can't get rid of.

Gray

Maybe she's just as upset about seeing you?

Corbin

Why would she be? She's the one who ended things between us.

CHAPTER Sixteen

John was in a black mood.

When he'd arrived home from the party earlier, he'd whipped off his tie and jacket, then yanked free the first two buttons on his shirt. He'd stared into his refrigerator, fuming, until he'd finally remembered that he wasn't hungry. Then he'd gone into his living room and turned on a Netflix series he'd been watching about two government agents. The show offered action, gun fights, and explosions.

This is television, he wanted to tell Nora. Slow-moving shows set long ago in Europe weren't entertaining. The actors looked like they were dressed for Halloween, and all they did was talk. Between their accents and their old-fashioned language, he had a hard time understanding what they were saying. He also had a hard time caring.

Even though his perfectly good show was on and a perfectly good interrogation scene was happening, John couldn't concentrate. He slid lower into his sofa and bent his elbow over his eyes.

An actor from *Northamptonshire* had come from England to be with Nora. And even though the show and the actor meant nothing to him, they obviously meant a lot to her.

Duncan plays the role of my favorite character. Nora's cheeks had been pink, and she'd been breathless when she'd introduced him. Duncan had stood next to her looking full of himself, and John had wanted to punch him in his English face.

Women all across America were in love with actors. It was what bankrolled the careers of Hollywood's leading men. What were the chances, though, that an actor would travel to see a female fan?

One in a thousand? A million? Yet he'd just watched it happen.

It sounded like Nora had been communicating with Duncan for years, like they messaged each other all the time. Duncan had even said that Nora talked to him about the Navy SEAL. The two of them had been talking to each other about *him*. What had Nora told Duncan? And if she'd told Duncan about him, why hadn't she told him about Duncan?

There was no doubt that Duncan had a thing for Nora and that the two of them were perfect for each other. Duncan was probably the type of man who'd enjoy making antique recipes and visiting museums.

Duncan was also the type of man who'd get to keep his eyesight.

Maybe Duncan's arrival was God's way of telling John to back off Nora. The timing, Duncan showing up when he had, made it look like that was exactly what God was saying.

However, John was in pretty close communication with God, and he didn't sense God leading him to back off. The idea of letting Duncan have Nora affected him like a hand gripping his throat.

He prowled from the sofa and stalked into the cold night air of his deck.

He'd waited to break up with Allie. Then, after he'd broken up with her, he'd waited again because he hadn't wanted to rush. If he'd called Nora the day after breaking up with Allie, it would have been disrespectful to both women, and it wouldn't have reflected well on the seriousness of his intentions toward Nora. He'd also waited because he'd been torn. He'd needed time to come to grips with the fact that he'd be asking Nora to date a man who was losing his sight. He'd wrestled with that. Was still wrestling with it.

In the end it didn't matter why he'd waited. Regardless of his reasons, he'd waited too long.

What was he going to do?

If Nora felt about him the way that he felt about her, then a visit from a British celebrity would make no difference. He could hold his silence and wait until Duncan left.

Only he'd never told her how he felt about her, nor explained his condition. Surely . . . surely she knew how he felt. Surely she'd been able to tell tonight how he felt.

But maybe not.

What was certain: Over the next few days, Nora would have to make decisions about Duncan and him without the benefit of complete information. His time in the Navy had taught him that disasters happened when people made decisions based on incomplete information.

Could he stand to wait and risk her choosing Duncan?

Could he step back and let Duncan have her? Was that what a truly unselfish man would do?

Could his pride stand it if he went to Nora and told her outright about his blindness and his feelings for her?

John had no answers.

The powerlessness and bitterness he'd been pushing down for months concerning his blindness gathered into a black hole of jealousy.

He'd waited too long.

"We haven't seen your sister since we parked," Duncan said to Nora. "Are you worried?"

"Not at all." Nora's breath came in puffs. They'd been hiking for well over an hour in the national forest. "If Britt can be believed and this alleged Wagonwheel Lake really is somewhere ahead of us, then she'll be waiting there. We'll probably find her wrangling dolphins."

Britt had gotten them going on the correct path, then left them in the dust kicked up by her hiking boots. Though they all carried a portion of their picnic lunch in three separate backpacks, Nora knew that Britt had given herself the heaviest one. It hadn't slowed her down.

"How about we stop and take a breather?" Nora suggested.

"Yes, please."

"Just because Britt's a specimen of adventurousness and athleticism doesn't mean we have to be."

"Hear, hear."

They sat on a log that had fallen parallel to the path. She handed him a bottled water, unscrewed the cap on her own, and listened as he continued to fill her in on the behind-the-scenes politics of *Northamptonshire*.

They'd been following a twisting path over tree roots and occasional trickles of water. It was so green here at the forest's base that it seemed almost otherworldly, more suited to fairies than humans. A haze the color of emerald tinged everything. Springy ferns blanketed the ground. Algae, moss, and lichen crept up tree trunks and fell from the branches like cobwebs. In the distance, Nora could hear the tumble of a river, a sound that only underscored the quiet of their bower of nature.

"On movie sets the writers are far down the chain of command," Duncan was saying. "But on television sets, the writers are king. Try as I might, I just haven't been able to get myself into the good graces of Hugh Mackinsby."

"I don't know about that. Your part is delicious."

"My part is small. I wish you could have been there during my meetings with the team when the series was in pre-production. There was such enthusiasm for Adolphus and his storyline. Such enthusiasm for me in the role. It was all optimism and great expectations."

"Do you think part of that was tied to the team's optimism and expectations for the show as a whole?"

He appeared to mull her question over.

"The show is outstanding," she stated. "It must be difficult for everyone involved to put out something so outstanding and not be immediately met with commercial success. Whatever amount of frustration you or the producers or the directors are experiencing, I share, because the show *should* be a runaway hit. It's that good. That deserving."

"I agree with you, of course. I've blown a gasket plenty of times over the status of the show. Ultimately I've had to make peace with the fact that no one actor can control the fate of an entire show. Not even me. I've given my role my level best. You know I have."

"I know you have, and it absolutely shows. You were nominated for an award by the British Academy of Film and Television, don't forget."

"That was two years ago, and I didn't win. Little good the nomination did me with Hugh, because he's yet to lift Adolphus up and bring him to the fore."

No one besides Duncan wanted additional screen time for Adolphus more than she did. However, Nora's sensible side wouldn't let her forget that Adolphus had been a secondary character from the start. Duncan had the exact same size role now that Hugh had allotted him in episode one, season one. It wasn't as if Duncan had been promised the moon and given a one-pound bag of moon dust. It was more that he'd been given a one-pound bag of moon dust, been thrilled with it at first, but grown disillusioned with it over time.

"It's difficult to be filled with hope when you accept a role," Duncan said, "and then to feel unappreciated as time goes by."

"You're not unappreciated by the Devotees."

He smiled at her gratefully. "You and that group have kept me going, Nora."

"You can count on us to continue supporting you."

Until now she'd only ever seen Duncan through the lens of a camera. It dazzled her to look at him without a filter. He wore an Adidas track suit with pant legs so slim-fitting they tapered inward over his calves. He'd double-knotted the laces on his pair of Pumas.

The getup read as European, yet not at all Adolphus-like. Adolphus wore muslin shirts, cravats, cutaway coats, breeches, boots.

All morning long she'd been startled by the contrasts between Duncan and Adolphus. It was ridiculous! Adolphus was the fictional creation of Hugh Mackinsby. Duncan was the person who brought Adolphus to life.

She'd had an online friendship with Duncan. Yet, in many ways, *Adolphus* was the man she knew inside and out, the man she loved.

Adolphus was a genius. He spoke with such speed and complexity that Nora often had to rewind and re-listen to his dialogue just to make sure she'd deciphered it correctly. She'd memorized some of his witticisms, and she and her fellow Devotees quoted them to one another.

Adolphus was brooding.

Adolphus was tortured by the tragic death of his mother during his boyhood and the abuse and neglect he'd endured in the aftermath.

Adolphus was quiet.

Duncan did not speak with great speed and complexity. Honestly, it wasn't humanly possible for *anyone* to speak off the top of their head the way Adolphus did. Not only could neither Duncan nor Nora aspire to Adolphus's level, but neither of them were even as witty in actual conversation as they were with one another online.

Duncan was not brooding. Quite the contrary. He was easy with people. Personable. Energetic, even.

Duncan wasn't tortured. He was the adored only son of a journalist mother and professor father. He'd been raised comfortably and with every advantage and opportunity.

Duncan was not quiet. In fact, the two of them had been talking without a moment's pause. She'd put in hours of conversation already today. Hours.

Duncan enjoyed verbally dissecting a subject down to the tiniest detail. Just when it seemed everything had been said that could be said, he'd pose a different way of looking at the subject, then consider it still more.

An overabundance of conversation was far preferable to having nothing to say. At the same time, Nora was accustomed to communicating with Duncan in snappy, bite-sized pieces. When their hike was over and they returned to Merryweather, she'd need a vacation of silence and a book in order to recover from all the talking.

John had said far less during their entire trip to Oregon than Duncan had said so far today.

John. The thought of him caused a *pang* deep in her chest. She'd heard nothing from him since last night. She'd gone over and back over how she'd reacted to Duncan's arrival at the party and John's subsequent departure from it.

She wished she hadn't called Duncan a celebrity. Also, it hadn't been necessary to say that he played the role of her *favorite* character. Other than those two regrets, she didn't see—short of shoving Duncan into the basement and hiding him—how she could have done things much differently. She'd had to bring him forward. Once she had, she'd asked John point-blank to stay and have cake with her. He was the one who'd refused.

Even so. She couldn't shake the feeling that she'd let John down. The way they'd left things last night had been hovering over her like a storm cloud.

"My contract is up after this season." Duncan nudged a pebble with the toe of his sneaker. "I may not renew. Let Mackinsby write me off. Then we'll see how he likes the great backlash he'll receive from fans."

If the Earl of Cumberly or Craddock were written off *Northamptonshire*, there would be as great a backlash as fans of a modest show could muster. Nora and the other women on Team Adolphus were a small minority. Backlash from them would be akin to a ripple in a pond.

"I'll die if Adolphus leaves the show," Nora said.

"You will?" he asked hopefully.

"Yes. Adolphus is a fantastic character, and you do an outstanding job playing him."

"There are several talented actors in the cast."

He was fishing for more compliments. She suspected that he didn't regard any of the other actors on the show to be as talented as he was. "Yes, several. But none who are as talented as you." The words made her feel a bit like the mirror in *Snow White*.

"Do you really think so?" he asked.

Must she tell him a million times? A billion? "Yes, I really think so." Surely other actors, secure actors, didn't require this much praise. Nor would secure actors probably have encouraged an actor/fan relationship like theirs in the first place.

"I don't know."

"You're adored by many, Duncan. Many. And there must be hundreds of actors who would covet your job."

"Thank you." He took her hand and squeezed it. "It's really good to talk to you, Nora. You get me. You understand. I think I just really needed this. To see you. To clear my head."

"Of course." Which did he need precisely? To see her? Or to clear his head? She'd known for some time that he relied on her support. She was a steady friend, an enthusiastic fan, a willing PR volunteer—all positions that his grandmother could just as easily fill. Did he feel differently toward her than he did his grandmother?

He broke the contact of their hands and passed over his half-finished water bottle. She dutifully zipped it into her backpack.

"Shall we forge on?" he asked.

"Let me get a picture of us first." This was the fifth picture of the two of them she'd taken. She was almost faint with desire to post one of the photos to the Devotees of Adolphus Brook group with a blithe status update along the lines of *Look who came to see me!*

Oh, the gloating. Oh, how she selfishly wanted to broadcast the message that, of all the Devotees, she was most special to their revered Duncan. The woman who'd been left by her fiancé for someone better was Duncan's favorite.

Nora typically uploaded share-worthy photos to social media within thirty seconds of having taken them. So far, though, she hadn't posted a single picture of herself with Duncan. She'd hesitated because she knew that a photo of the two of them together would give the Devotees a reason to resent her. She and the other members of the group had always enjoyed their like-minded and fruitless adoration of Duncan. A picture with Duncan would separate her out like a sheep that the herd pretended to be happy for but no longer liked.

She hadn't decided *not* to share pictures of her with Duncan. How could she not share them?! For the moment, she'd simply decided to wait and think longer about the pros and cons.

Nora extended her arm for a selfie and centered their images on the screen. Duncan adjusted the angle of his face and served up the bemused arch of his lips that she'd seen him serve up in dozens of photographs over the years. It was his patented smile. It was quite possibly the very same smile he gave his grandmother.

By the final night of Duncan's visit, Nora was ready to take a vow of silence. She'd gone to the Library on the Green early the past two mornings, crammed as much work as possible into a few hours, then spent the rest of her time with Duncan.

She'd driven him into the city, and they'd visited the Chihuly Garden and Glass exhibit at the Seattle Center, picked up coffees at the first-ever Starbucks, and walked up and down the aisles of Pike's Place famous seaside market. During every minute of their time together, they'd talked.

Talky, talkety, talk talk talk.

A dull fog had overtaken Nora's brain around noon today and steadily worsened. It was now seven forty-five in the evening, and she'd deposited Duncan at the house five minutes ago. Then she'd stolen away to her dad's hammock tucked into the woods near Bradfordwood's back terrace.

Her entire body felt drained dry. Sore eyes. Pesky headache. Heavy limbs.

She relaxed into the hammock, sinking into the blessed quiet the way she'd sink into a warm tub full of gleaming bubbles. She was desperate for cinnamon toast and tea chased by a Tylenol.

For her pajamas. For time spent burrowed under the covers with her novel. She'd head home and see to all of that. Just as soon as she could muster the energy.

Her phone binged. If Duncan had sent her a text, she might have to hurl her phone into the canal.

But it wasn't Duncan who'd sent the text.

Is it all right with you if I stop by tonight? John asked.

Her pulse kicked, then sped. This was the first she'd heard from him since Grandma's party. She'd been at war with herself over whether or not to reach out to him. She'd decided that if he hadn't contacted her by the time Duncan left tomorrow, then she'd contact him. Now this. Word from him. Praise God.

Of course! she typed. *I haven't forgotten about the talk we didn't get a chance to have the other night.*

I haven't forgotten either.

I live at 12 Blackberry Lane, Merryweather. What time?

Thirty minutes?

Perfect.

Suddenly she didn't feel especially drained. Nor terribly interested in following through on the vow of silence thing. She slid behind the wheel of her car and checked her reflection in her visor mirror. It had rained today, so even though she'd blown her hair dry this morning the way Javier had instructed, the style now looked mussed. Her makeup wasn't bad, just mostly gone. Her pale pink skinny jeans, new Tretorn sneakers, and white cotton top were decent. These days, she only had decent outfits thanks to Willow. She finger-combed her hair, applied lip gloss, and started home.

The sky darkened into a deeper and deeper shade of ebony as she drove. What did John want to talk to her about, exactly? Dating her? Please please please. Could he be . . . returning to the Navy? Moving away? Did he need to confess a secret about his book or movie? Was there something about Allie they needed to discuss? Had he fallen in love with someone else entirely—not her and not Allie? Her experience with The Dreaded Harrison assured her that such a thing was possible. Was something the matter with one of

John's family members? Or maybe he wanted to talk to her about hiring her to do more research. Into his parents' ancestry, perhaps?

Her tires rumbled over gravel as she turned off the road onto her driveway, which snaked through pine trees. She'd almost reached her house when her headlights sliced across John, leaning against her front porch post, waiting for her. He wore a black T-shirt and jeans. His arms were crossed, and he'd bent one leg and planted the sole of his black work boot against the wood behind him.

Buckets of gravy, she thought nervously and with no small amount of awe, *John is handsome.*

Also, extraordinarily punctual.

Ten minutes early, actually. He must have been in Merryweather when he'd texted her.

She climbed from her car and walked toward him.

He pushed away from the post and stood tall and resolute, hands in his pockets. The wind ruffled through his hair. His arresting features were lean and firm, his dark eyelashes the only incongruously soft aspect of an otherwise utterly masculine face.

"Well, hello there," she said, perhaps a tad too breezily. She came to a halt before him.

"Hi."

"You're early."

Laughter creases grooved the skin at the outside of his eyes. Those creases melted her heart to the consistency of a chocolate lava cake.

"I'm always early," he said.

"Very true." She was sorry that he'd been standing alone in the dark. She started to apologize, then caught herself. She was early, too. He'd just been earlier.

"I won't keep you long," he said.

Keep me. How about forever? Does keeping me forever sound about right? "Stay as long as you'd like. I'm glad to see you, John."

Looking down at his feet, he shifted his weight. "I . . ."

She waited, trying to interpret his sudden discomfort.

He lifted his head. His gaze met hers. "I'm going blind."

Her body froze while her mind whirred to absorb the statement. What he'd said didn't want to compute. John? Was going blind?

"That's what I . . ." His words disappeared into silence.

John was a specimen of fitness. His gorgeous eyes, his unbearably gorgeous eyes, could not be failing him.

"That's what I wanted to talk to you about," he said. "I wanted you to know."

• • •

Quote from Uncommon Courage*:*

> "You don't fully know yourself and what you're capable of until you're faced with the worst. The worst shows you who you are."

• • •

Text message from Duncan to Nora:

Thank you for today. I loved every minute of it because every minute was spent with you. You're an outstanding hostess, Miss Lawrence.

CHAPTER Seventeen

John heard Nora's phone chime from inside her purse. She gave no evidence of having heard. Her attention stayed wholly focused on him and the confession he'd just made.

"Oh, John." He didn't hear pity in the words, just empathy. Even so, this conversation was agonizing for him.

He'd driven here because, in the end, he hadn't heard God telling him to step aside and give Nora over to Duncan. If anything, he'd heard God prodding him to act. So he'd come, knowing she might already be in love with Duncan. He was determined to tell her the truth anyway. Then let her decide.

"Come inside." She took hold of his forearm as if it was the most natural thing in the world, then tugged him onto her small front porch. He wondered with dark humor whether she thought he already needed her to lead him around.

She kept one hand on his arm while digging in her purse for her keys with her other hand. In response to her touch, need stirred within him like a tiger waking from sleep. He stared hard at the wooden exterior of her house, struggling for control.

She'd painted her house hunter green with white trim. Green and white. He attempted to concentrate on that.

Once they were both inside, she released him to flick on lights. He drew in a deep, uneven inhale.

Her house was small. The dimensions were more suited to an apartment than a freestanding home. From his position, he could see all there was to see of the open-concept living areas.

Nora moved into her kitchen and ran water into a kettle. "My sisters call this place the Bookish Cottage. For obvious reasons."

Bookshelves covered almost every wall from floor to ceiling. Two light green chairs, an ottoman, and a television filled her living room. The chairs were the only green things in the space. Everything else was either red, white, blue, or a girly pattern that mixed those three colors. Several pieces of furniture and some of the decorations had that distressed, antique look he'd never liked.

Still, he liked Nora's house. He liked it because it was *her*.

"I found this place five years ago," she told him. "I love it except that I've run out of bookshelf space again, so I'm going to have to declare eminent domain on yet another wall. I don't have many walls left. Soon I'll have books as a kitchen backsplash."

Light shone along strands of her hair. Her diamond circle earrings glittered. The short ruffle sleeves of her shirt kept fluttering around her slender shoulders. She looked like spring after a long, gray winter. He couldn't think of anything . . . not one thing . . . to say.

Her phone chimed again. She ignored it again.

"I'm going to make us tea." She set the kettle into a machine. "I know you think you don't like tea, but since you're in my house and therefore my captive, I'm making you tea. You'll see how delicious it can be."

Something here was delicious, that was for sure.

"This is my tea maker, and it's genius because the basket rises and lowers to infuse the tea just so. Different varieties need different brew times and temperatures and with this, I'm able to program all that in."

He nodded. She didn't seem to require him to say much, which he appreciated. He set a hip against her table and watched her.

"I use loose tea leaves, of course, and I craft my own blends. I think tonight calls for something sweet and soothing."

Something here was sweet and soothing, that was for sure. "Okay."

She pulled a loaf of white bread from the cupboard. "I'm also going to make us cinnamon toast. To go with our tea. Does that sound all right?"

"What, no scones?"

"What do you know about scones, John Lawson?"

"Only that some women eat them with tea."

She laughed. "Scones would be ideal, I concede. I love scones, but since I have no scones, I'm making us cinnamon toast. Not just any cinnamon toast but the kind my mom used to make for me when I was sick." She set four pieces of bread on a cookie sheet and spread butter over them. "While I'm making this you can begin to tell me what's going on with your vision."

He hesitated.

"Go on." She spun the butter knife in an encouraging motion.

"About four months ago, I was at my parents' house when I noticed that their Venetian blinds didn't look straight to me. They looked wavy in the middle."

"But they weren't wavy? They just appeared that way to you?"

"Right. So I went to see an ophthalmologist. He found a pattern of small white dots on my retinas."

She regarded him for a long moment, then sprinkled sugar and cinnamon over the buttered bread. She lit her oven's broiler and slid the cookie sheet in.

Her phone chimed for the third time since he'd arrived. "Are you going to check that?" he asked. "It might be the Englishman."

"I can check it later."

"Or it might be an emergency."

"I can check it now." She picked up her phone. "It's the Englishman." After clicking the tab on the phone's side to silence it, she set it facedown and stooped to peek at the toast. "Continue with what you were saying."

"The ophthalmologist suspected that I might have something called Malattia Leventinese. A DNA test confirmed that I did."

She pulled the toast from the oven, then arranged the slices on a plate. Once she'd poured tea into mugs, she placed everything on a tray. He came forward and lifted the tray for her.

"It's a beautiful night." She preceded him into the living room and opened the French doors that led to a patio at the back of the house. "Let's sit outside."

Two Adirondack chairs waited beneath the halo of an outdoor light. Her deck descended two more levels, following the slope of the hill toward what must be the canal. He'd seen on the GPS map that her house stood in an isolated spot not far from the canal. During daylight hours, she no doubt had a view of the water.

It seemed that they both liked houses out of sight of any neighbor, but within sight of water.

Sight. That word. While her house and his would always have views of water, he himself would not.

He set the tray on the small table between the chairs.

She instructed him to make himself comfortable, ducked inside, and reappeared with two throw blankets. She offered him one.

"No thanks." He leaned into one of the chairs and bent an arm back, setting his hand behind his head.

"Don't you get cold?" she asked.

"Not often." He'd endured his share of harsh conditions. He didn't need a blanket to keep warm on a summer night.

She unfurled the blankets with a flick and tucked them around herself as she settled in her chair.

He was struck by how much he liked to watch her. Just that. Just to watch her made him happy and brought him peace.

"Try the tea and toast." She picked up her mug.

"The toast is delicious." And it was. Soft on the bottom with a warm, brown crust of sugar and cinnamon on top.

"The tea's delicious, too," she informed him.

"Aren't I the one who's supposed to compliment the tea?"

"It's rooibos, with berries, blossoms, and a dash of vanilla, if you must know." She slanted him a stern look from beneath her brows, and he almost burst out laughing. "Try it already."

The tea didn't taste or smell like any tea he'd had before. It smelled like vanilla and flowers. It was full of flavor but also subtle. Not at all bitter. "It's very good."

"Thank you." She gave him an I-told-you-so look over the rim of her mug. Steam rose in front of her features. She took another sip.

He wasn't used to caring this much for a woman or to the vulnerability that brought with it.

"I haven't heard of Malattia Leventinese before." She pronounced it perfectly, which showed him she'd been listening earlier.

"I hadn't heard of it either until my doctor told me about it. It's a form of macular degeneration."

"Which is?"

"Macular degeneration is vision loss in the center of the field of vision that's usually age-related."

"But in your case, it's not age-related."

"No. Malattia Leventinese can strike teenagers. People with it usually notice symptoms before the age of forty."

"What do the doctors say about your prognosis?"

"My vision will get worse and worse. There are treatments that can provide some benefits but nothing that can stop it. Nothing that can reverse it."

Her stare didn't waver. "Do they expect your vision to deteriorate quickly or slowly?"

"It depends. With this condition, they're concerned about the possibility of some sort of hemorrhage and also something to do with red blood cells. Those complications can happen, and if they happen to me my eyesight will go down fast."

"And if those complications don't happen?"

"Then my eyesight will deteriorate more slowly."

"Slowly across the rest of your life slowly? Or slowly over the next five years slowly?"

"They don't know. It just depends."

"Does it hurt?"

"No." She was his friend, and he trusted her. He was surprised to realize that the conversation had grown less agonizing for him. Explaining this to her was beginning to feel like lifting a mountain he'd grown tired of carrying off his shoulders.

He polished off the first piece of toast and started on the second.

She watched him with a soft expression as he took another drink of her tea. "Our trip to Oregon," she said. "You told me that your employees needed your car. Was that true? Or were you not comfortable driving to Oregon and back because of your vision?"

Nora was smart. Too smart for his comfort at times. "I drive myself around this part of Washington fine. My vision's at 20/40 right now, so I wear glasses when I drive to bring it closer to 20/20 or 20/30. But my eyesight is still blurry in the center."

She nodded.

"They've taught me how to turn my head and look out of the sides of my eyes at the road. But I'm not used to it yet. There was no way I was driving you all the way to Oregon like that. I wouldn't . . ." *put you at risk. Not for any reason.* "I'm sorry I lied. I wasn't ready to tell you the truth."

"I'm glad you were ready tonight." She rested her shoulder into the chair's back and turned toward him. The blankets wrapped around her lower half. "Who else knows?"

"My family. Allie."

A pause. "You said that a DNA test confirmed that you had Malattia Leventinese," she said. "Does that mean that the condition is inherited?"

"Exactly."

"And naturally you'd want a medical history. So it was your diagnosis that motivated you to search for your birth mother."

"Yes." He finished the toast and brushed the crumbs from his hands. "I'd been interested in locating my birth mother for a long time, but when I found out about my eyesight it pushed me to take action." He wanted to know which parent he'd inherited it from. He wanted to know how that parent's eyesight was at their age. How any grandparents or great-aunts or uncles with the disease were doing. Whether he had half-siblings with the condition.

"Is Malattia Leventinese something that both parents have to be carriers of? Or just one parent?"

"Just one. If either parent has the gene mutation that causes it, then each of their children has a 50 percent chance of inheriting the same gene mutation."

"What about kids who don't inherit the gene mutation? Can they still pass it along to their kids?"

"No." Was she grasping what his genetic history meant for his future? "If I hadn't noticed the change in my vision, I wouldn't have known about the condition, and I might have gone on to marry and have kids of my own. But now I do know." He turned his focus upward. Around and above them, dark trees towered. "Just like I had a 50 percent chance of inheriting this, any child of mine would have a 50 percent chance of inheriting it from me."

Silence.

It was strange to feel a sense of loss over something that didn't exist. Lots of people must experience that feeling. People who became paralyzed must mourn the mobility they could have had. People who were told they had a short time to live must mourn the years they wouldn't receive. People who lost loved ones must mourn the life they'd planned to live with that person in it.

Those situations were all far worse than his. But John's situation was what he had in front of him to deal with. He was sorry for the vision he wouldn't get to keep. And he was sorry, very sorry, for the children he wouldn't get to have. "I wouldn't risk passing this down to an innocent child." The wind in the branches made a swishing sound.

"Wouldn't you?" she asked thoughtfully.

"No." His muscles tightened reflexively.

"I have a confession," she whispered.

He gazed at her.

"I don't know what to say. I'm racking my brain, trying to think of something that might make you feel better." She wrinkled her forehead. "I'm usually great at knowing what to say and when to say it. My intuition for these things is *usually* excellent. For instance, with one person I might sense that they needed to hear me say, 'This diagnosis stinks and I just want you to know that I'm with you in your anger and sorrow.' With another person I might say, 'This diagnosis might be indubitable, but I know you. And believe me when I say that your life, your one-of-a-kind life, will still be full of wonder and beauty, even with this diagnosis. That's indubitable, too.' With another I might say, 'Let's get a second and third opinion, then make a list of exactly what we're going to do to fight this.' Which of those would you most like to hear, John? Because I mean every word of each of them."

A grin tugged at his lips. He liked that Nora had confessed her indecision about what to say instead of rattling off what she thought he wanted to hear. "Did you just use the word *indubitable*?"

"Indubitable was the perfect word in that context. It communicated my meaning exactly."

"Have I ever told you that I like your vocabulary?"

She blinked. "No. You like it?"

"I really like it."

They held eye contact across the space that separated their chairs. His blood began to pump with awareness.

"What can I say to make you feel better?" she asked.

"What you said already made me feel better."

"What did I say that had that effect? Indubitable?"

"Exactly."

"Indubitable, John. Indubitable. Indubitable."

He chuckled.

"*Indubitable.*" She smiled at him.

Her smile made him hope. It tempted him to think that there might be a future for the two of them. That everything really might turn out all right, because of her.

Her.

The need within him grew so physically powerful that a bolt of fear chased it. He pushed from his chair. He should go.

She slanted her face to him questioningly. "Are you getting up to get more tea or are you abruptly departing?"

"I'm abruptly departing. And I think that's the first time in my life I've ever used the word *abruptly*."

Her blankets dropped from her as she rose. "Feel free to stay. I have enough tea leaves to last for several more pots."

"I didn't mean to keep you long. Even this long."

"Why is it that people you want to stay always insist on leaving early and people you're ready to usher out always linger and linger?"

She'd been honest with him just now. Her honesty felt like an invitation to be equally honest with her. A heavy pause stretched between them.

"I want to go out with you, Nora," he said bluntly.

Her lips parted.

"I want us to be together," he added, just so there'd be no misunderstanding. He didn't want her thinking he was asking her out on another paid research assignment. "I felt like you had a right to know these things so you could make an informed decision about me. And the Englishman."

"Oh."

She didn't rush to tell him she didn't like Duncan, which made his gut knot. "Take your time. Think on it. If you'd rather we be friends, I'll understand. No hard feelings." Even as he said the noble thing, some *very* hard feelings—so hard their edges were as sharp as swords—dug into him. "When you've decided, call me or text me or drop by my house."

"Drop by? Really?"

"Of course. Anytime."

She peered at him, a beautiful redheaded statue in pink pants who'd been shocked into silence.

"Thanks for the tea and the toast," he said.

"You're welcome."

"Good night."

He was halfway through the back doors when she said, "John?"

He glanced at her.

"Indubitable."

He dipped his chin and left.

Nora's hands came up to cover the lower half of her face. She couldn't move. Couldn't believe that John had just said what he'd said to her.

"If you'd rather we be friends, I'll understand. . . ."

No, John. She almost dissolved into hysterical laughter. *I wouldn't rather we be friends.* He was certifiably impossible not to want. She'd wanted him—to like her, kiss her, be her boyfriend—since the first moment she'd seen him. Of course she had! She was a spinster librarian. The difficult thing to comprehend was that *he'd* want to be more than friends with *her*.

But . . . it seemed he did.

"Great Scott," she whispered.

Since the day she'd received his text at Sweet Art, her longings had been trying to coax her brain into thinking that Britt's theory might be right. That John had texted her because he was interested. But she'd been terrified, frankly, to give those longings a toehold. Only now did she dare believe it. The realization that he liked her cascaded through her like champagne.

He'd told her he'd come tonight to provide her with information so that she could make an informed decision. He'd encouraged her to take her time, and then, before she'd collected herself enough to form the words that might have convinced him to stay, he'd gone.

He'd behaved like a man who'd had months to consider his condition, knew how difficult the subject was, and fully expected her to think through everything carefully before deciding whether or not to invest her heart in him.

The fact that he'd taken pains to tell her all this before so much as going on a single date spoke volumes about his character. He was nothing like the shady guys who hid everything about themselves until their girlfriends fell in love with them. Then divulged that they had a criminal record, a stalker ex-wife, loads of debt, a drinking problem, and cooties.

Nora folded the throw blankets and returned them to the wicker basket inside. She carried the tray to her sink and went to work straightening her kitchen.

She respected John's thoughtful, deliberate approach. The genetic eye condition he'd just described was an incredibly serious thing. She could imagine how the news that he had Malattia Leventinese must have jarred him because she'd once been jarred, too—by Harrison. The shocks she and John had received in their lives had meant, for both of them, that their futures wouldn't look the way they'd hoped or expected.

John's future *literally* would not look the way he'd expected.

So many, many blessings in Nora's life had flowed to her through her ability to see. The view of the canal from her house filled her with pleasure. Reading was her greatest joy. Watching *Northamptonshire*. Looking at the beloved buildings in her historical village, each one with a history and charm of its own, ranked right up there. So did staring at John.

She relied on her vision in order to accomplish almost every aspect of her work. Her vision gave her independence and autonomy.

The coming decrease in his independence and autonomy was probably at the core of what John was working through at the moment. He wasn't a regular guy. He was a man so physically superior that he'd been part of one of the most elite fighting forces on the planet. His aura of proficiency had been one of the first things she'd noticed about him.

The idea of *this particular man* having to accept *this particular fate* caused pain to scrape against her like the tines of a fork. No doubt, he was grappling with who he'd be once diminished eyesight took away some of the things he'd built his identity on.

She slotted dishes into the dishwasher.

John had a flaw. She marveled over the fact that his imperfection didn't diminish him in her eyes. If anything, she felt more connected to him than she had before because, tonight, he'd finally let her in. He'd been real with her, and now she understood his truth that much better.

No matter how fabulously perfect John had appeared, or how much she'd enjoyed putting him on a pedestal, she'd understood from the start that he could not possibly *be* perfect.

He was close. She smiled to herself. He was very close. Only make-believe men like Adolphus Brook were perfect.

Just like every other human being, John had faults. He was a man facing a struggle, a struggle she could perhaps help him with—and God knew how much she loved to be helpful.

So, no. His weakness did not dissuade her. She was crazy about so many of his qualities, too many to count, that had nothing to do with his ability to fell dragons. In some deep, intrinsic way, she and John were at heart level a matched pair. His deficiencies and proficiencies and her deficiencies and proficiencies had been constructed to click together like two Legos.

She wanted to date him. Badly, she wanted it.

However, she'd had very little time to comprehend what the reality of blindness would entail. She'd respond to his thoughtfulness and deliberation with thoughtfulness and deliberation of her own.

She left a night-light on in her kitchen, like always. After double checking to make sure that all the doors were locked, she got water flowing into her bathtub. She added a squirt of bubble bath and lowered in. No need of a book tonight, thanks. Her mind was overfull as it was.

She was a researcher. Before she saw John next, she'd do a copious amount of research into Malattia Leventinese. She'd find out what life was like for those with impaired vision and what their loved ones could do to support them. She'd also find out more about John's reproductive options.

John had been powerless to opt in or opt out of his fate, which likely explained why he'd gone to great pains to give her a way to opt out and why he wanted to opt out on behalf of his future children.

However, when he'd informed her of his refusal to father children, it had seemed to Nora that she was hearing his grief talking. In time, he might change his mind.

Or he very well might not.

Ever since her engagement went kaput, she'd assigned herself to the role of doting, single aunt to her future nieces and nephews. Just the prospect of becoming John's girlfriend was blowing her mind at present. Imagining herself and John as a married couple who wanted to have children together felt utterly fantastical. If that pie-in-the-sky thing ever were to happen, and he didn't want to have biological children—then yes, she could see how she would mourn that. If married to him, then she'd want their babies to be his and her babies. Sure.

On the other hand, if they loved each other enough to get married, then she knew herself well enough to know that she'd be willing to make sacrifices for him. That's what love did. That's what love was.

On the whole, a hazy, potential future that included parenthood was just too remote to be of much consequence to her now. In the here and now, she was deciding yes or no to a boyfriend. The ability to sire children was not a quality she deemed important in a boyfriend.

Again, though. This was all very new. She'd think on it. She'd pray on it.

Skin pink and dry, she went to her dresser and slid out her pajama drawer. Her pajamas with the Adolphus quote waited on top.

To be as forthright toward Duncan as John had just been toward her, she really did need to speak with Duncan first thing tomorrow and make sure they were both in agreement as to the status of their relationship. At times over the past few days, she'd suspected that Duncan liked her as more than a superfan.

She bypassed her Adolphus pajamas and selected the pair that had arrived in the mail last week. The drawstring bottoms were pink gingham. The matching cotton T-shirt was emblazoned with the words *U.S. NAVY SEALS. The only easy day was yesterday.*

• • •

Phone conversation between Allie and her best friend, Lizzie:

Allie: I was just going through my hallway closet and guess what I found? Full scuba diving gear! Mask, fins, regulator, tank!

Lizzie: Why is this worthy of such an excited tone of voice?

Allie: I've been racking my brain for a reason to see John again that would allow me to appear as if I don't care about our breakup and have gone on to be fabulous without him. Men can never resist that in a woman, can they? Fabulousness without them?

Lizzie: Nope. They never can resist that.

Allie: This news is worthy of an excited tone of voice because this scuba gear belongs to *John*. A few months ago we went scuba diving, and he told me to hang on to the equipment until we went scuba diving together again. I stashed the stuff in a bag in the closet and forgot about it. But now I'm honor-bound to visit him so that I can return his gear. Aren't I?

Lizzie: Yes. I approve. You have my official endorsement.

• • •

Email from Grandma to Willow, Nora, and Britt:

Girls, I've been suffering from constipation ever since that very expensive party you threw for me the other night. I think this is the fault of that extremely rich cake. Have any of you been experiencing similar difficulties? If so, I insist you use milk of magnesia. Under no circumstances should you resort to an enema.

Sincerely, Grandma

• • •

Email from Britt to Willow and Nora:

Constipation!!! From a cake? I'm highly offended on behalf of my top-notch cake. I'm thinking about purchasing an enema just to spite Grandma.

• • •

Email from Willow to Nora and Britt:

If I had to guess I'd say that the disgruntlement Grandma's been swallowing is the source of her constipation. I've been eating leftover slices of your top-notch cake daily without complication.

• • •

Email from Nora to Willow and Britt:

I'm unable to work up any annoyance toward Grandma at the moment because John came by to ask me out an hour and a half ago. My psyche is too busy being overjoyed.

• • •

Email from Britt to Nora and Willow:

Nora, you're a hunk magnet! I suggest you take the Navy SEAL straight to the nearest wedding chapel.

• • •

Email from Willow to Nora and Britt:

I concur with Britt about the wedding chapel. Just be sure to think it through before you decide to live dangerously and let Britt bake your wedding cake.

p.s. What are you going to do about the cute British guy?

CHAPTER
Eighteen

Duncan scooted his chair closer to Nora's. "I've loved spending time with you these last few days."

"Likewise."

"We've always had a great rapport online. You're stellar in cyberspace." The word *stellar* sounded charmingly crisp and hard-edged spoken in his British accent.

"You're stellar in cyberspace, too. Only it doesn't come out as cute when I say it. Stellar," she said, employing her best imitation British accent.

Instead of making him breakfast this morning, she'd collected Duncan at Bradfordwood and driven him to The Griddle, her favorite breakfast restaurant in Merryweather. Lots of old brick, a fireplace, and plenty of dark wood surrounded them. She'd very much like to enjoy the cozy ambience and the plate of food their waitress had just set before her. Huge biscuits sat beside an over-easy egg, hash browns, and bacon. Eating breakfast out was somewhat akin to eating chocolate at the beach . . . a luxury. Steam twirled upward from the food, begging her to dig in.

Except Duncan was staring at her with an intensity that required her full attention. Mirth still lingered at his lips. "Here's the thing . . ." His voice took on a husky, conspirational timbre.

Uh-oh. Dread zinged through Nora.

"Even though you're stellar in cyberspace," he said, "I had no way of knowing how endearing you'd be in person. Until this trip."

"Thank you!"

"You're endearing, and you're a beauty," he stated.

Nora took a sip of coffee. Whenever she ordered coffee instead of tea, it was very much a desperate times/desperate measures type of situation. She'd lain in bed, an expression of dreamy amazement on her face, her thoughts twisting like a corkscrew, for hours last night after John's visit. Thus, she was functioning on four hours of sleep. She knew she'd need caffeine and lots of it in order to survive this breakfast and the unceasing talking that awaited her between here and the airport, where they were headed next.

Duncan placed a hand on the table and turned it palm up, then slanted his handsome head and gave her the smile he employed for photographs.

Reluctance pricked her. Was it too late for her to text Duncan, claim an illness, and cancel this breakfast?

This is what adult women do, Nora. They deal with uncomfortable situations in mature ways. She placed her hand in his, while simultaneously wondering if holding his hand was the mature thing to do. Holding Duncan's hand wasn't terribly disloyal to John, was it? It felt like it might be, yet she hadn't gone out (yet) on a single date with John. Plus, Duncan might be wanting to hold her hand because he harbored the same kind of affection toward her that he harbored toward his grandmother.

"Do you remember messaging me not so long ago to say that if Adolphus noticed Lucy's existence, she would be his?" he asked.

"Mmm?"

"Heart and soul."

"I said that?"

"Always and forever."

She feigned surprised pleasure. "Are Adolphus and Lucy finally getting together on the show?" Her deliberate misunderstanding was an extremely wimpy way to buy time.

"You know I can't divulge upcoming plot twists. My lips are sealed about Adolphus and Lucy."

How about you allow me to unseal mine so I can dig into these biscuits? The floury, fresh-out-of-the-oven smell of them was making her stomach weep. Slightly desperate for a coffee refill, she tried to catch the waitress's eye.

"The point I'm trying to make is that *I've* noticed *your* existence, Miss Lawrence."

Nora forced her attention to him. There'd been a time when she'd danced around her house each and every time he'd called her Miss Lawrence. Now it annoyed the tar out of her. Miss Lawrence was an intelligent woman who was wasting her life pining for a fantasy.

Duncan gave her an expression akin to that of a parent leading their kids into the living room on Christmas morning to see Santa's haul. Self-satisfied. Benevolent. Expectant.

Then he leaned his face toward hers. Not quickly. Slowly. Did . . . did he mean to kiss her? Before he could, she reared back.

He stopped his progress. Confusion tweaked his forehead.

"I'm sorry." Her hand was still ensconced within his. She slipped it free, then tucked her hair behind her ears. "I may not have handled that well."

"Aw" he said as if she were a child who'd done something adorable. "Of course you're nervous."

He thought she was rattled by the supreme magnitude of his interest in her. She understood his deduction. It was quite preposterous to think that she, Nora Bradford, would reject famous actor Duncan Bartholomew.

His affection for her complimented her. His talent impressed her. But she didn't want to kiss him. If Adolphus Brook or John Lawson pulled her into, say, a quiet alcove and set her against a wall and pressed their hands to the plaster on both sides of her head and met her eyes and leaned in, she'd yearn to be kissed by them. She'd tunnel her hands into their hair and pull them to her. She'd combust with desire.

Duncan was a friendly, insecure, and enormously gifted man. Whenever he went into a funk over things that didn't go his way, he relied on her for encouragement. Whenever he required extra effort from his fandom, he depended on her as his best soldier. She was a woman who loved to be needed. But in the end, she didn't want to be needed by a boyfriend in those specific ways.

Duncan looked young to her, sitting there in front of his plate of pancakes. His cheeks were smooth. His build youthful. He was two years younger than she was, she remembered. And an only child.

More age would benefit him. More weathering. More of the kind of life experiences that would force him to realize that he might not be the center of everyone's universe.

She liked Duncan a great deal. But, no. She did not want to kiss him.

"Let's try that again, shall we?" he murmured and once again began leaning into her personal space.

"No," she said calmly.

He halted.

"I didn't scoot back just now because I was nervous, Duncan. I did it because I view you as a friend."

A beat of quiet. "Only as a friend?"

"Only as a friend."

For such a good actor, he was having a hard time covering his astonishment. She bit back an inappropriate giggle. "The two of us are better as friends than as anything else. You're too famous for me. Too good-looking." She spoke guilelessly, as if unaware of the fact that she was working him over with flattery. If he had any sense, he'd call her on it. But he seemed to be receiving the thick flattery as if it were his due. "You're also a resident of a country that's very far away. You know how I prefer to be realistic."

As she said it, she recognized it to be true.

Realistic.

For the first time in three years, she wanted the real man down the road more than the fictional man on the small screen. Real men were dangerous. They could shred your heart and decimate your trust. But real men, with their weaknesses and their strengths, were also the ones who could eat cinnamon toast with you and take you to hotels in Oregon that overlooked a valley of treasures. Real men were the ones who could smile with you and listen to you and hold you. Real men were the ones brave women entered into relationships with—even if relationships were sometimes messy and without guarantees.

Her book-loving, PBS-drama-loving soul wanted to refute it. The fictional men she'd fallen in love with congregated in her imagination, Adolphus Brook right at the apex of them. *But, but,* they seemed to sputter, *look at us. Remember us. We're perfect.*

Yes, she patiently responded. *And John's imperfect. But, you see, it was his admission of his imperfection that won me so completely. I'm imperfect, too.*

"Don't you agree?" Nora asked him. "I could never fit into your life."

He considered her.

"You know it's true," she prodded. "I could never fit."

He shrugged. "You may have a point."

"Of course I do. I'm a very sensible person. I always have a point. Now, dig into those pancakes and tell me more about your summer shooting schedule for the show and what the Devotees can do to promote it."

He headed down the conversational track she'd provided.

Nora would not share a single photo of herself and Duncan with the Devotees. It was enough that her sisters and John had seen Duncan. They could attest to the fact that for a few days the actor who played her favorite character on her favorite show had entered into her life in Merryweather, Washington. She hadn't dreamed it. He'd been here.

He'd wanted her.

And she'd turned him, her fantasy man, down.

John could look at himself in the mirror because he was pretty sure he'd done the right thing when he'd told Nora about his eyesight and the future he was facing.

It turned out that doing the right thing was cold comfort.

Almost three days had passed since his visit to her house, and he'd yet to hear from her.

He'd hiked to the top of Mount Lewis and now stood, arms crossed, staring hard at Lake Shore Pine far below. His house and the boats enjoying a Saturday afternoon on the water looked toy-sized.

Every day he spent time committing the sight of things to memory. Sometimes he'd catch himself doing it even when he hadn't planned to. The thing he'd been staring at the most since his diagnosis was one of the things he loved the most and would miss looking at the most: this place. This lake that his grandfather had introduced him to, where he'd learned to drive a boat, where his connection to the water had begun, where he'd felt completely at home.

He drew in a painful breath of fresh, clean air.

When he and Nora had been searching for Sherry, Nora had helped him forget about his diagnosis. Now she was the one keeping his diagnosis at the front of his thoughts because he didn't know what Nora was going to do with the information he'd given her.

She might choose for him. She might choose against him. She might send him a text message saying she cared about him. She might call him and tell him in a sad tone why they were better off as friends. She might show up at his house and throw her arms around him. She might ask him to meet her at the village, then greet him with a pitying look in her eyes.

For the past three days, his hope and his pessimism had been like two monsters locked in a never-ending fight.

Three days wasn't a long period of time. Rationally, John knew this. He was the one who'd told her to take her time, so he could expect her to take her time—

Why on earth had he told her to take her time? He'd been trying to be gentlemanly. The truth was, he didn't want her to take her time. He couldn't stand for her to. Time was passing the way it had during BUD/S, every hour a marathon.

He lifted his face toward the sky and spent long minutes praying, asking God to get his head and his heart right, asking for God's will to be done.

It didn't seem to help.

Frowning, he began walking toward home.

She'd likely already chosen Duncan. He needed to prepare himself for that because not very many women would want to date a man who was going blind. It wasn't like he and Nora were already in love or married and she didn't have a way out. They hadn't even started dating, and he'd already given her a very easy way out.

He might as well have put up a flashing neon sign that read, *This way to exit my life*.

He'd done the right thing, but he didn't want the self-respect that came from knowing he'd done the right thing. He wanted Nora.

Nora had concocted a delicious little fantasy about John. In the fantasy, the uncertainty of whether or not she was going to accept or reject him was driving him crazy.

It was quite beguiling, really. The idea of big, strong Navy SEAL John Lawson stalking around his modern-day mansion, racked with frustrated adoration for her. Her! The fact that her fantasy was totally unlikely made it that much more delectable.

It was Sunday. She attended church, then went out to lunch with Grandma and her sisters. When she returned home, she picked up a book but saw nothing on her bookmarked page except John. After rereading the same paragraph three times, she set the book aside and arrived at the conclusion that four days of research, thought, and prayer over John was the most she could cobble together. The common sense part of her couldn't talk the romantic part of her into waiting any longer to seek John out.

He'd invited her to drop by his house—*anytime*, he'd said—so that was what she'd do. She'd drive there today. The topic of their dating life had been important enough to him to honor with a visit. She should be bold in the same way. A visit was more personal than a mere phone call or text message. Plus, as a huge added benefit, she'd get to see John. She was dying to see John.

Nora changed into clothes she considered to be her cutest, but that simultaneously didn't make her look like she was trying too hard. A loose sky-blue tank, a long necklace, and jeans, accessorized by a spritz of perfume.

On her way to Shore Pine, she made one small detour to the Hartnett Chapel and performed her customary inspection of the chapel's interior.

She'd spent the days since Duncan's departure working furiously to catch up on everything that had gone undone at the Library on the Green during her time as Duncan's tour guide. The Summer Antique Fair was now less than eight weeks away, and she had a mountain of things to do in preparation.

When Nora hadn't been working these past few days, she'd been combing through article after article about Malattia Leventinese. She'd read case studies. Medical journals. And every other source the Internet provided on the subject of blindness.

Knowledge was power. In this case, the knowledge she'd accumulated lent considerable power to the certainty that had begun to take root in her the moment John had told her he felt she had the right to make an informed decision about him.

Well, she could confidently say that she'd informed herself.

She closed the chapel's door behind her and rested a hand lovingly on the weathered wood of the handrail that invited parishioners up the chapel's front steps.

John's diagnosis hadn't been the only thing she'd mulled over while considering the prospect of dating him. She'd also thought a lot about the fact that his relationship with Allie had ended recently. She'd contemplated both parts of that less-than-ideal situation. John's relationship had ended. And it had ended recently.

The "it had ended" part forced Nora to acknowledge that she had no assurance that things between herself and John would end any differently than they had for Allie and John. Statistically, each new dating relationship was much more likely to end in a breakup than in a happily ever after. Right? The woman who'd insulated herself from dating for years needed to step out from behind her insulation and accept that potential consequence.

The recent ending of John's relationship with Allie made Nora think about her dad, who'd rushed into a relationship with her mom after Sylvie had left him with Willow.

Nora couldn't bring herself to label her dad's actions as disastrous, exactly. He'd been happy with her mom, for one thing. And Nora wouldn't be alive if not for their relationship. However, both her friends' and sisters' dating experiences—and the consensus of the culture at large—suggested that rebound romances weren't a great idea.

Sylvie's abandonment had devastated her father. He probably should have taken more time to recover from that before pursuing anyone else.

John's case was different than her dad's. John didn't have a child. And he didn't seem devastated by his breakup with Allie. He'd told Nora at the party that he and Allie got along well but that things had never been very serious between them. Which she hoped to be true because selfishly it made her heart hurt to think about John having loved Allie deeply.

Nora lifted her gaze to the cerulean sky above, dotted with ribbons of happy late-afternoon clouds. Then she faced the little church. Six years ago, when Mr. Hartnett had first informed Nora that he would not sell his chapel to her, Nora had decided to find another chapel for her village.

Since then, she'd found five chapels. Some of them had been prettier than this one. Some had been in better condition. Every one of them would have worked wonderfully well for her village. But whenever it had come time for her to buy one of the five inarguably good chapels, she'd pulled back. Following through on a purchase hadn't felt right to her because none of them had been *this* chapel. She loved this chapel in a way that was inexplicable.

Her heart was, very simply, set on it.

Her feelings for John were identical to her feelings for this chapel.

Her heart was, very simply, set on him.

Perhaps both in spite of and because of his shortcomings.

That he might break her heart wasn't enough to dissuade her. That he'd broken up with Allie just weeks ago wasn't enough to dissuade her, either. What could she do about that? Postpone contact between herself and John? And make herself unbearably impatient in the process? Give him time to forget about her and start dating someone else?

No and no.

She'd try her best to be smart and self-controlled. To hang on to her wisdom and judgment. To protect herself as much as she could. To take things with John very slowly and carefully.

Except . . . she'd been smart and slow and careful with Harrison, too. She'd made the best possible decisions, and even so her romance with Harrison had ended with her crying in the shower late at night for weeks upon weeks.

She never wanted to go back to crying in her shower. To living in a fog of sadness. To dashed dreams. Because of love.

Yet if you were going to care about someone, then you also had to open yourself to loss. Caring meant risk. The only alternative was never to care about anyone again.

Nora wanted the chance to care about John, no matter the risk.

Because her heart was set on him.

She climbed into her car and zipped along the road toward his house. The Indigo Girls song "Closer to Fine" poured from the car's speakers, and Nora sang along gamely, even though her confidence began to falter as she neared John's house.

He's stalking around his mansion, racked with frustrated adoration, remember?

She turned onto his private road. Maybe she should have sent a text message letting him know she was thinking about stopping by. Had she chosen the correct move? Drat her dating inexperience!

She approached his house for the second time in her life and spotted, for the second time in her life, a silver Audi parked outside.

Allie was here.

She sucked in a gasping breath as if she'd been stabbed. What . . . what was Allie doing here? She and John hadn't—they could not have—gotten back together. Could they?

She'd picked a terrible time to tell John she'd decided to date him. There was no way she was going to stammer out her intentions in front of Allie.

Just as she reached forward to shift her car into reverse and execute a three-point turn, Allie and John exited his front door. Allie turned to grin at John, and the movement sent the long, dark blond strands of her hair fanning outward before they resettled themselves over her chest.

A terrible lurch of jealousy and dismay stunned Nora into immobility.

She knew exactly when John caught sight of her, because he stopped suddenly. Guiltily, it seemed.

He was not stalking around his mansion, racked with frustrated adoration like he was supposed to be.

Had she waited too long? Until now, she'd suspected that she'd erred the other way. That the time she'd taken, that he'd asked her to take, had been a touch too short. It could be, though, that she'd gotten it all disastrously wrong and Allie had capitalized on Nora's mistake, swooping in to steal Nora's man . . . who'd been Allie's man first. . . . So did that make him Allie's by rights?

Part of her wanted to say nothing and simply accelerate toward Merryweather. That response would be so telling, though, so humiliating. She had a great deal of practice at retaining her dignity in the face of rejection. She could muscle through a performance if needed.

Perhaps it wouldn't be needed. Allie was here, and that looked bad. However, it wasn't like she'd caught the two of them kissing. Nora refused to jump to the wrong conclusion like leading ladies in romantic movies were so fond of doing.

She parked and stepped from her car, her legs trembling imperceptibly.

Allie's expression remained smooth as she and John approached. In contrast, John's expression was shuttered. Nora's heart slipped another notch.

"Hi, Nora," Allie said. "How've you been?"

"I've been well," Nora answered, relieved that her tone didn't betray her turmoil. "And yourself?"

"I've been enjoying my summer. Isn't this weather awesome?"

"Awesome."

"It really is." Allie looked between John and Nora, understanding dawning in her eyes. "Well, I have dinner plans back in Tacoma tonight, so I'd better head that way."

"Take care," John said, voice neutral.

"Will do. You too."

When John said nothing more, Nora noticed Allie's shoulders droop a degree. It seemed Allie wasn't quite as carefree as she'd first appeared, as someone who'd just reunited with an ex-boyfriend would be.

Allie made her way to her car. "Bye!" she called.

"Bye," John and Nora said. Neither of them moved, not a flicker of an eyelash, not a covert glance at each other. Nothing, until they both lifted a hand to wave at Allie, who drove past them, then disappeared from sight.

• • •

Text message from Duncan's personal assistant to Duncan:

Personal Assistant
Did a romance materialize between you and the American?

Duncan
She did have aspirations of a romance between us. But in the end, I realized that she wasn't really my type.

CHAPTER Nineteen

You could have cut the tension between Nora and John with the proverbial knife.

Nora counted out a slow *one, two, three, four, five* inside her head. Keeping her attention trained on the spot where Allie's car had vanished, she calmly asked, "What was that about?"

"Allie came by to return some scuba gear of mine."

John gestured up the path, inviting her without words to precede him to his house. She started in that direction, and he fell into step behind her. Was it literally out the door with one woman and in with the next?

Did she dare believe that Allie had only come by to return something? The sag in Allie's shoulders assured Nora that her visit to John had been about more than scuba gear on Allie's end. "Really?" Nora asked gently. "She only came by to return gear? That's all it was?"

"That's all it was."

"Do you regret your breakup?"

"No."

Their footsteps made almost no sound as they followed the sleek strips of concrete that formed his walkway.

"Allie and I are better as friends," he said.

"I think Allie might still want to date you, though."

Nora stopped walking and turned to face him. Energy jolted through her at the power of their eye contact.

"I don't know whether or not Allie still wants to date me. If she does, she didn't tell me so, and I'm glad she didn't. I think God has other plans for her. And me."

In the serious contours of his face, Nora could see the wear his prognosis and his future and maybe his search for his birth mother had chiseled there. She could also see that he was telling the truth. Allie had come by to return something, and that was all her visit had been. For him, anyway.

This time, *this time*, could it be that the man she wanted was actually going to choose her? With a depth of yearning she hadn't allowed herself to truly feel until this moment, Nora longed for him to choose her.

They stood a few yards from his open front door, glorious sunshine pouring over them. She could see the kaleidoscope of muted greens, browns, and tans that made up the colors of his eyes. His cheeks were slightly scruffy with five-o'clock shadow.

"There is someone I want to date." He looked directly at her with both raw need and vulnerability. "I don't know, though, if she wants to date me."

"She does," Nora said.

A fissure of amazement showed in his expression. "She does?"

"She does." She stepped forward, narrowing the distance between them to inches.

He lifted his hands slowly, reading every nuance of her expression as he did so. Reverently, he edged aside the fall of her hair so that his fingers skimmed both sides of her neck. Then his palms rested there, cradling her head and jaw with exquisite gentleness, as if she was precious to him.

The feel of his rough, masculine fingers against her skin sent a thrill of goose bumps racing down her arms. He could probably detect the thrumming of her pulse in her veins. Where had her breath gone?

He dipped his head toward hers, stayed himself, then asked her a question with a slight lift of one eyebrow. *Do you want this*? He was an experienced man. Confident. Direct. In no hurry. And unwilling to come on too strong too fast and rattle her.

She answered with a wobbly smile. *Yes! Yes, John*.

Her hands rose of their own accord to wrap around his forearms. The scent of bergamot enfolded her, then their lips met with wonder, exploration, devotion.

Desire drew at her middle. Tenderness for him outran her ability to call it back. This was a lot for a bluestocking to take in. She leaned back only when she desperately needed air to her brain.

John's hands remained on her neck. One of his thumbs rubbed down an inch, up an inch.

She might pass out—

She would not pass out! She continued to coax air to and from her lungs. She should say something, but what? What should she, could she, say in the face of that epic kiss?

John appeared wholly calm.

She spoke the first thought that sailed by. "Is the someone we were talking about just now, the someone you want to date . . . is she me, Nora?" She grinned unsteadily. "Just thought I'd double check."

John tilted back his head and laughed. He glanced down at her and laughed more. Never before had she heard him laugh in this deep, rumbling, irrepressible way. "Did you say your name was Nora?"

"Yes."

"Well, shoot. My vision's a lot worse than I'd realized." He hadn't moved back at all. There was still only a sliver of space between their bodies. "How's your vision?"

"Outstanding."

"Because I'm not Duncan. I'm John."

"Well, shoot," she said with feeling, imitating him. "Are you sure?"

"Completely sure. I'm insulted, by the way, that you'd get me confused with a short guy who wears a girly scarf."

"My mistake."

Humor tugging at his mouth, he kissed her again. "I'm glad we got this straightened out." He spoke in a sexy whisper against her lips.

"Me too."

"Nora?" Another kiss.

"Mmm?"

Two more kisses.

He pulled back. His eyes had darkened to a hazy, unfocused hue. "I know exactly who you are."

She fought the urge to break into piteous happy tears. Nodding, she said, "So . . . I *am* the someone you were speaking of earlier?"

"Yes. You're my someone."

Her mouth tingled from his kisses. "You're my someone, too."

He gave her a kiss as light as the brush of satin on satin. Then he hugged her against his chest, his arms locking around her. In response, she laid her cheek against his heart and interlaced her hands behind the small of his back. She wanted to stay right here, like this, with him forever.

One minute swept into two. Birds trilled. In the distance, a boat motor rumbled.

He'd. Kissed. Her. She was in John's arms. She was his someone.

She peered up at him. "Thank you for coming over the other night and telling me all that you did."

"My diagnosis didn't scare you off?"

"No."

"It's not a pretty diagnosis, Nora."

"There are things about my life that aren't pretty, either."

"I don't want . . . my eyesight to end up having a negative effect on you."

"And I don't want either of us to worry about that at this point. What I've learned," she thought back to the loss of her mother and her broken engagement, "is that the past might be challenging and the future might be unsure. And that's okay. The present is all we're given, anyway. When we get to the future, God will be there. He'll supply whatever we need for each day."

Time elongated as he watched her. She didn't have words equal to the task of explaining to him what a blessing he was to her.

"Since the present is all we have . . ." he said.

"Yes?"

"Are you ready for our first date?"

"What? Now?"

"Now."

"Most definitely. Now would be perfect."

Their transportation for their first date? John's boat.

Nora sat in the passenger seat wearing one of his ball caps in order to keep her hair from whipping around her head. An expanse of glinting water fringed with timbered hills surrounded her, though she found it difficult to admire the surroundings when she could, instead, watch John.

He drove a boat like he'd been doing so since birth. All easy, relaxed know-how. The wind pushed his shirt flush against him, flapping it a little so that she could see a wedge of bare, smooth skin at his lower back. His sunglasses reflected her image dimly back at her in shades of dark gray.

They docked at Shore Pine's marina and ate dinner at a restaurant on the wharf that served crab and potatoes and corn on sheets of white butcher paper. They laughed and talked and Nora tried, really tried, to wrap her mind around the miraculous fact that the two of them were out together on a date.

In the restroom she looked at her reflection while washing her hands and saw that she was smiling a huge, dopey smile. It wouldn't leave. It kept returning like a stray cat that had been served milk.

At the chapel earlier today, she'd determined that she'd be smart about John. Careful! For goodness' sake, she needed to rein in her rampant imagination. This was only their first date.

After the return boat ride to his house, he lit his outdoor fireplace, and the two of them sat in a settee facing it. Beyond her view of his feet and her feet resting side by side on the coffee table, both sets crossed at the ankles, the sky eased from sunset colors, to deepening dusk, to inky blackness pinpricked by stars. The sounds of nature and the crackle of the fire provided a background soundtrack for their conversation. They held hands and, occasionally, they kissed. She couldn't believe it when she realized it was two in the morning.

He walked her to her car.

Despite the late hour, she left him regretfully. Very, very regretfully.

All the way home, she wore the huge, dopey smile.

This deluge of happiness was not to be trusted, she knew. Her past love life and her sisters' love lives had taught her that any relationship's initial bout of infatuation could not be counted upon.

But the part of her that was doing the emotional equivalent of a salsa dance and singing *John likes me, John likes me, John likes me* did not want to hear caution.

Not tonight.

Tonight, he'd told her that she was his someone.

John stood in front of his outdoor fireplace, hands in his pockets, head full of Nora, attention trained on the last of the glowing logs.

Hours ago, when he'd first seen Nora sitting in her car outside his house, her face had looked so serious that he'd been sure she'd come to tell him no. But, incredibly, she'd come to tell him yes.

This—*she*—was the first good thing that had happened to him since the day he'd met with his ophthalmologist months ago. The whole time she'd been here this evening, he'd been astonished by the fact that she'd come.

He hadn't frightened her off. He wasn't alone. The two of them had finally come to a place where they were free to date each other without guilt.

The librarian with the house full of books who liked boring TV was independent, sweet, and an unbelievable kisser. For all his experience, he'd never been as rattled by the power of a kiss as he'd been tonight.

He didn't believe in fate, unless fate was another name for God's plans. If it was, then every part of being with Nora this evening had felt like fate. Like a *yes* and a *thank God* and a *finally*, deep within.

Nora was the silver lining to his worst cloud, a silver lining so strong that it lessened the threat of the darkness.

The next morning, Nora's office door rushed open. Willow and Britt filled the opening.

Nora swiveled her desk chair in their direction. "To what do I owe this pleasure?" she asked, though she could guess.

After her very late night with John, she'd slept in more than she usually did on weekday mornings. She'd arrived at the Library on the Green two hours ago, around ten.

"You're dating John?" Britt asked.

"I'm guessing that you already know that I am," Nora answered. "Because you're both here just twenty minutes after I sent you a text about him. What sort of transportation moves that fast? Monorail?"

Her sisters made themselves comfortable on the patterned chairs opposite Nora's desk just as Nikki made an appearance. "You're dating the Navy SEAL?" Her question dripped with disbelief.

"Well, we've only been on one date so far, but I guess you could say that John and I are dating."

Nikki released a garbled death scream, then pantomimed pulling a knife out of her chest.

"We're happy for Nora," Britt informed Nikki. "We're here to be supportive and encouraging."

"Oh." Nikki straightened. "Except it's hard to be supportive about your boss dating the man that you've been having a meaningful relationship with during every REM cycle of sleep."

Britt and Willow laughed.

"He's gorgeous," Nikki said to Nora. "I didn't think you had it in you, to date a man like that."

"But you suggested to me once that I move heaven and earth to make him mine."

"Yes, but in my heart of hearts I thought you'd fail, hon."

More laughter from Britt and Willow.

"I'm touched by your confidence," Nora said.

Nikki drummed her fingers on the flare of her hip. "I'd like to take a look at the Navy SEAL's abs sometime. You know, as a job benefit."

"I can't guarantee that specific job benefit."

"Then I can't guarantee that I'll stay on here at Merryweather Historical Village."

"I'd hate to lose your accounting skills," Nora said. "But I'll get by."

"That face of his!" Nikki said dreamily. "It's just so—"

"Would you mind going downstairs and checking on Mr. Cummings?" Nora asked. "He's looking through church records."

"Fine. Is the Navy SEAL—"

"How about we all call him John from now on?"

"Will John be coming by here any time soon?"

"Tonight. At five thirty."

Waggling her eyebrows, Nikki turned and made her way downstairs.

"Tell us all," Willow said.

Nora filled them in on the details of her magnificent evening. "It was just a date," she felt compelled to say in conclusion. She didn't want them to get their hopes up.

"It sounds like a great first date," Willow pronounced.

"I agree," Britt said.

"Is it wrong of me to want to call attention to my excellent makeover skills?" Willow asked Britt.

"Very wrong," Britt answered.

Willow flourished her hands in Nora's direction. "The evidence speaks for itself. As soon as I completed the Enhancing of Nora, two very eligible bachelors beat a path to her door."

"Is it wrong of me to want to call attention to the fact that Nora never would have met John if I hadn't talked her into coming with me to a staged emergency?" Britt asked.

"Very wrong," Willow answered.

"Is it wrong of me to want to remind you that it was me, just me and my charming personality, who won John over in the end?"

"Not wrong at all," Willow answered kindly. "This is a very exciting development."

Both her sisters beamed at her. Nora hadn't realized how happy they'd be about this. Had they secretly been feeling sorry for her these past three years? The suspicion jabbed her like a needle. She'd thought she'd been projecting contentment to them.

"What's going to happen next?" Britt asked.

"He texted to ask if I was free after work, and I said that I was and he said he'd come here to meet me."

Willow gave a low whistle. "It sounds like he's eager to see you again."

"I'm not sure. I—I can't speak for him." She struggled to keep the huge, dopey smile at bay.

"*Oooh-ooo!*" Willow and Britt responded as if they were both thirteen.

"Nora," Mrs. Williams said later that day, near closing time. "I believe I may have contracted scurvy." The elderly woman, a hypochondriac and museum regular, gave Nora a look of great sorrow. "Don't get too close, dear. I wouldn't want you to catch it."

"I don't think scurvy's contagious," Nora assured her.

"I've already come down with the symptom of fatigue. I'm expecting the joint pain to set in at any moment."

Mrs. Williams was a living example of exactly why typing your symptoms into an Internet search engine was a ghastly idea. "I'm sorry to hear that."

"Before I'm bedridden, I'd like to go back through Merryweather's early burial documents to see if I can discover what became of little Bucky, Arthur Thacker's youngest." She wrapped a hand around Nora's wrist. "Bucky's descendants might be living right next door to me, and I wouldn't know." Her wrinkled lips pursed. "Come to think of it, I hope they don't live right next door. My next-door neighbors sometimes leave beer bottles in their grass and don't prune their azaleas the way they should. Bucky's descendants are welcome to live two doors down. The couple that lives there knows how to prune their azaleas."

Nora settled Mrs. Williams at one of the library's tables and brought out the requested records. Just as she was heading back to her office, she caught sight of something beyond the windows on the side facing the green. She waited. There it was again. A football sailing by. Then again, sailing by going the other way.

She moved to the window. Randall *and John* were throwing a football back and forth.

John had on jeans and a lightweight dark-gray sweater. The sight of him throwing a football with Randall caused fondness to sink into her like honey into hot tea, every molecule of it absorbing until it changed her substance.

In between throws, Randall gestured with his hands as he spoke to John. John smiled in response.

She let herself out the library's front door and approached John and Randall, her hands stuck into the back pockets of her white pants. The toes of her silver flats sparkled against the grass. "Hi, guys."

Immediately, John turned. He held the football clasped against his thigh and gazed at her as if it had been a year since he'd seen her instead of hours. Was he having difficulty focusing on her precisely?

She drew nearer. "How are you?"

"I'm doing well." His mouth curved, and she knew that he *could* see her clearly now. The things they'd shared last night, a secret knowledge, passed between them.

"You've met Randall."

"Yeah. He was throwing the ball in the air and catching it when I walked up, so I asked if I could join him."

She hooked a thumb toward John. "How is he, Randall? Can he hang with your skills? Or does he need to be demoted to toddler ball?"

John snorted.

"He can hang," Randall said. "Um, Ms. Bradford? Can you move out of the way so we can keep going?"

"Don't bite the hand that feeds you hot chocolate with mini marshmallows, my young friend," Nora said.

"Clearly, Randall already likes me best," John said just loud enough for her to hear. The sound of his voice pitched low like that brought to mind the things he'd said to her last night in the very same tone. *I know exactly who you are.*

"Any right-minded boy would like you best," she said.

"You're my favorite, though," he said, meeting her eyes.

Cue huge, dopey smile. Her cheeks heated with a blush.

"She can join us," John called to Randall.

"Aww," Randall protested.

"Hot chocolate," Nora warned the kid. "And mini marshmallows."

They formed a triangle. John sent the ball arcing through the air in a perfect spiral. Randall caught it and threw it to her, then she threw to John.

The three of them talked and lazily passed the ball while townspeople and tourists milled into and out of the village shops. It was all pretty perfect, as far as Nora was concerned.

Finally, Randall looked at his watch, caught the football, and approached them.

"My grandmother's expecting me home soon. So I better go."

"Do you need a ride?" John asked. "To your grandmother's?"

"No, I always walk."

"Okay."

Randall stuck out his skinny arm. "It was nice to meet you," he said to John solemnly.

"You too." They shook hands, and Randall even managed to hold John's eye contact for the better part of a second.

"See you later, Ms. Bradford." He gave her an awkward one-armed hug.

"See you." She hugged him back. Then he loped off, a boy and his football.

"I remember that Randall was at the library the first day I came to the village," John said.

"He's here several days a week. The village is his hangout spot."

"He picked a good hangout spot."

"He picked a good guy to throw a football with. That was probably the highlight of his week."

John angled to face her more fully. "Have you finished your work for the day?"

"I have."

"Are you up for giving me a tour of the buildings?"

"Of course." Nora adored talking about her village but took care not to prattle on about it because she knew she had the potential to get swept away by fervor and end up boring people. That John had actually *requested* a tour was as delicious to her as one of Britt's truffles. "Do you want the free tour of the village or the very expensive, very detailed, history-packed ten-dollar tour?"

"The ten-dollar tour. I want to see your village."

He'd put slight emphasis on the word *see*. Ah. So he wanted to take in the details of it now, while he still could. Which explained the concentrated expression on his face earlier, when he'd first seen her. And the way he'd looked at the sunset last night. And his careful study of the view off the lodge's balcony in Oregon.

"When you're fighting unconsciousness during my lecture about western migration," she said, "just remember that you requested the ten-dollar tour."

"I like to live dangerously."

"All right, then." She smiled at him.

"One thing first?"

"Sure."

"I brought the letter I wrote to Sherry." He pulled an envelope from his back pocket. "Would you be willing to read it before I mail it?"

"I'd love to."

He handed her the envelope. He'd already affixed a stamp and addressed it to Sherry in neat handwriting.

They sat on one of the benches facing the green, and she spread the letter carefully across her knees. She read it twice. Her chest tightened more and more with every word because she so desperately wanted his search to end well for him.

What he'd written and how he'd written it made it clear that he'd implemented the suggestions in the reference material she'd sent him. He'd succeeded at condensing his life onto a single plain-spoken sheet of paper. He'd put no guilt, pressure, or accusation on Sherry.

Finding John's birth mother had not only cost the two of them a lot of hours and effort, but Nora knew that it had taken an emotional toll on John, as well. In the end they'd succeeded at their task, but as soon as Sherry received this letter, the power would shift to her. The decision to respond or not respond to John would be hers. This search could still result in a dead end, a possibility that left Nora longing to scribble a note of her own onto the letter. Something along the lines of, *John is a good man. He won't overstep. He simply wants a meeting and a medical history, and he deserves for something to go right at this particular point in his life so please call him. Please do.*

Their best hope was that Sherry had long been interested in reconnecting with her birth son and would thus reply quickly to his letter. Nora hadn't forgotten, however, that John had told her long ago that he'd checked the registry that connected birth parents who want to locate their adopted children with adopted children who want to locate their birth parents. Sherry had not been listed.

"I think it's a wonderful letter," she said truthfully and passed it back. "In my opinion, you worded it exactly right."

He nodded and sealed the envelope's flap. "Is there a mailbox nearby?"

"Yes, we have one here at the village. Are you . . . ready to mail it? Right now?" He'd had Sherry's address in hand for well over a month. For reasons of his own, he'd waited to send his letter, and she didn't want to rush him at this point. This was a no-going-back kind of letter to mail.

"I'm ready."

"How about I say a prayer over it? To give it a good send-off?"

"I'd like that."

She intertwined her fingers with his. "Lord, prepare Sherry's heart to receive this letter. Go with it in power. We know that in all things you work for the good of those who love you, so I'm stepping out in faith, believing that John's search will ultimately be for his good and Sherry's good, too. Amen."

"Amen," he whispered. He met her eyes. "Thank you."

She wrapped a hand around his elbow as they walked to the mailbox situated between The Pie Emporium and the General Store.

John opened the slot and without hesitation slid the letter in. *Whoosh*. Gone.

He'd set the ball rolling, and it couldn't be stopped.

• • •

Text message from Britt to Nora:

Britt
I'm racked with curiosity about Willow and Corbin Stewart. There were a lot of sparks in the air between them at Grandma's party. Do you think we should talk to her about him? Or would that be too painful?

Nora
I think we should wait and let her discuss him with us when she's ready.

• • •

Text message from Willow to Nora:

Willow

Are we supposed to go on forever pretending that Zander and Britt are nothing more than friends, simply because the two of them are so bent on pretending? Zander's unhappy, and it's starting to make me irritable. Do you think we should talk to Britt? Or would that ruin everything?

Nora

I think we should wait and let her discuss him with us when she's ready.

CHAPTER Twenty

The next night, John and Nora stood in the parking lot at a restaurant called Gino's, delaying their good-bye. He had his back up against his Suburban, Nora in his arms. She'd set her feet in between his much larger ones, and he'd tilted his head down to watch her.

She was finishing a story about her sisters and a prank the three of them had pulled when they were kids. The sound of her voice, her scent, the softness of her body, her smile. All of it was working magic on him.

After she'd given him a tour of the historical village yesterday, they'd shared a take-out dinner at her house. Today, when he'd offered to drive to Merryweather after work again, she'd volunteered to make the trip to Shore Pine instead. They'd walked down Main Street and back, stopping at each of the stores she'd wanted to visit, then eaten homemade ravioli followed by cheesecake at Gino's.

The wind pulled a piece of red hair across her face. Gently, he caught it and smoothed it back as she continued talking.

I love her, he thought.

I love her.

Sometimes, when something was right, you just knew. All those years ago, when his friend had suggested the SEALs to him, it had been the same way. He'd known right away that the SEALs were for him. For the second time in his life, he was experiencing that same unexplainable certainty.

He'd started falling for Nora the day they'd knocked on doors on Regent Drive and she'd jokingly told him he was as intimidating as a torpedo. His feelings for her had been growing roots ever since, stretching into the corners of him, tunneling so deep they couldn't be pulled out.

He'd never loved any of the women he'd dated in the past. He'd liked them. He'd been physically attracted to them. He'd cared. But this was as different from those other times as black from white.

She finished telling him her story and laughed.

He smiled at her, emotion gusting through him. He hadn't cried since he was a child, but tears were threatening at the back of his eyes now, gathering like storm clouds.

He could feel soul-deep devotion steal over his heart. Hear it in the thundering of his pulse. He lowered his head, pausing when their profiles were just millimeters apart. Her lips came open with a quickly indrawn breath that caused him to groan.

He closed his eyes and kissed her while need roared through his bloodstream. He held himself ruthlessly in check. She was much smaller than he was, but he was powerfully aware that he was the one completely at her mercy.

If he had Nora in his life, then no matter what came with his vision or with his search for Sherry, he could face it. Which was why he'd finally been able to mail the letter to Sherry yesterday. He could deal with his future because he'd still have her, the most important thing—

A warning bell sounded deep within him. It was wrong to rely that much on Nora. On anyone. He needed to watch himself, to make sure he kept God as his most important thing.

He wrapped his arms more tightly around Nora, drawing her closer, determined to shelter her from the cold and anything else that could ever hurt her.

The next morning on his way to work, John stopped at a red light and reached into the door pocket next to his seat in search of a scratch piece of paper. He wanted to jot down a reminder about the emergency preparedness presentation he'd be giving to city officials in Chicago in a few weeks.

He pulled out the first thing he touched and saw that it was the kind of paper sleeve that the teller at the bank gives you when you withdraw cash. His brow furrowed. He couldn't remember withdrawing cash and putting it there—

Wait. He flipped it over. On the back he'd written, *I noticed that you hadn't cashed my checks.*

This was the money he'd given Nora. He ran his thumb along the edge of the bills stuffed inside the sleeve. He didn't have to count them to know that she hadn't kept a single one.

The light turned green, and he eased forward. Nora had snuck into his car and left the money in the side pocket for him to eventually find.

"Nora," he growled. That stubborn, stubborn, unbelievably stubborn woman. Even as he thought it, though, he wanted to laugh.

She was about to find out just how stubborn *he* could be.

At some point during the first week after they'd become super couple Jora instead of just John and Nora, Nora suggested they take turns planning how they spent their time together. One day, she'd choose what they would do. The next day, he would. It seemed to her like a brain flash. They were very different people with histories and hobbies that hardly overlapped at all. What better way to introduce each other to the things they enjoyed?

They may have been kissing when Nora suggested the taking turns thing. And the kissing may have made John more amenable to the idea than he would have been otherwise.

The next day, John took her kayaking.

"I'm not speedy," she called to him, "but you have to admit that I'm surprisingly good for a beginner."

"You're very good."

To her untrained eye, John could pass for an Olympic kayaker. Seriously. That's how effortless this appeared to be for him.

"Although," she said, "it's probably pretty hard to fail at sitting in a stable little boat and holding a paddle. All beginner kayakers probably surprise themselves with how good they are."

"You're an excellent beginner."

She followed him down a narrow inlet that crooked like a finger away from the hand of Lake Shore Pine. The sound of rippling water filled her ears, and the air smelled like cedar thanks to the fallen tree up the bank on her right.

She'd tried kayaking once with Grandma when she'd been nine and hated it. Grandma had complained the whole time about how much her bottom hurt due to the hard kayak seat. When Nora had piped up with a complaint about her own uncomfortable bottom, Grandma had given her a sermon about how the Lord hadn't sent Nora to this earth to be comfortable. Kayaking with John didn't even belong in the same solar system as kayaking with Grandma.

Her only small . . . okay, not so small . . . worry was that John would spend his turns taking her on a group of excursions entitled The Things I Always Do With Every Girlfriend.

He wasn't, was he?

Because she didn't want to go on that particular group of excursions.

He owned three kayaks and had transported hers to the water with the kind of familiarity that made her think he often let guests borrow them. That thought was immediately chased by images of him kayaking with other women.

She should let go of her dumb concerns and fully embrace the present. Yet imagining him kayaking these same waters with past girlfriends gnawed at her every time she glanced at John and saw again how painfully handsome he looked in his T-shirt and baseball cap.

"Did you go kayaking with Allie?" she heard herself ask.

In response, he immediately dipped an oar and turned his boat diagonally across the water so that he could study her.

"You did, didn't you?" she said.

"Yes."

"I'm guessing she wasn't a beginner and that she was more than surprisingly good."

"You're right."

Pain nicked her. It served her right! She shouldn't have mentioned Allie. A fully confident woman wouldn't have. It was just that she really didn't want to become another tally mark on John's long list of girlfriends.

"Allie was great at kayaking." He gave the tip of her boat a tug and slid her in beside him. "But she wasn't you."

The sides of their kayaks bumped. With a huff of startled laughter, Nora caught the lip of his seat to steady herself. She didn't want the *surprisingly good* beginner to pitch headfirst into the water right in front of him.

He looked at her with utter seriousness, as if determined to communicate clearly. "There's no comparison between the two of you in my mind, Nora. The dullest moment with you—"

"With me, there's never a dull moment." She gave what she hoped to be a persuasive smile.

"Shut up and let me compliment you." Humor ghosted across his lips. "The dullest moment with you is one hundred times better than my best moment with any of my past girlfriends."

Her heart expanded wildly with joy and hope.

"I didn't have a choice about when in my life I'd meet you, Nora. If I'd had a choice, I would have chosen to meet you years ago."

"Oh."

"Before you, I was making decisions with the information I had available at the time. Now everything's different. Because of you. Okay?"

"Okay," she whispered.

Into their second week of dating, John still hadn't received a response from Sherry.

When it was Nora's turn to plan their date, she decided to introduce John (indoctrinate him?) to her love of antique recipes. She pulled her wooden recipe box forward to the edge of her kitchen counter.

John regarded it like he would a homework assignment. "You're going to make me cook?"

She tipped open the lid. "I'm going to do you the honor of letting you cook *with me*." Her growing trust in his affection had been bringing out her sassy side. "Might I remind you that your dullest moment with me is one hundred times better than your best moment with your past girlfriends?"

He slanted a look at her. "Did you memorize what I said?"

"I memorized it all right." She slipped out a recipe and handed it to him. "I collect old recipes. All of these were handwritten at least one hundred years ago. Each one is like a time capsule." She flicked through a few of her scrupulously organized tabs. "I have recipes for a wide variety of things. Punch, soups, dessert, soap, candles."

"Have you tried them all?"

"Every one. Prior to you, I had a lot of time on my hands," she said dryly. "So? What would you like to make? I'll let you choose."

"Dessert."

They studied the dessert recipes one by one. When he came to the one for peach cobbler he held it up. "Now we're talking."

They made a grocery store run, returned to the Bookish Cottage, and scrubbed their hands. Once they had the peaches, sugar, and water simmering in a saucepan, they turned their attention to the all-important pie crust.

John worked the rolling pin back and forth over the dough the way Nora demonstrated. "I've never used a rolling pin before."

"Then you're overdue."

"Do I look like a girl?"

She giggled. "You most definitely do not look like a girl."

He dipped his pointer finger in the open sugar bag, then swiped it across her cheekbone.

"Excuse you!" she protested.

"Oops," he said. "My mistake. Let me get that." He bent his head and kissed the sugar away.

She went still, butterflies swarming in her stomach.

He dipped his finger back into the sugar.

"That's unhygienic," she said weakly.

"I'll buy you another bag."

"Big spender."

He left a trail of sugar crystals along one side of her forehead, then kissed them away.

"You're turning out to be . . ." she breathed, "a very good baker."

"I never thought I'd like baking." He swept sugar along the bridge of her nose. His lips followed. "But I do."

"I do, too. . . . That is . . . um. I can't remember what I was saying."

His sugar-covered finger glided across her bottom lip. "Sorry," he whispered. "I'm clumsy today."

"Unforgivably clumsy," she managed. Then he kissed the sugar away from her bottom lip, and she knew, she knew with unshakable conviction, that this kiss was sweeter than the sweetest antique recipe for peach cobbler could ever be.

Into their third week of dating, John still hadn't received a response from Sherry.

When it was John's turn to plan their date, he signed Nora up to volunteer again at one of his emergency training drills. Knowing she was present made running his course graduates through their paces *a lot* more enjoyable for John.

Today's session was taking place on the floor of his building arranged to look like a mall. A wide hallway ran down the center with "stores" located on both sides.

John followed two of his students into the store Nora had been assigned to. A man and woman stood behind the counter. His trainees led them out.

Nora, however, was nowhere to be seen. He walked deeper into the space, searching the corners for a small, crouched form. He'd had the sprinklers recalibrated after the last incident, so no water fell today. However, special-effect fog hung in the air just like it had the day they'd met.

He still didn't see her. He checked under the cashier's counter. Empty. He opened one of the closet doors. Empty. He opened the second closet and found her sitting on the floor, knees drawn up, arms locked around them. Her eyes sparkled with challenge. "Well, shucks. It seems your trainees overlooked me yet again."

"I can't imagine how they could have missed you."

"Me neither."

He stepped to the side in a silent invitation to exit, exactly as he'd done that first day. "This way."

She peered up at him with a pretend expression of shock. Slowly, she blinked.

"Ma'am." He spoke with fake firmness, trying hard to keep a straight face. It wouldn't be easy to explain to his employees, students, and volunteers why he'd been laughing during the final stages of a staged terrorist takeover of a mall.

She stuck out her chin and remained exactly where she was, so he went to a knee and held out his arms. She scooted toward him much more willingly than a survivor would have. He pressed to his feet and carried her into the hazy interior of the store.

This was the second time he'd rescued her but, in truth, Nora was the one rescuing him.

"Sorry about my slow response time back there," she said, mimicking the first words she'd spoken to him.

He halted and kissed her. It wasn't a quick kiss. He made good, thorough work of it. Then he strode, with her in his arms, into the central part of the mall.

"You can put me down now," she whispered.

"What's that you say?"

"I'll walk."

"Too late."

"John! I don't want everyone to see me being carried out by you. *Again.*"

He smiled wickedly. "Too late."

Two days later, Nora made an exquisitely frustrating discovery.

She was sitting at her desk scrolling through a spreadsheet that detailed the monthly budget for the Friends of Merryweather Historical Village, a volunteer group of village enthusiasts bent on finding new and delightful ways to support Nora's endeavor. The income and expense columns followed an uneventful trajectory, right up until she saw that someone had made an online donation to the Friends of Merryweather Historical Village in the exact amount, down to the dollar, of what Nora had charged John for her help with his birth mother search.

Wait! *What?*

"John," she hissed savagely.

The Friends of Merryweather Historical Village were not controlled by her. They valued her as a member of their group, and she attended all their meetings. But they were a separate entity. She couldn't take that money from them and thrust it back at John. He'd given her the money in a way that made it impossible to give back.

"Did you mention John?" Nikki called from the adjoining room. "I was just daydreaming that I was bobbing at sea in a life preserver, and he was lowering out of a helicopter to save me."

"Get your own boyfriend!" Nora hollered.

"I'd rather have yours," Nikki answered.

Nora snatched up her phone and texted John. *Did you make a donation recently to the Friends of Merryweather Historical Village?*

He responded immediately. *That's really not my style, Nora. I prefer to give to Christian or veteran's charities.*

John Truman Lawson, you're diabolical!

I don't see how giving to Christian or veteran's charities is diabolical.

I wanted to donate my help to you just like I do to every other person who walks in the door of this library! Her fingers jabbed quickly at the letters. *I wanted to donate my help to you MORE than I've ever wanted to donate it to anyone.*

Just think of all the things the Friends of Whatever Whatever will be able to do thanks to whoever gave that generous gift. You should be more civic-minded.

I'm the most civic-minded person in Merryweather!

You know what?

What?

Checkmate, Nora. Checkmate.

Into their fourth week of dating, John still hadn't received a response from Sherry.

When it was Nora's turn to plan their date, she took John to a dinner party at Harrison and Rory's.

She'd purchased a flowy peach sundress for the occasion. Willow had been over in the afternoon with Ben & Jerry's and had offered to style Nora's hair. Thus, she wore a thin gold headband and a low, loose bun at the nape of her neck. She had a crush on her high-heeled espadrilles. Best of all, her hand was intertwined with John's as they made their way up the walkway to Harrison and Rory's two-story colonial.

The roiling hurt, bitterness, and betrayal she'd been battling since the day Harrison had broken her heart had at last faded to an echo.

"Why are we doing this again?" John asked. His business shirt looked very crisp and white against the skin of his throat and face. "I don't want to spend time with your ex-boyfriend."

"We're doing this because Harrison and Rory are impossible to avoid. Merryweather is a small town. They live here and I live here, and if I spun in a circle with my arms outstretched like Julie Andrews in *The Sound of Music*, I'd be hard-pressed not to hit one of them."

"Tell me you didn't just make a *Sound of Music* reference."

She drew him to a halt so she could explain what needed to be explained before they reached the door. "Against all natural laws, Harrison and Rory continue to go out of their way to be nice to me and to invite me to their events. I don't know if it's motivated by guilt or misguided pity or genuine kindness. Probably a little of all three."

"I might be hard-pressed not to hit one of them. And not because I'll be spinning around like Julie Andrews."

A few weeks back, Harrison and Rory had sent her a gorgeous invitation to this evening's Midsummer's Night Soiree. The invite had offered her the opportunity to bring a guest. Because she was dating John, she'd taken them up on their invite and the "plus one."

"I turned down as many invitations as I could over the years, but I couldn't decline them all because I didn't want them to think I was rude or so gutted that I couldn't bear to see them. I said yes to tonight because I'm petty enough to want to show you off." She straightened his collar. "Maybe now they won't imagine I'm home alone sniveling into embroidered handkerchiefs."

"Did you just say embroidered handkerchiefs?"

"Maybe now they'll stop sending me invitations. But even if they keep sending me invitations, I promise that I won't make you attend any other event that they host. Just this one dinner."

"I haven't met Harrison yet, but I can tell you that I don't like him, and that I won't like him because he broke his engagement to you."

"The thing is, though, Harrison *was* honest with me back then. Also, I really do think he was genuinely sorry about what he put me through." As sorry as a man who lands a lovely, stylish wife who's a mite too good for him can be, anyway. Nora set her palms on John's chest, feeling his body's heat, marveling afresh that she had the privilege to touch him.

"I still don't like him," he stated.

His animosity toward Harrison probably shouldn't please her as much as it did. "Let's go in so that I can gloat over you. We'll enjoy what's going to be a fantastic meal. Then we'll go."

They rang the doorbell. Rory answered.

Rory appeared to be just weeks shy of her due date. Only she could look as fresh and darling as she did at such an advanced stage of pregnancy. "Good to see you, Nora. . . ." Her greeting trailed off when she spotted John. Her artfully eye-shadowed eyes widened.

Could it be, Rory, that you're astonished by John's incredible appeal? Nora wanted to ask.

"Come in." Rory motioned them inside her beautiful, tasteful foyer.

"I'd like you to meet my boyfriend," Nora said, "John Lawson."

Nora could feel surprise rolling off Rory in waves, though Rory was too sophisticated to gawk or allow the conversation to lag. She and John chatted amiably.

My boyfriend, Nora had called him.

She and John had spent part of every day together since their first kiss, with the exception of the three miserable days earlier this week when he'd traveled to Chicago for work. When they'd parted, she'd kissed him as if he was never coming back. While he'd been gone, missing him had felt like a backpack she'd been made to carry around. When he'd returned, she'd kissed him like he'd been raised from the dead.

She hadn't known that three days apart from someone could feel like three months. That distance could physically hurt. The only beauty in their separation, the only solace in it, had been that John had felt exactly the same way.

They'd never had a conversation in which they'd put a label on their relationship, which was fine with her. She didn't need a label for it at this point because she believed that they already understood each other very well.

She knew they were exclusive. She knew he felt deeply about her. His actions and her actions and the way they were with each other was enough. It was way, way better than enough, actually. It was beyond what she'd expected for herself, ever. It was new and blissful and heady and it made her heart ache with joy. They were dating. They were dating, and it was more romantic and wonderful than any movie she'd ever seen and any book she'd ever read.

It was also as scary as scary could be, emotionally. She was trying her best to be wise. Not to rush. Not to get ahead of herself and fall crazily in love with this man she'd only been dating for a matter of weeks. It was just that what was happening within her at times felt next to impossible to control. Like attempting to hold back an avalanche. How was she supposed to pace the rate at which she fell for him?

Over the last week or so, John had started introducing her to people as his girlfriend, which had given her the courage to introduce him in kind just now.

My boyfriend.

"Hon?" Harrison's voice called from the region of the kitchen. "Do we have any more toothpicks to use on the antipasto brochettes?"

"I think so," Rory answered. "Come say hi to Nora."

Harrison appeared, and Nora felt John stiffen. Her ex-fiancé had on a gingham Vineyard Vines shirt, flat-front khaki shorts, and slip-on loafers.

"I'll go look for the toothpicks," Rory said to Harrison, "so you can visit with Nora and her boyfriend."

Harrison's forward motion stuttered.

Could it be, Harrison, that you're astonished by John's incredible appeal?

"Glad you could come." Harrison gave her a polite hug during which their chests came nowhere near touching. Then he shook John's hand with more enthusiasm than necessary as the two men exchanged names. "What do you do, John?"

"I own Lawson Training in Shore Pine."

"I'm not familiar with it. What kind of training do you offer there?"

"Emergency preparedness and response."

"Great, great."

"What do you do?" John asked tersely.

"I practice orthodontics at the office I founded. It's meaningful to own a business here in the community where I was raised. To give back. Nora and I"—he gently squeezed her elbow—"have known each other a long time. We're both invested here."

John set his mouth in a flat line.

"We just received our plaque," Harrison said to her. "The one we received from the city because of our Best of Merryweather recognition?"

"Oh, sure."

"We already have it hanging proudly in our waiting room."

Men. So tiresome. What was with their irrepressible need to beat their chests in front of one another? *You work there? Well, I work here! You drive that? I drive this! You vacationed there? I vacationed here! That's your golf handicap? Here's mine! Chuckle chuckle chuckle.*

"Come this way," Harrison said. "I'd like to show you the fireplace we just had re-rocked." He kept up a steady stream of subtly self-congratulatory talk.

For the next half hour, the ten guests mingled with Rory and Harrison in their beautiful and tasteful den and kitchen. Folk rock played softly. Antipasto brochettes circulated.

Then they all moved into a dining room swathed in decorations that paid homage to Shakespeare's *A Midsummer Night's Dream*. Two light fixtures dripped sparkling beads. Vases of varying heights held flower arrangements in shades of plum, pink, and deep red. Actual, honest-to-goodness moss served as placemats and wooden slabs served as chargers. The plates and goblets shone matte-gold. In the center of every place setting rested a tropical leaf as big as a child's head on which had been written the dinner menu in scrolling calligraphy.

Nora heard John grumble something dark under his breath and had to bite her lip to keep a giggle at bay. No doubt, the table had already been photographed extensively for the *Say Yes to Beauty* blog.

When they took their seats according to their place cards, it became apparent that Harrison and Rory had assumed Nora's guest would be female, because single guys were sitting on both

Nora's side and John's side. The single guy next to Nora had a trendy beard and hair shaved on the sides and slicked back on top.

She had to hand it to Rory. He wasn't bad. He was fairly eligible. It was just that he wasn't John. Every man other than John, including the formidable Adolphus Brook, had now become a pale, watery also-ran.

Before they began eating, Rory took out her huge Nikon and snapped candids. She repeated the process after the first course arrived.

"What in the world is she doing?" John asked, bending his head near Nora's shoulder. She could feel his breath on her skin. Tingles flowed down to her fingertips in response.

"Shooting pictures for her very successful blog."

"What am I supposed to do? Look at her? Not look at her?"

"Either. So long as you appear to be having an amazing time."

"The fact that she's taking pictures is making it hard for me to have an amazing time."

"Therein lies the rub."

"This will be my one and only visit here," he vowed.

"Aye, aye, captain."

"Harrison's a tool."

She glanced in Harrison's direction and caught him watching John with a troubled expression. The grim cast of his jaw may have indicated a twinge of . . . jealousy? "I know now what I didn't back then," Nora said. "Harrison wasn't the one for me."

"No. He didn't deserve you."

She met John's eyes.

"I don't deserve you either," he said. "But I'm smarter than he is because I know better than to let you go."

At work the following Monday morning, John was making his way through his email inbox when he spotted a name that caused his heart to miss a beat.

From: Sherry Thompson

Subject: Meeting

He leaned back in his chair, letting his hands fall away from the keyboard. He stared at her name.

For as long as he could remember, he'd thought about finding his birth mother. And now, suddenly, here was an email from her. He was thirty-three years old and for the first time in his life had received a communication from his biological mother.

The familiar need for information about his heritage and his medical information still existed within him. However, over the past four weeks since he'd mailed his letter to her, he'd gotten used to *not hearing* from Sherry.

He'd stopped thinking every phone call was from her. He'd stopped bracing himself every time he opened his mailbox or email. He'd adjusted to Sherry's silence, mostly because his time, energy, and thoughts had been focused on Nora.

He planted his elbows on his desk and rested his forehead on the heels of his hands. He prayed until the commotion within him calmed. Then he lifted his head. And opened her email.

John,

Thank you for your letter. It was so good to learn about you and your life.

My husband and I saw *Uncommon Courage* when it came out. We had no idea, of course, that you were related in any way to me. I'm amazed by the fact that you are the John Lawson of the movie and book. Your accomplishments are truly impressive, and I'm more pleased than I can express by the success you've made of yourself.

I appreciate the courtesy you extended to me when you assured me that the next communication between us would be mine. That was both respectful and thoughtful.

Contact between us is difficult for me. Because of that, after receiving your letter, I took some time to decide how best to respond. In the end, I've come to hope that it might be beneficial to us both to meet in person. I'd like to answer the questions that you very understandably have and I'd like to explain my situation to you.

I'm free this Thursday or next Tuesday for lunch. Perhaps we can meet at The Grapevine restaurant, which is located between where you live in Shore Pine and where I live in Aberdeen. Let me know if either of those dates or that location is convenient for you.

Sincerely, Sherry

• • •

Text message from John to Nora:

John

I just received an email from Sherry. She suggested we meet for lunch this Thursday or next Tuesday at The Grapevine. According to my phone map, it looks like The Grapevine is on the outskirts of the town of McCleary. Will either of those times work for you? I'd really like for you to come.

Nora

John! Oh my goodness! I'm surreptitiously texting during a town council meeting on tourism. I'll call you as soon as this meeting wraps. I'm visiting a caterer in Olympia Thursday morning to discuss the Antique Fair, so I can drive to The Grapevine and meet you there in plenty of time to have lunch with Sherry. But please don't feel obligated to include me.

John

I don't feel obligated. I want you there.

• • •

Sherry,

Thank you for your email. Lunch this Thursday at The Grapevine will work for me. Is it all right with you if I bring my girlfriend?

She's a genealogist and was instrumental in my search to locate you.

—John

• • •

John,

If you feel comfortable with your girlfriend being there, then it's certainly all right with me if she joins us for lunch. I'll make a reservation at The Grapevine for noon on Thursday. I'll wear a bright pink scarf so you'll be able to identify me.

Sincerely, Sherry

CHAPTER

Twenty-one

Outings that begin with a sullen grandmother and a Russian housekeeper cannot be expected to end well. Willow believed this maxim in theory. Yet that didn't stop her from continually testing it in practice.

"The state of church music in this day and age deeply saddens me," Grandma proclaimed. Her small frame was belted into the passenger seat of Willow's Range Rover.

"Um-hmm," Valentina murmured consolingly from the back seat.

"The great old hymns of our faith have stood for generations. Some were written by the likes of St. Francis of Assisi and Martin Luther. But are we singing them in our churches anymore?"

"Sometimes." Willow injected a bright note into her voice.

"No, we are not," Grandma answered. "Hymnals are being replaced by computer lyrics on awful electronic screens. Excellent classical music is being replaced with songs no one's ever heard. We're expected to sing a simple chorus over and over again ad nauseam in a monotone." She sucked air disapprovingly through her lips.

"Mmm," Valentina offered in sorrowful commiseration.

"They've done away with hymnals at four out of Merryweather's five churches," Grandma continued. "My own Grace Church is the only one that hasn't fallen to temptation. Our building is one hundred years old, Willow! Imagine erecting a screen in such a beautiful sanctuary and expecting us to accept modern rock-and-roll tunes. I've already told the pastor that it'll only happen over my dead body."

"I'm sure he was thankful for the feedback."

Grandma would be hosting her church's knitting group at her house tomorrow. Apparently her friend June had been on deck to host, but when June had been stricken with a shingles flare-up, Grandma had felt duty-bound to offer her home as a substitute location. Last night she'd stopped by Bradfordwood and told the tale of woe to Willow and Britt. Britt had said with incredible acting skill and a tone ripe with regret, "I'd offer to make all the food for the get-together, but I wouldn't want to constipate anyone."

Thus, Willow and Valentina had ridden to Grandma's rescue this afternoon to cook, clean, polish the silver, and set the table for tomorrow's gathering. Now it was nearing dinnertime, and Willow had packed the two older women into her car. They needed food. But before they hit the Edge of the Woods Bakery and Tearoom, Grandma had insisted on one quick stop.

Willow pulled up in front of Nora's Bookish Cottage. A new custom-painted dark-matte-gray Lincoln Navigator was already parked there. "It looks like Nora has company."

"Her new boyfriend?" Grandma asked.

"I assume so."

"Is he a Christian?"

"You know that he is. I've heard you ask this question of Nora at least twice."

"I tend to doubt the salvation of good-looking men."

Laughter burst from Willow. She went around and helped Grandma from the car. "God doesn't look at the outside, remember? He looks at the heart."

"Yes, but it's easier for a camel to go through the eye of a needle than for someone who is handsome to enter the kingdom of God."

The three of them made their way up the walkway. "It's easier for a camel to go through the eye of a needle than for someone who is *rich* to enter the kingdom of God," Willow corrected. "That's what that verse says."

"What's true of rich men is doubly true of handsome men who are also rich. They're prone to vanity and promiscuity and greed. It's hard on me to have my granddaughter dating someone who looks like that."

"He's a national hero!" Willow opened the front door a crack and called, "Hello," in a carrying voice. She wanted to give Nora and John plenty of warning should they be making out.

"Hello?" Nora called back.

"Grandma and Valentina and I stopped by because Grandma wants to give you something." Willow led the older women toward the living room—

Her gait cut to a halt.

Nora and John were inside. Fine. As expected. But Corbin was with them, too. *Corbin.* The three of them were on their feet in front of the spots where they'd no doubt been sitting moments ago.

Corbin regarded her levelly, his features defensive. He had on track pants and a well-worn Nike T-shirt. He'd been wearing a suit the night of Grandma's birthday, but today he looked like a man you could snuggle up with. Lay your head on. Watch a movie with while you both talked back to the screen and laughed and ate homemade nachos.

She'd once snuggled with him and laid her head on him and watched movies with him while eating nachos.

Seeing him was like a javelin to the chest.

"Hello." Willow attempted to appear unbothered by the javelin.

John and Corbin greeted them and Nora came forward to give out hugs. She shot Willow a look of silent apology.

"Nora." Grandma drew herself upright. "I'd like to give you this hymnal." She handed Nora the book. "Soon the hymnal will be a thing of the past and all the beautiful, beautiful songs inside it will be forgotten and unappreciated. I hope I can trust you to keep this safe in your little library."

"You can trust me to keep it safe." Nora accepted the hymnal then motioned toward the living area. "Would you like to sit down? Can I get you anything?"

"No, no," Grandma replied. "We're on our way to the tearoom."

"Valentina, can I get you anything?"

"I good, miss! Good." Valentina's circular face beamed.

"You've been helping Grandma get ready for tomorrow, right?" Nora asked Valentina. "That was nice of you and Willow."

"Yes, yes. The weather so nice! Sunny!"

As usual, Valentina's answers didn't quite match up with their questions. Having a conversation with her could be like reading *Alice in Wonderland*. You were charmed, but you also couldn't help but wonder if you might be on drugs.

Grandma, bolstered by the fresh audience, gave a repeat airing of her grievances against electronic screens and modern worship songs. The guys listened politely. Willow avoided looking at Corbin while trying not to look as if she was avoiding looking at Corbin.

Ever since she'd been confronted with him at Grandma's party, he'd been hovering just beneath her thoughts. She kept shoving him away, yet he kept hovering. Several times she'd spotted him around town or on the road and been besieged by turmoil, only to realize whoever she'd spotted wasn't Corbin after all. She hadn't been sleeping as well as she normally did, either. And her typical calm felt just beyond the reach of her fingertips.

Willow allowed herself one cautious peek in his direction. His body was still as mercilessly fit as it had been when they'd been together. She'd always loved his body. She was tall, but he'd towered over her in the best way. Not too tall. Not too brawny. Just deliciously right.

To her everlasting shame, she found that she still loved his body.

She moved her attention from Corbin to Nora. Willow had been advising her sister to take things slow with John. It was a difficult balance beam to walk because she didn't want to come across as meddlesome or bossy or pessimistic. However, she earnestly *did* want to impart to Nora the knowledge that experience had carved into her.

She and Corbin had not taken things slow. They'd only dated for a few months, but they'd been going at one hundred miles per hour the entire time. When you crashed into a wall going that speed, it hurt.

She didn't want that for Nora. Nor did she want to stand here, her ex-boyfriend's presence viscerally reminding her how alone and bitter she was while Nora and John broadcasted extreme happiness. She clearly wasn't a good person, because she had an urge to grab her sister's shoulders and inform her that her romance with John couldn't possibly go anywhere so long as John had Corbin as a friend.

She felt as if she'd caught Nora red-handed being cordial to the enemy. Had Nora been hanging out with Corbin regularly and hiding it from her?

Mercifully, Grandma kept the visit short.

Back in the car, the road skimming beneath them and Willow's emotions a lump in her throat, her phone chimed to signal a text.

At a stoplight, Willow checked it. From Nora. *I'm really sorry about that. John and Corbin had been at the gym, and Corbin dropped John off here afterward.*

Willow set the phone aside without replying.

"Is John's tall friend a Christian?" Grandma asked.

"I don't know."

"It would definitely be easier for him to go through the eye of a needle than to enter the kingdom of God."

Nora arrived at The Grapevine ten minutes prior to John's scheduled lunch with Sherry. His Suburban already waited in the parking lot, so she pulled in next to him. In under thirty seconds, she was out of her car, he was out of his, and he'd wrapped her in a hug.

He bent his head and pressed his face near where her shoulder met her neck. She could feel banked tension in his body. "Have you been here long?" she asked.

"A couple of minutes."

"Have you seen anyone wearing a bright pink scarf enter the restaurant?"

"No. Either we arrived first or Sherry arrived very early."

She leaned back to study his face. "How are you feeling?"

He shifted, interlacing his fingers at the small of her back. "I'm feeling like I can't believe this is finally happening. All my life I've wondered about her."

It was hard to imagine growing up with an empty box inside you that needed answers neither you nor your parents had access to. John had spent his whole life that way. For decades, it was what he'd known. And now—suddenly—he was going to meet the person who could give him those answers.

For John, today was like the metal piece that held up the center of a teeter-totter. Before, the teeter-totter had slanted down in one direction. After today, it would slant down in the opposite direction. Today was the fulcrum.

"Are you nervous?" Nora asked.

"Not really."

She wished she could say the same. Her stomach had been jumpy all day because she so badly wanted this meeting to go well for him.

"I'm glad this isn't going to drag out any longer," he said. "I'm ready to get this done."

"Understandable." Delicately, she combed her fingers through the hair at the back of his neck, smoothing it into place. He'd worn a simple navy crewneck sweater and jeans with his Red Wing boots. His jaw was smooth and clean-shaven.

He always looked great, even without effort. But she could tell that he had put in effort today, which caused protectiveness of him to swell within her. John had once vanquished terrorists intent on killing him and the people he'd been guarding. She couldn't even vanquish the to-be-read pile of books on her nightstand. It was ridiculous to feel protectively toward him. It was also unavoidable.

John had shown her Sherry's emails. In writing, Sherry had come across as a careful, circumspect, gracious woman. Nora didn't think Sherry had proposed today's meeting for her own sake but for John's, which said a lot about her generosity.

However, the fact that she'd written to John that "contact between us is difficult for me" concerned Nora. John had told Nora that he had no expectations for a future relationship between himself and Sherry. In this case, though, Nora's book knowledge of the adoption triad—adoptees, birth parents, and adoptive parents—was a liability. She knew that a sense of rejection, of being unwanted, could plague adoptees. Especially male adoptees.

It sent a chill down her every time she entertained the possibility of Sherry unwittingly or wittingly making John feel unwanted. Like a boxer who'd recently taken a hard right to the chin, John was already staggering from the diagnosis concerning his vision. He needed time to regain his footing, not another hard right.

She held his face in her hands and kissed him.

He meant more to her than she'd yet been able to successfully articulate either to him or to herself. He was her boyfriend, but he'd also become one of her closest friends. Their relationship was the sweetest joy of her days. Her most precious possession. "What time is it?" she asked.

"It's five till." They stepped apart, hands still linked. She clicked her key fob once to lock her car, then again for good measure. Together, Nora and John walked toward the restaurant beneath a pale blue sky.

The Grapevine was the type of place that reveled in warm weather because it had as many tables outdoors as it did in. The passageway that led from the sidewalk to the outdoor seating gave her a view of a space reminiscent of the children's book *The Secret Garden*. It was enclosed on one side by the restaurant and on the other sides by walls covered in ivy. A fountain occupied the middle of the courtyard. Ferns and tall pots of pink and red flowers clustered in the corners.

They entered The Grapevine's interior. While John gave the

hostess his name and Sherry's name, Nora's attention combed anxiously over the diners filling the indoor space. No woman in a pink scarf.

Her heart started to race. *Nora! This isn't your reunion. You're supposed to be here to support John, to be steady.*

"Right this way," the hostess said. She picked up two menus and led them outside.

As soon as John stepped into the courtyard, he saw her.

Sherry sat at a table near the back corner. She wore a pink scarf and a white shirt with its collar turned up. As they approached, she rose, her face softening with emotions he couldn't name. "John," she said quietly, opening her arms.

He hugged her. She was several inches shorter than he was, but her arms were strong around him. When other people would have pulled away, she gripped him tighter, and he realized that the hug wasn't a greeting so much as a conversation. She was communicating to him that she hadn't forgotten him and that it was good to see him for the second time in his life. He communicated the same to her.

Here she was, at last. Sherry. His birth mother.

John waited, holding her patiently until she was ready to release him. When she moved away, she smiled at him for a long moment through watery eyes. Then they all took their seats.

"I don't often cry," she told him.

Nora had a tissue ready. "Here you are."

"Thank you." Sherry took it and dabbed her eyes. "My. Forgive me. I'm more overcome by . . . this than I thought I would be."

"I understand," Nora said, and he was grateful he'd brought Nora. No one was better at dealing with women's feelings than other women.

"I'm Sherry."

"Nora. It's nice to meet you."

"It's nice to meet you, too."

Sherry reminded John of Laura Bush. She had the same brown hair styled in the same classy, conservative way. She was close in age to his mom, and he could easily picture Sherry as one of his mom's friends from church or work or the group she played tennis with on Saturdays. Sherry's diamond earrings, ring, and clothes suggested that she had both means and good taste.

"You look like my dad and my brother Jeff," Sherry said to him.

He couldn't see himself in Sherry at all except in her brown hair and maybe her eyes. Were her eyes hazel? They were. Like his.

This was *strange*. This was like wishing all your life that you could meet a fictional character . . . say, Luke Skywalker. And then one sunny summer day, you found yourself sitting at a table across from Luke Skywalker.

Sherry was studying him intently, too. "This is hard to believe."

"It is," he agreed. "Thank you for answering my letter."

"You're welcome."

A male waiter arrived and it took effort for John to collect his thoughts enough to say that he wanted to drink water. Nora chatted with the waiter, asking him which lunch dishes he recommended. The normalcy of their exchange settled John.

"Would it be all right if we order now?" Nora asked the waiter.

He said that it was. Sherry ordered. Nora ordered the dish the waiter had recommended.

"Two of those, please," John said, though he didn't feel like eating. The waiter moved off.

"Tell me about your family, John." Sherry had excellent posture. She sat very straight and still, hands in her lap.

He told her about his parents and his younger sister.

"They sound wonderful," she said.

"They are."

"I'm glad to know that you were raised by people like them."

"What about you, Sherry?" Nora asked. "I'd love to know about your family."

"My husband's name is Ed. He's an engineer. We have two children together. Our oldest is Lauren, who's twenty-six. She works as a consultant in San Francisco. She's engaged to be married."

"How nice," Nora said.

"Our son, Ben, is twenty-two. He's finishing up at Gonzaga University. They're both doing very well."

"That's wonderful to hear," Nora said.

A brief pause. "I—I know that you have a lot of questions, John. About me. About your birth. I . . ." She drew in a long breath, looking between him and Nora. "I thought perhaps I should start at the beginning, so you can know a little about my background. Would that be all right?"

"That would be great," Nora answered in a tone that assured her she could begin her story anywhere she liked.

"Sure," John said.

"I'm from Bend, Oregon," Sherry said. "Did you already know that?"

"We did," Nora answered.

"My parents were and are wonderful people. Their faith is the central pillar of their lives. They were strict and protective of me when I was growing up. But good, too. Always good."

John dipped his chin.

"I attended Portland State," Sherry continued. "After I graduated from there, I got a teaching job in Shelton. My parents were happy with that because they wanted me to live with family, and my aunt Deborah, my dad's sister, lived in Shelton at that time. I was thrilled to move in with Deborah because she was one of my favorite people. She was successful and independent and, in my eyes, forward-thinking compared to my parents. She and I had always been close."

"We visited the house you and Deborah lived in," John said.

"Did you? Ah." Sherry seemed to lose herself in memories for a moment before refocusing on him. "When I became pregnant, I'd just turned twenty-two and I was *terrified*. I don't think there's any way to explain to you how terrified I was, how distraught. I didn't know what to do. Every time I thought about how my parents and brother might react if I told them the news, my head would spin."

Sherry quieted as their waiter delivered their drink order, then continued talking in her articulate, measured way once he was gone.

"I couldn't bear the thought of how upset my parents would be and how mortifying it would be for them to have to share the news of my pregnancy with our extended family and their friends. So I decided not to tell them." Frown lines marked her forehead. "Later, much later, when my own daughter was twenty-two, I realized how foolish I'd been. Of course I should have told my parents about my pregnancy. *Of course* I should have. Their love for me would have been strong enough to bear the truth." Regret filled her expression. "My only explanation is that back then, the scared twenty-two-year-old I was couldn't face telling them."

"I understand," John said. And he did. "I don't blame you. For anything."

"I decided to put you up for adoption," she said with a faint rasp in her voice, "because I wanted you to have the best life possible, and I realized that I couldn't give that to you."

"That's exactly what my mom and dad always told me about you."

"God bless them." Moisture filled her eyes again. "And thank you, John. For not blaming me. I carry guilt about what happened."

"Don't."

Nora squeezed Sherry's hand. Strength appeared to flow through the contact from Nora into Sherry. When Nora let go, Sherry had herself back under control.

"How were you able to keep your parents from finding out about your pregnancy?" Nora asked.

"Deborah helped me. Because of her help, it wasn't very hard, actually. I was already living several hours away from my mom and dad. I visited Bend when I was three or four months along but not yet showing. Then summer vacation arrived, and Deborah and I told them that I'd received a last-minute invitation to teach summer school in Minnesota. That was a lie. I stayed right where

I was in Shelton with Deborah until the baby—John was born. Deborah was a lifeline for me in those days. She went with me to my obstetrician's visits and helped me research adoption agencies. She was with me, the only one with me, during labor and delivery."

"Were you able to spend time with John after he was born?"

"I got to hold you for about an hour." Sherry looked at him as if searching his features for the baby she remembered. "You were a big baby. Beautiful. Perfectly healthy. With a cry as loud as your silences were quiet."

He didn't know what to say. His mom had taken hundreds of baby pictures of him, so he knew what Sherry had seen when she'd looked at him as a newborn. He also knew what he'd looked like at every age after that, which was knowledge Sherry didn't have.

"We know from John's birth certificate that you named him Mark Lucas," Nora said.

"Yes. Lucas is my father's name. And Mark was my favorite boy's name."

"Did you continue teaching in Shelton?" John asked.

"No. A few weeks after the adoption, I returned to Oregon. I moved in with close friends in Grants Pass and got a job teaching second grade. A year or so later I met Ed at church, and we started dating. As things grew more serious between Ed and me, I wrestled with whether or not to tell him about the pregnancy and the baby I gave up."

Sherry took a sip of water. The cup trembled slightly before she set it down. "When I was pregnant, I thought I'd be able to deliver the baby, then go on with life as if nothing had happened. Instead, I couldn't forget any of it. Keeping it secret from my family hadn't made it go away. Every single day I was aware that there was a little boy walking around in the world somewhere that I'd given birth to but knew nothing about." She sighed. "I thought I'd be able to push down the things that had happened to me, but I couldn't. The things that happen to us in our lives *happen*. They won't and can't be pushed down."

John had thought plenty about Sherry and how this reunion

might affect her. He'd expected this meeting to be difficult for her, and it seemed that it was. He hadn't thought enough, however, about how living with her decision might have affected her across the years since she'd made her choice. He'd been too focused on how her choice had impacted him.

"It got to a point," Sherry said, "when I realized I was falling in love with Ed and he with me, and I knew I had to tell him. It still makes me cry to think about the grace he immediately extended to me. He was so supportive. He *is* so supportive. He's always assured me that he's fine with me telling my parents, my extended family, and our kids. But I never have told them. Deborah and Ed are the only ones who know."

John had run all the scenarios in his mind so he'd half-expected this news. He'd already told her he didn't blame her, and wouldn't start blaming her or judging her now. Still, it was hard to hear her say that she hadn't told her legitimate children about him, her illegitimate child.

"I never made a conscious decision *not* to tell Lauren and Ben. It was more a question of . . . when." Sherry looked to Nora. "Do you tell a toddler that you once had a baby you gave away? Do you look into the trusting face of an elementary school girl and tell her? Do you tell your son when he's a teenager and already full of reasons not to like you?"

"I don't know," Nora answered kindly, honestly.

"The right moment never came," Sherry said. "If I told my kids and my parents and the rest of my family now, I'm afraid that their perception of me would change. They'd no doubt be angry with me for keeping something this important from them for so long. And they'd have a right to be angry." She took another sip of water. "I wish I'd told everyone about the pregnancy right from the beginning. Instead of trusting the people closest to me with the truth, I covered everything up. I made a big mistake."

"We all make mistakes," John said.

"My big mistake explains why I said in my email to you, John, that contact between us would be difficult."

He nodded. Sherry had given him a great deal of information, but she'd said nothing yet about his birth father and her relationship with him. And he'd said nothing yet about his diagnosis. Both subjects needed to be addressed. "A few months ago I learned that I have an inherited eye condition called Malattia Leventinese, which is partly why I wanted to contact you. Have you ever heard of it?"

"No," she said with concerned surprise. "I haven't."

"It causes vision loss."

"I'm so sorry, John. You said that it was inherited. So is it . . . the kind of thing that can hide for generations and then crop up?"

"No. Not everyone in a family that's affected by it will have it. But a lot of people will. About half. You would know if it's in your family."

"No one in my family has it."

He took a second to absorb that. "What that means is that I inherited it from my biological father."

Sherry flinched.

"I apologize for bringing him up, but I'd appreciate the chance to get a medical history from you and from him."

"Of course. That makes sense. Only . . ." She smoothed her fingers along the corner of the table over and over. "Are you sure you want to know about him?"

"I'm very sure," he said without hesitation.

She dropped her hands back into her lap. He watched her grip her wrist reflexively. "The thing is . . . it's not a . . . pleasant story. I've thought about whether or not to discuss it with you, and I still don't know if I should. I just . . . I'm unsure. I don't want to hurt you."

His muscles tightened with worry. She wouldn't withhold the identity of his birth father from him, surely. "If Malattia Leventinese doesn't run in your family, then it must have come from my biological father," he said calmly. "I can't contact him or his relatives about the condition unless I know who he is."

She swallowed. "Yes, but I'm afraid that it will be difficult for you to hear about him. That it will cause you unnecessary pain."

What could have happened between Sherry and his father? Dread began to simmer within him. "I'd still like to know."

Her eyes held a world of pain and indecision. "Are you very, very sure?"

"Yes." He'd faced plenty of challenging things in his life. No part of him wanted to shy away from this. "It's important for me to know who both my parents are."

Sherry spoke carefully, as if each word were a stepping-stone in a stream she had to cross. "The winter after I moved in with Deborah, I went hiking alone on one of the trails outside of Shelton." He read apology in her face. "I'd been walking for about twenty minutes when I . . ." Her voice faded to nothing. She cleared her throat. She was still gripping one wrist, so tightly her knuckles had whitened. "I was pulled off the path by a man," she finally managed to say.

No, John thought.

"He dragged me out of sight." Her voice shook. Sorrow weighted her frown. "He put duct tape over my mouth and around my wrists. He . . ." Her gaze slid from his.

No, he wanted to yell. *No!*

Nora was dead quiet. He couldn't stand to look at her.

"He took advantage of me." He could hear growing courage in Sherry's tone even as his own courage drained out of him. "Af—afterward, I managed to get myself back to the house. Deborah took me to the hospital." She paused to inhale and exhale. Once. Twice.

"I was treated and evidence was taken and stored. I'd hardly even seen the man's face because he was pressing my cheek into the dirt the whole time, but I answered the detective's questions as best I could."

John couldn't speak.

"The man who attacked me raped five more women over the next five years," Sherry said. "His final victim was a woman named Robin Bradford. Her, he killed. She was only twenty-five, and she was the mother of two little girls."

John felt like he was going to vomit. He couldn't breathe. He couldn't move. He sat motionless while everything inside him tore apart.

"I'm thankful now that I allowed the nurses to take, um, evidence, because when they finally caught the man who'd done it, that evidence helped put him away. His name was Brian Raymond."

John's heart beat in hollow, aching thuds.

"A month after the attack," Sherry said, "I found out I was pregnant."

Through the rush of awful thoughts filling his brain, John understood, in a distant way, how hard it must have been for Sherry to tell him this. Yet she was looking at him like she wanted to extend compassion, not like she expected to receive it. "I'm so sorry, John. I wish the facts were different. I know how terrible they are."

"It's okay," he said hoarsely. "Thank you for telling me." He was too devastated to say anything else. He regretted that he couldn't find more words, better words. Why—why wasn't Nora saying anything? It took all John had to glance at her.

Nora's skin had paled. As if in answer to his gaze, she turned and met his eyes. In her face he saw two things. Horror. And disgust.

He reached toward her, and she jerked instinctively back.

He pushed to his feet so quickly that the legs of his chair made a loud scraping sound. "I'm sorry," he told Sherry with a voice like sandpaper. "I can't stay."

"I understand," Sherry assured him.

"I'm sorry," he said again.

"It's all right."

"John," Nora said urgently.

He didn't answer. He stalked from the restaurant without once looking back.

Nora balanced her palms on the table and rose halfway to standing as she watched John leave. Should she go after him? Or give him room? She wanted to go after him, but doing so would mean leaving Sherry here alone after Sherry had just finished trusting them with her traumatic story.

Gradually, filled with numbing gray shock, Nora lowered into her chair. John's biological father had raped Sherry. John's biological father had raped and killed Nora's mother. Her lovely sweet *mother*. John's biological father was the monster who'd stolen her mother's chance to live, to be a mother to her.

That man's blood flowed in John's veins.

But John . . . John was good. Had he seen just now what she'd been thinking? He'd definitely seen how she'd recoiled. She'd been processing. She'd needed a minute to get her thoughts right.

Panic and remorse swirled inside her. She hadn't guarded herself like she should have. What had her response betrayed to him?

Vaguely, she became aware of Sherry's gentle hand on her arm. Sherry's words. "Nora? Are you all right?"

"I think so."

"Here. Drink some water."

Nora sat back and took two long sips of icy water while Sherry watched anxiously. "Better?"

"Yes."

"I'm not surprised that John needed space. Imagine the shock of finding out that you were conceived that way." She clicked her tongue. "Ever since I received his letter, I've been praying about whether to meet with John and whether to tell him about the circumstances of his birth. I hope I made the right choice."

"I think you did. You warned him, Sherry. John was the one who decided that he wanted to know."

Sherry appeared to think through Nora's statement, and then, in the relaxing of her posture, to accept it. "Between you and me, I almost had an abortion when I found out I was expecting. I even went to the clinic and sat in the waiting room, but I couldn't go through with it. The Holy Spirit spoke to me in a powerful way, and there was just no way I could . . . go through with it. What I didn't get a chance to say to John just now is that I'm thankful that I carried him and gave birth to him. Will you tell him that for me?"

"I will if you want me to, but I think it might mean a lot to John if you told him yourself through a phone call or email or letter."

She paused. "You're right. I'll tell him." Sherry surveyed Nora's face. "Are you sure you're feeling okay? You're very pale."

Sherry deserved an explanation. "Part of why . . ." She licked her lips. "Part of why John reacted the way that he did is because my mother was Robin Bradford."

Sherry blanched. "No."

"My mother was killed by Brian Raymond, and John knows that." Grief scored Nora. Grief for John and the misery intertwined with the truth of his conception.

• • •

Text message from Nora to John:

Please call me.

CHAPTER Twenty-two

John was shaking.

He noticed it as he peeled off his clothing and yanked on his swim trunks. He was shaking. Add it to the list of things that were very, very wrong with him.

He reached his dock, walked to its end, and dove into the lake. His arms sliced the water as he swam, hard, toward nowhere.

His life was the result of an act of violence. A man his mother hadn't known, a stranger, had physically overpowered and violated her.

And he was the outcome.

A lot of babies were put up for adoption by young, unmarried mothers because they were unwanted. Sherry had been young and unmarried when she'd had him, so he'd assumed he'd been unwanted. But this?

He'd been far more than an accidental mistake. The sex hadn't been consensual, which made his conception a horrible injustice.

He couldn't imagine why she hadn't aborted him. Agony gripped him when he thought of what it must have been like for her to have her rapist's child growing inside of her.

Half of what made up his physical body—his bones and blood and organs and skin—had come from a serial rapist and murderer.

Brian Raymond had raped Sherry and killed Nora's mother.

And that man made up half of who he was.

As if he could outswim the facts, he pushed himself harder. His burning muscles and rasping breath made him feel no better, yet he continued because he didn't know what else to do, had nowhere else to go. All his life, water had calmed him. After leaving Sherry and Nora he'd made his way straight to the lake, because he'd known that if anything could help, it was water. But there was no help to be found today. Not even here.

His sight was deteriorating because of a condition he'd inherited from his father. His father had left a mark of both symbolic and literal darkness on John. His blindness wasn't something he could escape. It *was* coming for him, and every day that he lived with impaired vision was a day that he'd be reminded who had saddled him with it.

There had been times when he'd been conflicted about whether or not to continue his search for his birth mother. But every time he'd chosen to move forward. Even today at the restaurant, Sherry had cautioned him. She'd asked him again and again if he was sure he wanted to know. He could have turned back. He hadn't, and now he couldn't unknow what he knew.

He had the answers he'd valued so highly, and they sickened him.

All his life, his mom and dad had been carefully building his identity like a statue made of stones. One stone here. One stone there. The things Sherry had told him today had jerked away the largest of the foundational stones and brought the whole structure crashing down.

Who am I?

He was the son of an evil man.

He stopped swimming and treaded water. Gasping for air, he looked back toward shore. He'd crossed a long distance, but this new perspective changed nothing about the landscape filling his head.

He couldn't see his house very well because his central vision had gone blurry. But he could make out its long, modern lines against the green of the hill. He lived in a very expensive house that his famous heroism had bought. People paid him ridiculous amounts of money to speak to their groups. Strangers lined up for the opportunity to shake his hand and take pictures with him and have him sign their books and DVDs of *Uncommon Courage*. When he'd met the President of the United States, *he* was the one who'd been thanked and admired.

What a joke.

An instinct to flee coursed through him so strongly he could taste it. He angled his body to the side, searching for somewhere to hide. He found nothing. Again he twisted. Again. Again. But his body was suspended in water. There was nothing to stand on. Nowhere to hide. Nowhere to run.

He swam in the direction of his dock, the memory of Nora's expression seared into his brain. He could see it in detail. Her brown eyes. Red hair. Milky skin. It had been like a slap to see her face, the face that had looked at him with such softness, staring at him with hatred. To watch her jerk back when he'd reached out.

On the day that his father had ripped her mother from her, Nora's life had changed in a way that could never be repaired or made right. Mothers were not replaceable. He got it.

He couldn't fault Nora. He understood what she'd felt after Sherry had told them that Brian Raymond was his father, because it was exactly the same thing he'd felt.

Still . . . it wrecked him to know that he loved her but that she'd been horrified by him. These last weeks it had seemed to him that everything in his life had brought him to this time and place for *her*. She was the hope and beauty and color in his days. She was priceless to him.

If the thing that had come between them had been something he could fight, he'd do whatever was needed to defeat it so they could be together. He'd travel anywhere. He'd empty his bank accounts. He'd sacrifice his body. He'd give up his future. But the valley that had opened between himself and Nora today wasn't something that he could fight. He was as powerless to change the things that had happened in the past as she was.

Up until today, it had been an ongoing struggle to think of asking her to love a man who was blind, who would not father children. Those things had already been too much to ask. This was a whole new level of impossible.

He hadn't told her that he loved her yet because he'd wanted to wait a reasonable amount of time. He'd been set on doing everything right with her.

He didn't know if it made it better or worse . . . the fact that he hadn't told her he loved her. It would probably make things better for her. But worse for him, because now it was too late to tell her.

When he reached the dock, he barely managed to haul his exhausted body onto its surface. He lay on his back, knees bent, feet on the rough wood, chest heaving.

He stayed on the dock so long that the sun began to arch toward the horizon. When cold finally drove him indoors, he purposely avoided looking at his cell phone. He'd silenced it before leaving The Grapevine.

He went to the shower in his master bathroom and stood beneath the spray for a long time, hoping it might warm him. It was no use. The cold was in his bones.

At his desk in his home office, he ran computer searches for information on Brian Raymond. His stomach churned and a headache beat against his skull. The things Brian Raymond had done disgusted him, but he continued until he'd read everything he could find on the man.

By then it was late.

He didn't turn a single light either on or off. He simply picked up his phone, went to his room, and fell onto his bed. He bent his elbow over his forehead, debating whether he could afford not to look at his phone until tomorrow. He didn't want to let the world in. Thing was, he had no house phone, so his family used his cell number when they wanted to reach him. His mom would worry if she couldn't get ahold of him after a few hours of trying.

He checked his phone and, sure enough, saw that his mom had left him a voicemail. She wanted to know what he'd like for lunch when he came over next Saturday. He sent her a text requesting lasagna.

He'd received a few work-related texts, voicemails, and emails, a text from Corbin, and a text from Nora that she must have sent thirty minutes after he'd left the restaurant. More recently, she'd sent a second text. *John?* was all it said.

Nora.

Pain and fury toward God fisted viciously around John's heart. Why had God allowed a man like Brian Raymond to conceive a child? And in that way? Why? It wasn't right. Sherry had been an innocent twenty-two-year-old. Why hadn't God protected her from Brian—or at the very least from pregnancy? John couldn't find any justice or fairness or grace in what had happened to Sherry.

And why, when he himself had had a 50 percent chance of inheriting a gene mutation from Brian, had God allowed him to inherit it? John had trusted God. He'd tried to glorify Him through his life, his company, his book, his speaking.

Sherry had received a rapist's baby.

And he'd received a diagnosis of blindness and a heritage that separated him from Nora.

What good, exactly, had Sherry's faith and his faith done them? Where had their all-powerful God been when they'd needed Him?

Before he mailed the letter to Sherry, Nora had prayed that his search for his birth mother would ultimately be for his good and Sherry's good. God had turned His back on her prayer.

Scowling fiercely, miserable inside, John wrote, deleted, started again, and deleted a response to Nora. Finally he sent, *I'm fine*, not true, *I just need time to deal with this. I know it's a lot to ask, but I'd appreciate it if you could give me four or five days. I'm doing my best to get my head around the things Sherry told us today, but it's a lot.*

After he hit send, scrolling dots appeared, letting him know that Nora was reading what he'd written. A few minutes later her response came through. *Just know that I care about you and that I'm thinking about you and praying for you.*

The words turned like a pocketknife in his midsection. Her kindness—or maybe pity?—made him feel all the blacker. With a growl, he tossed the phone a few feet away from him on the bed.

The memory of how Nora had looked at him after Sherry had told them that Brian was his father rose again and again in his thoughts. He couldn't stand to see it anymore. He wanted to shove everyone and everything away and be left alone.

In a failed bid to comfort herself, Nora had taken a bath, donned pajamas, put in the DVD of *Northamptonshire* season one, eaten a bowl of ice cream, and pulled a throw blanket over herself. None of it had successfully comforted her.

She was trapped in a mire of shock, fear, and suffocating regret.

The text she'd just received from John had reassured her that he was alive, which was good. But it had also informed her that he didn't want to see her, which was very bad.

She was no expert on healthy dating relationships, but she suspected that boyfriends and girlfriends were supposed to share their pain with each other, not shut each other out.

Could she really blame John for wanting time, though? Could she? Considering what he'd learned today, his request made sense.

In the hours since lunch . . . Honestly, it didn't really deserve the title of "lunch" since no food had been eaten. When their dishes had arrived, Nora and Sherry had immediately requested to-go containers because neither of them had been able to think about eating. When the waiter had brought them the containers, he'd informed them that the bill and tip had already been taken care of. John had paid both on his way out.

In the hours since their non-lunch, Nora had thought through the similarities between her mother and Sherry. Both women had lived in the same region of Washington, the region that Brian Raymond once prowled. Both women had been pretty twentysomethings at the time they were assaulted, just like Brian Raymond's other victims. Both women had gone walking alone.

She was a researcher, trained to take the smallest clues and grasp the secrets they might point to, yet she'd never once imagined that Brian Raymond could be John's father. Never. She'd known that John's father's name was left off of his birth certificate and adoption information sheet. Perhaps, if she'd viewed that detail as darkly ominous, then maybe . . .

But no. That clue had been entirely too obscure. She was sorry she hadn't seen Sherry's revelation coming—felt guilty that she hadn't—because if she had, she could have protected John somewhat from today's blindside.

She herself was having a brutal time accepting the fact that Brian Raymond, the person she'd always known as her mother's murderer, was also John's biological father—and she wasn't the one who'd discovered she was related to Brian. She could only imagine the difficulty John must be having and would continue to have with these new facts.

Robin, Nora's mother. Sherry, John's mother. Both women victims of the same man.

When she and John had been in The Grapevine's parking lot together, she'd hoped the meeting wouldn't hit John with another hard right to the chin. But in the end, John *had* been hit again. And now? He must be reeling.

His request for time was most likely for the best. At the moment, her emotions were a heaving muddle. It would be better, much better, to wait and see him again once they both had themselves back together and could view things in their proper perspective.

Only . . . since their first kiss, they'd spent time together every single day, except for when he'd been in Chicago. Even then, they'd been in touch often through phone calls and text messages.

Thus the fact that he wanted time apart stung unbearably. He didn't want to see her. And she feared he didn't want to see her, in part, because of how she'd reacted in those first moments after Sherry's revelation.

Her eyes filled with tears, blurring a scene of Adolphus talking with Lucy.

Time apart would be good! Yes, she'd miss him. She'd miss him like a person missed air when underwater. But she *could* fix this. She was smart and perfectly capable of figuring out how to get her relationship with John back on track. She'd figure out what needed to be done and said, and she'd do and say those things. Everything would be fine. She'd solve this. There was no reason to feel terrified down to the marrow of her bones that she'd lost everything they'd shared.

But she *was* terrified.

Down to the marrow of her bones.

John didn't leave his property for four days.

For every hour of those four days, the thought of Nora was like a burning coal in his stomach.

Not once in that time did he return to the lake. He slept like he'd been drugged and had a hard time forcing himself out of bed. He watched whole seasons of television shows on Netflix. He researched the bios of serial rapists online and read articles that dissected their psyches. He showered, but he couldn't be bothered to shave. He avoided exercise. He ate cereal or frozen food or more cereal. He let go of as many of his responsibilities at work as he could. What were they going to do about it, fire him? He owned the company. Over the years, he'd assembled a strong team of employees at Lawson Training. They could easily get by without him for a while, a fact that should have come as a relief but only made him feel worse.

More than once, he stood in front of his bathroom mirror peering at the face his birth parents had given him and feeling depression crawl over his mind and body.

He was no longer a SEAL. No longer the man who'd gone on that mission to Yemen. Back then, he'd known who he was. He'd liked that version of himself far more than he liked himself now.

He'd aged. He was going blind. He was on this earth because of rape.

When he finally backed his Plymouth out of his garage on Monday afternoon, he did so in order to attend the meeting he'd set up with Brian Raymond's mother.

Sherry had been difficult to find. But Brian Raymond's mother, Irene, had been easy. She'd been interviewed recently for an article about Brian's crime spree. The reporter had listed her as Irene Dewberry, age eighty-one, of Shelton. He'd located her through a simple telephone search. When he'd called and explained his identity, she immediately invited him to visit.

Weeds sprouted from sidewalk cracks on Irene's street. The bright yellow paint covering the buildings of her aging retirement community was working so hard to be happy that it had the opposite effect.

John spoke with the receptionist, then waited in the Activities Room, a space full of fake wood tables and the smell of Lysol. When he spotted a woman approaching, he stood.

Her white hair was cut no-nonsense short around a plain face free of makeup. She had on a cheap-looking floral cotton shirt, gray pants, and shoes that reminded him of something a nurse might wear. Bags of flesh swung from the bottom of her upper arms.

"I'm Irene." She offered a hand and gave his a firm shake.

"John."

She nodded, and they sat.

Her shrewd, dark eyes were set into skin webbed with wrinkles. She looked to him like a woman who'd lived through more than her share of trials and come through them toughened but unbroken. Her body might have softened with age, but he sensed that her will was as hard as a steel pipe. "Discovering that Brian was your father must have come as a shock to you," she said.

"It did."

"Discovering that Brian fathered you has come as a shock to me."

"I'm sure it has."

"It never occurred to me to think that Brian might have a child." She set her lips in a straight line. Her attention raked over his face.

He said nothing. He had no interest in hurting Irene by admitting that his gut wrenched every time he thought about having her awful son as his biological father.

"Have you had time to educate yourself about Brian and his crimes?" she asked.

"I educated myself as much as I could. The articles I read didn't say much about his childhood."

"And you'd like to know about it?"

"I would."

She rested one forearm on the table's surface. Her thumb circled the pad of her second finger. "I was married to Brian's father, Darrel, for about a year. He was a terrible man, and I can't say I was much better back then. After Brian was born, I struggled with alcoholism on and off for ten years or so." Her gaze didn't flinch. "I was young and stupid."

He waited while she seemed to collect her thoughts.

"I married Charlie Dewberry when I was thirty. Together, we had three children. We were married forty-eight years before he passed away, God rest his soul." She waited with pointed silence.

"God rest his soul," John said.

"Marrying a decent person makes a lot of difference," Irene stated. "Charlie was decent. Our family life wasn't perfect, but at least our kids came up in a house that was safe and stable." She scratched the side of her jaw. "The same can't be said of Brian."

John had no plans to pity Brian. He'd come today strictly for information. Maybe he was punishing himself, but if there was a reason why Brian had become what he'd become, John needed to know it.

"Brian was a quiet boy. Good-looking. Introverted. Intense. I can't remember him ever being carefree. He was always suspicious. Up until he was ten, back during my heavy drinking years before I met Charlie, I left Brian with Darrel a lot . . . which is one of the greatest regrets of my life. When Brian was little, he'd cry when I made him go to Darrel's. But when he got to be about five or so, he stopped crying altogether. I'd take him to his father's house, and he'd walk in without a word. He was at Darrel's the night Darrel killed himself."

Brian's history and Sherry's history were tangled together with his own history. Ugly or not, this story was a part of his story.

"As a teenager Brian was secretive," Irene continued. "He withdrew from me and Charlie and the younger kids. I knew that something was off with him, but whenever I tried to talk to him about it, he shut me out. I remember telling Charlie not to worry about it, that Brian was just a moody teenager. You see, it was easier on me to believe that than to deal with the truth. I had a full-time job and little kids to take care of, so I let Brian be because at least he wasn't an additional drain on my time or energy. He kept to himself. He handled his schoolwork and minded our rules." She coughed dryly.

"Can I get you something?" John asked.

"I wouldn't say no to a Diet Coke."

John went to the soda dispenser situated along one wall and filled a glass with ice and Diet Coke. He handed it to Irene, then returned to his chair.

"I drink Diet Coke faster than cars drink gas, and I'm as healthy as a horse. Don't believe it when people tell you Diet Coke isn't good for you."

"Okay." John found that he didn't hate the gruff woman before him. In fact, he felt almost unwillingly connected to her by the link they both had to Brian. Neither of them had wanted Brian to be vicious. But that hadn't been for them to decide. The evil Brian had done wasn't debatable or changeable. Brian *had* been vicious, and now neither of them could escape that fact or their tie to him.

When her glass was half empty, Irene set it aside and squinted at it. "The worst time of my life was after Brian's arrest, when we found out what he'd done. Many of our friends and family members turned on Charlie and me—me especially. I just about drowned in guilt and blame. I hated what he'd done to those women, but I attended his trial and visited him in jail and sent him the things they allowed me to send him, because after everything was said and done, he was still my son. When he committed suicide in prison, I grieved for him with a mother's love. . . . I've never forgotten what he was like when he was an innocent little boy." She tapped her temple and looked to John. "I never will forget."

Uncomfortable quiet settled between them.

"At some point along the way, the police allowed me to look at one of the notebooks they'd found in Brian's apartment," she said. "It was a kind of diary. He'd written in it and drawn in it a lot, too. In that notebook he said that he'd been sexually abused many times by Darrel's brother." Her eyes blazed. "I didn't know that. If I'd known that, I wouldn't have made Brian go to Darrel's. I would have gotten sober and protected Brian the way I should have. Of course I would have. If I'd known."

When John didn't reply, she asked, "Do you have questions for me?"

"Just one. I have an eye condition called Malattia Leventinese. Do any of your family members have it?"

She regarded him seriously. "I'm sorry to hear that you have Malattia Leventinese."

He gave a nod.

"I didn't inherit it," she told him. "But my father had it. So did his grandmother. And one of my brothers. And four of my nieces and nephews."

Her words were the answer to one of the primary questions that had sent him searching for his birth mother in the first place. He only wished the answers he'd collected hadn't come at such a high price. "In that case, there's a lot more I'd like to know. I'm hoping to put together a medical history for myself."

"Ask away, John. I'll do whatever I can to help."

She'd done it. Nora had managed to give John five days of privacy. They'd been five *rotten* days, but she'd survived them (barely) and was now about to send him a text message. She couldn't bear to wait any longer.

She anxiously paced her back porch, phone in one hand, the thumb of her other hand clamped between her teeth.

Ever since she'd filled her sisters in on her ill-fated non-lunch with John and Sherry, Willow and Britt had been working to prevent her from overdosing on tea and heartache. One or both of them had kept her company each evening after work. Britt had made steady deliveries of chocolate, and Willow had gifted her with expensive bubble bath and a new pair of shoes. They kept telling her that all would be well and that John would come around, that a separation of five days wouldn't break a relationship as solid as her relationship with John.

But only Nora had seen what he'd looked like when he'd discovered the identity of his father. Only she knew how uncharacteristic it was for him to stalk out of a restaurant, then send a text hours later asking for distance. Only she knew the struggle he'd gone through simply to come to a place where, because of his diagnosis, he'd allowed himself to let her in at all.

And only she knew how much she loved John.

His absence had focused a spotlight on the depth and breadth and tenacity of her feelings for him. It had clarified for her exactly what she felt for him.

Love. Love was what she felt.

The factual nature of that was exhilarating and terrifying.

She'd filled the past five days with a great deal of research salted with prayer. Since sleep had served her divorce papers without her consent, she'd read late into the night each evening. She'd finished four books written by relationship experts on the topic of overcoming conflict. She even reread *Uncommon Courage* to hunt for insights into John she may have missed the first time.

Dutifully, she'd prayed each morning. She'd asked God to forgive her for wanting John so badly when she knew very well she ought to be finding completeness in God alone.

She'd also asked God to forgive her for reacting to Sherry's revelation the way that she had because—yes—for a moment there she'd been horrified by the identity of John's father and by John himself. Worse, John had been able to tell.

Her reaction had been thoughtless and selfish. God offered her grace at every turn, yet as soon as she'd had the chance to offer John grace, she'd failed.

Nora stopped pacing, screwed her eyes shut, and sent the simple text message she'd composed to John. *How are you? I miss you, and I'd really like to see you.*

She waited one hour. Then two. Six.

She collected a matched set of twenty-four heartbroken hours. And still, he did not respond.

• • •

Facebook message from Duncan to Nora:

DUNCAN: I haven't heard from you lately, Librarian Extraordinaire. How are things between yourself and the Navy SEAL? Still continuing along a blissful course?

NORA: I'm afraid we've hit a bit of a rough patch.

DUNCAN: That's a shame. Sorry to hear it.

NORA: Never fear! I have the situation in hand. I'll fix it.

DUNCAN: Why don't you come see me and take your mind off of him? London is glorious this time of year. I'll squire you around to all the touristy spots. We can drink tea and see shows. With any luck, you may even be able to join me on the set.

NORA: That's a very kind offer. Thank you! For now, though, I'm completely focused on getting myself and John back onto our "blissful course," as you so aptly put it.

DUNCAN: And if things don't work out . . . ?

NORA: I'm not yet willing to contemplate that possibility.

• • •

Letter from Irene to her deceased husband, Charlie:

Sweetheart,

You always managed to see optimism in me. But even when I was a girl, I think a part of me was already old and pessimistic. Well, this old, pessimistic woman got to see a miracle yesterday.

A son. Of Brian's. A miracle son. And he's good. When I told Patti Jo his name, she went to her bookshelf and pulled out a book that must have cost thirty-five dollars. Charlie, the book's about him. Brian's boy, John. He's a veteran.

I now understand why God kept me alive, even though I didn't much want to go on living after you died. It was so I could meet this boy who's now a man. Through all these years, despite my sins and Brian's sins, God was at work. God had mercy on me, and yesterday, He let me see how He's been working.

I only wish that you'd been with me to see him, too.

I love you, Charlie. Always.

—Irene

CHAPTER Twenty-three

When a full day had come and gone since Nora had sent her unanswered text message to John, she sent another. *Are you okay, John? I'm worried about you.*

An hour passed without a reply. Nora spent that hour at her desk in her office at the Library on the Green trying and failing to accomplish work. She assumed there were plenty of girlfriends across America who were experiencing relationship problems and still managing to get an iota of work accomplished.

Alas, she was not in that group.

She dialed John's number. His phone rang four times then went to voicemail. "This is John Lawson. I'm sorry, I can't come to the phone right now. Please leave a message."

Nora hung up halfway through the beep. The sound of his voice was so sexy and familiar that stupid tears rushed to her eyes.

She was closing down her computer—no sense sitting here doing nothing of value—when her phone dinged. A text from John.

You don't need to worry about me, he'd typed. *I just need more time.*

Not a single one of the books on conflict had recommended the silent treatment. None! The silent treatment was death to a relationship. All the experts advocated deep, respectful, face-to-face conversations in which both partners communicated their feelings openly. She and John required a deep, respectful, face-to-face conversation! *We need to talk. I'm coming over*, she wrote.

No need.

She blinked with dismay at his words.

John was shutting her out. She'd been sticking up for him in her own mind, rationalizing his silence as best she could. She'd reacted to his withdrawal from her with six days of scared, hoping-for-the-best quiet. Now he was asking for even more time. More time wouldn't help.

They had to address what he was going through and deal with it together. They simply . . . had to. *You've been warned*, she replied to him via text. *I'm coming over.*

On the drive to Shore Pine, Nora battled her frustration and fear. The experts recommended that couples converse when both parties were calm. Calm would be good.

She decided that she'd lead with an apology for how she'd treated him that day at The Grapevine. Then she'd ask him to share his heart with her. Then she'd share hers. Then they'd discuss their issues, and they'd kiss and maybe cry and everything would be all right. These were the bright hours at the end of a beautiful waning day at the end of a beautiful waning summer that they *should* be enjoying together, she and John.

Turning off the main road onto his private driveway, Nora braced herself for the sight of him. He'd likely be waiting for her on his front lawn with his arms crossed.

However, when she pulled up, she saw no sign of him. She tamped down her jittery nerves, lifted her chin, walked to his door, and rang his doorbell.

He didn't answer.

She knocked with three composed knocks.

A full minute went by. His front door remained smoothly indifferent to her presence. She didn't want to believe that their relationship had deteriorated to the point that he wasn't going to open his door to her. Perhaps he wasn't at home? Perhaps he was working late?

But she'd told him she was coming. If he'd been at work during their exchange of text messages, he should have said so.

She tried the knob. Locked. She rang the doorbell and knocked again. Nothing.

She walked around the side of his house, hunting for unlatched windows she could tug open and crawl through. Who locked all their windows on a summer evening when they could instead be enjoying breezes off the lake? John, apparently.

She'd be able to get in via his back deck. He kept the doors there open almost all of the time. When she reached the back of his house, though, she found it as shuttered as everything else. She couldn't spot a single interior light. Facing the lake, she shaded her eyes. His boat was moored at the dock. No John.

She continued around the far side of the house, stopping only when she spotted a rock that looked as though it was begging to be thrown. She was usually a mild-mannered librarian, but nothing about this situation or her love for John was usual. Since the experts would definitely, definitely frown at her for throwing a rock through John's window, she opted to send him one last text message. Her fingers trembled as she typed. *I'm not going anywhere until I talk to you.*

She stomped along the small path that ran parallel to the side of his house, head down, mouth set in a belligerent line. If he didn't answer her text, she'd be forced to reconsider rock throwing. John might be the former SEAL, but she was the one who was about to dig in and fight—

"Nora."

Her face jerked up.

He stood ten yards or so in front of her with deep-green pine trees at his back. His feet were bare. He had on black basketball shorts and a slightly wrinkled gray T-shirt with the SEAL trident imprinted on it over his heart. A short beard covered cheeks that had hollowed since the last time she'd seen him. His hair was in disarray.

He didn't look like *her* John. He looked like the toughened, proven, intimidating man she'd first seen at Lawson Training.

She could see at a glance that he wasn't doing well, which caused her indignation to crack and compassion to flood into her like water into a ruptured boat. The girl who loved to be helpful desperately wanted to help him. But she could only do that if he'd let her. Her instinct was to go to him and bend her fingers into his hair and plead, *Let me help you.* But his expression warned her, when she'd advanced to within a few yards of him, to come no farther.

Say you're sorry, Nora. Lead with that. Then ask him to share what's on his heart. Remember? Except . . . memories of him were crowding into her head and his distress was confusing her heart. "I . . . haven't seen that T-shirt before," she said.

John drew his eyebrows together. Seeing Nora again was pure torture. He felt like he couldn't get enough air into his lungs, and her first words to him had been about his T-shirt?

"I might have been able to see that shirt if you'd invited me over at some point during the past six days," she said mildly.

He remained silent.

"But you didn't. Invite me over."

"No." The word came out raspy.

She took a step toward him, and he took a step back. Instantly, she stopped.

The thin straps of her white sundress ran over the smooth skin of her shoulders. She wore her hair down, and she had on tiny gold sandals. She looked healthy and clean, and she made him feel worse and dirty and if she came any closer, he didn't know what he'd do. Wrap her in his arms? Ruin the separation between them with hard, deep kisses? Beg her to look past his faults?

He hadn't known what to do about Nora since receiving her text message yesterday and her messages today. He didn't see how they could be together, but he wanted to drink a bottle of whiskey every time he thought about breaking up with her.

Since she'd rung his doorbell, he'd been sitting in his media room with his head in his hands, fingertips digging into his scalp, caught between wanting back what they'd had and knowing there was no going back. "Are you here to break up with me?" he asked.

Her face went smooth with shock. "*No*." She started to speak. Appeared to think better of it. Started again. "There are . . . a hundred reasons why I wouldn't want to break up with you, John. I stayed away these past six days because you asked me to and because I was honoring your request. I didn't stay away because I wanted to. I'm here because I couldn't go another hour without seeing you. Without apologizing to you."

He stiffened. "You don't have anything to apologize for."

"Yes, I do. I reacted badly when Sherry told us about Brian, and I'm really sorry."

"Your reaction was normal, Nora."

"No, it wasn't. We both know that I reacted badly. It took me longer than it should have to get my mind right after Sherry told us about Brian."

"I don't expect you to ever get your mind right about it."

"John," she said firmly. "Stop talking like that and listen to me. Hear me. I'm sorry for how I looked at you. For how I jerked away from you. I want you to know that that wasn't my true reaction."

He scowled at her in confusion.

"That was only my *first* reaction," she said. "Not my truest."

Many of the articles John had read about Brian Raymond had included pictures of Nora's mother. Robin looked the way murder victims always look in pictures. Young and sweet and tragic. Nora resembled her. They had the same forehead, and Nora's face was shaped just like her mother's.

His heart and his body ached with love for Nora. But this situation was *messed up*, because looking at Nora filled his mind with thoughts of Robin and how she'd been murdered and by whom. He felt bad enough as it was. He didn't want to be reminded that he was the son of a murderer every time he looked at Nora.

"John?" Nora asked.

"Every time you look at me from now on you'll see Brian Raymond," he said.

"No, I won't."

"Yes, you will."

"I see *you* when I look at you, John. And you're wonderful."

"Then I'm the one who's screwed up, because I *do* see Brian Raymond when I look at myself, and I see your mother when I look at you."

"You're going to have to choose not to see them."

"I *did* choose not to see them. But they're there anyway."

They stared at each other, the air snapping with invisible sparks.

Just days ago he'd had the right to touch her, to hold her, kiss her. Now it felt as though a wall of glass separated them, as thick and real as the glass panels that separated his living room from his deck.

She straightened tall, her fingers curling into fists. "You're not responsible for what Brian did. What happened a generation ago has nothing to do with you or me."

"No? What about the Scripture verse that says that children will be punished to the third and fourth generation for the sins of their parents? That would explain why I'm losing my sight, wouldn't it?"

Her mouth came open. "No! John . . . Let's go inside. We can talk through all of this, okay? I think that's what might help—"

"I can't. I'm sorry, but I can't"—he gestured back and forth between them—"do this."

"Yes, you can." Her voice wobbled, and he hated himself for upsetting her.

"No, I can't. I don't know who I am," he confessed to her with painful honesty. "I need to figure it out before I can think. Before I can see you or myself clearly."

"I can help you figure it out," she whispered, taking a step toward him.

He lifted a staying hand.

Her movement cut to a halt.

"I need to be alone," he said more harshly than he'd intended.

None of this was her fault. He knew it wasn't, and he didn't want to hurt her. Ever. But her goodness was making him sick with his own darkness. Her mother's face, looking out at him from her eyes, was damning him. "I just . . . I need to be alone. I'm sorry."

"Don't do this."

Time unwound, one second pulling into the next, before he turned, walked into his house, and locked his door. He stood in his foyer, arms crossed, trying to hold himself together while a storm howled within. He willed Nora to leave, because he couldn't take it if she knocked again or said anything more or looked at him with that shattered expression.

When he heard her car start, he closed his eyes. Not with relief. With crushing loss.

He knew a thing or two about killing, and he wished he could kill Brian himself. He envisioned doing it. He thought in detail about exactly how he'd do it.

But the reality was that he'd been born too late to rescue Sherry or Robin or to kill Brian. Brian had taken his own life and was now just as dead as Nora's mother.

Nora drove to the Bookish Cottage like a carrier pigeon flying instinctively home for protection and safety.

Her throat throbbed with unshed tears, and her pulse beat a depressing cadence in her ears. *Keep it together*, she kept telling herself. *Keep it together, Nora.*

She parked, made her way around the side of her house, and tossed her purse and keys onto her Adirondack chairs as she passed her deck. She kept walking until she reached the place where the grass and moss of her hill gave way to the strip of wet, rocky earth that rimmed the Hood Canal.

"I don't know who I am," John had said to her, and he'd looked and sounded anguished when he'd said it. He'd had no idea how appealing he was to her with his rugged body and his past glories and his vulnerabilities and his honor.

She'd tried to tell him that he was wonderful, but telling him he was wonderful had been like throwing a pebble into the Grand Canyon. Too little. No impact. She'd wanted to say so much more than she had. She'd wanted to refute the Bible verse he'd thrown at her to support the suggestion that God might be punishing him for the sins of his parents. She'd wanted to explain that his tarnished conception and fading eyesight were like age cracks in the surface of a Monet. If you had the intelligence to view the painting the right way, the cracks didn't keep it from being what it was—a masterpiece.

Clearly, John hadn't been ready to hear any of that.

She ran her hands down her face. Let her arms fall.

This struggle John was facing was bigger than she was. Far bigger than he was, too. She loved him, but she didn't have the power to help him. This crisis was about his identity. This was about what was true and what was a lie. This was a battle of light and dark and, as such, was far, far above her pay grade.

She knew the One, though, who specialized in battles between light and dark.

She lowered onto the ground, letting her dress bell outward over her crossed legs, not caring that the damp would stain the fabric. She cleared her mind, preparing to pray for John. But what the Lord laid bare before her, with startling clarity, was . . .

Herself. Her own mistakes.

The day of her shopping trip to Seattle, she'd acknowledged that she had issues with letting God take control and issues with her singlehood. But her response to those realizations had largely been a self-help type of response. *Choose contentment! Get your head straight about your singleness, Nora. Repair your self-image with a makeover.*

When she'd started dating John, she'd loaded yet more responsibilities onto her own shoulders. *Be smart, Nora. Protect yourself as much as you can. Take things slowly!* And then, when her relationship with John had encountered its first trial, *Make it right, Nora. Fix it.*

Fresh certainty locked into place within her as she took in the details of her surroundings. She could not fix what was broken inside herself through self-help. She could not fix what was broken between herself and John through earnestness or well-meaning effort. She'd tried.

She'd failed miserably.

Three years ago she'd stepped to the helm and taken hold of the ship's wheel of her life because it had no longer seemed safe to trust wholly in God. Since then, she'd attempted nothing larger than what her own human abilities could accomplish.

From this vantage point, however, she could see that her broken engagement hadn't been an oversight on God's part. He hadn't fallen down on the job of running her life and accidentally let pain devour her.

That season of grief and dashed dreams, the season when she'd declared God to be the most unworthy of her trust, was actually the season when He'd been the very *most* worthy of her trust. He'd known that Harrison was not the man for her. Through her broken engagement, He'd been safeguarding her. But she hadn't had the eyes to see it at the time. So, in her fear, she'd made God small.

She couldn't continue managing five aspects of her life while delegating two to God. She couldn't continue managing even two aspects of her life while delegating five to God. It couldn't be Christ's will plus her will. It had to be Christ alone.

Either He was the one at the helm, steering the ship's wheel of her life, or she was.

Terror gathered, shaking and icy in her midsection. She wanted to draw back and protect herself from this precipice she'd come to because . . . what if He didn't take her where she wanted to go? What if the future God had for her didn't include John? Not a single fiber of her wanted that outcome. But if that was what happened . . .

Then Christ alone would be enough.

What if she never married?

Then Christ alone would be enough.

What if something terrible happened to one of her family members? Or her village went bankrupt? Or she was handed a diagnosis that rocked her the way John's diagnosis had rocked him?

Then. Christ. Alone. Would be enough.

When she was scared or disappointed or racked with sorrow—that's exactly when He would be the most trustworthy. In faith, she'd need to hold on to that truth regardless of what her eyes could see.

Nora dug her hands into the grass and pebbles, then bent her head. "You are trustworthy," she whispered unevenly. "*You are trustworthy.*" She said it again and again, letting the chorus seep into her quavering heart and hungry soul. "I trust you with everything. My whole life. I want your will, Lord. Not mine. Just . . ." Her voice broke. "Just Christ alone. That's what I choose. You're enough."

She prayed as hard as she'd ever prayed. Tears slipped down her cheeks as she humbled herself before the King of the Universe, God on His throne. He was not small at all, the way she'd tried to make Him. He was huge. The biggest thing there was.

She confessed her weaknesses and pleaded for His forgiveness. She thanked Him for His goodness. And she begged Him to fight for John.

"Remind John who he is. Remind him what his true identity is in you. Love John. Rescue John. You're the only one who can."

• • •

Letter from Sherry to John:

John,

Since we met the other day, my heart has been lighter in some ways than it has been since the day the nurse carried you out of my hospital room. In other ways, my heart has been heavy because I know the things I told you about Brian Raymond were very difficult for you to hear.

As you know, I'm no stranger to very difficult things. I can tell you unequivocally that there is joy and love and family and a future on the far side of difficult things. But, perhaps even more applicable to you in this moment, there is also peace, through the Lord's provision, in the midst of difficult things. And that's the sweetest peace there is.

You see, we so often long for a change in our circumstances. What's ultimately of more value is God's ability to strengthen us with power through His Spirit, so that we'll be able to deal with the circumstances He doesn't change. We can deal with them, John, if we have His supernatural power on our side.

I want you to know that I never regretted my decision to carry you and give birth to you. I've always been certain, ever since the day you were born, that I got that part right.

As I write this, I'm filled with gratitude to God because He led me to make the choices that, in turn, led you into the future He had for you. You were His son far more than you were ever my son, and God the Father was looking out for you every step of the way.

It's clear to me that God placed you in the earthly family He meant for you to have. Now that I'm the age that I am and have experienced a few decades of motherhood, I'm sorry that I wasn't the one who raised you. I'm sorry for all I missed, for all the things you and I didn't experience together. Yet I acknowledge that the role of mother was not the role God had for me concerning you. I'm honored that He saw fit to give me the small part in your life that He gave me, and I'm amazed by the outstanding things He's done through you. I'm full of expectation for the things He's yet to do.

I'd like for us to stay in contact, but only if that's all right with you.

Sincerely,
Sherry

CHAPTER
Twenty-four

Two days after Nora's visit to John's house, her sisters, Grandma, Valentina, and Zander arrived at the Bookish Cottage bearing a pot of clam chowder, sourdough bread, and sympathy.

In no time they had the chowder bubbling on Nora's stove and the bread in the oven. Delicious smells and happy conversation threaded through the air while Nora leaned against her table, watching them and wondering whether she was up for the company of cheerful people.

Her heartfelt prayer the day before yesterday had been a turning point. But already God was showing her that her prayer was a starting line, not a finish line. She'd given the situation with John to God—she'd given *everything* to God—but that didn't mean her thorniest emotions had been swept away. She continued to wrestle with sorrow and doubt. Her old patterns still beckoned. *Take control! Do something to repair your romance with John*, they kept insisting. But those weren't God's voices. Those were her worries talking. All she could hear God saying so far was *Trust me*.

She wasn't accustomed to trusting. This situation with John was going to require not just a daily surrendering, but maybe an hourly surrendering. Maybe a minute-by-minute surrendering.

There was peace to be found in surrendering. There *was*. But the Holy Spirit's peace, at this particular point in her life, was a hard-earned peace accompanied by tears.

"I told the children's minister that I'd teach sixth grade," Grandma said to Valentina and Nora in a resigned tone. Despite the August evening beyond the walls of the cottage, she'd swathed herself in Old Musty. "No one else stepped forward because no one else wants to teach sixth-grade Sunday school. I don't want to teach it either." Dramatic sigh. "I, however, understand the meaning of duty. Too few understand the meaning of duty anymore."

Nora could always count on Grandma, at least, not to be cheerful.

"Children that age and I have never gotten along," Grandma said.

"Good, miss," Valentina replied.

Grandma's eyes narrowed as she scrutinized Nora's face. "You look tired."

"Yes!" Valentina exclaimed. "So pretty."

Willow captured Nora by the wrist. "Excuse us for a moment. I just remembered that I need to ask Nora and Britt about something." She grabbed Britt's wrist, too, and led them both into Nora's bedroom, then closed the door behind them. She wrapped Nora in a hug that smelled like a very expensive floral arrangement. "How are you doing?"

"Pretty well." Nora took a seat on her bed.

Willow settled into the room's one chair. Britt sat cross-legged on the floor with her back against the wall.

"When you visited John, did you say you were sorry, like you'd been wanting to say?" Willow asked.

"I did, but he said I had nothing to be sorry about . . . which made it really hard to apologize fully, because we didn't agree on the premise."

Willow scrunched her nose. "Men. They're so strange."

"He said he wants to be alone," Nora informed them.

Her sisters let that sink in.

"How did he look?" Britt asked.

"Sexy. Um, did I just say that out loud? I meant to say distraught. He looked sexy distraught."

"Well," Willow said, "none of us have ever had to deal with a secret like the one he's having to deal with about his birth parents. Who are we to judge how he handles it? More time alone might be what he needs."

"Nah," Britt said. "He's sexy *distraught*, remember? He could be sinking into depression."

"I think it's more constructive to look on the bright side," Willow said.

"What are you going to do?" Britt asked Nora.

Nora knotted her hands in her lap. "Pray. And pray some more."

"Is it too late to choose the cute British guy?" Britt asked.

"Britt!" Willow scolded.

Nora considered her younger sister. "I don't want the cute British guy. I want John."

"Part of your frustration this last week," Willow stated reasonably, "has been about your inability to say to John the things you wanted to say. Even though you saw him the other day, it sounds to me like you were still unable to say those things."

"True."

"What about writing him a letter, then? Would that help? You can collect all your thoughts and articulate everything you want to communicate. He can read it when he's ready to read it. And when he reads it, it might make a difference. But even if it doesn't, you'll have the satisfaction of knowing you said what you needed to say."

Nora exhaled gradually. For the first time since her prayer the day before yesterday, she sensed a *yes* deep within. The idea of a letter felt immediately right.

"It's not a bad idea," Britt said.

Zander opened the door and peered at them from the threshold, one hand on the knob. "Plotting world takeover?"

"If so," Willow responded, "the only thing we agree on so far is that men are strange."

"Not all men are strange," Zander replied. "Only the ones who can fell dragons. They're not normal." He looked to Britt. "Do you want me to take the bread out of the oven or does it need more time?"

"You can take it out now. Thank you."

Willow regarded Britt with confusion. "I've said twice now that men are strange. You haven't said *amen* either of those times, which is weird."

"I'm not feeling as dismissive of the unfairer sex as I often do." Britt smiled. "I met someone yesterday."

Nora tensed. So did Zander.

Was it necessary for Britt to meet her next crush at this catastrophic moment in Nora's own love life? She didn't know if she could hold up her "I'm so happy for you" end of the conversation each time Britt mentioned her fantastic new man.

"Who is this person?" Willow asked.

"Let's just say that he's handsome and charming and that I'm excited about our date tomorrow. Though I'm certain he'll drive me crazy a few months down the road, and I'll be forced to send him packing, at which time I'll be firmly back in the men-are-strange camp."

Zander's face whitened. Mouth set grimly, he made his way in the direction of the kitchen.

"Even if you will be forced to send him packing in a few months, he sounds nice. . . ." Nora tried.

"You don't have to pretend to be excited about him," Britt told her.

"I don't? You'll give me a pass today?"

"Yes. Today, I'll give you a pass."

John did not enjoy dropping bombshells on his mom and dad. He'd done so months ago when he'd told them about his diagnosis. Now, he'd just finished telling them about Sherry and Brian Raymond. Another bombshell.

They were both regarding him with a mix of shock and sympathy.

He'd arrived early at his parents' house for his family's scheduled Saturday lunch. He'd arrived so early that the table was only halfway set and his sister and her husband weren't expected to arrive for another half an hour.

The three of them—he, his mom, and his dad—were sitting in the sunken den at the back of the house he'd grown up in. Vacuum tracks marked the room's beige carpeting. His mom kept the house tidy and updated. Always had.

He could hear the tick of the wall-mounted kitchen clock and smell homemade lasagna. He knew the sounds, smells, and objects of this house very, very well. This was home.

"We were never told about any of that," his mom said in response to the bombshell about Sherry and Brian.

"I know."

His dad cleared his throat. John's father talked easily about every subject except feelings—his own or other people's. Whenever he had to address anything emotional, he became so awkward it was like he had a marble in his mouth. "I'm sorry you had to find out something like that, son. I . . ." More throat clearing. "I wish your search for these . . . people would've ended better."

"I do, too," his mom said.

"I don't want either of you to worry about this. I told you I'd found Sherry's address and planned to send her a letter, so I wanted to let you know what happened. That's all."

John's mom and dad had tried for three years to have a child of their own before a doctor had informed them that it would be impossible. He was well aware that they hadn't had an opportunity to have a biological child of their own, just like he hadn't had an opportunity to be raised by people he was genetically connected to. They'd all experienced loss. And they'd all experienced gain when they'd been given to each other.

"Are you all right? About this?" his mom asked.

Since his meeting with Sherry and Nora at The Grapevine, he'd been falling down a black, endless cave. No eyesight to rely on. No Nora. No goodness of his own to hold on to. Then, yesterday, he'd received a letter from Sherry. He'd reread it over and over. Her words were like a branch sticking out of the wall of the cave. He'd grabbed the branch, and it had slowed his fall. Was he *all right*, though? He debated how to answer and decided on the truth. "No. Not yet."

His mom leaned forward. "John, don't let what happened between Sherry and Brian determine how you feel about yourself. Okay?"

He remained silent.

"You're in Christ, so you're a new creation. The old has gone. The new is here. The old has gone, honey."

He held her gaze. The kitchen clock ticked.

"I remember when you were literally a new creation. We saw you for the first time when you were five days old." She tipped her head and smiled affectionately. "I wish we knew someone with a newborn." She turned to his dad. "Who do we know who has a newborn grandbaby? Marcy?"

"I don't think Marcy's newborn grandbaby will be interested in joining us for lasagna," his dad said dryly.

"Anyway." His mom focused again on John. "I wish I had a newborn here to show you. I wish you could look into the face of a five-day-old baby. If you could, you'd see how helpless and tiny and innocent they are. They're all those things, aren't they, Ray?"

"All those things."

"But especially innocent. Whatever Brian Raymond did, you were innocent of it, John. You're a man now, but you're as much a new creation today as you were when you were young. You know that already. Of course you know that, but I feel compelled to say it. And here's another thing I feel compelled to say, even though I've said it a hundred times."

John waited, guilty and hopeful and uncertain.

"We prayed for you." His mom looked directly at him. "You're God's answer to our prayer, John. You're our son, and we couldn't love you more than we do."

"Yeah," his dad said gruffly.

"I love you, too," John said.

Tears pooled in his mom's eyes.

"Mom," John said with a trace of warning. He didn't want her to break down into a full-blown cry.

Though his dad looked like a panicking horse around the eyes, he reached across the loveseat they were sitting on and took her hand.

"I know, I know." She gave a shaky laugh. "It's okay. These are happy tears."

"I'm off on Thursday, John. I could drive out to Shore Pine and we could do a little fishing," his dad offered.

"Sure. Anytime."

"Who do we know who could recommend a psychologist, Ray?"

"I don't need a psychologist," John stated. Though he was scared he might.

"It wouldn't hurt to talk to someone, honey." His mom started in on a story about her friend Denise's daughter who'd been treated by a wonderful doctor when she'd been suffering from postpartum depression.

His parents were trying to help him. His dad the way he knew, by inviting him to go fishing. His mom the way she knew. They were trying to help him because he was their son and they loved him and that's what parents did for their kids—they helped and they loved.

He saw the two of them, then. He saw their imperfections and their quirks and their good, good hearts.

His mom, with her gentle hands and slender build and plain hairstyle. She had a tendency to get flustered when stressed, but she could beat them all at Scrabble. She was an excellent cook. A volunteer at the church ministry that provided clothing to families in need. She was such an understanding elementary school vice principal that kids always left her office smiling, regardless of why they'd been sent there.

His dad, with his broad chest and thick graying hair, was the best fisherman John had ever met. A genius at predicting the weather.

Prone to accidentally letting a swear word fly when the Seahawks fumbled. The person everyone called to help them move because he'd always come, work hard, and never complain.

He remembered his mom laying a washcloth on his head in the middle of the night when he was sick. He remembered his dad grounding him for missing his curfew. He remembered them sticking a candle in his favorite breakfast, blueberry pancakes, every year on his birthday.

They'd supported him at every school program and every sports banquet. They'd just about bankrupted themselves paying for baseball and driving him to tournaments. They'd sat in their fold-up bleacher seats at his games wearing the T-shirts and hats of his team.

Would Brian Raymond's outcome have been different if he'd been adopted at birth by Christian people as decent as these?

Probably.

John had gone on a search for his parents. And he'd found them.

Here they were.

Here is where they'd always been.

Miles to the south, Nora smoothed the blank sheets of stationery resting on the table before her. She chewed on her bottom lip. She tapped her pen.

God was calling her to follow through on Willow's idea to write John a letter. She'd been praying about it, and she knew what He was asking her to say.

It was just that . . .

Great Scott! This terrified her. She drew in a breath, collected her bravery, and started writing.

John,

I'm a history lover, but I have to confess that I'm not much of a letter writer. I'm an email sender. I'm a texter and Facebook messenger. But for you, I'm sitting here with stationery in front of me and a pen in my hand. Hang on to your hat, John. I'm writing you a letter.

Our last meeting didn't go well, and I've been thinking nonstop about a lot of things ever since. Actually, I've been thinking nonstop about a lot of things ever since our lunch with Sherry.

The Lord says in the Bible that justice is His. You're familiar with that verse, right?

There's evil in the world, but in the end, God assures us that the light will win out over the darkness. Justice will be His.

Brian Raymond raped six women. But do you know how many people you saved, John? In the Yemen mission alone you're documented with saving eleven lives. I don't know much about your other missions. I'd like to. I know enough to guess that eleven isn't the total number you saved during your career with the SEALs.

Can you glimpse God's justice at work?

Brian injured six people. But you, Brian's son, saved eleven.

Justice was the Lord's.

And then, shortly after you were handed a diagnosis that came to you because of Brian Raymond, God made a way for the two of us to meet.

I thought our meeting was a coincidence, just like the coincidental meetings that led so many of my friends to their boyfriends. But after Sherry told us what she told us, it's no longer possible for me to see our meeting as accidental.

All along, God knew you were Brian's son and He knew I was my mother's daughter. I believe that He brought us together on purpose, which explains why we're such a good match even though we're not much of a match on paper at all. Before the two of us learned that we were connected by Brian Raymond, God was already redeeming the awful things that happened to our mothers through our relationship.

Justice was the Lord's.

You told me the other day that you see my mother when you look at me and Brian Raymond when you look at yourself. Now that I've had time to think about it fully, I'd respond to you differently. I'd respond to that statement by saying, great.

Great!

Look at me and see my mother and marvel at the way God is vindicating her loss. Look at yourself and see Brian and remember how God was able to take what Brian did with evil intentions and turn it to good.

I'll admit to you that after my broken engagement, I'd come to expect very little from God. But since I met you, I've seen that He CAN do big things. That He IS doing big things. That I should expect the miraculous from Him. And that He's worthy of my trust.

He's been telling me that I can't fix this situation between us on my own. He's also been telling me that expecting Him to do big things isn't enough. He expects me to do big things when He asks me to. Which frightens me.

I refuse to be cautious about this. I refuse to be scared.

Well . . . maybe I'm a little scared. But I'm working on it.

Here's the BIG, not-cautious thing I need to say to you, John. . . .

I love you.

Regardless of anything. The fact that Brian Raymond is your biological father. My insecurities. Your eyesight. My fears. What the future may or may not hold. Or the fact that you very well might reject me.

I need to tell you that, no matter what, I love you.

—Nora

CHAPTER Twenty-five

John lowered Nora's letter. He stood in his foyer, on the spot where he'd been standing when he'd looked through his mail.

Carefully, he set her handwritten pages on his entry table. Then he walked to his bedroom and turned on his bathroom shower. While he waited for the water to warm, blocks began to fall within him. One after another. Like stacks of children's building blocks crashing down. Unstoppable.

When the water was hot, he stepped in, set his palms on the tiles, leaned into his arms, and cried. Sobs wracked his big body. He cried for Sherry and Nora's mother and the other women. He cried because his eyesight was fading. He cried for the children he wouldn't have. But most of all, he cried because Nora loved him, and he felt so unworthy of it and so incredibly relieved.

She loved him.

When he stepped from the shower, he felt clean on the inside for the first time since his meeting with Sherry. His eyes were scratchy and his throat hurt, but he was lighter. Hollowed out and ready to start over.

He pulled on a pair of track pants and returned to his foyer. He read Nora's letter a second time. He turned over everything she'd said in his mind. Then read it again.

He carried the pages to the back of the house.

Today, he'd finally felt well enough to return to work. If Sherry's letter had been the branch he'd grabbed to slow his fall down the endless cave, then his visit to his parents the day before yesterday had been a rope. And Nora's letter . . . Nora's letter was like a hand reaching down into the shadows and pulling him up.

It was near dinnertime, but the gray clouds pressing low over Lake Shore Pine made the hour feel later. Wind tossed light rain against his windows with a soft tapping sound.

He read the letter again, then placed it on the kitchen table. For the first time since he'd come inside the day Sherry had told him about Brian, he unlatched his back doors and shoved them along their track.

Outside, rain that wasn't warm or cold peppered his face, chest, hair. He took the path to the water, continuing until he'd reached his dock's farthest point.

Choppy whitecaps marked the lake's navy-blue surface.

To survive as a SEAL he'd had to find a core of toughness, independence, and fierce confidence within himself. Back then, it had sometimes seemed like he'd be able to build his identity on those qualities and on the things he'd achieved after leaving the teams.

But then he'd been hit back-to-back by his diagnosis and the news that Brian Raymond was his father.

The old things, the things he'd been holding on to for a long time, had been stripped away. He couldn't base his identity on the people he'd come from, or his abilities, or his health, or even on Nora.

All those things could be taken away. None of those things were at the core of who a person—who he—was.

Here I am, he said to God. *I'm a sinner who's been forgiven by you and who's loved by you. That's the only identity I have left to claim.*

It turned out that was the only identity he needed. The only identity that would last.

It was freeing to recognize how short he fell, how totally inadequate he was. It meant that John didn't have to work hard to be accepted by God. Even when he'd been at his best, his efforts never would have made him good enough for God. They definitely wouldn't make him good enough now.

Jesus was the only good one. Everything John had received was a straight-up gift.

He didn't agree with all of God's choices. There was much that made him angry, that he didn't understand, that seemed unfair. However, in addition to giving him grace, God had also seen fit to give him Nora. God had given him Nora, and it was hard to argue with that. Difficulties had come his way, but so had *she*.

It was a bargain he could accept.

Nora loved him.

I need to tell you that, no matter what, I love you.

That was what she'd written, and it seemed like a miracle. Maybe it was a miracle.

What could he do to answer her letter? He wanted to tell her "I love you, too" in a way that would be impossible to misunderstand.

He was ready to do his own big thing.

For her.

Nora's employees stood in a predawn huddle in the parking lot of the Library on the Green wearing colonial clothing. Nora hurried toward them carrying a huge thermos of coffee in one hand and a box of cinnamon-sugar donuts in the other. She'd wedged cups and a stack of napkins under one arm.

Today was the opening day of the Summer Antique Fair they'd been planning for months. The Fair would open at nine, and they had a great deal to do between now and then.

"I come bearing apology gifts," Nora announced. "I know it's unforgivable of me to ask you all to arrive here at six."

"Completely unforgivable," Nikki confirmed.

Nora set the coffee, donuts, cups, and napkins on the hood of Nikki's Camry.

"I only got four hours of sleep last night," Amy said dolefully, reaching for the coffee. "I stayed up helping Grace with a report that had to be emailed by midnight last night. What sort of teacher asks students to email in reports by midnight?"

"What sort of mom helps her perfectly capable seventeen-year-old daughter with her report?" Nikki asked.

"The good type," Blake answered. "I only got four hours of sleep, too, because my friend and I were making plans for the Hayride of Horror we're doing for Halloween. There'll be a lot of disgusting gore. It'll be sweet."

"I wish I'd only gotten four hours of sleep because I'd been up most of the night—for all the right reasons—with a new husband." Nikki worked on a donut, bright pink lips speckled with sugar. "I need a new husband bad."

Nora swiveled at the sound of a car. Willow's familiar Range Rover pulled up and she and Britt climbed out. They were both dressed in light jackets to combat the early-morning chill.

"Your sisters always look so young and fresh," Amy said wistfully.

"I know," Nora answered. "It's revolting."

"It's outstanding," Blake insisted. "*They're* outstanding."

"This is a surprise," Nora called to them as they neared.

"It's your big day. We thought you could use a few extra hands," Willow said.

"Thank you." Nora was genuinely touched. Her sisters loved her more than she'd realized if they were willing to show up for unpaid duty at six in the morning.

Nora had eaten her donut on the way here in the car, so she retrieved her trusty tote bag from her trunk and extracted a clipboard and pen. She went through three pages of notes with the group, stopping whenever anyone had a question or discussion was needed to iron out a detail. The sky began to lighten to pearly gray in the east.

She was just wrapping up the final item when a small figure came jogging toward them. "Randall?"

"Good morning, Ms. Bradford."

"Are you here to help, too?"

He shrugged. "I guess."

There wasn't any guessing about it. He prided himself on the role he played within the world of the village. That he'd gotten himself out of bed at this hour proved it. Nora handed him the last donut.

These people were her people. Her misery over John had heightened her appreciation of her family and friends.

Almost two weeks had passed since she'd written and mailed John her letter. She'd yet to hear anything. She had no way of knowing if he'd read it. And if he had read it, whether or not he'd balled it in his fist and thrown it in the trash.

She didn't regret sending it. She'd felt led to do it, and Willow had been right—it had been important for her to voice what she'd so dearly wanted to voice. At the same time, it was harrowing to put yourself out there the way she had in her letter. Whenever she thought about the fact that she'd told John outright that she loved him, her muscles clenched as if bracing against a blow.

"Okay!" Nora said. "Are you all clear on what you'll be doing?"

"Clear!" Nikki jerked upright and gave a crisp salute.

Randall put one thin arm forward. "Awesome Antique Fair on three," he instructed. The rest of them laid their hands on top of his. "One, two, three."

"Awesome Antique Fair!" they all shouted, then headed in separate directions.

Nora's sisters kept pace with her as she took the path along the side of the library toward the central green. She fumbled in her purse for her key ring so that she'd be able to unlock the library's door. When she found it, she turned toward the library. As she lifted her head, keys in hand, something off to the side caught her eye. The ground lights framing the long, rectangular swath of grass glowed prettily against the dew. Her attention followed the lights all the way to the end of the green where . . .

Where . . .

Nora came to an instantaneous stop.

At the far end of the green, where a blank space had always been, stood a chapel.

Her jaw sagged. Fingers of early-morning light reached across the horizon to tip the chapel's spire and roofline. This wasn't just any chapel.

This was the Hartnett Chapel. Her chapel. The chapel she'd loved for so long and wanted for so long. And like a dream, like an optical illusion, like a mirage, there it was, placed precisely in the spot she'd saved for it.

Astonishment sifted over her. She blinked, but the chapel didn't disappear. A pair of birds flew past the quaint structure, winging heavenward.

She moved forward a step. Concentrating hard, she could just make out a figure on the chapel's porch. A male figure.

She covered her mouth with her hands. Her heart leapt, then beat furiously.

"Maybe you should go over and say hello," Willow said gently.

Nora had temporarily forgotten her sisters' existence, but they were standing just behind her, watching her with excitement. Several yards behind them, her employees had gathered. Nikki gave her an enthusiastic thumbs-up.

Her sisters had . . . maybe all of them had . . . known about this.

Of course. John wouldn't have been able to move a building onto her property without the help of her family and employees.

"Let me hold your bag." Britt extended a hand, and Nora numbly passed it over.

"Keys," Willow said.

She passed them over, too. "Thank you," Nora said.

"Thank him," her sisters said in unison, then looked at each other and said what they'd always said when they were kids. "Jinx!"

Nora set off toward the chapel on legs that had gone weak and wobbly. *Oh my goodness, oh my goodness, oh my goodness.*

She didn't think boyfriends were in the habit of having historic chapels moved to their girlfriend's villages unless they wanted to give their girlfriend her dream come true. And boyfriends didn't typically want to give girlfriends their dream come true unless they really, really liked them.

As Nora drew nearer, she could see that the chapel sat on the steel beams and specially made dollies the house-moving company used to transport buildings. The Hartnett Chapel had been lifted from Mr. Hartnett's property, trucked here, and—at some point since she'd left work last night—deposited in Merryweather Historical Village. It lacked nothing but a fresh foundation. Once she had that laid, it could be lowered into its new permanent location.

John leaned against the siding next to the chapel's peaked front door wearing a black jacket, cargo pants, work boots. He hadn't shaved this morning, but his cheeks were much smoother than the last time she'd seen him. Though his eyes were tired, they were no longer ravaged by fury and hurt.

He pushed away from the wall as she mounted the portable wooden steps that led to the raised chapel. Nora stopped. They faced each other while a breeze slipped past. Distantly, a rooster crowed.

No, his eyes were no longer ravaged. Not at all. The hazel depths were warm and at peace. He looked thoroughly pleased with himself for having pulled off such a major surprise.

"Did you steal Mr. Hartnett's chapel when he wasn't looking?"

John broke into a full-fledged grin complete with crinkly eyes and a dimple.

Nora's joy careened upward.

"Mr. Hartnett's son served in the Navy," John said. "He was injured at sea, but thankfully survived. You could say that Mr. Hartnett has a fondness for veterans."

"Does he?"

"Yes. Plus, he read my book."

Nora gave a soft, breathless laugh.

"He was surprisingly open to the idea of selling me the chapel."

"John! I . . ." She gaped at him. "I adore this chapel."

"I know."

"I can't believe Mr. Hartnett sold it to you. And I really can't believe that you brought it here. For me."

"Believe it."

"How did you . . . ?" Her thoughts spun as she tried to imagine how he'd managed this. She knew exactly what transporting a building entailed. A great deal of planning, coordination, and money.

"I contacted Nikki, and she introduced me to Hal at the house relocation company you use. Your sisters, Hal, Nikki, Mr. Hartnett, and I have been working on this project together for the last ten days."

Speechless, Nora gestured to the beloved bell tower, the beloved door, the beloved windows. Then she let her arms drop and focused solely on John. "Thank you. Those two words sound incredibly inadequate to me in this moment but I can't think of better ones. So. Wow. Just . . . thank you."

He extended a hand to her. She placed her hand in his, and the sensation of his warm fingers enclosing hers caused emotion to clog her throat.

"You're welcome," he murmured and gave a gentle tug. Her body settled against his and there it was, that mystical *click* between them. That fated, meant-to-be feeling.

"I missed you," she said.

"I missed you, too."

She rested her palms on the cool, slick fabric of his jacket. Beneath the layers of his clothing, she could feel the unyielding planes of his chest. "It seems indubitable that you read my letter."

He laughed. "My favorite word."

She smiled. "Indubitable."

"You're right. I read your letter."

She looked into his eyes, and he looked into hers.

"I'm sorry," he said solemnly. "I'm sorry for the way I acted when you came to see me."

"You were struggling."

"That's no excuse. Can you forgive me?"

"Yes," she said. "Can you forgive me for how I responded that day at The Grapevine? Please?"

"Yes."

A gap of quiet.

"After I read your letter," John said, "I wanted to find a way to answer it that would be . . ." Humor creased his expression. "Indubitable."

"Mission accomplished. This is the best reply to a letter I've ever received. This is the best gift I've ever received, period."

"You're the best gift I've ever received," he said. "I love you."

Bliss suffused her. Tingling bliss. "You do?"

"I do," he vowed.

"I love you, too."

"The past might be challenging, and the future might be unsure. And that's okay. The present is all we're given, anyway. Right?"

He'd quoted something she'd said to him after their first kiss. "Right."

"If I have you"—his voice turned rough—"here in the present, then I have all that I could hope for, Nora." He moved his hands into her hair and set their foreheads together. Their breath mingled and her eyes drifted closed and she never wanted to forget how she felt in this moment.

Then his lips met hers and they were kissing and this moment—*this moment!*—was even better than the last.

This was the moment, kissing John here on the porch of her dream come true, that she never wanted to forget. Not for as long as she lived.

"Ah, Sovereign Lord,
you have made the heavens
and the earth
by your great power
and outstretched arm.
Nothing is too hard for you."

JEREMIAH 32:17

Questions for Conversation

1. Are you adopted? Or do you have any friends, family, or children who are? Has any adoptee in your circle ever searched for their birth mother or birth father? Why or why not? What was the outcome of their search?

2. Nora is the middle of three sisters. Do you have sisters? What is your favorite aspect of sisterhood? What's one aspect of sisterhood you find challenging?

3. Were you surprised by any of the turns that the plot of *True to You* took? If so, what surprised you?

4. Throughout the course of the story, John struggles to accept the diagnosis he's been given. Have you struggled to accept a diagnosis, or a difficulty, or a desert season of some kind in your own life?

5. The theme of *True to You* is truth. During the course of the story, Nora and John have to dig beneath the falsehoods they've believed to find the truth beneath. Can you name

some of the instances of False versus True that Becky touched on in this novel?

6. Which characters or situations in the novel made you laugh?

7. Which aspects of Nora's bookish, history-loving personality did you relate to most?

8. In her letter to John, Sherry writes, ". . . we so often long for a change in our circumstances. What's ultimately of more value is God's ability to strengthen us with power through His Spirit, so that we'll be able to deal with the circumstances He doesn't change." Can you share a time when you found this to be true in your own life?

9. *True to You* is set in Washington, and scenes in the novel take place at Bradfordwood, Merryweather Historical Village, and John's modern house on Lake Shore Pine. What did the setting add to the experience of reading *True to You*?

10. Which moments in *True to You* did you find particularly romantic?

Becky Wade is a native of California who attended Baylor University, met and married a Texan, and moved to Dallas. She published historical romances for the general market, then put her career on hold for several years to care for her children. When God called her back to writing, Becky knew He meant for her to turn her attention to Christian fiction. Her humorous, heart-pounding contemporary romance novels have won the Carol Award, the INSPY Award, and the Inspirational Reader's Choice Award for Romance. Becky lives in Dallas, Texas, with her husband and three children.

To find out more about Becky and her books,
visit www.beckywade.com.

Sign up for Becky's newsletter!

For the latest news about her upcoming books, sneak peeks of yet-to-be-published chapters, and exclusive giveaways, subscribe to Becky's free quarterly e-newsletter:
www.beckywade.com/home/contact-me

Are you social media savvy?

Connect with Becky on Facebook at:
facebook.com/authorbeckywade

Twitter person? #great
twitter.com/beckywadewriter

Crafty, Pinterest type?
pinterest.com/beckywadewriter

Instagram photo fan?
instagram.com/beckywadewriter

If you enjoyed *True to You*, you may also like . . .

NFL star Gray Fowler is receiving death threats. When his team hires a security detail, Gray can't imagine what a woman half his size can do to protect him. But former Marine Dru Porter is, in fact, more than capable. As danger rises, can Dru and Gray entrust their lives to one another?

Her One and Only by Becky Wade
beckywade.com

After a red carpet accident leaves her blackballed, Lauren Summers would do almost anything for another chance at her dream of a career in fashion. Does that include making a deal with a reporter to befriend a former Hollywood star, learn her secrets—and then betray her trust?

Fading Starlight by Kathryn Cushman
kathryncushman.com

BETHANYHOUSE

Stay up to date on your favorite books and authors with our free e-newsletters. Sign up today at bethanyhouse.com.

Find us on Facebook. facebook.com/bethanyhousepublishers

Free exclusive resources for your book group! bethanyhouse.com/anopenbook

More Contemporary Fiction from Bethany House

On a visit home to Maple Valley, Iowa, political speechwriter Logan Walker meets intriguing reporter Amelia Bentley. She wants his help on a story, and he wants to get to know her better. But sooner or later, he'll have to tell her that he's here to sell the newspaper she's trying to save.

Like Never Before by Melissa Tagg
melissatagg.com

When a wedding-planning gig brings single mom Julia Dare to the Caliente Springs resort, she learns that her college sweetheart, Zeke Monroe, is the manager. As they work together on the event, Zeke and Julia are pushed to their limits both personally and professionally.

Someone Like You by Victoria Bylin
victoriabylin.com

Perla Phillips has carried a secret for over sixty years. When she sees her granddaughter Ella struggling, Perla decides to share her story—then suffers a stroke. As Ella and her aunt look into Perla's past, they'll learn more than they expected about Perla, faith, and each other.

A Tapestry of Secrets by Sarah Loudin Thomas
sarahloudinthomas.com